Praise for P. J. Alderman's
Haunting Jordan...

"Lush, descriptive writing is the hallmark of
P. J. Alderman's novel *Haunting Jordan*."
—DIANE MOTT DAVIDSON

... and her RITA-nominated debut,
A Killing Tide

"Tense and riveting, Alderman's debut delivers."
—COLLEEN THOMPSON, bestselling author of
Beneath Bone Lake

"Suspense, romance, and a setting so well-drawn, you'll
feel like you're there—Alderman delivers it all.
An outstanding debut!"
—MARILYN PAPPANO, award-winning author of
Forbidden Stranger

"Alderman's debut is a heart-thumping, quick-paced
novel that will keep you on your toes. With an intricate
plot, a complicated love story, and strong characters, this
book possesses the winning formula for this genre."
—Romantic Times Book Reviews

"A phenomenal debut novel combining suspense and
romance against the backdrop of the sea."
—Amazon (5 stars)

"You have a winner. . . . I stayed up until after midnight
to finish it. . . . I love that pooch!!! I'm looking forward to
future books by you—write fast!" —CINDI STREICHER,
Bookseller of the Year Award winner

Haunting Jordan

A Novel of Suspense

P. J. Alderman

BANTAM BOOKS
NEW YORK

Haunting Jordan is a work of fiction. Names, characters, places, and incidents either are the product of the author's imagination or are used fictitiously. Any resemblance to actual persons, living or dead, events, or locales is entirely coincidental.

A Bantam Books Mass Market Original

Copyright © 2009 by P. J. Alderman

Published in the United States by Bantam Books, an imprint of The Random House Publishing Group, a division of Random House, Inc., New York.

BANTAM BOOKS and the rooster colophon are registered trademarks of Random House, Inc.

978-0-553-59210-8

Cover illustration: Fernando Juarez

Printed in the United States of America

www.bantamdell.com

2 4 6 8 9 7 5 3 1

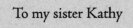
To my sister Kathy

Acknowledgments

THANKS to the following: Donnell, Kathy, and Julie, for reading and providing invaluable feedback when I most needed it. Thanks also to Margaret Benton, Faren Bachelis, and Randall Klein, for helping me find my way through the editorial process.

Thanks to Pamela Beason of Sirius Investigations, Bellingham, Washington, for her valuable insight into police investigations and interrogations.

A very special thanks to Amy Atwell, critique partner extraordinaire and valued friend—I couldn't have done it without you.

And last but not least, thanks to Kevan Lyon, my fabulous agent, and to Kate Miciak, my incomparable editor, who believed in this series and provided the support to make it happen.

Haunting Jordan

The Ransom

Port Chatham, Washington
June 6, 1890

HER satin shoes left damning footprints in the pearlescent dew on the moonlit garden path. The herb beds she fled past announced their presence in cloying waves—the spice of mint here, the pungency of rosemary there. Under the spreading branches of a magnolia tree, she paused, trembling, and glanced over her shoulder. Shadows danced on the breeze, chasing a shower of blossoms across the empty garden.

He hadn't followed her.

Before long, though, she'd be missed. And once Seavey discovered her absence, he'd hunt her down. No one would stop him, she realized bitterly—he was above the law.

I mustn't think about that now. I'm Charlotte's only hope.

Taking a deep breath, she slipped through the hedge at the back of the garden and crossed to the street, walking rapidly toward the bluff.

An onshore wind flattened the waves on Admiralty Inlet, blowing the clouds from the sky and chilling her soul. On any other evening, she could've counted on Port

Chatham's mercurial weather to camouflage her escape. But not tonight.

Beneath the brilliance of the stars, the town's waterfront stretched below her. A dozen schooners anchored in the harbor, rocking gently on a sea of silver, rigging draped from their masts like black filigree. Once upon a time, the stately ships had called out to her, whispering of romance and adventure. Now she couldn't stand to look at them.

She turned right at the next corner, breaking into a run before forcing herself to drop back to a more sedate pace. *I must act natural. I must look as if I haven't a care in the world.*

Her neighbors' cottages stood dark and silent behind picket fences and tidy gardens, their owners still in attendance at the soirée. Though she was more than a block away, she could hear the laughter and music spilling from the Canby mansion, the syncopated rhythms of Scott Joplin's ragtime pulsing along her raw nerves.

For the other guests, the party had been an opportunity to share an evening with Port Chatham's social elite, its powerful politicians and businessmen. But for her, the dinner had turned into an agonizing game of nerves, each course of rich food an obstacle to overcome. And Seavey had relished in her discomfort, leaning back with savage grace in his chair, his pale gray eyes watching her swallow her terror with every bite of salmon in dill sauce, every spoonful of floating island.

God *damn* his soul. Had his men beaten Charlotte, or worse? Was Charlotte lying right this moment, bound and gagged, in the filth and pitch-black terrors of the tunnels?

Reaching into the hidden pocket she'd sewn into her skirt, she clutched the roll of money. She couldn't let her imagination run wild with possibilities—she knew what she had to do.

At the top of the bluff, she stepped onto the footbridge that would take her down to the waterfront, treading carefully on dew-slick wood. The wind howled, buffeting the trestle. A gust tore at the silk skirts of her evening gown as if it were trying to drag her back from an unknown precipice. *Drunken sailors and soiled doves are the denizens of the waterfront*, it seemed to scream, *not decent people like you.*

Leaving the footbridge behind, she crossed the two blocks to the bay. Choosing the muddy streets over the louder boardwalks that fronted the business establishments, she used the faint illumination of the occasional gaslight lantern to light her way.

Honky-tonk and laughter spilled from a saloon, and she avoided the pool of light from its open doors. At the end of the wharf, a six-masted schooner towered over her, armed thugs patrolling its decks to keep the crew from deserting. When a guard stopped and stared down at her, shifting his rifle, she quickened her pace.

She darted past abandoned buildings charred by fire, all too aware she was most exposed in this recently leveled stretch of waterfront. The stench of scorched wood and damp ash assaulted her, forcing her to breathe through her mouth. The tragedy marked the beginning of her nightmare, she realized. *If only I'd stayed home that night.*

The odor of brackish salt water was stronger now. Out

on the bay, the oars of an unseen Whitehall boat slapped the water rhythmically. She could make out dark, prone forms on the beach, revelers blinded or passed out from one too many glasses of the corn liquor served by saloons and houses of ill repute. A shadowy figure moved among them, rifling through pockets. Farther down, two people lay entwined, groping silently and urgently. Heat warmed her cheeks, and she averted her gaze.

Turning away from the water, she slipped past a deserted City Hall, clinging to the buildings' shadows. When a group of sailors approached, shouting and staggering, she ducked into the alley. Catching a glimpse of their faces in the moonlight, she had to stop herself from gasping. They were so young, their faces still unlined in the innocence of youth. Just boys, perhaps thrilled to taste their first hint of danger, heedless of the perils.

A shoe scraped on gravel, and she whirled, peering into the darkness. Had Seavey followed her after all? Had he tracked her down like an animal, intending to corner her in the darkened alley? Oh, how he'd like that. She'd seen it in his eyes every time he'd looked at her. She was his prey—she'd known the moment they first met.

A shadow shifted.

She leapt across the alley, into the pool of green light at the rear entrance of Port Chatham's most infamous house of ill repute. Her pursuer's footsteps quickened until he was directly behind her.

Raising her fists, Hattie Longren pounded on the door, her screams rending the hushed violence of the night.

Chapter 1

Port Chatham, Washington
June, present day

JORDAN Marsh stood in the middle of the street, staring aghast at her new home. Across twelve feet of uneven pavement and a weed-choked patch of lawn sat Longren House, the nineteenth-century Queen Anne she'd bought on what could only be described as—though she normally tried to avoid the term—an *insane* whim.

Crisp air, washed clean from last night's rain, brought into sharp relief decorative tracery hanging askew from the domed turret. Bright sun highlighted chunks of paint peeling from the columns of the wraparound porch that—she tilted her head—sagged. Behind a railing missing every third baluster, a broken swing had been shoved against the front bay window, which sported an ugly crack running diagonally its entire length.

Holy God. I don't even own a hammer.

While she'd been going through the inevitable hassles of closing down her therapy practice in Los Angeles and packing to move, Longren House had been a daily reminder of the new life she'd planned for herself. A simpler, quieter life—an antidote to the hell she'd lived through for the last year. A fantasy of peaceful, solitary days spent wallpapering a few rooms, perhaps rehanging the porch swing she'd always dreamed of owning.

What on earth had she been thinking? That watching a few reruns of *This Old House* qualified her to handle a historic-home remodel?

She counted the faded colors gracing the exterior, punctuating each numeral with a fingertip pointed midair at a section of siding, or what was left of it. "Thirteen goddamn colors of paint!" Just the thought of matching such a color scheme in modern paints had her lightheaded.

A huge, shaggy dog lying in front of the door raised its head and grinned at her, tail thumping, looking for all the world as if it belonged there. And for a brief moment, she could envision the house as she'd dreamed it would look after it was refurbished. "Like a real home," she murmured. "With a front porch swing for visiting neighbors and a friendly dog."

A door slammed down the block, and a dark-haired man wearing a cable-knit sweater and jeans jogged down the front steps of the house on the corner. Zeroing in on the tray of coffee cups he balanced in one hand, she recalled that in her haste to hit the road, she hadn't stopped for her requisite morning cup.

Local Man Assaulted by Caffeine-Deprived Lunatic

If she gave in to impulse, that's what tomorrow morning's newspaper headlines would read. Not, she reminded herself firmly, that she was a person who typically gave in to impulses.

Caffeinated beverages notwithstanding, though, he looked...interesting. Broad shoulders, and a confident, ground-eating stride. Definitely...

She gave herself a shake. Nope. Gazing was *not* in the cards. According to her Four-Point Plan for Personal Renewal, *gazing* was on hold for at least six months. Then she could *look but not touch* for another six. She'd laid it all out, written it all down. She had a plan, and she was sticking to it. Remodel first.

As soon as she bought a hammer. And a paintbrush or three.

She forced her attention back to her house. Leaning forward on her toes, she squinted to see whether lack of focus improved it. The driver of an approaching car tapped its horn, evidently afraid she would fling herself into its oncoming path.

The idea had merit.

Okay, so the house needed a little work. But she'd fallen in love with that crazy witch's cap perched atop the turret, the arched entryway and the gingerbread trim, the utter *wackiness* of its architecture. She didn't care whether it tumbled down around her—for the first time in her life, she had a real home.

Complete with a dog, it seemed.

"Nice bones."

Her head whipped around. Her new neighbor stood just a few feet away.

He gestured with the tray. "The house," he clarified in a deep baritone, smiling slightly, his blue eyes crinkling at the corners. "One of the few examples of stick-built Queen Anne architecture left standing in Port Chatham. She's a real beauty, isn't she?"

Jordan frowned. Even with the aid of fuzzy focus, the house wasn't yet close to a "beauty." But, hey, maybe he was an architect who recognized potential.

The aroma of fresh-roasted coffee and steamed milk wafted over her, and her eyes crossed.

"Can I ask what your interest is in her?" he asked.

"What? Oh." Jordan cleared her throat. "I bought her."

"Ah." He looked squarely at Jordan, not concealing his curiosity. Up close, his face was rugged and lived-in... and appealing. "You must be the psychologist from Los Angeles."

Her surprise must have shown on her face.

"Sorry." He shrugged, smiling sheepishly. "Small towns and all that." He extended a hand. "Jase Cunningham."

"Jordan Marsh." His grip was warm and firm.

"So you'll be setting up shop here in town?"

"No, at least, not right away." Perhaps not ever, though she wasn't admitting that yet, even to herself. "I'm taking a year off to work on the house."

"You're planning to fix her up?"

She nodded.

"Good."

"I need to buy a hammer," she blurted out.

He rubbed his chin thoughtfully. "The purchase of a hammer is a symbolic act. It is not to be taken lightly."

She narrowed her gaze. Okay, scratch *architect*. Maybe he was one of those artisans who worked on historic homes. Maybe he had a lot of hammers. Maybe he named them.

He came to some kind of conclusion with a nod. "Talk to Ed at Port Chatham Hardware out on the highway, and tell him I sent you. He'll get you set up properly."

"Um, thanks."

He pried one of the cups from its holder and handed it to her. She clutched it with both hands, giving him a look of such profound gratitude that he grinned. "You seem a little shell-shocked—it's the least I can do. Welcome to the neighborhood."

"Thanks again."

He waved a hand as he started down the street.

"Hey," she yelled, and he turned back, raising an eyebrow. "Do you know who owns the dog?"

"Nope. Never seen him before."

* * *

JORDAN watched for a moment longer, then shook her head. *Four-Point Plan for Personal Renewal*. Time to review the salient points.

As she walked over to her Toyota Prius, she took a sip of the coffee, which she discovered was an excellent latte. The man obviously knew his java. Shifting the cup to her left hand, she opened the trunk and hauled out her bag.

The hairs on the back of her neck suddenly rose, and she glanced around. The neighborhood of turn-of-the-twentieth-century homes seemed unusually deserted, the street empty and desolate with its cracked pavement and faded markings. Why weren't more people outside, taking advantage of the fine summer day?

She studied the vacant windows of the surrounding houses, keeping her expression nonchalant. No doubt a neighbor was watching her from inside one of them. After all, this was a small town—people were bound to be curious about the recently widowed psychologist moving to their neighborhood.

From the foliage of the maple tree, a songbird trilled enthusiastically, mocking her uneasiness. Shrugging, she gripped the handle of her bag and rolled it across the uneven lawn, banging it up the front steps.

The dog scrambled to its feet, ears perked. It had the black and tan coloring of a German shepherd, but its blocky build and thick, shaggy hair reminded her of a much larger breed. Definitely a classic mutt. A very *large male* mutt. She held out her hand for him to sniff.

Setting her bag down, she hunted through her pockets for the key the real estate agent had given her. After several tries, the lock gave with a screech and the beveled-glass door swung inward.

She looked down at the dog. "Excuse me."

He cocked his head.

"Shoo?" She wiggled her fingers, and when that had no effect, she managed to look stern. "Go home!"

He didn't budge.

She sighed. "I absolutely *cannot* get attached to you—someone owns you, I'm sure of it. I'm not letting you inside."

He barked, and she jumped a foot. Then he trotted into the foyer.

"Right," she muttered.

She set her bag inside the door, then slowly turned in a semicircle. The carved mahogany staircase that had made her hyperventilate when she'd first laid eyes on it rose in a graceful curve to the second floor, its risers covered by a faded, robin's-egg-blue runner worn through at the front edges. To her right stood the parlor with its bay window looking onto the front porch; to her left, the library that had been the second reason she'd lost her mind and written an obscenely large check.

"God." She sagged against the arched doorway to the library, staring at the cream-colored area rug. "That may be an Aubusson. Did I even notice that when I was here before?"

Nails clicking on the oak parquet flooring, the dog came to stand next to her, sniffing the stale air. She rubbed his head. "If you pee on that rug," she warned, "we'll have words. No marking your territory, even if it is the male imperative."

He looked insulted and returned to lie down by the front door.

The house had the empty silence of disuse, as if it had been waiting far too long for her arrival. She climbed the stairs, brushing cobwebs off the dusty railing. High up in the stairwell, sun shone through a small dormer window, turning the tracks her fingers made a burnished gold. Dust motes spiraled upward, floating on air currents warmed by shafts of sunlight.

She walked into the front bedroom, a giant, dimly lit cavern, the formality of its frescoed ceiling relieved by the cozy window seat in the turret. The room stood empty, its wide-planked floor scratched and bare, and the air was even staler than it had been downstairs.

After three tries, she found a window that wasn't painted shut. Fresh air blew in on a cool breeze, banishing the odors of must and mildew. She'd start cleaning in here first so that she wouldn't have to put her sleeping bag down in the dust. She'd packed only the essentials for the trip—casual clothes, an espresso maker, books. The movers wouldn't be here for another day or two, so she'd be roughing it until then.

Bracing her knee on the worn velvet seat cushion, she gazed down at the street through the leafy boughs of the maple tree. The neighborhood was quiet, filled with quaint, carefully tended houses and mature trees, reminiscent of small-town America from a bygone era. Ryland would have hated this place, she mused, as much as she was drawn to it.

The dog trotted up the stairs but stopped short of coming into the room, watching her hopefully with soft, liquid brown eyes. She straightened, sighing. "You really *do* need to go home."

Walking over to him, she rubbed his head some more, then ran a hand down his back. She could feel every joint of his spine, she realized in horror. Whoever owned him certainly didn't deserve him. "Come on, fella. Let's find you something to eat."

She bounded down the stairs. Glancing into the library as she walked past, she noted what she estimated to be a few thousand books stacked in random piles and jammed into glass-fronted bookcases. A wingback chair sat in the center of the room, flanked by a rickety pedestal table and a floor lamp with a leaded-glass shade. Across the room, a huge oak desk sat stacked with more books and yellowed newspapers. But it was the French doors on the opposite wall that beckoned.

She held up a hand to the dog. "I'll only be a moment..."

The doors swung open onto a stone patio tangled with weeds. An intoxicatingly sweet scent blew in, and she ventured out a few steps and looked up, trying to locate its source. She gasped. Wisteria covered the entire side of the house. Its cascading lilac flowers drowned her in fragrance.

"Oh...*oh!*" She knelt and wrapped her arms around the dog's neck.

In her mind's eye, she could see the garden as it would be when she cleaned it up—overflowing with flowers, bounded by bentwood fencing lush with climbing roses blooming in a riot of pink and white. What she'd felt the first time she'd seen the house had been a serious crush, but this...this was *love*.

"I'll be okay," she sniffed, burying her face in the dog's fur and pushing back the ever-present grief. "We'll be just fine."

"Hello?" The call came from the front hall.

"Coming!" She stood, swiping at tears, and crossed the library. Through the window, she spied a police cruiser parked at the front curb. *Damn.*

A woman stood inside the door, her gaze as sharp as the razor cut of her chin-length ash-blond hair. She spied Jordan. "Oh, good. I was afraid Sandy—the real estate agent—had left the door open. You must be the psychologist."

Though dressed casually in pressed jeans and a tailored jacket, she reminded Jordan of a Scandinavian Valkyrie—around six feet tall, she estimated, athletic and imposing as hell. Jordan had had her fill of cops in the last few months, asking questions for which she had no answers, treating her as if she were a criminal.

The Valkyrie thrust out a hand nearly twice the size of her own. "Darcy Moran. Port Chatham chief of police."

Chief of police. Even worse. Jordan reluctantly introduced herself. "What can I do for you, Chief Moran?"

"Make it Darcy. Stopped by to welcome you to the neighborhood."

Jordan relaxed marginally. "Thanks."

Darcy jerked her head toward the front door. "Looks like you could use some help carrying boxes."

"That's okay. You don't—" She was talking to empty space. The woman was already at the curb, pulling boxes from the trunk of Jordan's Prius.

Jordan followed at a more leisurely pace. "Slow day?" she asked wryly.

"Waiting for the tourists to wake up and hit the

streets." Darcy shoved a box into her arms, then picked up two more. "Where do you want these?"

"Um, the kitchen?"

They carried the boxes down the hall to the roomy country kitchen at the back of the house.

"When did you hit town?" Darcy asked over her shoulder as she deposited her boxes on the warped linoleum counter and headed back outside.

Jordan had to trot to keep up. "This morning. I'm a bit overwhelmed."

"Buyer's remorse." Darcy handed her another box. "You'll get over it."

"The wisteria's helping."

"Yeah, it's cool. Bit of a pain to keep in check, though."

It took only two more trips to empty the car. "See?" Darcy dusted off her hands. "Much easier when someone helps."

Jordan eyed her, trying to catch her breath. "Anyone ever compare you to a human cyclone?"

"I may have heard similar comments a time or two. Got anything to drink?"

Jordan rummaged in the ice chest they'd brought in, coming up with a soda. Then she found a bowl and headed for the sink. Nothing but a hiss of air came out when she turned the faucet handle, so she uncapped a bottle of Evian and poured it into the bowl for the dog. Unwrapping the all-natural chicken breast she'd been saving for a sandwich, she held it out to him. He scarfed it down in one gulp, then looked at her expectantly.

"I've been trying to catch up with that dog all week."

Darcy flipped open her cellphone. "Let me put in a call to Animal Control—"

He lowered his head and whined.

"No!"

Darcy paused, her finger poised over the keypad, brows raised.

"He's mine," Jordan improvised.

"Uh-huh. Didn't you say you just drove in this morning?"

"Minor technicality," she replied brightly. "Why don't we take our drinks and go sit out front? I've always wanted a front stoop to sit on." Without waiting for an answer, she grabbed Darcy's soda can, leaving her to follow.

"So what made you decide on Port Chatham?" Darcy asked once they were settled on the porch steps.

"An acquaintance of mine gave me tickets to last year's jazz concert. A few days in town was all it took to hook me on the idea of moving up here. Are you familiar with the Ted Rawlins Trio?"

Darcy nodded. "Rawlins is the friend? I've heard him play—he's very good. I think he purchased a summer home south of town on the golf course, didn't he?"

"He comes up every summer, as far as I know."

"How long are you planning to stay in town? Will Longren House be your vacation home, or your primary residence?"

The police chief was grilling her—and not all that subtly, either. Jordan kept her answers friendly. "I'll be here at least a year, maybe more, depending on how the remodel goes. And no, I don't plan to split my time—I'm gone from L.A. for good, I think." She shrugged. "We'll see. I want to research the house's history, plan the remodel right. Got any suggestions on where to start?"

"County. They might even have a copy of the original plans." Darcy propped an elbow on the top step. "If memory serves, a Captain Charles Longren built the place for his bride, Hattie, in the late 1800s. Hattie didn't live here all that long, though. There've been a number of owners over the years—"

Her cellphone wailed, startling Jordan.

After a brief conversation, Darcy hung up, sighing. "I've got to head back to the station."

"Your phone is programmed for Miles Davis?"

"Of course. We take our jazz seriously around here." Darcy drained her soda and stood, then studied Jordan for a moment. "So I'm betting you weren't the one who cut the brake lines on your husband's Beemer."

"No, I wasn't." Jordan managed to keep her tone matter-of-fact.

Darcy nodded. "Needed to ask."

"I can give you the name of the detective in L.A. who is handling the case. I'm sure he'll be glad to fill you in."

"Not necessary. The LAPD has already been in contact to say you're part of an ongoing investigation. It got me curious, so I asked a few questions."

Jordan didn't respond—over the past few months she'd learned not to volunteer information.

They walked to the curb, Darcy in the lead. "Listen,

why don't you drop by the pub tonight? I'll introduce you around."

"Pub?"

"The neighborhood hangout, over on the main drag. Come to think of it, your buddy Rawlins is slated to perform there tomorrow night. It's a laid-back place—the food is great and Jase doesn't water the drinks."

So he owned a pub. "I met him a bit ago, I think. Dark, wavy hair, killer blue eyes—"

"—and sexy as all hell? Yep, that's Jase." She flashed a grin, and Jordan relented, smiling back. "Seeing as how you don't strike me as a black widow in training," Darcy added, "I'll also mention that Jase is unattached."

Jordan held up a hand like a traffic cop. "Not on the agenda anytime soon."

"Good thing you've adopted a dog to keep you company, then." Darcy opened the door of the police cruiser. "Hey, do you like to hike? I'm always looking for new blood, and there's a great trek out on Dungeness Spit if we time the tides right."

Jordan had a sudden vision of being dragged, breathless, along a boulder-strewn promontory. "We'll see."

"Wise to be cautious." Darcy's grin broadened. "Talk to Jase—he'll tell you I don't lose too many of my hiking buddies. Well, just the uncoordinated ones."

Jordan shook her head, amused in spite of herself. "Thanks for the help unpacking the car."

"No problem. We tend to do for each other around here. Give it a couple of days and you'll be buried in food from the various welcoming committees."

"You live here in the neighborhood?"

"Two streets over—the Gothic Revival in the middle of the block."

Jordan must have looked perplexed.

"Blue with white trim, clean, symmetrical lines, a couple of Adirondacks on the porch," Darcy elaborated. "None of those frilly cottage garden flowers. You can't miss it."

She started to climb into the driver's seat, then paused, angling her head to look up at the second floor of Longren House. "So which bedroom are you planning to commandeer?"

"The front one. It's the largest, and the window seat in the turret is pretty hard to resist."

"You might want to rethink that if you plan on getting a good night's sleep."

"Why?"

"You mean Sandy didn't tell you?" Darcy shook her head in apparent disgust. "Back around the turn of the last century, Hattie Longren was bludgeoned to death in that very room."

Chapter 2

AS the police cruiser disappeared around the corner, Jordan squeezed her eyes shut.

"Okay," she muttered. "Murder definitely constitutes a giant checkmark in the buyer's remorse column."

But now that she thought about it, she'd been able to buy Longren House for a lot less than other homes for sale in town. Not that writing the amount on the check hadn't caused her serious heartburn at the time, but still, she remembered having one of those niggling feelings...

Abruptly, she sat down on the curb and scrubbed her face with both hands. When it came to dealing with the unintended consequences of impulsive acts, murder—even one a century old—bumped the thirteen colors of paint and sagging porch all the way down to the white noise level. She was a therapist, for chrissakes. She strongly believed in, and practiced, Rational Therapy. So how in God's name had she considered it *rational* to act so impulsively?

A small, hysterical laugh escaped. And what were the damn odds that she would buy a house tainted by murder? No one would believe it was mere coincidence. She had no problem envisioning *that* headline:

Suspected Black Widow Fascinated by Murder Buys Longren House

No wonder the police chief had shown up on her doorstep twenty minutes after she'd hit town.

She really needed to work on the gullibility issue. Not that this would be the first time she'd fallen prey—witness her seven-year marriage to one of L.A.'s smoothest operators. She'd had no clue of the double life he'd led; she'd actually believed him when he'd said he had to work late all those evenings.

She sighed. No matter what Ryland's faults had been—and they'd turned out to be legion—he hadn't deserved to die. And though she might've fantasized a time or two about wringing his neck, she hadn't actually given in to impulse, regardless of what the L.A. cops believed.

The dog sat next to her, whining, and licked her cheek. She threw an arm around his neck and hugged him. "I'm okay," she reassured him. "But thanks for asking."

Then she rolled her eyes. "Great," she muttered. "I'm thanking a dog."

Definitely time to take charge. She couldn't do anything about the past, but the future . . . well, she'd keep a low profile, work on the house, and pray the LAPD would look at other suspects. As far as they knew, she didn't have a strong motive to kill Ryland, what with the divorce almost final. They'd bought her reasoning.

At least, she thought they had.

And as for the murder that had taken place in Longren House, she'd simply ignore it. It had nothing to do with her.

As she used to tell her patients, *Focus on today, and tomorrow will take care of itself. Ignore that little voice inside your head whispering they're out to get you. Avoid the urge to put foil on your windows.*

Unpack. Review the Four-Point Plan. In light of the day's events, consider modification of the FPP. Make a list for the hardware store.

"An ancient murder will *not* stop me from loving this place," she told the dog, "and it will *not* make me start obsessing again."

"*Raaooooow.*"

"After all, it was a really long time ago, right?"

"*Rooooo.*"

"Precisely."

She dragged a bucket of cleaning supplies from the backseat of the car and headed inside.

* * *

IT took her an hour, crawling among the lethal brambles along the back kitchen wall, to locate the water main and turn it on, then flip the circuit breaker on the electric panel. While she waited for hot water, she grabbed a packet of dust cloths and a bottle of lemon oil and headed back upstairs.

She hesitated at the door to the front bedroom. Then she scolded herself for being ridiculous. The fantasy of whiling away the hours in the window seat with a good book definitely trumped an old homicide.

First thing in the morning, though, she'd head over to the county offices, maybe even check the local newspaper archives. She had to admit, she was curious about what had happened to Hattie Longren.

Had the murder been a random act by a drifter? Or committed in a moment of passion by someone close to her? Had she known she would die beforehand? For that matter, had Ryland known—in those last seconds as his car plunged into the ravine—that *he* would die?

Jordan halted halfway across the room, shuddering at the morbid direction of her thoughts. Forcing herself to focus on the present, she waited to see whether she felt anything from the room, like old, malevolent vibes. People always swore they could feel the remnants of the violence—even decades later—in a room where a crime had occurred.

She cocked her head . . . Nope, nothing. All she felt was that she'd finally come home, that *this* was the house she belonged in, not in the ultramodern condominium in Malibu that Ryland had talked her into buying.

After securing her shoulder-length hair with claw clips, she grabbed a dust cloth and got down to work, chasing away personal demons along with the cobwebs. The dog lay down in the doorway to watch her.

It took her a while to notice that he wasn't coming into the room. She paused while unrolling her sleeping bag in front of the window seat and, bending over, slapped her hands on her knees. "C'mere, sweetie."

He lowered his ears and thumped his tail on the floor.

She injected a firm note into her voice. "*Come.*"

He stood and disappeared down the hall.

"Clearly I have a bright future ahead of me as a dog trainer," she muttered, rising to follow.

She found him sitting in the middle of the bedroom at the back of the house. When she entered, he barked and grinned, his tongue lolling.

The room was full of light and charming with its angled ceilings and faded floral wallpaper, some of it even still hanging. The dormer window that looked down on the overgrown backyard opened without much protest.

In the winter when the leaves had fallen from the trees, the view of Admiralty Inlet and the shipping lanes would be stunning. She couldn't help but wonder if Hattie Longren had stood in this very spot more than a century ago, watching for her husband's ship on the horizon.

Directly below, through the boughs of a magnolia tree, she could still see the faint outline of the garden's original beds, which would've been filled with herbs and flowers and vegetables. The debris-covered remains of a flagstone path led around to the side, probably to the patio off the library. Once restored to its original design...

The dog whined, capturing her attention. He stood at a closet door, scratching. Walking over, she opened it, revealing a funky, oddly shaped triangle built into the corner of the room. After sniffing excitedly, the dog started scratching the inside back wall, so she dropped to her knees to see what had captured his interest. Prying away a loose board, she spied a tattered edge of lace and reached for it. The lace was attached to an old porcelain doll.

"Well, well," she murmured, carefully removing the doll from its hiding place. "How did you know it was there, fella?"

Sitting on the floor, she smoothed its dress, yellowed by time, using her thumb to wipe a smudge off the doll's chipped, rosy cheek. Had this been Hattie's daughter's room? If so, what had happened to her after Hattie's death?

"*Yoooo-hooooooooo?*"

The trill came from downstairs, startling Jordan, and she scowled. Where was that peace and quiet she'd moved to a small town to find?

"Anybody home?" The voice was closer and more insistent now, at the foot of the stairs.

Sighing, she set the doll on the lower shelf and stood. Heading for the hall, she looked back for the dog, but he'd disappeared. "Smart," she muttered under her breath.

At the top of the stairs she skidded to a halt, gaping.

Two women stood in the lower hall, dressed in vintage clothing. One, in her forties, wore a full-length, forest-green silk dress with a fitted velvet bodice that dropped into a curved vee over her slim hips. Her narrow shoulders were covered by a cape of the same velvet trimmed in black, and she'd pinned her brown hair up in an elaborately coiffed style that Jordan figured had to be historically accurate. The second woman, fair-haired and younger by perhaps a decade, was dressed less sedately. Her pale blue silk gown sported a small bustle and a daring neckline.

"There you are." The older of the two smiled up at her. "I hope we're not disturbing?" When Jordan continued to stare, slack-jawed, the woman laughed self-consciously. "I'm Nora. And this is my sister, Delia. We're docents at the Port Chatham Historical Society. We must have given you quite a shock."

"Ah. Um, no. Sorry." Jordan loped down the stairs. "Your costumes are fabulous."

They glanced at each other, smiling.

"Thank you." Nora smoothed her skirts with slender, pale hands. "It's best to look the part, we always say. Don't we, Delia?"

Delia turned in a circle to show off her gown. "What do you think?" Her eyes, which were a perfect match for her dress, gleamed with mischief. "I'm trying to convince Nora that fashion had nothing to do with comfort in those days. She's been reading about the rational dress movement that was touted back then by a few radical old stick-in-the-muds."

"Hmmph." Nora looked down her nose. "The rational dress movement was very forward thinking. Women actually damaged their internal organs by wearing corsets and carrying around so much weight in all those bustles and petticoats."

"Most women were looking for a husband and wanted to display their assets to best advantage. Just because a few old biddies were lecturing on the dangers of corsets—"

"The new, less restrictive styles were just as flattering—"

"Bull!"

Jordan, fearing the onset of whiplash, cleared her throat. "Um, I'd offer you ladies some refreshments, but I'm afraid all I have is—"

"Who would want to look *that* straitlaced?" Delia snapped, rolling right over her. "Men weren't looking for *sedate*." She sniffed, turning her attention to Jordan. "You don't happen to have any *Vanity Fair* magazines, do you?"

Jordan hesitated, baffled by the question.

"Can't you see she hasn't even moved in yet?" Nora chided her sister. "Magazines would be the very last thing she'd unpack."

"Nonsense. Anyone who keeps up on fashion would have one or two magazines with them for the long trip up here, now, wouldn't they? And she did travel all the way from California."

"Ah, well—"

"Delia." Nora ignored Jordan's attempted reply. "Quit harassing the poor girl."

Delia pouted.

Jordan couldn't remember the last time anyone had referred to her as a "girl," but she had to admit that it beat "black widow" hands down. She pasted an apologetic smile on her face. "I'm afraid I really don't pay much attention to fashion," she said, gesturing at her jeans, which looked "vintage" only because of the number of washings they'd endured. "About those refreshments—"

"We brought treats!" Delia lit up, her moods fluctuating at the speed of a teenager's. "A chocolate cake! We put it in the kitchen."

"How kind of you. Let me find some paper plates. But first, would you like a tour of the house?"

"Don't go to the trouble," Nora told her firmly. "We've seen it many times."

"That makes sense." Jordan led the way toward the kitchen. "I suppose Port Chatham has a historic homes tour, right? And the prior owners would've had the place on the tour, what with the murder and all."

She heard a gasp behind her; she turned to find Delia halted, tears in her eyes.

"There, there." Nora rushed to put an arm around her sister's shoulders. "She's extremely sensitive," she confided to Jordan. "She cries over the sad stories associated with some of the homes here in town."

"I'm so sorry. Can I get anything? Perhaps some water?"

"No, we're fine. Your comment took us by surprise, that's all."

"So you know all about the murder?"

"Of course. Poor Hattie. Such a tragedy it was. Killed by the man she loved, they say . . ." Nora handed Delia a handkerchief, her own expression bereft. "But we never really believed the official story, now, did we?"

"*No.*" Delia blew her nose loudly. "Frank *loved* Hattie. He *never* would have killed her."

"Though it's true we don't really know for certain—"

"I do! He was a *wonderful* man. He didn't have a violent bone in his body."

Nora sent her sister a sharp look. "Well, perhaps, though it would hardly seem so from the newspaper accounts." Her hand sliced through the air impatiently. "The fact is, I've always suspected Seavey."

"Who is—was—Seavey?" Jordan asked, intrigued.

"Well, I don't think he did it," Delia insisted. "Even if he was a bad man."

"He was a *vile* man. Anyone can see that from—"

"But he worshipped Hattie—"

"He most certainly did *not*!"

"Cake," Jordan said grimly. "In the kitchen. Now."

Nora jumped. "We have to be going." She pointed Delia in the direction of the front door.

"No—wait," Jordan said hastily. *Right. Scare off the sweet little local ladies. That'll endear you to the neighborhood.* "I'm sorry for sounding abrupt—it's just that I've already had a long drive and . . . Please stay."

"No, we mustn't keep you." Nora nudged her sister forward. "We just stopped by to bring you a few historical documents we thought you might enjoy. They're on the counter next to the cake. You'll return them to us at the Society when you're through with them, won't you?"

"Of course. How thoughtful of you. In fact, I'm eager to visit and go through your collection." Jordan waved a hand. "I'm determined to fix the old place up. I'd love to see some pictures from when it was new, plus any articles that might have appeared at the time in the local newspapers."

Evidently she'd said the right thing, because both women beamed at her.

"And we'd love to be of help!" Delia gushed. "It's so important to preserve our heritage, don't you think?"

"Absolutely." Relieved, Jordan walked them to the door. "Are you sure I can't interest you in some cake? I can't possibly eat it all by myself."

"No, we'll . . . get out of your hair!" Delia giggled, looking pleased with herself, and Nora chuckled indulgently.

Jordan looked from one to the other, not getting their joke. Did her hair look that bad? She resisted the urge to raise a hand and check. "Well, thanks again. I'll stop by tomorrow. What time do you open?"

"Around ten," Nora replied. "Do you know where the research center is?"

"I have a map—I'll find it."

Jordan closed the door behind them. Leaning against it, she shook her head, amused. Given their argumentative communication style, she'd wager her Prius that those two had been living together for a *very* long time.

Walking back to the kitchen, she spied a cake box on the counter next to a jumble of newspaper clippings and papers. Peeking inside, she swiped a bit of frosting. "Oh. Yum." Devil's food with cream cheese fudge frosting.

One side of the cake was smashed—she wondered whether they'd dropped it on the way over. She shrugged, smiling, and licked more frosting off her finger.

As she walked back down the hallway to the foot of

the stairs, she looked up. "You can come out now," she called. "They're gone."

The dog stuck his head around the banister, unrepentant.

"Traitor."

* * *

JORDAN spent the next several hours hauling, sweeping, and mopping. By late afternoon, she had generated a recycle pile of respectable size and felt the need for sustenance that didn't contain sugar.

After explaining the concept of leash laws to the dog, who sat and listened with exaggerated patience, she tied a piece of rope she'd found in the butler's pantry around his neck. He barked at her, no matter how firmly she tugged on the rope, until she folded it and held it out. Taking it gently from her, he held it in his mouth and trotted out the front door, pausing to look over his shoulder. She shook her head and hurried obediently after him.

"We need to have a discussion regarding names," she said as they proceeded down the sidewalk. "I refuse to call you Dog—it's demeaning. What about...hmm... Spike?"

"*Raaoomph!*"

"Hey, he's a great director—you could do worse. But I'll keep thinking."

The afternoon had turned warm, and she tugged off her sweatshirt and tied it around her waist. As she walked, she soaked up the atmosphere along with the rays.

Port Chatham sat on a bluff on the northernmost tip of the Olympic Peninsula, surrounded by the glistening waters of Puget Sound. The town's historic waterfront faced Port Chatham Bay on a narrow strip of low-lying land only a few blocks wide. The rest of the town—the majority of its residential areas—had been built on the bluffs overlooking downtown.

Around each corner, Jordan was confronted with yet a different view of the shipping lanes and the islands that dotted Puget Sound. To the east, a few blocks off the brow of the hill, she could see the ferry making its way across Admiralty Inlet to Whidbey Island.

Her neighborhood consisted of blocks of historic homes surrounding a small, satellite business district that spread outward from a central intersection of two arterial streets. As always, she was struck by the clash of old and new—well-cared-for homes that made her feel as though she'd stepped back a hundred years in time juxtaposed with the jarring presence of modern businesses, telephone poles, and parked cars.

A block down, a young man sat on a sagging couch on the front porch of a small cottage, playing jazz on his guitar—a song that combined elements of blues and fusion. A young girl wearing a vintage dress sat at his feet, softly humming her own tune while she played with an antique doll.

Just beyond the cottage stood a lovingly tended old home, painted lemon yellow with aubergine accents and surrounded by a white picket fence smothered in pink climbing roses. Jordan smiled and waved at the elderly couple sitting in the gently swaying porch swing, holding hands. The man put out his foot to halt the swing, surprise showing on his face, but his wife returned Jordan's smile with a nod.

The grocery was one block up and two over, and it seemed to be a neighborhood hub of sorts. She'd discovered the small business district when she'd stayed at a bed-and-breakfast down the block, on her trip to town the prior summer. Between jazz performances at the local taverns, she'd sat outside the bakery and had coffee, then wandered down the quiet back streets, exchanging greetings with friendly locals who'd been out watering their lawns or walking their dogs. She remembered thinking at the time that she'd possibly found a community that could be her salvation. Her impression hadn't changed.

The dog sat down to wait outside the grocery, his leash still in his mouth. She didn't even attempt to tie him to the bicycle stand.

Though the building was new, the grocery fit into the neighborhood with its homey atmosphere, appealing displays of organic produce, and quaint hand-lettered signs. Leaded-glass windows of abstract design flooded the interior with light, and customers sat in a loft over the deli, reading the newspaper while they ate their sandwiches.

The aisles were stocked with standard fare plus an impressive selection of gourmet and organic foods that promised to do serious damage to Jordan's monthly budget. She dumped canned organic dog food, a box of whole-grain cereal, milk, and a bag of coffee into her basket, plus a deli-packed serving of vegetarian lasagna for dinner. Snagging a bottle of Pinot Noir, she headed for the checkout.

Halfway there she halted and backtracked to add a wedge of imported French triple-cream Brie, fancy crackers, and more sliced chicken breast, muttering to herself the entire time about a lack of self-discipline. After a chat with the checkout clerk about the fire a few years back that had destroyed the original historic building, she and the dog headed back home.

Pulling paper plates from one of the boxes on the kitchen counter, Jordan fixed a sandwich, dividing the chicken breast heavily in favor of the dog. Opening a can of dog food that looked more appealing than her own recipe for beef stew, she added its contents to the plate, placing it on the floor. The food disappeared with alarming speed.

While she munched on her sandwich, she rifled through the stack of papers left by Nora and Delia. The ladies had provided a mix of old newspaper articles about the murder and what appeared to be pages from a diary. She wedged the papers under one elbow, picked up a book on Port Chatham's history she'd bought at a local bookstore during her last trip to town, and headed outside to sit on the front stoop. Though she felt more exposed than she liked—as if someone were still watching her—she'd be damned if anyone would stop her from enjoying her own porch.

According to the clerk at the grocery, fire had played an

important role in the town's history. Torn over what to read first, she finally set aside the ladies' papers and propped the book on her knees, flipping through until she found a chapter on historic fires. The author had interspersed text with pictures of the valiant fire crews, standing somberly in their old-fashioned uniforms and helmets.

A photocopied newspaper article on a huge waterfront fire caught her eye, and she settled down to read, the dog snoozing in the sun at her feet.

The Great Fire

May 25, 1890, two weeks earlier

"THEY say an entire block is already in flames," Hattie Longren murmured to Eleanor Canby. "Five are dead, with more to be found."

Though midnight had come and gone, they stood next to the bell tower at the top of the bluff with their neighbors, watching as the inferno raged below them on the waterfront. Orange flames leapt high against a smoke-filled, black sky, writhing and reaching out on the wind.

"Good riddance, I say." Eleanor folded her arms over her ample bosom. Tall and matronly, she wore her gray serge as if it were a suit of armor in a war against loose morals. "We both know that area was nothing but saloons and brothels."

As the owner of the *Port Chatham Weekly Gazette*, Eleanor frequently wrote editorials with strong views regarding the lawlessness and temptations of the waterfront. Rigid, old-fashioned views, in Hattie's opinion.

She shivered, holding the folds of her cape tightly

closed against the damp night air. "No one deserves to die that way."

The bell had begun ringing at ten, a full half hour after the first spiral of smoke had been spotted, according to one neighbor. The blaze had quickly spread. Hattie suspected the fire was no accident, and that the initial report had been intentionally delayed. Someone had been sending a message: *Do as we say, or see your business destroyed.* But whoever had started the fire hadn't counted on the strong wind from the south, and other businesses were now at risk.

A murmur rose from the crowd as several adjoining buildings, black silhouettes half eaten through, teetered, then fell, consumed instantly in a roiling mass of crimson sparks. A silver stream of salt water arced from a tugboat anchored in the harbor, dousing roofs and flooding the streets. Hattie could see the dark shapes of men racing to and fro in a desperate attempt to save the records from City Hall. Working to save City Hall, but making no effort to save the people in buildings facing the waterfront, she thought in disgust.

"Will the fire spread up here?" Charlotte's delicate features were pale from anxiety.

"No." Hattie placed a hand on her sister's trembling shoulder. "There's no chance of that. They'll have it under control before then."

"Don't be too sure," Eleanor retorted. "Sparks could find their way to us."

"If they do, we'll extinguish them," Hattie said firmly. At the impressionable age of fifteen, Charlotte was prone to wild mood swings. Hattie didn't need her frightened by Eleanor's tendency toward dour predictions.

After their parents died in a carriage accident in Boston, Charlotte and her beloved lady's maid, Tabitha, had come to live with Hattie. Charlotte had proven to be more of a handful than Hattie had anticipated. *Charlotte yearns for adventure as you once did*, their mother had written in a letter to be delivered upon the event of her death, *but she hasn't your innate good judgment. We're counting on you to keep her safe.*

Innate good judgment. Hattie sighed. If only her mother knew the truth about her short marriage. The tension between her and Charles had driven him to sea, where he perished at the hands of a mutinous crew, leaving her with a struggling shipping business she was ill prepared to manage. And now she had Charlotte depending on her as well. A familiar sense of panic threatened to overwhelm her.

"That fire was started by a drunken prostitute, mark my words." Eleanor's voice snapped her back to the present. "I can find no sympathy for those of her ilk. Painted harlots, flaunting their wares and infatuating our decent young men, plying them with corn liquor until they don't know their own minds!"

"Bull," Hattie said, earning herself a sharp look from Eleanor. But Hattie knew well the intertwined cycles of poverty and cruelty—her mother had run a clinic in Boston's Back Bay. "It's the supposedly decent men of this town who are preying on helpless women."

"You don't know what you're saying."

Hattie shrugged off Eleanor's look of condemnation. "What about Jessie? Hasn't he been seen in the Green Light?"

Eleanor's mouth thinned at the mention of her youngest. Young, handsome, and possessing an easy charm he couldn't have inherited from his mother, Jessie was well known around town for his wild ways.

"Jessie is no longer welcome in our home, and the Green Light is nothing but a stench in the nostrils of decent citizens," she replied.

"But don't you worry that among the dead tonight might be other sons of prominent families?" Hattie asked quietly. "That fire was deliberately set."

"*Ssshhh!*" Eleanor glanced over her shoulder. "You can't make statements like that in public."

"Why not? You know it's true."

Eleanor stiffened. "My reporters have already determined that the fire started in a house of ill repute. May they all reap what they sow!"

Hattie raised an eyebrow. "You sound like a temperance lecturer."

"And what of it? John Gough and his disciples have much to say that is worth listening to." Eleanor's voice had risen, and several in the crowd nodded their agreement. She looked gratified, as if the fire were proof of her belief that the waterfront was populated by the devil's own.

Hattie shook her head but dropped the subject, knowing it was futile to think she could change Eleanor's mind.

Mayor Payton's buckboard clattered to a halt behind them, its matched pair of bays wild-eyed from the smoke.

Short and barrel-chested, Payton struggled to control the lunging horses.

"We need every able-bodied man!" he shouted, his silver handlebar mustache streaked with soot. "Customs House and City Hall are threatened!"

Hattie turned to Charlotte. "Go quickly and rouse Tabitha."

"What do you think you're doing?" Eleanor spat as Charlotte dashed off. "Women like us don't go to the waterfront—not if we want our reputations to remain intact."

"Nonsense," Hattie replied. "I need to check on my sailing crews, some of whom could be trapped inside burning buildings. They're my responsibility now." Though she felt a twinge of foreboding, she kept her voice confident. "We'll be perfectly safe. The police are standing guard throughout the area."

"But think what you'll be subjecting the girls to!"

"They'll be fine—I'll be there to chaperone them. And it will be an excellent learning experience for them, helping those less fortunate than themselves."

Eleanor huffed. "This is outrageous behavior for a widow so recently in mourning."

"No one will think ill of me if I go down to help." Hattie stared Eleanor down. "Will you do nothing, then?"

"I've dispatched a reporter and photographer to the scene. I have no intention of personally mingling with the criminal elements."

"Many of those *criminal elements* are men regularly invited into the better homes in this town, men who don't admit to having their hands dirtied by the proceeds of the very saloons and brothels they rail against."

"Talk like that will not endear you to your neighbors," Eleanor admonished in a low voice.

Charlotte and Tabitha ran toward them, buckets in their hands. Resolute, Hattie turned her back on Eleanor and went to meet the girls by the buckboard, taking hold of the extra buckets.

"Help us up," she ordered the man sitting closest to them.

* * *

HUGE, glowing cinders flew overhead as the wagon rolled to a stop in front of City Hall. Across the street, flames shot through the roofs of several two-story wooden buildings, and the window frames of others were already smoking. Every few moments, Hattie heard the sound of plate glass shattering. It was hot, so hot that even from where she sat, her dress felt on fire next to her skin.

Men begrimed with smoke and soot dragged boxes from City Hall, while policemen pulled furniture from the adjacent courthouse. The town's new hose cart stopped next to their buckboard, pulled by a huge, black draft horse and several runners. Firemen raced to unwind the hose.

In front of the Green Light, a man in a preacher's frock coat held up a Bible and cried, "This fire was visited upon us by the wrath of God!"

A policeman headed in his direction, looking irritated. *Good*, Hattie thought as she climbed down.

Her first order of business was to find her manager, Clive Johnson. "This way, girls."

They ran toward the harbor, their long skirts dragging through blackened puddles of water. Men rushed past them, shouting at them to get out of the way. As they rounded the corner, Hattie thrust out her arm to stop Charlotte and Tabitha.

Fire roared the length of the block. Dozens of half-dressed women stood crying in groups on the beach below the wharf, their white chemises now soot-streaked and torn, their hair falling in disarray around their faces. Others ran to the water's edge with buckets, then back to fling water onto the burning structures. Sailors dragged crates of corn liquor from a burning saloon, while more men used axes to break the front windows of the general store and retrieve clothing and tins of food.

"Those women aren't dressed," Tabitha said in a low voice, glancing nervously at the prostitutes. "And the men..."

"Never mind that now." Hattie folded back her mourning veil so that she could see better.

Dear God.

At least a dozen buildings were completely engulfed. Next to where they stood, flames ate through the huge, white block letters of the words Stable and Livery painted on the wooden plank siding of a building. Hattie heard the screams of horses still trapped inside their stalls, then saw several lunge from the smoke-filled interior.

"Get back!" She yanked the girls out of the path of the horses.

Two men ran from the building, fiery beams crashing behind them as the structure collapsed.

Hattie took a calming breath. She scanned the crowd on the beach, spying Clive Johnson standing among them. "Wait here," she told the girls.

As she approached, Johnson, a portly man of average height, thinning hair, and unexceptional features, exclaimed, "Mrs. Longren! What're you doin' down here?"

"Checking on the status of my sailing crews. I trust you've ensured they are safe?"

He gave her an odd look, then shrugged. "I reckon."

"Please locate them and verify their safety. Order them to assist in the firefighting, if they aren't doing so already. And send someone out to the ships immediately. Have the first mates bring the skeleton crews onshore to help fight the fire."

He shook his head. "I ain't leavin' the ships unguarded."

She controlled a flush of irritation. In recent weeks, she'd come to expect his attempts to undermine her authority, but they still rankled. "And if we don't halt this fire," she countered in a sharp tone, "there won't be any boardinghouses left standing to shelter the crews who sail those ships. Now do as I say."

Without waiting for a response, she turned her back on him, pretending not to hear the derogatory comment he made under his breath, then searched the crowd for someone in authority. Her gaze landed on an older woman of imposing height, dressed in a midnight blue gown of the finest silk and brocade, standing ten yards away.

Walking over, she touched the woman's shoulder. "Excuse me!"

The woman turned. Upon closer viewing, her features, though not beautiful, were arresting, and she exuded an air of authority. Her makeup was smudged, revealing lines caused by years of hard living, but her eyes were sharp and alert.

After looking Hattie up and down, she frowned. "Can't you see we're busy? We sure as hell don't need some temperance lecturer underfoot!"

Hattie stood her ground. "I'm Hattie Longren, and those girls"—she pointed—"are Charlotte Walker, my sister, and her maid, Tabitha. We're here to help."

The woman ignored her outstretched hand. "So?"

Hattie hesitated, then turned toward the crowd on the beach. "Ladies!" she shouted. "Form a line between the bay and the saloon. Two at the shore, handing full buckets up the line, and two at the front, emptying them. We can pass the empties back down the same line."

The prostitutes stayed where they were, afraid to follow her instructions until the woman jerked her head and said grudgingly, "Do as she says."

In no time, they were tossing water on the flames now pouring from the front door of the saloon. But they might as well have been pouring it on a teaspoon at a time—the fire devoured the water without so much as a hiss.

The woman stood next to Hattie at the front of the line, sweat creating dark patches on their dresses as they worked. After the third time Hattie's hands brushed against the woman's, she turned to give Hattie an assessing look. "I'm Mona Starr, proprietress of the Green Light."

Hattie's eyes widened. Port Chatham's most notorious madam. Hattie had heard it whispered that without the philanthropic efforts of the woman standing next to her, the town couldn't boast about its grand opera hall, or even its new courthouse. Rumor was that Mona Starr also stood between her girls and any man who would abuse them—that prostitutes lined up to work under her patronage.

"I don't imagine hoity-toity types like you should be touching my kind," Mona observed.

"I'm not worried." Hattie took an overflowing bucket from her, slopping some of it down the front of her dress.

Mona looked surprised, then pursed her lips. "You must be Charles Longren's widow."

"Yes." Hattie noticed men hauling crates of liquor down the block. "Where are they taking those?" she asked, pointing.

"The tunnels."

Intrigued, she followed their progress. Before his death, Charles had related stories of sailors imprisoned in underground caverns until shanghaiers could negotiate their passage on the next ship leaving port, and of young girls, kidnapped and sold into prostitution.

Shivering, she turned to search for Charlotte and Tabitha, relieved when she located them farther down the bucket line, near the beach. The chief of police—a somber, intimidating man named John Greeley who had been outside City Hall when they'd arrived—now stood next to Charlotte, his expression watchful and ... proprietary, Hattie realized. She frowned.

Mona glanced in the direction of her gaze. "Don't you worry about your girls—Greeley will keep them safe from harm."

"Charlotte is so young."

"Many of my girls are younger."

Hattie shook her head.

"Your husband was a customer at the Green Light for a time." At her stunned look, Mona laughed. "Honey, you'd be surprised who visits my girls. I train 'em good, and the men can't resist. They just don't get the same kind of attention at home."

"You must be mistaken," Hattie said firmly.

Mona studied her for a moment before handing over an empty bucket. "Charles Longren wasn't a nice man."

Hattie stiffened. "I beg your pardon? My husband was well regarded."

Mona hesitated, then shrugged. "My mistake."

Hattie would have pressed the point, but a man who stood observing her across the street on the beach caught her eye. Tall and slender, he wore his evening clothes with a casual elegance at odds with his surroundings. Two burly, rough-looking men stood on either side of him, their expressions watchful. The man dipped his head in acknowledgment, staring steadily at her, a slight smile curving his lips.

"Who is that?" she asked, suddenly uneasy.

Mona spared him no more than a glance as she tossed the next bucket of water. "He owns a hotel and some boardinghouses down here."

Hattie tried to place him. "I think I've seen him before—perhaps at a dinner at someone's house."

Mona shook her head. "If you do run across him, you'd best steer clear, you hear?"

Two prostitutes burst from the front door of a brothel on the far side of the saloon, falling to their knees and coughing. Hattie ran over to pull them to safety. She heard a scream and looked up. A woman stood in the second-story window, frantically jerking at the iron bars trapping her. Her eyes pleading, she slid from sight. Impulsively, lifting an arm to protect her face, Hattie darted inside.

Lung-searing heat and thick black smoke instantly enveloped her. Pulling her cloak over her head, she worked her way up the stairs, holding her skirts away from flames licking at the risers. She found the woman in the front room, crumpled below the window. When she shook the woman's shoulder, she stirred and moaned, then coughed.

"Come with me!" Hattie shouted, helping her to her feet.

They crept back along the wall to the stairs, Hattie's

arm around the woman's waist for support. Chunks of burning roof crashed around them as they stumbled down the steps and outside. The woman collapsed on the front porch, her eyes rolling up into her head.

"Hattie!" Charlotte cried, starting forward, but Greeley grabbed her arms.

Hattie doubled over, coughing and slapping at the flames eating the hem of her dress. She tried to drag the unconscious woman away from the flames, but the woman was heavyset and limp, a deadweight.

"Help me move her," Hattie rasped to the other prostitutes.

All three of them tugged, but at best, they moved her a few feet at a time. Fire exploded above them, hot glass raining down, and the women screamed and ran. Hattie locked her hands around the woman's wrists. Using her own weight to drag the woman backward, she stumbled and fell into the mud, only to rise and try again.

Large hands gripped her waist, picking her up effortlessly and setting her down several yards away. The man she'd seen across the street stood facing her. His fingers radiated warmth through the fabric of her dress, but his eyes were as pale and cold as the water in the harbor on a cloudy day. "She's not worth it," he said. "Come away, before you get hurt."

"I'm not leaving her!"

He studied Hattie for a moment. "Remy, Max." He jerked his head at the woman. "Carry her over to the beach."

The two bodyguards picked up and carried the

woman, dumping her none too gently on the sand twenty yards away. Hattie glared at the man still holding her. "Tell your men to have a care, sir!"

He merely shrugged as if her response amused him.

She stepped away, but before she could reach the woman, a large man wearing a work shirt and overalls walked over and knelt down to examine her.

"I'll take care of her," he said quietly. Smoothing the woman's hair out of her face, he placed gentle fingers against her neck, feeling for a pulse.

The man in evening attire seized Hattie's arm and led her several yards down the street, his bodyguards flanking them. Then he stopped to face her.

"You shouldn't be down here, Mrs. Longren. This is no place for a woman as fine as yourself."

She raised her chin. "You have the advantage, sir."

"I usually do." He bowed mockingly from the waist. "The name's Seavey. Mike Seavey."

Chapter 3

LATER that same evening, because Jordan felt like staying home by herself, she made it a goal to put on a bit of makeup and go socialize. With the press hounding her 24/7 in L.A., she'd become increasingly isolated. Even worse, she'd gotten used to the isolation. She was in danger of becoming a certified loner, and if her treatment of the day's visitors was any indication, her social skills were rapidly deteriorating.

Not to mention the fact that she'd felt perfectly comfortable having several long, involved conversations with a dog. *That* had to stop.

"What about Duke?" she asked as they left the house and headed for the business district. "As in Duke Ellington?"

The dog gave her what she now recognized as The Look, comprising equal parts derision and personal affront.

"Okay, okay, I'll keep working on it."

The sky to the west had faded from fuchsia to purple,

creating deep shadows in the yards of the houses she passed. Down at the end of her block, at the bluff's edge, the triangular-shaped silhouette of the old wooden bell tower she'd read about partially blocked her view of the buildings downtown. Lights glowed from the buildings' windows, and she caught herself automatically thinking the illumination came from gaslight lamps.

She shivered. The evening had turned surprisingly chilly, and the cropped jean jacket she'd put on over her tank top was no protection against the damp and cold coming off the water. She paused not far from the grocery and looked back in the direction from which they'd come. Echoing her uneasiness, the dog growled low in his throat.

Throughout the day, she'd been unable to shake the feeling of being watched. She was beginning to believe her new neighborhood might harbor a sexual predator. Then again, perhaps the paparazzi had followed her north.

Except for a gray-haired woman dressed in a dark blue cashmere skirt and flowing cape, the street stood empty, its businesses closed for the evening. The woman glanced in Jordan's direction, but when she smiled back in greeting, the woman didn't appear to notice.

Still unsettled, Jordan placed a hand on the dog's neck. "Come on, fella. Our imaginations are in overdrive."

The pub sat midway through the first block off the main intersection of the arterial leading down to the waterfront. The building was flanked by a bakery, its wood-slatted shelves empty for the evening, and a small print

shop displaying colorful greeting cards in its front window. Despite the cool temperatures, the pub's oak plank
door stood open, releasing onto the sidewalk bluesy
strains of piano overlaid with murmured conversation.
All That Jazz glowed in neon in the window. The dog
trotted inside, slipping through her fingers when she tried
to grab him.

"Don't worry, no one minds." Darcy waved her over to
a table next to a huge fireplace constructed of rugged slabs
of gray granite. Flames burned cheerfully, crackling and
spitting the occasional glowing ember at the wrought-
iron screen.

Jordan slid into the captain's chair Darcy shoved out
with a foot, and the dog collapsed on the floor between
them. She took a moment to shake off her moodiness
from the walk over, then glanced around the room.

Massive beams, looking well over a century old, ran
perpendicular to the fireplace chimney, supporting an
arched brick ceiling. Dark green leather booths sat
against distressed brick walls and mixed with varnished
oak tables scattered in cozy seating arrangements. The
works of local artists were prominently displayed. Jordan
noticed she wasn't the only one who'd brought a dog.

The pub was surprisingly full, its clientele mixed—
some young enough to be college students, others closer
to Jordan's age, still dressed in their work clothes and
clearly tradesmen. Even the personal styles were eclectic—
everything from dreadlocks to old-fashioned, elaborate
French twists paired with vintage clothing.

Patrons stood at a baroque-style mahogany bar that

ran the length of the room, chatting among themselves with the ease of longtime acquaintance. Others crowded around tables or jammed into booths, sharing pitchers of beer over some hotly debated topic.

"Hey, everybody!" Darcy yelled. "This is Jordan. She bought Longren House. Jordan, this is everyone."

Jordan acknowledged several "hi's" with a smile, noting the curious but polite scrutiny she was receiving.

A tall, thin man with a silver ponytail and a diamond stud in his left ear came over to the table. He introduced himself as Bill, the bartender, and took her order for white wine.

"Friendly place," she noted to Darcy, relaxing into the captain's chair.

"Would I steer you wrong?" Off-duty, Darcy looked only slightly less intimidating, dressed in boot-cut jeans that emphasized her long legs and a soft, sea green sweater that turned her hazel eyes the color of old moss. "Wait'll you try the food." She forked up a bit of fresh mozzarella, tomato, and basil vinaigrette from her plate for Jordan to taste.

The flavors exploded on Jordan's tongue. "*Oh.*" She closed her eyes to savor the moment.

"Kathleen makes the mozzarella from scratch each day, and she grows the basil out back. Jase has threatened to commit suicide if she ever leaves to open her own restaurant."

Jordan couldn't stop herself from looking around for him. She found him seated behind a shiny black grand piano on a small stage in the back corner. Glancing up from the keyboard, he gave her a slow smile and launched into a mellow tune she recognized.

Not only did he own the pub, he played jazz piano. She did *not* need to discover that fact. "FPP," she muttered under her breath.

"What's that?" Darcy asked.

"You have hearing like a bat's," Jordan complained, then sighed. "Four-Point Plan. It's my way of dealing with everything that's happened in the past year, starting with a grief stage."

Darcy snorted. "You're grieving for a jerk who lost his license to practice by bedding his patients?" Catching Jordan's wary look, she held up both hands. "Hey, don't look at me like that. One of the guys Googled you."

"Terrific."

"Hell, most folks in here figure if you killed your ex, you were entitled."

Jordan choked on her wine, and Darcy leaned over to pound on her back, nearly slamming her face-first into the table.

"So much for living a quiet life of anonymity," Jordan rasped when she could finally talk.

"If you wanted anonymity, you should've moved to another city. Everyone knows everyone else's business in a small town, and you're the most exciting thing to happen around here in years."

And to think she'd taken those politely curious looks at face value.

"Cheer up," Darcy said. "Half the men in here believe that if they get involved with you, they might end up dead. The rest are turned on by the possibilities." She took a drink from her beer mug. "Of course, the fact that you bought Longren House has them a bit twitchy, but adopting the dog helped."

It was on the tip of Jordan's tongue to ask which group Jase fell into. She drank down half her wine in one gulp instead.

"I don't suppose you have any theories as to who *did* kill your hubby?" Darcy asked.

"The list of possible suspects is long," Jordan replied wryly.

"And you being the spouse—"

"Soon-to-be ex," Jordan corrected her, "which diluted my motive."

Darcy shrugged. "Depends on whether you were getting screwed in the settlement." She waited, her expression expectant, and when Jordan didn't confirm or deny, she asked bluntly, "Were you?"

Jordan continued to hesitate. No matter how friendly Darcy seemed, Jordan couldn't trust that anything she confided would be kept confidential. "No," she said finally, keeping it simple.

Darcy drank more beer, her gaze still assessing. "Whatever you aren't telling me, you can bet the cops in L.A. picked up on as well."

Jordan remained silent, striving to look unconcerned, and Darcy shook her head.

Jase ended his song with a glissando that ran the length of the keyboard, drifting away to enthusiastic applause, then rose from the piano. A group of men at a nearby table caught his nod, rising to carry their drinks and instruments up onstage, unpacking a bass fiddle, a sax, and two horns. Apparently, they were to be treated to live jazz. Jordan decided she could easily become addicted to evenings spent here, even if it meant putting up with a few questions from the resident cop.

"So what have the welcoming committees brought so far?" Darcy asked.

"Chocolate cake, sugar cookies, and a salmon loaf," Jordan answered, relieved by the change of subject.

"Salmon loaf is classier than a tuna casserole. Let me guess—Betty from down the block?"

"I think so—I had trouble keeping track." Jordan remembered a question she wanted to ask. "What's a colorist? She—Betty—mentioned one when we were standing outside this afternoon."

Darcy scooted around in her chair. "Yo, Tom?" A bearded, red-haired mountain of a man at the bar raised his eyebrows. "Jordan wants to know about colorists." He nodded and headed toward their table, beer mug in hand.

"Tom's the great-grandson of one of Port Chatham's most famous police chiefs," Darcy said by way of introduction.

"Really?" Jordan shook his hand. "What time frame?"

"Late 1800s," Tom rumbled, his soft voice at odds with his bulk. He pulled out the chair next to Darcy, settling in. "My great-granddaddy was smitten with Hattie Longren's sister, Charlotte, for a while, according to the diaries he left behind. At least, until Charlotte turned to prostitution, which cooled his ardor a bit."

"I read about her this afternoon." The doll the dog had found evidently belonged to Charlotte, not a daughter. "She became a prostitute at the Green Light after Hattie was killed, correct?"

He nodded. "Bad luck ran in that family, that's for sure. Charles Longren perished at sea, leaving Hattie in charge of his shipping empire, but then Hattie was murdered not too long after. Once Hattie was gone, Charlotte was too young to run the business and had no way to survive. She ended up dead on the waterfront not too many years later."

"Tom's a history buff, like many of the descendants of the original families here in town," Darcy explained. She eyed Jordan curiously. "You've already started researching?"

"A couple of ladies brought me a stack of papers they thought I'd want to read. Newspaper accounts of the murder and so on." Jordan shook her head. "From what I was able to glean, the man who hanged for Hattie's murder was someone with whom she had a close relationship. Pretty sad."

Tom leaned back, balancing his mug on the arm of his chair. "That jibes with my great-granddaddy's account."

"The man was a union representative, correct?"

"I think so. Frank Lewis enjoyed a certain amount of fame—or notoriety, depending on your perspective—for writing about the sailors' plight in the union magazine of the time, the *Seacoast Journal*. The union and the shanghaiers were always at odds—both vying for the same berths with the shipping lines. And, of course, the shanghaiers had a lot to lose if the union got a toehold in the business."

"The opinion of the ladies who brought me the articles was that Frank Lewis might've been falsely accused," Jordan said.

Tom frowned, stroking his neatly trimmed beard. "I seem to remember some speculation that he'd been framed as a way to neutralize him because of his influence on the waterfront. The shanghaiers continually looked for a way to get rid of him, that's for sure. He was highly educated—his columns in the *Seacoast* regularly documented the brutality and illegal practices of both the shipping masters and the shanghaiers. But as for whether he was ultimately wrongly convicted, I wouldn't know about that."

Belatedly, Jordan realized she had suggested that his relative, the police chief, might've bungled the investigation. "I didn't mean any disrespect."

Tom shrugged. "None taken. People around here love to speculate about past events. Though it certainly seems like that old murder affected the lives of a lot of people, and not in a good way. My great-granddaddy never really got over losing Charlotte, and not too long after the trial, he was killed in the line of duty. I've always wondered whether his grief had made him careless." He sat in pensive silence for a moment, then took a long drink of his beer. "You asked about colorists."

"Yes."

"We've only got two in town who specialize in color schemes for the Painted Ladies."

Jordan looked at him blankly, then the light dawned. "The Victorians?"

"Yeah. Colorists consult with you to design historically accurate colors by customizing modern paint. I'm one, and the other is Holt Stilwell, who's standing over there at the end of the bar."

She craned her neck to get a glimpse of a broad-shouldered man with a bleached buzz cut who was chatting up two young women. Aviator sunglasses hung from the neck of his muscle shirt, which exposed arms indicating that he bench-pressed somewhere around a gazillion pounds. Jordan had never been attracted to big, beefy types—her taste ran more to the lean, angular builds of men like . . . well, Jase. Dammit.

"Best to stick with Tom," Darcy muttered. "Stilwell is one of the main reasons I contribute heavily each year to the National Organization for Women."

Tom grinned behind his beer mug. "He's a talented colorist, but he does have a certain reputation with the ladies."

"And it's all bad." Darcy scowled. "I'd love to run that son of a bitch in for being a misogynist and a womanizer, but unfortunately there's no law against treating women like shit. And he's too clever to get caught physically abusing anyone he lures back to his rat-infested dump."

"So tell us what you really think." Jase had walked up while she was talking, and he rubbed her shoulder affectionately, smiling at her.

At some point during the day, he'd exchanged the cable-knit sweater for a midnight-blue Henley T-shirt that emphasized his shoulders and lean build. Pulling out the chair next to Jordan, he was careful not to hit the dog, who was sound asleep.

"Best not to encourage Darcy." Tom winked. "Before you know it, she'll have Stilwell facedown on the bar, handcuffed."

"That would be police brutality," Darcy said, her tone prim.

"Darlin'." Tom grinned, placing a hand over his heart, and she rolled her eyes.

"Justice, perhaps, in Stilwell's case," Jase pointed out.

Jordan noted the easy camaraderie among the three and felt a moment of envy. In the past year, with her increasing isolation from friends and family, she'd lost any sense of comfort or intimacy she'd had with others. She missed it.

"What you really need, though, before you start thinking about painting, is a master plan for the renovation," Tom said, bringing the conversation back on topic. "You should assess the damage to the house and come up with a prioritized list of the repairs. There could be structural or mechanical problems that should be addressed first, or possibly problems that'll cause continued deterioration and need to be fixed immediately."

Jordan hadn't thought of that—he was probably right. The simple remodel she'd envisioned was becoming more complex by the moment. "Can you recommend someone for that?"

"I can come by tomorrow and get you started in the right direction, if you want," Tom replied. "Jase and I are both fairly knowledgeable when it comes to the old homes, and we know most of the folks here in town who work on the renovations—many are regulars here at the pub. You had an inspection done before you bought the place?"

"Yes."

"Well, there you go. We can start with the inspector's report. Shouldn't be that difficult to get a handle on the work required, though with old homes like yours, there are always a few surprises along the way."

Jase leaned in close to pick up Jordan's empty wineglass. "Another?"

"Yes, thanks." She smiled at him, then a thought occurred to her. "Would Holt Stilwell watch someone from afar?"

Darcy shook her head. "He's not that subtle. Why?"

Jordan shrugged. "I felt a little creeped out today, like someone was watching me. You don't have problems with anyone in this neighborhood, do you?"

"Not that we know of."

Jase frowned as he set a full glass before her and returned to his seat. "Did you see anyone?"

She shook her head. "I'm probably overreacting, given recent events."

"Maybe." Darcy drummed her fingers on the table. "Then again, I'm thinking you've got the training in abnormal behaviors to pick up on something like that before the ordinary citizen would. I'll take a look through the incident reports and see whether anything leaps out. For now, keep the dog close."

"And let me know when you're ready to leave," Jase added. "I'll walk you home."

"No!"

He gave her an odd look, and she felt heat color her cheeks. "I mean, no thanks, really, that's not necessary."

He continued to hesitate. "Then why don't I drop by tomorrow morning with Tom and check on you? We can point you toward the right people to hire, and so on."

"Works for me," Tom added.

Jordan quickly agreed. "Can we make it afternoon, though? I'd planned to visit the Historical Society at ten."

"Their museum downtown is open," Darcy said, "though it won't do you any good—they don't keep the archives at that location. But if you mean the place out on the airport cutoff road, it's closed down for remodeling."

"You must be thinking of a different place. Nora and Delia—the ones who brought me the papers?—told me to meet them there in the morning."

The three of them exchanged perplexed looks.

"Nora and Delia are vacationing in the South of France," Jase said. "I got a postcard from them just today."

Jordan shrugged. "So maybe they beat the postcard home. Unless this town has two sets of sisters named Nora and Delia, they were at the house this afternoon— they brought me a chocolate cake."

Darcy sent a silent look to Jase, and Tom rubbed his jaw.

"What?" Jordan asked.

"I stopped and checked the Historical Society building not two hours ago, on my usual rounds," Darcy said. "It's boarded up, and the sign says that it won't reopen for at least three months. All the employees have been laid off for the summer, which is why Nora and Delia decided to take a long vacation . . ." She trailed off. "Well, hell."

Jordan stared at them. "Nora is around five-six with light brown hair," she clarified, "and Delia is blond with blue eyes. Right? They wear vintage clothing?"

"Nope. Nora is in her eighties," Jase corrected, "and Delia's not much younger. They're both gray-haired."

"I don't friggin' believe this!" Darcy grumped. "I've been wanting to meet up with these two for eight damn years, and *you* get to see them on your first day in town."

Jase and Tom grinned, which seemed to make Darcy even madder.

Totally confused, Jordan said, "Clue me in here, guys."

"You might want to drink some more of that wine," Jase suggested, his blue eyes twinkling.

"You had a visit, all right," Darcy said dourly, "but not from the Hapley sisters."

"Well, then, *who?*" Jordan asked, exasperated.

"Most likely," Jase replied, "the ghosts of Hattie Longren and Charlotte Walker."

Chapter 4

"YEAH, right." Jordan chuckled. No one joined in. "Oh, come on."

Darcy cleared her throat. "Evidently Sandy failed to mention a few of the more unique aspects of Longren House."

"Is this some sort of joke?"

"No."

Jordan shifted in her chair as she looked around the table. All three looked completely earnest. "*Seriously*, people don't really believe in ghosts. *I* don't believe in ghosts."

"We like to think we're open-minded on the subject," Jase allowed. "After all, there're a lot of 'em around."

In a matter of moments, the atmosphere in the pub had gone from cozy and welcoming to surreal. The dog woke up and looked at her.

She propped her elbows on the table. "Okay, here's the deal: Most of the time, when folks tell me they're seeing things that can't be real? I, like, refer them to a psychiatrist who can prescribe antipsychotic meds."

"Questionable strategy," Tom pointed out. "You'd have to dope up half the town."

"Cute." Jordan pinched the bridge of her nose. "You're serious."

"Well...yeah." Darcy shrugged. "We've heard about Hattie and Charlotte for years, though this is the first time we've heard anyone has talked to them."

"You think that because Hattie Longren was murdered in my house, she—what—roams the halls at night, clanking her boyfriend's prison chains and moaning?"

"She's being sarcastic," Darcy explained to the others.

"My coping skills are stretched a bit thin these days, and I'm not feeling all that flexible about sharing my house with a couple of ghosts!" Jordan's voice rose, and there was a lull in the conversation as patrons craned their necks to look at her.

She took a deep breath, then another, holding up a hand. "Where I come from," she said, lowering her voice, "California has real estate disclosure forms—TDS, SSD, and SPQ." She ticked them off on shaking fingers. "You're required to disclose even the smallest things, like whether there's a children's playground nearby that the buyer would consider too noisy, for chrissakes. You're *required* to tell the buyer about bad things. *Ghosts*"—she paused for emphasis—"are *bad* things!"

"Actually, many of the old homes are thought to be haunted," Darcy said. "So people don't necessarily think a resident ghost or two is all that awful."

"Okay, 'normal,' then. Ghosts aren't normal. And I make a point of dealing in 'normal.'"

"In this town, we prefer 'quirky' over 'normal.'" Jase laid a soothing hand on Jordan's shoulder. "Bill? Bring me a brandy, would you?"

"Hattie and Charlotte are known for their pranks more than anything else," Tom continued. "While the prior owners were living there and operating a B and B, the ghosts used to run the guests off in droves. It put the owners out of business."

"Gee, how reassuring."

"They're probably more reasonable if you don't do things they object to," Darcy assured her. "From all accounts, they *really* didn't want Longren House turned into a B and B."

"So you think they impersonated Nora and Delia as some kind of prank?" Jordan shook her head, still not believing she was having this conversation. "Follow the logic—why would they do something like that? I'm not buying it."

"They've gotten some pretty negative reactions over the years," Tom said.

"Imagine my surprise."

Darcy grinned. "They probably figured it was better to disguise themselves this time. At least, until you'd gotten settled and they knew what your intentions were."

Jordan studied each of their faces. They appeared to be accepting Darcy's explanation as plausible—even Jase. She shook her head back and forth. "No, no, no. I'm calling the real estate agent. I want those disclosure forms."

"What good will they do you now?" Tom asked pragmatically.

"How the hell should I know?" Jordan gulped down the brandy Jase handed her. "Hey, I've got it." She waved the brandy snifter in the air. "Since you all are so fond of your ghosts, maybe the local judge is a true believer and will let me back out of the sale."

"Now you're *really* being sarcastic," Darcy said.

"It's a gift," Jordan snapped.

"You might as well accept the inevitable."

A new thought occurred to her. "Oh, God, I get it now." She stood abruptly, feeling ill. The dog leapt to his feet. "This is all a ruse, isn't it?" She folded the rope and put it in his mouth. "You thought you could be entertained at my expense."

"Whoa. Wait a minute." Darcy's amusement faded. "We didn't think that at all."

"Then it's my notoriety—that I'm suspected of murder." Hands shaking, Jordan fumbled for money to pay the bill. "You don't want someone like me in your town."

"That's *not* it." Darcy hesitated. "Okay, I admit that maybe some people might have thought that as a psychologist, you'd cope better with the ghosts...I mean, what with your ability to be empathetic—"

"Shut up, Darcy," Jase said pleasantly. He turned to Jordan, his expression apologetic. "Please, stay and enjoy the music."

Jordan shook her head mutely, throwing cash on the table.

"Look," he explained quietly. "Most people only catch an occasional or fleeting glimpse of ghosts. We didn't even know for sure that you'd ever see them, and we certainly didn't think you'd be able to converse with them."

"Hell," Darcy said, "I'm flat-out envious. I'd love to be able to talk to them."

"They're probably thrilled to finally have someone to talk to," Tom added.

Jordan backed away. "I'll prove you all wrong. When I get to the research center tomorrow, it will be open, and Nora and Delia will be waiting for me."

"Then why don't I walk you home," Jase suggested, standing, "and check the place out? Just so you'll feel safe tonight."

"I don't think so." Tears burned behind her eyes. Would she ever learn not to be so damn trusting?

She turned and walked out, the dog at her heels, leaving the three of them staring after her with what appeared to be concerned looks on their faces.

Too bad she knew better.

* * *

TEN minutes later, Jordan stood in her front yard, hugging herself, afraid to go inside. She half wished she'd taken Jase up on his offer. Their story was crazy, but... well, it made a weird sort of sense. Nora and Delia *had* been pretty strange, she had to admit.

As she replayed the conversation from earlier that afternoon inside her head, she realized many of the things they'd said could be interpreted in a different light. Take Delia's argument, for example, that Frank would never have murdered Hattie. She had sounded as if she'd actually known him. And then there was the odd hair comment, which might indicate they didn't understand modern speech idioms.

Jordan blew out a breath. This was crazy. Nuts. She was making something out of nothing. Pretty soon, *she'd* be the one she referred to a psychiatrist for meds.

She took a deep breath, threw back her shoulders, and climbed the porch steps, reaching out to open the door for the dog. He trotted right in, unconcerned.

"See?" she muttered. "Nothing to worry about." She fumbled for the light switch, turning on several lights, including the chandelier high up in the stairwell before she located the one in the hall. She left them all blazing.

Standing just inside the door, she listened.

Nothing.

The house was quiet...settled. No creaks or groans, no moans...no goddamn ghosts. Just in case, though, she looked around for something she could use as a weapon.

Clutching a library lamp in front of her with both hands, she crept down the hallway to the kitchen. On the way, she didn't walk through any cold spots, which—if she remembered correctly from movies she'd seen—were supposed to be a sign of spectral activity. She did, however, jump a foot when a floorboard creaked loudly, almost losing her grip on the lamp.

She reached inside the kitchen door and flipped on the light switch, then walked to the center of the room. "If you're here, I frigging *dare* you to come out!" she said in a loud voice.

Silence.

There, that proved it. No ghosts.

"Uh-ohhh. We've been outed." The whisper came from several feet behind her.

Jordan whirled, the lamp dropping with a deafening crash. The air sort of shimmered in the middle of the kitchen, and the two women materialized before her.

Charlotte's image faded in and out like a spastic highway construction warning light, but Hattie's was clear as a bell. At least Hattie had the decency to look chagrined.

Jordan glanced around surreptitiously for the dog, hoping for some protection, but he'd disappeared. She hyperventilated.

"Paper bag"—she gasped, waving her hands wildly—"cupboard."

Charlotte floated over to the sink, her blue satin slippers barely touching the floor. The cupboard door slammed open and a paper bag flew through the air. Jordan managed to snag it as it winged past her.

She collapsed onto a kitchen chair and breathed into the bag, eyes closed. The bent lamp leapt from the floor to the table, wildly teetering back and forth on its base before settling. A hand patted her lightly on her shoulder, the feeling somewhat akin to static electricity crawling across her skin. The hairs on the back of her neck rose.

"You keep your paper bags by the kitchen sink?" Charlotte asked. "That's what the butler's pantry is for."

"Now, Charlotte, don't nag," Hattie admonished, rubbing Jordan's shoulder. "We can worry about the arrangement of the kitchen later—Jordan's had a fright."

"Well, she doesn't want to unpack and arrange things in here twice, does she?"

"Nevertheless, she has plenty of time to think about where she'll put her kitchen items," Hattie said, her tone firm.

"I'm only trying to be helpful."

Jordan raised her head to stare blearily at Charlotte. She was pouting again, which seemed to be her perpetual state. Something to look forward to, if Jordan had to live with her. On that note, she closed her eyes again.

"Can't you see she's shaken?" Hattie continued. "No one thinks about organizing their cupboards when they're in shock."

"A stylish home, along with a keen sense of fashion, are critical foundations of a well-ordered life—"

Jordan stood on shaky legs and walked over to the open cupboard. She dry-swallowed three tablets from the aspirin bottle she'd put in there earlier. Why the *hell* hadn't she thought to pack something stronger?

"And look at *that*!" Charlotte's tone was outraged. "She's got *medicine* in there. Everyone knows herbal tinctures should be kept well away from the preparation of the food."

"Times have changed," Jordan managed. "Why don't you two teleport yourselves to the local home improvement store? They're probably still open, and you can check out the latest kitchen designs. That'll give me the time I need to pack my bags and check into a hotel."

"There's no cause to get testy," Hattie said mildly. "Or to leave. We have no intention of harming you."

"Yeah, right. I've heard you two are a real joy to live with." Jordan gripped the edge of the counter with one hand to hold herself up, since her knees were still nonfunctional. Though the roaring in her ears had begun to subside, she breathed into the paper bag again for good measure.

Charlotte sniffed. "If you're referring to the prior inhabitants who ran that wretched boardinghouse—"

"Bed-and-breakfast," Hattie corrected.

"—they got what they deserved. Why, they were considering knocking down the wall between the parlor and front hall!"

"Hell, no wonder you drove them to financial ruin," Jordan muttered. "World peace hung in the balance."

"Well, of course it didn't . . . Oh, you meant that as a joke."

Jordan could feel herself crashing as the adrenaline seeped away. "I don't suppose I can talk you two into leaving for the evening and coming back in the morning, after I've had eight hours of sleep and some caffeine and can cope better?"

They glanced at each other with confused expressions. "We live here," Hattie said. "Where would we go? You can't really mean that you want to turn us away from our home."

"That would be tragic," Jordan said grimly, then snapped her fingers. "Got it! What about a portal? Didn't I read somewhere that ghosts have portals, like little holes in the wall? You two could disappear into one and then I could stuff a rag into it."

Charlotte folded her arms. "That's insulting."

"Well, what, then? Am I supposed to just accept that I'm now rooming with you two? And what have you done with my dog?"

"He's around." Hattie waved a hand. "Actually, we're glad you finally arrived. It's been hard to steal enough food for him. If you take the same item often enough, people notice. The poor thing has been getting thinner and thinner."

"And we're still developing our powers," Charlotte confided, her image brightening, then fading, as if on cue. "We signed up for the seminar as soon as we heard you bought our house, but our instructor said it takes a lot of practice to perfect telekinesis."

"Sorry about the smashed cake," Hattie added. "We tried."

Jordan rubbed her forehead. The aspirin wasn't even going to make a dent. "So what *do* you want? Approval of the renovation plans?"

Hattie hesitated, then put an arm around Charlotte, who pressed trembling lips together and nodded encouragingly.

"We want you to solve my murder."

A Crisis of Confidence

BY dawn, the fire had been contained to two blocks facing the harbor, sparing City Hall. Nine were dead, scores more injured. Overhead, the sky slowly lightened to streaks of pale pink and bluish gray, marred only occasionally by black wisps of smoke. Hattie dropped a bucket in the mud at her feet and rubbed the small of her back, gazing past smoldering ruins to the harbor.

Ships lay quietly, anchored on glassy water reflecting the colors of the early morning light. Yet the harbor already resonated with the cries of first mates, ordering crews up masts to secure sails against the growing threat of clouds on the horizon. Wind and rain would move onshore before noon.

Since moving to Port Chatham, gauging the weather had become second nature. Until recently, she would've checked the harbor throughout the day, hoping to catch a glimpse of Charles's ship on the horizon. A dense bank of clouds such as the one visible this morning would've meant his return would be delayed. Even now, Admiralty

Inlet was unusually empty of ships—none would set sail until the storm had passed.

Though it had been weeks since Hattie had received word of Charles's death in the South Seas, she still found herself unconsciously searching the waters for his barque. She hadn't had his body to lay to rest, nor any way to properly grieve. It was as if he'd sailed out of the harbor and would return any day now. She felt like an interloper, running his business. An interloper, yet one with responsibilities, she reminded herself.

Given the threatening weather, she'd have to order Clive Johnson to return the crews to their schooners. No doubt he'd take the opportunity to point out that if they'd been on board throughout the night, they would already have the rigging secured. But at the moment, she was simply too tired to care about his barbed criticisms.

Turning toward the beach, she spied Charlotte and Tabitha curled up together on a blanket, sound asleep, their faces showing the same signs of exhaustion she was certain could be seen on her own, their dresses as soiled and soaked with muddy water as hers. Chief Greeley, though busy throughout the night, had never wandered far from Charlotte's side. Even now, he stood watch. Hattie was grateful, yet uneasy. Greeley was big and stern looking, and she'd never observed in him any evidence of good humor. Charlotte was far too fragile for a hard man like Greeley.

"Ma'am?" Two of Mona's girls stood a few feet away, holding folded blankets from the Green Light.

She walked over to take them. "Thank you," she said gently.

They dipped in nervous curtsies and fled, but not before Hattie had noticed the newly healed cuts and bruises on the smaller of the two. She wanted to inquire about the girl's injuries, to ask if she needed help, but she suspected her questions would only serve to frighten the two even more.

"They aren't comfortable around respectable women of means," Mona explained as she approached. The hard lines in her face were more deeply pronounced in the morning light.

Hattie remembered Eleanor's earlier warnings and condemnation, and her expression turned wry. "My position in society may be more precarious than you realize."

"And you haven't improved it, coming down here to help," Mona concluded astutely.

"If so, I can't worry about it."

"Perhaps you would be wise to return home now that the fire is out."

Hattie shook her head. "I'm not leaving while people still need tending." She held out the blankets. "If you'll pass these out, I'll see whether the hand pump on that well across the street is still working. The injured need water."

Mona studied her for a moment, then shrugged. She cast a look at the rapidly darkening western sky. "We'd best hurry—that storm may put out the rest of the fire, but it will bring its own form of misery. We'll have to use the tunnels for the supplies, and move the injured to the

Green Light. We can access the tunnels from the basement of Seavey's hotel."

Hattie surreptitiously glanced toward the beach, where he still stood with his bodyguards. He'd watched her all night long, making her shiver more than once from the weight of his gaze.

From what little Charles had told her about his business, Port Chatham's booming shipping industry relied on a steady supply of sailors. Shanghaiers like Seavey either worked in concert with boardinghouse operators to provide crews to the shipping masters or, in some cases, owned the boardinghouses outright. The tunnels supposedly served as a temporary prison for those least willing to go along with the shanghaiers' demands.

"Charles told me he refused to pay the shanghaiers for his crews," she said now.

Mona snorted her disbelief. "It's common practice with all the shipping companies, your husband's included. How do you think he got the crews he needed to run that many ships? And with some sailors turning to the union, cheap crews are more scarce than ever." She glanced around, then continued before Hattie could argue, keeping her voice low. "Rumor is now that Seavey has the local shanghaiing business all but tied up he's moved on to kidnapping young girls."

"*What? He ransoms them?*"

"He sells them into prostitution rings operating in the Far East. Young white virgins are in great demand over there."

"But if everyone knows what he's doing, why don't the police raid the tunnels?" Hattie asked, sickened.

"When someone up on the hill is kidnapped, the police might investigate, though they would have trouble finding enough proof to convict. But most of the time, they look the other way." Mona's tone was bitter. "Prostitutes don't matter."

Hattie had heard similar complaints regarding lack of police protection from women down on their luck back East—a hard truth of the times she had trouble accepting. Shuddering, she glanced over to reassure herself that Charlotte and Tabitha were still safe. No wonder Greeley had been so attentive.

"I trust I don't have to tell you to never let your girls go out without a chaperone—even in your immediate neighborhood," Mona said. "Even respectable business establishments in your neighborhood have been targeted."

"No, I'm insistent that the girls are always accompanied by an adult."

"Good. I'll talk to Seavey about storing supplies in the tunnels after I distribute these." She took the blankets. "I don't want you wandering down to that end of the street."

"Nonsense—"

"No." Mona was adamant. "You listen to me. You and the girls have been in far greater danger than you realize. Seavey's utterly ruthless. And those two thugs he has with him? You don't want to know what they've done to the girls they've gotten hold of." Her expression softened. "Look, you helped us last night, and we're grateful. But don't be a fool—you have no experience with men like

Seavey. Take water to the injured, if you feel you must—you're safe enough on the beach. But stay away from the tunnels."

Hattie wanted to protest, to point out that as owner of a shipping business, she would eventually have to cope with the dangers of the waterfront. That as the daughter of parents who had regularly ventured into the slums of Boston to provide medical care, she knew a thing or two about what she might encounter. But she'd gone cold at the image of Charlotte and Tabitha in the hands of Seavey's thugs.

Mona was right—she didn't have any experience with men like Seavey. Or with running a waterfront business. She didn't just feel like an interloper—she felt completely out of her element.

A fact Clive Johnson relished in reminding her of daily.

* * *

ONCE she'd filled a bucket from the well and hunted through the piles of merchandise from the general store for a cup, she carried both across the street. As the fire had burned lower, people had started small bonfires along the beach for warmth and were now huddled around them, their hands spread over the flames. She spied Mona moving from one group to the next, distributing the blankets.

People huddled under blankets, their faces lined with the strain of their ordeal. Conversation trailed off to tense silence whenever Hattie approached, but she persisted, knowing they needed the water she offered. Some refused outright, but others accepted the cup, their eyes remaining wary as they drank.

The workman who had tended to the prostitute she'd pulled from the fire stopped to help her hold the head of a burn victim so that she could trickle water into his mouth. "I'm Frank," he said as he gently lowered the man back to the ground with large, capable hands. "And you are?"

"Hattie," she replied softly. Under the circumstances, it didn't seem right to insist he address her formally. She noted the care with which he tucked a blanket around the man.

"Well, Hattie, it's a good deed you've done tonight," he said, leaning back on his heels and smiling tiredly. "Though folks are acting wary, they won't forget that one of you from the hilltop area came down here."

She shrugged. "More should have been willing to help. 'The good we secure for ourselves is precarious and uncertain until it is secured for all of us. . . .' "

"Jane Addams," he said, nodding. "Apt."

"You know of her work?" Hattie was surprised.

His expression turned wry. "Just because I don't live on the hill doesn't mean I don't stay abreast of social reform. Hull House has been an exceptionally successful settlement house for the unfortunate back East."

"Yes, of course," Hattie said quickly, embarrassed that she'd allowed herself to be misled by his appearance into thinking he was uninformed. Indeed, she should have immediately noticed his intelligent eyes and educated speech patterns. Yet given his muscular build and work clothes, he certainly didn't fit the mold of a refined man of letters who spent his days reading in the library.

"We need to move the injured to the Green Light," she said. "Do you know of any men who can help transport the ones who can't walk on their own?"

He nodded, waving over several who stood close by. After explaining the situation, he quickly had a system set up whereby he and Hattie would give the victims water and check their condition, then indicate who should be moved.

She followed him down the beach to kneel by the next victim. "Are you a doctor?" she asked, finding herself more curious about him than polite society dictated she should be.

Frank shot her a look of disbelief. "Hardly. It's rare that we can get a doctor to treat anyone down here. We've learned to rely on ourselves."

"But you're from back East? Your accent..." His voice, though rough in timbre, bore the unmistakable broad vowels of New York or perhaps New Jersey.

"You've a good ear." He checked the victim's bandaged hands, then told the man that he would hold the cup for him. "I hail from New York City—I'm a union man," he explained.

"Oh."

Charles had spoken disparagingly of the local union movement, claiming a small group of men had set up their own shipping office and were challenging the shipping masters, demanding outrageous wages and special treatment for union sailors. She'd refrained from arguing with him, even if it had gone against what she'd been raised to believe about the rights of workers. As it was, she and Charles had had enough contentiousness in their marriage.

Also strengthening her decision to remain silent, however, had been the recent newspaper accounts of violent clashes between the union representatives and the shipping masters. The latest had occurred when union members had thrown rocks at a boardinghouse that was supposedly run by a shanghaier. Eleanor had written numerous editorials openly condemning the union's condoning of such violence.

Frank glanced up. "Don't believe the mistruths you read in the local newspaper editorials," he warned, uncannily reading her mind. "I was shanghaied off the New York docks, so I have firsthand knowledge of how sailors are treated."

"My husband was a shipping master as well as a ship's captain," Hattie informed him coolly.

"I'm sorry," he said, catching her use of past tense. "I'm sure he wasn't happy about the formation of the union, since it meant money out of his pocket. But it's necessary."

"Charles always claimed that if he had supported the union, he would have lost his contracts to provide crews to the ships' captains, as well as any chance he had of finding crews for his own ships."

"I'm not surprised. Most of your social acquaintances,

with few exceptions, look the other way, unofficially sanctioning the shanghaiers' brutal methods."

Hattie bristled. "Failing to support the union doesn't necessarily mean that Charles and his business associates supported the shanghaiers. Charles always said that it's the union that isn't doing the sailors any favors."

"I'm sure that's what your husband wanted you to believe." Frank took the cup from her and crouched to hold it to a woman's lips, softly urging her to drink. "But someone has to stand up to such a corrupt system. If unchecked, the already brutal treatment of sailors will only get worse."

"But you *would* say that, wouldn't you?" she argued, increasingly upset yet not really understanding why. "To salve your conscience when you resort to violence."

Her comment appeared to amuse him. "What's the matter, Hattie? Are you not as open-minded as you thought? Does it bother you to see an educated man fight for the rights of sailors?"

"Of course not! My family had a long history of philanthropy in Boston."

"Really?" He straightened and took a step forward, standing too close for her comfort. "Then is it that you find yourself agreeing with me, even though I'm willing to resort to violence for the right cause?" he asked softly, holding her startled gaze. "Is that what's making you argue so vehemently the views of a dead husband who probably never deserved your loyalty, even when he was alive?"

She gasped. "Why, you—" She stopped herself, saying coldly, "You overstep, sir!"

"Is this man bothering you, Mrs. Longren?" They both turned to see Chief Greeley approaching, his expression hard.

Hattie took in the look of animosity that passed between the two men. "No. No . . . I'm unharmed."

"Ah. Longren Shipping, is it?" Frank stepped back, his expression cooling. "If you want to learn what goes on down here, *Mrs. Longren,* read the *Seacoast Journal.* The 'Red Letters' column documents the true accounts of people who have been severely mistreated in the course of doing business with Longren Shipping. Or better yet, ask your man Johnson, if you think you'll get a truthful answer from him."

"How *dare* you imply—"

"That's enough, Lewis." Greeley spoke in a steely tone, and Hattie jerked at the mention of his name, water sloshing over the side of her bucket.

"Lewis," she repeated numbly. "Frank *Lewis.*"

He reached for the bucket. "Yes. What of it?"

The bucket fell to the ground as she hit him, hands fisted on his chest. "*You* are responsible for my husband's death! You incited his crew to riot—"

"Mrs. Longren!" Greeley stepped between them and grabbed both her arms. "Control yourself!"

"Let her go, Greeley," Frank said quietly, his gaze holding regret but no hint of remorse. "Though it seems there are circumstances under which Mrs. Longren believes violence is appropriate after all."

"You watch your mouth," Greeley snapped, "or I'll have you arrested."

Frank shrugged and leaned down to pick up the empty bucket, giving Hattie a long, quiet look in the process. "I'll just refill this and get back to my work."

Suddenly aware of the silence around her, Hattie turned. People stood staring at her—Seavey with his slightly mocking smile, Clive Johnson, his face reflecting anger and resentment. Even Mona, who'd warmed up to her during the night, now appeared cautious and withdrawn. But it was the pity she read in Frank Lewis's expression that she couldn't bear.

Pulling away from Greeley, she raised her chin. "Thank you for your intervention, Chief Greeley, but I'll be fine now."

He shook his head, again taking her arm to lead her to where Charlotte and Tabitha stood. "You have no idea what you've done, Mrs. Longren, exposing your girls to the waterfront. For God's sake, look at yourself, woman." He gestured at her stained and scorched dress. "If you want to parade around in public in such an unkempt manner, I can't stop you. But allowing Charlotte to do so is inexcusable. Take her home and make certain her maid attends to her promptly. And see that she doesn't continue to wear dresses that are so suggestive. A high-standing collar would have been more seemly."

Hattie trembled but refused to back down. "Though I appreciate your vigilance, I will be the judge of what is appropriate dress for my charges."

"If that judgment is as flawed in matters of social decorum as it has been throughout this night," he retorted, "you'd do well to seek the advice of Eleanor Canby and others in your neighborhood."

Suddenly too exhausted to form a suitable response, she turned to the girls, who had watched the altercation with growing alarm. It had begun to rain—large, cold drops that would soak them through before they reached the house. Hattie gestured for them to head in the direction of the footbridge.

"Leave the day-to-day running of your husband's business to your manager, Mrs. Longren," Greeley called after her, loudly enough for all to hear. "Don't bring Charlotte down here again."

Chapter 5

JUST great.

**Black Widow Works to Solve
Century-Old Murder,
Easily Slipping into the Mind of a
Deranged Killer**

After a sleepless night, Jordan stood on the front porch, cellphone in hand. Sunlight filtered through decorative scrollwork, highlighting the iridescent pink petals of the few roses that struggled to bloom along the foundation. The dog was stretched out at her feet, his head propped on the seat of the broken swing, snoring.

Although it was not yet midmorning, several of her neighbors were out, working in their yards or walking their dogs. She'd greeted a couple of people as they passed by, but they hadn't stopped to introduce themselves. Down the block, a lawn mower kicked on, drowning out the birds singing in the trees. Though she was certain it was her imagination, she thought she could already smell the newly mown grass.

All in all, it was an idyllic tableau.

She scowled, focusing on the peeling paint and rotting wood beneath her feet while she speed-dialed her therapist.

She and Carol had gone through school together, roomed together, and practiced therapy techniques on each other. Carol was her best friend and had been there for her, unconditionally, during the last year.

"I need you to prescribe Librium," she said without preamble when Carol answered. "I'm experiencing a psychotic break, but I have a plan to deal with it."

"Good morning, Jordan," Carol said, placid as always. "You're adjusting well to your new environment, I take it."

"Will you prescribe the Librium or not?" Jordan stalked down the hall to the kitchen, almost mowing down Hattie and Charlotte, who were practicing cotillion steps to "Rhyme and Reason" by the Dave Matthews Band, booming at earsplitting volume on her portable CD player.

"Jordan!" Charlotte cried. "Quick! Go find someone to fill out the foursome!"

"Now, Charlotte . . ." Hattie began.

Jordan hastily palmed the lower half of the cellphone. "*Ssshhhhh!*"

"You called *me*, remember?" Carol said, sounding irritated.

"Sorry." Jordan retrieved the old spatula she'd discovered at the back of a drawer and grabbed a bucket, retreating to the relative safety of the porch. Breakfast had been more of a debacle than the last six months in L.A. combined, and the ghosts' attempts to use her espresso machine didn't even bear thinking about.

"Get me those meds," she told Carol grimly.

"What's this about?"

"I don't want to talk about it."

Her friend's sigh huffed into the phone. "You want me to prescribe a powerful, habit-forming antianxiety medication without explaining why. Let me think... No. Sign up for a yoga class."

"It's either drugs or sell the house, and I love the house." Jordan targeted a curl of dingy white paint roughly the size of some third world nations.

"You aren't having a psychotic break," Carol said, her desk chair creaking the way it did when she swiveled to prop her Gucci platform sandals on her antique needle-point footstool. "Okay, correction. If you *are* having a psychotic break, it's caused by your impulsive decision to remodel a century-old house, a decision which all along I suspected indicates a deeply disturbed mind. After all, who willingly puts up with Sheetrock dust?"

"The walls are plaster, not Sheetrock. And I'm *not* impulsive."

"Uh-huh. Denial is such an underrated emotion."

Jordan chose to ignore that. "This has nothing to do with purchasing the house." Well, sort of. The ghosts and the house were related, but this was really about her inability to distinguish fantasy from reality. "I'm telling you, I'm having a psychotic break."

"You aren't even capable of having one. You worship at the altar of 'well adjusted.' Now, what's really going on?"

Jordan closed her eyes for a moment, then scraped furiously. "I'm seeing ghosts."

"Get *out!*" Carol sounded delighted. "You bought a haunted house?"

"*I did not buy a haunted house.* I'm simply seeing things that aren't there, having *conversations* with the things that aren't there, and fixing fucking *breakfast* for the things that aren't there. I'm in the initial stage of a major psychosis, probably manifesting itself as a delusional disorder, but I can—"

"Who are they?"

"What?" Jordan paused, thrown off stride. "Oh. Two women who lived in the house in the late 1800s." Then she added darkly, "*Not that they actually exist.* Can we please stay on topic here? I need those meds."

"You're the most rational person I know," Carol retorted. "Freakily, you haven't even exhibited much emotional trauma in the past year, even though Ryland cheated on you with size-two starlets, willingly fed you to the paparazzi, then had the nerve to get murdered in a way that made you the prime suspect. At the very least, you could've had the decency to check yourself into a spa and demand herbal wraps. So trust me, you'll take a ghost or two right in stride."

"Will you *listen* to yourself? Our training is grounded in science. *There. Are. No. Ghosts.* I'm having delusions."

"Bullshit. You haven't exhibited any of the early symptoms of a delusional disorder; ergo, you don't have one."

"I've been under a lot of stress, okay? And delusions can be triggered by stress."

"Jordan." Carol's voice turned firm. "You know better than to self-diagnose. What do the ghosts want from you?"

"What makes you think they want anything?" Jordan asked suspiciously, the spatula halting on an upswing.

"Well, that's why ghosts hang around, isn't it? Because of some unresolved issue?"

Jordan ripped a huge chunk of paint off the top edge of the column and dropped it into the bucket, then eyed the chunks hanging from the board-and-batten porch ceiling. "*Hypothetically speaking*, they want me to help them solve an old murder."

"Cool! Who got murdered?"

"One of the ghosts. She doesn't think the guy who hanged for it did it." Though Jordan had her doubts. She'd spent the wee hours of the night reading the rest of the papers the ghosts had brought her, and according to Hattie's diary, Frank Lewis had outweighed her by at least eighty pounds. He also had a history of violence. Jordan could easily envision him killing in a moment of rage.

Hypothetically speaking.

"With your background in psychology, it makes perfect sense that they'd ask you to investigate," Carol was reasoning out loud. "I get called all the time to do psychiatric evaluations of inmates."

"You know I'm taking time off from my practice, and you know the reasons why."

Carol snorted. "I know the bullshit explanation you gave me."

"Come on. If I can't even recognize my own husband's pathological tendencies, how can I expect my patients to trust my judgment? How can I trust my judgment?"

"My answer to that remains unchanged. Anyone can be fooled, especially when their emotions are involved. There's no correlation between what happened with Ryland and the excellent work you've done with patients."

"But I'm a proponent of Rational Therapy, for chrissakes. Somehow, researching an old murder based on my own delusions doesn't seem all that rational."

"Rational Therapy works for your patients, but what you need to do in this situation is take a leap of faith." Carol's tone was astonishingly matter-of-fact.

"You can't honestly tell me you believe in ghosts."

"Why not? Our professional training has nothing to do with believing in the possibility of alternative energy forms. I think you'll be dynamite at profiling, and investigating an old murder is the perfect interim project for you."

Jordan gave the phone a dirty look, then jammed it between her chin and her neck so that she could use both hands to climb onto the railing. Wrapping one arm around the column for support, she swiped at a hanging paint chunk with the spatula, missing by several inches.

"Speaking of investigating, your pal Detective Drake has been sniffing around, asking questions."

Jordan tensed, almost losing her balance, then barely managed not to shriek when she felt a warm, steadying hand on her calf. Jase stood below her, the corners of his eyes crinkling with amusement.

Hell. "What did Drake want to know?" she asked Carol, keeping her tone neutral and her wary gaze on Jase.

"Whether I thought the divorce would've gone through without a hitch, whether you were having financial problems, whether I'd witnessed any recent fights between you and Ryland, stuff like that. I told him I couldn't answer without violating doctor-patient privilege."

Jordan relaxed a bit.

The night of the accident, she'd called Carol and her divorce attorney, wanting both of them present when Drake questioned her. But Carol—whom she'd confided in later that night—was the only person who knew the details of what had really happened just before Ryland's death. If Drake ever found out, Jordan had no doubt an arrest warrant would be issued within hours.

"Thanks," she told Carol now, her tone heartfelt.

"No problem. But if I were you, I'd start thinking about replacing your divorce lawyer with a criminal defense attorney. Conspicuously absent from Drake's list were any questions regarding the victims of Ryland's rampant libido."

Jase held out a hand to help Jordan climb down, then handed her a latte. She smiled her thanks, though her stomach had started doing flip-flops at Carol's mention of a defense attorney. "I gave Drake plenty of names to investigate."

"Yeah, well, I don't think he was listening. Have you talked to your family about all this?"

"Of course not. You know what their reaction would be—Mom would fret and lose sleep and drive Dad nuts in the process, and Lindsay would harangue me about how bad choices lead to bad consequences."

Carol harrumphed. "Your sister could take a few lessons in how to be supportive. I was hoping something this serious would bring her around."

"Maybe." She and Lindsay had been on the outs for years; Jordan's expectations on that front were far lower than Carol's.

The dog finally awakened, leaping to his feet and barking at Jase. Jordan grabbed him by the ruff. "Sit." He ignored her, placing his massive paws on Jase's shoulders and licking his face. Jase chuckled and rubbed behind the dog's ears.

"Is that a *dog*?" Carol asked.

"Yes."

"So someone's there with you?"

"No," Jordan lied.

"Well then, whose dog is it?"

"Oh. Mine, I guess. He seems to have come with the house."

"You've adopted a dog." Carol sounded positively smug. "How psychologically healthy of you. Ghosts *and* a dog."

"You aren't exactly being supportive here."

"Consider this a growth experience," Carol suggested

in her best therapist voice. "Talk to the ghosts, get to know the ghosts, *bond* with the ghosts."

"And to think you are my closest friend," Jordan said bitterly, causing Jase to grin.

Carol's tone turned serious. "Watch your back, sweetie. Drake wants to close the book on you, and he's a by-the-book kind of guy. I wouldn't be surprised if he had you under surveillance."

"If he does, the local cops don't know about it," she said, then winced when she realized how that must sound to Jase.

She was fairly certain Darcy would've mentioned any surveillance, but then again, perhaps she was trusting Darcy more than she should. Being under surveillance did jibe with her feeling of being watched, unless—and she'd wondered about this during the night—her edginess could be attributed to the presence of the ghosts. But that assumed there actually *were* ghosts, which there weren't.

Her brain hurt.

"Gotta go—patient's here," Carol said. "Seriously, do you need me to come up there?"

"No."

"You're okay?"

"Everything's under control," Jordan lied, then said goodbye. Flipping the phone shut, she turned to face Jase. "Just how much of that did you hear?"

"Quite a bit," he said cheerfully. Slouching against the railing with latte in hand, ankles crossed, he looked comfortably at home on her porch. This morning's Henley

T-shirt was faded, his jeans ripped. His strong jawline was shadowed with day-old beard.

"I felt bad about how things were left last night," he said by way of apology, "so I thought I'd offer my services."

She took a sip of her coffee, giving him a sidelong glance as she went back to tearing off paint chips. "You'll help me find a ghost buster?"

" 'Fraid not." He smiled. "I gather Hattie and Charlotte want you to investigate the murder?"

"Assuming you buy the premise that they exist, yes."

"Hmm." He drank from his cup thoughtfully. "Why doesn't Hattie already know who murdered her?"

Jordan had asked the same question last night. "From what I gather, there's this whole afterlife process—" She stopped, realizing how crazy she sounded. "Let's just say it takes a while to . . . metamorphose, so Hattie wasn't immediately available to see her murderer."

Jase accepted her explanation without blinking. "Was Charlotte in the house?"

"Yes, but asleep. And before you ask, so was the housekeeper. She heard nothing until Frank Lewis, the union man, woke her to tell her what had happened." Jordan shrugged. "Odds really are good that Frank did it—he was in the house when it happened."

"But logically speaking, if he did, Hattie wouldn't need you to solve her murder. Ghosts typically remain on our plane for a reason."

Jordan gave him a "get real" look. "Even if I have been asked to investigate Hattie's murder, it would be virtually impossible. It's not as if any potential witnesses are still alive, and the court records probably aren't even available."

"It was common practice back then to keep diaries— even for men, right? I'm betting if you can lay your hands on Tom's great-grandfather's, you'll find he wrote about the case in detail. After all, it would've been a high point in his career to catch the perpetrator of a society murder."

"Maybe." Jordan was unconvinced.

"Plus, there will be old newspaper accounts available," Jase pointed out. "It's really too bad the Hapleys are out of the country. The historical society is the obvious place to start your search, what with its archives of newspapers, photos, and family documents."

"But you said yourself there's no one around who can get me inside the building."

He frowned. "It's possible we could sweet-talk Darcy into it...wait. Charlotte has to know something about the original investigation, right? She would've still been alive during the trial."

"Yeah, what the hell, just ask the ghosts," Jordan grumbled. "I'm trying to rationalize my way out of this."

He managed to look amused and sympathetic at the same time. "Probably won't be successful with that."

Jordan shot him a narrow look and picked up the spatula with the intent of going back to her scraping, but he leaned in close, gently prying it from her grasp. "Philosophically, I'm against gouging hundred-year-old wood, no matter what the provocation. And you should be wearing a mask—this old paint probably has lead in it. Which brings me to the reason I dropped by." He tossed the spatula into the bucket, then pushed away from the railing. "I've only got a couple of hours before suppliers start making deliveries, so let's get a move on."

"Where are we going?" she asked warily.

"I'm going to advise you in the purchase of a hammer." His voice was grave, but his eyes held a definite twinkle.

He jogged down the steps and held open the passenger door of his pickup, one eyebrow raised. The dog trotted over and jumped in without a backward glance, but Jordan already knew what kind of scruples he had.

She hung back. "Are you certain you want to help me purchase tools that can be wielded as deadly weapons?"

He smiled, but his gaze remained serious. "I'll take my chances."

Dammit.

Chapter 6

THEY returned from the hardware store just before noon with a truckload of tools, Jordan's bank account balance substantially depleted.

Jase had introduced her to Ed, a small, wizened man with a handlebar mustache who had greeted Jase as if he were a long-lost friend. Despite Jase's personal avowals, Ed had eyed her with deep suspicion.

"You sure about her?" he'd asked Jase outright.

"She's already talked to Hattie and Charlotte."

"Oh, well then." Ed had nodded, and Jordan had resisted the temptation to roll her eyes.

She was now the proud owner of three ladders—a six-foot, a ten-foot, and an extension; a pile of books on historical renovation Jase had insisted were required reading; at least four hammers, each of which—he had patiently explained—served very different purposes; and a few large, lethal-looking power saws and drills that he'd made her promise not to turn on until he could demonstrate their safe use.

"I *can* follow instructions," she said as they unloaded the shiny red tool chest she would use to store the smaller tools, a little miffed by his lack of confidence in her skills.

"Instructions are iffy, and I don't want to be the one hauling you into the ER, so humor me."

She would've continued to protest, but they were interrupted by the arrival of a middle-aged woman, conservatively dressed in cotton slacks and a short-sleeved knit top, walking across Jordan's front yard, carrying a foil-covered casserole dish.

"Hey, Felicia," Jase greeted her.

"Hey yourself." She returned his grin, then turned to Jordan, thrusting the casserole dish into her hands. "I'm Felicia Warren, your neighbor to the east." She waved at the pretty white bungalow next door surrounded by a white picket fence. "Welcome to the neighborhood."

"Thanks." Jordan had an immediate impression of cheerful, energetic, and down-to-earth. "Your yard is gorgeous." She'd noticed it the day before as she sat on her front stoop reading, wincing when she'd contrasted it with her overgrown, weed-ridden jungle.

Felicia's yard looked chaotic, but there the similarities ended. An artfully designed riot of flowers overflowed onto meandering stone paths, encouraging visitors to wander through and linger awhile on one of several bent-wood benches. No doubt Felicia was thrilled that someone would finally be taking care of the yard next to hers.

She beamed at Jordan's compliment. "I'm so pleased with it! Amanda, my daughter, handled all the planting and design. I taped her business card to the foil right on top of your dish." She pointed. "Amanda specializes in historical restorations."

Jordan retrieved the card, reading it. "I'll be sure to give her a call."

"No need—she'll be in contact," Felicia assured her.

"Felicia is a member of the Port Chatham Historic Preservation Committee," Jase put in.

Jordan perked up. "Really? Did you restore your own house?"

"Yes, with the help of my husband, who is an architect." Felicia smiled. "Of course, its time period is different from yours—Arts and Crafts, early 1900s. Once you're settled in, come by and I'll give you a tour."

"Actually, Felicia is the person you'll want to talk to, if you decide to apply to have Longren House listed on the historic register," Jase said. "And even if you don't go that route, she can provide all kinds of resources relating to historic preservation."

Felicia waved a hand, looking a bit embarrassed. "It's just that our group is connected with most of the other regional and national groups working on historic preservation," she explained. "Anyone on the committee can help you get started with all the paperwork."

"I'm just getting started," Jordan warned, a bit overwhelmed by their suggestions, "but I'm sure I'll have questions for you as I progress with the restoration of Longren House."

Felicia smiled reassuringly—no doubt she was used to seeing the growing panic on people's faces. "Restoring a home like Longren House is really a community project.

We love our old homes here in town!" She was obviously warming to her topic. "And the prior owners . . . well. Let's just say they weren't interested in preserving history. We all cheered when Hattie and Charlotte ran them off."

Jordan hadn't really thought about the remodel in those terms, but Felicia was right—the restoration of Longen House would affect the entire neighborhood, as well as enhance the town's appeal to visitors. If she could pull it off, and she was beginning to have doubts on that score.

"But really, Hattie and Charlotte will be far more able to answer your questions," Felicia continued, not seeming to notice Jordan's startled reaction. "And we all want you to know we think it's simply wonderful Hattie and Charlotte will now have someone to stand up for them."

Jordan slid her eyes toward Jase, who didn't look as if he thought she'd said anything out of the ordinary.

"Of course, we've been aware of how unhappy Hattie and Charlotte have been over the years," Felicia added. "I mean, we've all *sensed* it. But now that you're here, they'll be able to tell us what they need." When Jordan failed to respond, she rushed on a bit more nervously. "This, of course, represents a very unique opportunity. We won't be solely dependent on surviving documents or construction plans for the restoration."

Jordan cleared her throat. "Okay, wait a minute—"

"You'll have to excuse Jordan's reticence; she's still getting used to the idea of having Hattie and Charlotte around," Jase interrupted, ignoring Jordan's glare.

"Oh." Felicia looked momentarily confused. "*Ohhh*. You mean you didn't see ghosts when you lived in L.A.?"

"No. I saw a lot of strange things in L.A., but ghosts were not—"

"Well, that puts a new spin on things." Felicia frowned. "You must find this all very disconcerting."

"That would be an understatement," Jordan muttered. "Look, I'm still not convinced—"

"I'm sure Jordan would be glad to discuss this more with you after she gets unpacked," Jase said smoothly.

"Oh, of course." Felicia beamed at him. "Well then, I'll just be going." She turned to Jordan. "If there's *anything* you need, don't hesitate to trot over and knock on the door."

"Thanks again for the casserole," Jordan managed. "I'll be sure and return the dish."

Once Felicia was out of earshot, she looked at Jase. "Gee, thanks."

"No problem," he said, his expression amused. "Probably not a good idea to start off on the wrong foot with the local preservation group."

"So who else knows that I supposedly talk to ghosts?" she demanded.

"By now, I'd say most of the town. People have had most of last evening and this morning to get out the word. I'd already received several calls this morning before I dropped by, asking for details."

Jordan gaped at him. Clearly, living in a small town was going to take some getting used to. Even with the paparazzi tracking her every move in L.A., she'd had more privacy than this. Apparently, she'd moved from being in a fishbowl to being under a microscope.

"What did you tell the callers?" she asked uneasily.

"That if they wanted to know more, they should talk to you," he replied. "I don't gossip."

"Oh." She relaxed a bit. "Well. Okay, then."

"But I'm sure they found someone from the pub last night who would tell all," Jase added, dashing her hopes.

"So let me get this straight: Roughly half the town thinks I may have killed my husband, but *everyone* thinks I'm crazy and can see and talk to ghosts."

Jase nodded. "Though I'd phrase it slightly differently... People probably don't think you're crazy if you talk to ghosts."

"Oh, sure—*that* makes sense."

He eyed her, looking concerned. "You okay?"

"I'll get back to you on that." Shaking her head, she carried the casserole into the kitchen, then returned to help him unload the rest of her purchases from the truck.

Hattie and Charlotte watched avidly from the parlor window as she and Jase made trips from the truck to the front hall. He showed no indication that he had seen them, which had Jordan grinding her teeth.

"Are you sure something isn't wrong?" he asked while ripping open packages of screwdrivers and wrenches and organizing them in the tool chest.

"Not a thing."

He raised an eyebrow but didn't push the issue, handing her the shredded packaging. "These are the basic tools you'll need available for most small projects. As you prioritize and start the actual work, I can help you put together lists of additional supplies."

She mustered a smile. "I seem to be thanking you a lot."

"There'll be a pop quiz this evening on the first two books, including the one that explains the National Register of Historic Homes."

"Right." Her expression was wry as they walked out onto the front porch.

A late-model pale cream Cadillac edged up to the curb behind Jase's truck. A slender man of average height and carefully styled sandy hair climbed out, and she grinned, recognizing him.

"Jordan!" He loped onto the porch and enveloped her in a bear hug. "I heard you'd hit town."

When he would have held on a bit too long, Jordan stepped back, turning to include Jase. "I think you already know Ted Rawlins—"

"—of the Ted Rawlins Trio," Jase finished, introducing himself and shaking Ted's hand. "I've been expecting you."

"Well, this *is* convenient," Ted said. "I was on the way to your pub when I spied Jordan."

"I booked the trio for this evening," Jase told Jordan. His expression was curious. "I didn't realize you were connected to the L.A. jazz scene."

"I'm not, but I've heard the trio play a time or two." She quickly explained her acquaintance with Ted, omitting any details. "Ultimately, Ted's the reason I ended up in Port Chatham." Jordan turned back to him with a smile.

"But the festival is a month away. What're you doing in town so early?"

"I told you I bought a summer home up here. The band's been using it as a sound studio for the last month. And thanks to you, I landed a job teaching the seminars this year." He was referring to the work she'd done with him to help him iron out personality conflicts he'd had with colleagues in the music business. "Jordan, here, literally saved my life," he told Jase, who looked surprised.

"That's an overstatement," she protested.

"Not from where I sit," Ted said firmly, then his expression turned sober. "So how are you holding up? Any news on who might've killed Ryland?"

She shook her head. "Nothing so far."

"How about lunch tomorrow? You can bring me up-to-date."

"Why don't you drop by and I'll give you a quick tour instead? The movers will be here and it will be a zoo, but you'll enjoy seeing the house, I think."

If he was disappointed, he had the grace not to show it. "It's a date."

"And I can't wait to hear the trio play this evening," she quickly added, knowing he was still somewhat insecure about his comeback, even though his career showed every sign of a meteoric recovery.

"The pub's just around the corner," Jase added. "Give me another minute to wrap up here, and I'll be right behind you."

"Sounds good." Ted's tone was jovial. "Well. Tomorrow, then." With a casual wave, he returned to his car.

She could feel Jase's gaze on her as Ted drove away, but his next question was innocuous enough. "What time do the movers show up?"

"Early, hopefully." She needed to make a call and nail them down. "I haven't figured out where they can put everything—most of the rooms need a thorough cleaning, stripping, and painting before I can even put furniture in them."

"My advice? Pick a room that's a low priority and have the movers stack most of your belongings in there. That way, you can unpack and arrange as you have time, and as rooms are finished. Tom and I are always available to help you move the furniture later."

She nodded. "Good idea."

Jase leaned down to rub the dog's ears. "Have you picked out a name for him yet?"

"Worthless?" she said, only half joking. "He has a knack for abandoning me at key moments."

The dog lowered his head and whined, and Jase chuckled. "You've hurt his feelings."

She rolled her eyes and knelt to scratch the dog's stomach. "I wouldn't really name you Worthless," she assured him. "How about Oscar, after Oscar Peterson?"

He gave her The Look, then rolled onto his back.

After properly atoning for her sins, she stood and noted the time. "Can we put off the meeting with Tom until tomorrow? The day is getting away from me."

Jase nodded. "Why don't you come by this evening? I'll ask Tom to bring in his great-grandfather's diaries, and

I'm sure Darcy will want to hear all about your first day with the ghosts."

She watched him walk to his truck, oddly reluctant to see him leave.

FPP.

Shaking her head, she went inside to see whether Hattie and Charlotte had managed to conjure up lunch.

* * *

By midafternoon, Jordan had gotten hold of the movers—they would arrive first thing the next morning—and had accepted welcoming casseroles and desserts from several more neighbors who seemed definitely more pleased than worried about her arrival in town. Evidently, her ability to see and converse with ghosts rated higher than her homicidal tendencies. And at the rate the food was piling up, she'd have to throw a party just to clean out the pantry, though she was certain the dog was willing to consume more than his fair share.

The sight of that much food waiting to spoil, though, moved a functioning refrigerator to the top of her to-do list, so she scrubbed out the ancient Amana that had come with the house. Miraculously, when she plugged it in, it not only hummed enthusiastically but put out cold air. Though she had grim visions of the electric meter whirring faster than the speed of light, she had cold food storage and a way to make ice, so she wasn't complaining.

While she arranged the food in the fridge, she mulled over the latest plan that had been formulating in her mind. After all, she needed to start researching the house renovation, right? So if she just ignored *how* she gained access to the research, she was getting through her day productively and functioning normally. And if she happened to run across some old newspaper articles on the murder while she researched the house, it wouldn't hurt to read them, just to appease the ghosts. She could be productive *and* accommodating. Even proponents of Rational Therapy would be in awe of her ingenuity.

"Were you serious about getting me inside the Historical Society building?" she asked Hattie, who had been sitting at the kitchen table with Charlotte while Jordan worked on the fridge.

The ghosts glanced at each other.

"We'd have to break in!" Charlotte exclaimed. "It would give us an opportunity to test the strength of our telekinetic powers."

"Whoa," Jordan said, alarmed. "I can't be a party to breaking and entering—I'm already on the cops' radar." She received blank looks and tried again. "They're already paying attention to me because of my husband's death."

"Which is absurd," Hattie said stoutly. "Why, anyone could tell you aren't a murderess."

"If they try to arrest you," Charlotte added, her expression indignant, "we'll show *them*!"

Jordan didn't want to think about the ramifications of that remark. "But didn't you bring me papers from the Historical Society archives? How did you get in? Do you have a key?"

"Well, we don't have any trouble going through walls, though books and papers can't be transported that way..." Hattie hesitated, looking guilty. "The truth is, the papers were here in the library. Before Charlotte and our housekeeper, Sara, were forced to give up the house, they collected every bit of news they could find about the trial." At Jordan's glower, she spread her hands. "We couldn't count on you finding them on your own, at least not immediately. How long would it have taken you, given the state of disrepair the house is in, to focus on the books and papers in the library?"

Though she had a point, Jordan didn't feel like conceding it. "So your diaries are still here in the house after all these years?"

"Well, of course."

"Do you mind getting them for me?" Jordan asked through her teeth.

Hattie disappeared, then reappeared seconds later, just as several volumes landed with a dusty thud on the table.

Jordan picked one up and thumbed through it curiously. She didn't see any obvious entries about the house. Which, once she thought about it, made sense. Charles Longren had probably built the house in anticipation of traveling back East to find a bride. And that meant Hattie wouldn't have been in Port Chatham during its construction. Jordan still needed access to the newspaper archives. "So you can't get me inside the Historical Society without illegally breaking in?"

But she was talking to an empty room—the ghosts had disappeared.

Footsteps sounded in the hall, and Darcy walked into the kitchen, the dog at her heels. "You wanted me to unlock the Historical Society building for you?"

"How do you *do* that?" Jordan asked, spooked.

"Do what? I stopped by the pub for lunch, and Jase mentioned that you needed access to the archives."

"Oh. Never mind."

Darcy leaned against the kitchen counter, arms folded over the bulge of her shoulder holster. "You okay about last night? Jase thought you might still be a little shaken."

"I'm finding that 'okay' is a relative term," Jordan replied, and Darcy grinned. "Can't you get into trouble for letting me inside the building?"

She shrugged. "We're pretty loose around here, and the Hapleys would like the fact that I helped you out when they couldn't be here." She pushed away from the counter. "When do you want to head out there?"

"How about right now?"

* * *

AFTER clearing out the back of the Prius for the dog, Jordan folded down the backseats and made a bed out of a comforter she kept in the car for emergencies. But the dog didn't fit standing up, and he also couldn't jump in without banging his head on the ceiling. Since he outweighed her, she lifted his front paws in, then lifted and shoved his rear, then showed him how to scrunch down.

Once she had him settled, she dumped an armload of Hattie's diaries on the passenger seat, then followed

Darcy's police cruiser out to the highway on the east side of town, to a location not far from the regional airport. Traffic was light in Jordan's neighborhood, but when they turned onto the highway linking Port Chatham with the rest of the Olympic Peninsula, Jordan could see the impact tourists had in the summer months. Other than the ferry to Whidbey Island, the highway was Port Chatham's only link to civilization. As such, it was crowded not only with tourists but with service and logging trucks.

The Historical Society's building sat on a hillside with towering evergreens surrounding the parking lot. The architecture was plain—a one-story, cement block design. As a testament to the ongoing remodel, a large green construction waste bin sat not far from the front door, but there were no construction crews in sight. They parked their cars, Darcy waiting while Jordan cracked the windows for the dog, then they walked across the lot.

Darcy frowned at the sight of the piece of plywood that had evidently been nailed across the front door but now lay some distance away in the weeds on the edge of the parking lot. "I wonder how that happened."

Jordan glimpsed a blue dress inside the building. "Maybe one of the crew took it off temporarily," she prevaricated.

"That must be it." Darcy produced a ring of keys and unlocked the door.

Inside, the space was dim, musty, and torn apart. Display cases stood empty and shoved to one side, and the carpet had been rolled up, exposing the subflooring. Walls had been ripped open, wiring hanging loose, and windows had been boarded over, presumably to protect the glass.

Jordan sneezed twice.

"The air in here is a little thick," Darcy observed.

"So the archives are in the basement?" Jordan asked, waving a hand in front of her face and ignoring Hattie and Charlotte, who were lurking in the gloom on the far side of the room behind a display case.

"Yeah, the stairs to the basement are over there." Darcy pointed. "I need to make my rounds—will you be okay here by yourself?"

"Sure," Jordan said, relieved.

"Right. Back in a couple of hours, then?"

After Darcy let herself out, Jordan turned around. "I don't even want to know about the plywood."

Charlotte floated over the top of a display case, sniffing. "We were only trying to help."

Jordan climbed down the stairs, followed by the ghosts. She pushed aside a curtain of heavy construction plastic that had been hung to protect the basement's contents from the dust and dirt that accompanied any remodel. Charlotte stayed just long enough to retrieve a stack of historical fashion magazines and take them back upstairs.

"Which shelves hold the newspapers?" Jordan asked Hattie once they were standing in the midst of rows of metal stacks filled with boxes, books, and files. The construction of Longren House should have been a newsworthy event back then.

Hattie led her to the row next to the east wall.

"Eleanor Canby's newspaper—the *Port Chatham Weekly Gazette*—was the only one at the time."

Jordan ran her fingers along spines of the neatly labeled file boxes. "A woman owned the newspaper?"

Hattie nodded. "Eleanor was editor-in-chief of the *Gazette,* and a very important person in town. She held strong views. You've seen the large house down the block from us? The one with the sign out front?"

Jordan *had* noticed the place. Situated on a block of more modest cottages, it was hard to ignore. It was huge—three stories including the attic—and very formal in design. A historic marker graced the front yard. She'd been meaning to check it out but hadn't yet had the time.

"It's called Canby Mansion," Hattie said. "Eleanor's husband had his ship's carpenters handle all the finish work inside the house. It was considered a stunning accomplishment in its day. No one has ever figured out how they managed to disguise the support for the staircase. And the windows up above direct the sunlight onto friezes of different mythological figures, based on the month of the year—"

"Which dates should I be looking for?" Jordan interrupted, anxious to start reading.

"May 27, 1890. Charlotte used to love to go to Eleanor's soirées," Hattie continued. "They were the highlight of the Port Chatham social season." Her smile faded, replaced by sadness. "That is, until . . . well."

Jordan located several boxes for that year and pulled them off the shelf to stack them on a small desk next to the back wall. She blew dust off the desk and set down the materials. The only light came from a window high up on the wall, and since the lamp on the desk didn't work, she surmised that the electricity was turned off. Hunting through her purse, she located the small penlight she kept for such occasions, praying the batteries were still good.

Opening the first box, she carefully pulled out the stack of yellowed papers and set them down, gingerly leafing through them. By the time she realized Hattie had pointed her to a date right after the fire she'd read about the day before—not the date Longren House had been built—she was so engrossed in an editorial written by Eleanor Canby that she forgot all about her original quest.

Fall from Grace

May 27, 1890

Fiery Conflagration Consumes Two
Waterfront Blocks

It has been nearly six years since this community has been rocked by a deadly fire on the waterfront. Yet two nights ago we were once again confronted with the horrific consequences of the licentious behaviors of our waterfront denizens.

Certain residents of this town have suggested that this week's fire was started by businessmen who were "encouraging" waterfront proprietors to pay promptly on accounts due, "or else." Such residents would do well to get their facts straight before making these outlandish accusations against our upstanding businessmen. For it was revealed to this newspaper's reporter late yesterday morning that the fire was indeed started as the result of the actions taken by a woman of the most degraded form of humanity.

It is now known that a young man from an honorable family had been frequently observed in the company of the soiled dove and become completely besotted. Two nights ago, in a fit of lovesick delirium and insane with liquor no doubt supplied by her, the young man killed the fallen woman, then set fire to the bed on which she lay. One can only assume he was subsequently overcome with guilt for the shame his family would have to endure when the truth came out, for he then effectually killed himself by blowing his brains out. The resulting conflagration was responsible for the taking of seven other lives and untold losses to many of our businessmen.

Let this tragedy serve as a warning to residents who sympathize with the women who engage in such scarlet sins. Public sentiment should see to it that these women who entice our young men to the waterfront pay dearly for this recent, tragic turn of events.

Hattie set the editorial next to her coffee cup on the dining room table and rubbed her throbbing temples. Eleanor might as well have mentioned her by name. A number of their neighbors had witnessed her argument with Eleanor the night before last—they would have no trouble putting together that incident with Eleanor's pointed editorial.

The housekeeper placed an eggcup before Hattie, then arranged plates of orange wedges and biscuits within easy reach.

"Thank you, Sara." Though food held no appeal, she

managed a smile. Since Charles's death, Sara had made it her personal duty to look after Hattie and Charlotte.

The stout housekeeper frowned. "You'd best eat—it's past your normal breakfast time, and you're looking mighty peaked."

"It's just a slight headache. Perhaps you could bring me some of that new powder Eleanor smuggled in from Canada?"

Sara shook her head. "No, ma'am! My friend Alice who works for the Canbys? I set store by what she says, and she told me the smugglers sometimes substitute a much more dangerous drug, or even talcum powder. Why, just this last week, Mrs. Canby sickened from a bad batch. I'll brew you a cup of willow bark tea, instead."

"Very well," Hattie sighed, resigning herself to the bitter taste of the concoction.

The housekeeper stood, arms folded and gazing pointedly at Hattie's breakfast, leaving only after Hattie picked up her knife.

She sliced off the top of the boiled egg, salting it. But she found she couldn't stand the smell of it, so she moved it aside and added a small teaspoonful of the black currant jam they'd put up last fall to one of Sara's fluffy baking powder biscuits. Hattie clearly remembered the outing into the foothills of the Olympic Mountains to gather the precious wild berries—it had been one of the last times Charles had seemed relaxed in her company.

After only one small bite, however, she pushed back from the table, too restless to remain seated. Walking around the table to the matching oak sideboard, she retrieved a tray of small crystal vases and the basket of sweet peas she'd gathered from the garden before breakfast. She arranged the fragrant sprigs among the vases, then set a bouquet by each place setting, hoping the routine task would soothe her frazzled nerves.

Out in the front hall, the grandfather clock chimed nine times, its pendulous ticking unnaturally loud in the ensuing silence. In the back of the house, Hattie could hear Sara talking softly to Tabitha, instructing her to take a tray of tea up to Charlotte. It all seemed so normal, and yet Hattie felt as if everything had changed in some way she had yet to understand.

The events of the night of the fire still plagued her. *Had* the fire been started as Eleanor had reported? Hattie couldn't bring herself to believe it. And even if the fire had originated in a house of ill repute, it could've been started there with the intent of misleading the authorities. Placing the blame on the prostitutes ran counter to what she'd seen with her own eyes. And many illegal activities were carried out daily on the waterfront, any of which could've provided a motive for arson.

But why had Eleanor felt the need to publicly chastise her? Perhaps her mention of corruption had threatened Eleanor in some way. Or maybe Eleanor's pride had been damaged, and she'd simply wanted a public venue in which to retaliate.

Hattie stopped to consider, then shook her head. Though Eleanor was overly rigid and moralistic, she'd never been petty. No, it seemed far more likely that she had a stronger motive, and that she knew more about the activities on the waterfront than she let on.

As Hattie placed the last of the vases on the table, the image of Frank Lewis's expression of pity resurfaced. She hugged herself, turning to stare out the dining room window at the dew-laden garden, still untouched by the morning sun.

Though she'd been deeply offended by Lewis's accusations, he had raised questions in her mind about Charles—about his business and how he had treated people. And those questions were all jumbled together with her memories of her struggle to make their marriage work, of her resultant confusion when nothing she did seemed to get through to him.

Had she known Charles at all? Had she thirsted so much for adventure, as her mother had suggested, that she'd been blind to the kind of person he was? She could only hope she hadn't been that naïve or self-absorbed, but how could she be certain?

She'd found it puzzling that once they'd recited their vows, Charles had become distant and cold, the antithesis of the handsome, charming man who had courted her so determinedly in Boston. Yet it didn't necessarily follow that acting aloof or abrupt with her meant he would've done what Mona Starr and Frank Lewis claimed. And she could hardly take Lewis's word as gospel—he'd written the "Red Letters" column that had incited the crew on board Charles's ship to mutiny.

She worried her lower lip as she mentally reviewed the events of two nights ago. What she needed was proof.

She needed to know what kind of man she'd fallen in love with—whether Charles had been honorable, whether she was right to blame herself for having failed in their marriage. She wouldn't be capable of moving on until she had answers, and that meant taking a closer look at Charles's activities and business dealings, however distasteful she found the task to be.

She turned from the window to pace the length of the elegantly appointed room. This restlessness within her—her constant chafing against the restrictions of the mourning period and her overwhelming sense of being stifled—simply wouldn't ease. Was she merely being reckless, as it now appeared she'd been the night of the fire? Or were the questions that swirled through her mind, keeping her sleepless, legitimate?

The front door slammed, jolting her from her thoughts, and Sara entered the dining room carrying a huge package. "For you and the girls, Mrs. Longren," she said, placing it on the oak sideboard.

Curious, Hattie examined the parcel, which was wrapped in brown paper and tied with a pale pink ribbon. She opened the accompanying white linen envelope and withdrew a card. *To replace the dresses you ruined,* the scrawled message said, accompanied by Mona's bold signature at the bottom of the card.

Hattie placed it on the sideboard and unwrapped the package. Bolts of fabric tumbled into her arms—black mousseline de soie silk, blue India silk, forest-green French cashmere—all of the finest quality. Stunned, Hattie set them down and reached out a hand to the back of the closest chair to steady herself. The gift was extravagant...and yet thoughtful. Mona had included the mousseline de soie in deference to her mourning period, the more vibrant colors for the girls.

Charlotte chose that moment to sweep into the room, a carefree vision in her cheerful lemon-yellow muslin gown, her elaborately styled cascade of blond ringlets no doubt the result of Tabitha's painstaking efforts. The poor girl was probably slumped over the kitchen table, exhausted and useless to Sara for the foreseeable future, Hattie thought, sighing inwardly.

Spying the fabric, Charlotte shrieked and rushed over to run her hands over the mousseline de soie. "It's as soft as the most expensive muslin," she breathed. She lifted the bolt of India silk, which was a perfect match for her eyes, and hugged it to her chest. "Oh, Hattie! These will make such beautiful gowns!"

"We'll have to send Mona a note thanking her."

"We must invite her to tea!"

"I doubt she would come." When Charlotte looked confused, she explained gently. "She wouldn't want to jeopardize our reputations by coming to our home."

"But that's not fair!"

"No, it's not, though we can do little about it." Hattie reached for the cup of tea Sara had brought her, grimacing at its taste.

Voices floated in from the front hall, and Sara entered, followed by Police Chief Greeley, who hadn't waited to be formally announced. Tall and imposing in his black wool suit, he bowed from the waist. "Ladies."

Charlotte blushed prettily. "Chief Greeley!"

He smiled indulgently, then turned to Hattie. "Forgive me for calling so early, but I wanted to drop by on my way to the police station to make certain you ladies hadn't suffered any lingering effects from your ill-advised adventure."

"As you can see, we're perfectly fine," Hattie replied coolly. "But thank you for your concern."

Greeley took in Charlotte's attire. "Your gown is quite beautiful, Charlotte, as well as conservatively designed. You look very fetching in it."

"Thank you, Chief Greeley." Charlotte smiled brilliantly.

"Please call me John," he said gently, then asked Hattie, "I gather you took my advice to heart?"

As luck would have it, Charlotte *was* wearing one of her more demure gowns. Determined to avoid an argument, she didn't respond to Greeley's query, instead turning to the housekeeper. "Sara, please bring Chief Greeley some tea."

He shook his head. "No, thank you—I can't stay long."

"But surely you would sample one of Sara's marvelous biscuits," Charlotte exclaimed, then looked hesitant. "Unless you've already had breakfast?"

"No, I planned to purchase something from a street vendor."

"Oh, then you *must* stay! You can't work all day on an empty stomach."

Greeley raised a brow at Hattie, who nodded. "Charlotte is right, of course." She indicated that he take a seat at the table. "Sara, if you would quickly prepare something for the chief?"

"Yes, ma'am," Sara said, though she gave Greeley a cautious look.

He pulled out a chair and sat down, moving the bouquet of sweet peas aside and setting his gloves and hat in its place. With one hand, he adjusted the crease in his slacks to accommodate the pull across his legs, which Hattie noted were the size of tree trunks. The fabric of his wool vest pulled across his massive chest, straining the buttons. She hoped he didn't intend to breathe too deeply. The man was built like a lumberjack who'd eaten far too many meals of hardtack and bacon.

Because her inclination was to pace, Hattie pulled a large crystal vase from the sideboard's lower cupboard and set about filling it with long stems of yellow forsythia and pink plum blossoms.

Greeley spied the bolts of fabric. "Ah, I see you've even purchased fabric to add to Charlotte's wardrobe."

"The fabric is from Mona," Charlotte gushed, not noticing Hattie's wince. "Isn't it beautiful?"

"Mona *Starr*?" Greeley looked at Hattie in stunned disbelief.

"Our gowns were ruined while fighting the fire," Hattie explained as she placed a sprig of forsythia. "Mona was kind enough to send fabric to replace them."

The chief's face set in rigid lines. "Surely you can't think it appropriate to accept a gift from that woman."

Charlotte slipped into the chair closest to where Hattie stood, looking stricken. "But—"

"Mona only meant to thank us for our help," Hattie interrupted, placing a hand on Charlotte's shoulder. "And as you yourself have noted, we can put the fabric to good use in dresses for the girls."

Greeley snorted as Sara brought in his breakfast. "Come now, Mrs. Longren. Were I to see the material made into a dress for Charlotte, I could hardly forget where it came from."

"You can't possibly think it has been tainted in some way!"

"That is precisely what I believe." He buttered his biscuit, wielding the delicate silver butter knife like a plaster trowel, then added a large quantity of jam. "I find myself at a loss to understand how you could be so ignorant of social propriety."

"But Mrs. Starr is a generous benefactor in this town, is she not?"

Greeley waved a hand. "That is neither here nor there. The material should be returned at once or, more appropriately, discarded."

"Hattie . . ." Charlotte whispered.

"Please take the fabric into the parlor," Hattie told her, keeping her tone gentle, "then assist Sara in the kitchen."

Charlotte sent her a pleading glance, then gathered the bolts, curtsied, and fled.

Hattie turned back to her arrangement, willing her hands to remain steady. "I will of course take your opinions under advisement, Chief Greeley, but I won't have you upsetting Charlotte. She lost her parents not even a year ago, and she is emotionally fragile."

Greeley took his time finishing the biscuit, then leaned back and observed Hattie in a manner that set her teeth on edge. "It isn't my intent to upset Charlotte. On the contrary, I intend to court her."

Hattie barely managed to keep her horror hidden. After setting the vase in the center of the table, she returned to her chair, meeting his gaze steadily as she folded her hands in her lap. "I absolutely forbid any courtship, Chief Greeley. At fifteen, Charlotte is far too young to be thinking of marriage."

"Nonsense. Women frequently marry young," he returned calmly. "I find fifteen to be an ideal age—Charlotte is malleable and eager to please. And she can certainly benefit from the firm hand and clear guidance of a man of my stature."

"You mean she can benefit from a father figure, now that hers is gone." Hattie scoffed at the notion. "You have a decidedly patriarchal view of marriage. Women today consider that a poor basis for a fulfilling relationship."

"I'm at a loss to understand how I should view marriage any differently," he retorted, "since it is the way the institution has survived successfully throughout the ages."

"Patriarchal power and female subordination are hardly God-given patterns."

He waved an impatient hand. "I can only assume you've picked up these misguided notions from reading the recent anarchist feminist literature. If that is the case, then, frankly, the sooner Charlotte is married to me and away from your influence, the better."

When Hattie opened her mouth to furiously protest,

he held up a hand. "I also find it perplexing that you'd deny Charlotte the chance for a suitor who has the means to support her comfortably. Shouldn't you be considering what Charlotte wants and needs?"

"That is precisely what I am doing, taking into account her best interests! She is too young to make this decision on her own, and whether you like it or not, I am her legal guardian. I will determine who she sees and what she does."

He stood, bracing his hands on the table to lean over her, and she had a moment of unease.

"I know when a woman is attracted to me, Mrs. Longren," he said softly, anger radiating off him in waves. "Charlotte is as good as mine. Before you cross me in this, I suggest you give the matter some thought."

The image of Charlotte married at fifteen to a man such as Greeley made the bite of biscuit Hattie had managed to swallow threaten to come back up. Yet he was the chief of police and, as such, wielded tremendous power. She was forced to accept the wisdom of not refusing him outright.

"I will give you my answer within the week," she said, barely able to get the words out.

Greeley straightened, reaching for his hat and gloves. "Then I await your favorable decision."

She accompanied him into the front hall, the palms of her hands itching from the urge to shove him out the door.

He paused. "I hope you will also give grave consideration to my feelings about accepting any gift from Mona Starr. She is not someone you should encourage."

Hattie didn't reply, hoping he would take her silence on the matter as assent. Instead, she strove for a way to smooth things over. "Perhaps you would do me the honor of advising me on a different matter altogether, Chief Greeley. It has been hinted that my husband, Charles, was in the habit of paying the crimps for his sailing crews. Is that correct? Because if so, I will immediately direct Mr. Johnson to rectify the situation."

Greeley frowned down at her. "I thought you understood it is best to leave these matters to the discretion of your business manager."

"I can't ignore the fact that a business I now own might be condoning the brutal treatment of sailors. Surely you are as concerned as I am."

She'd neatly turned the tables on him, and his expression spoke volumes. "If you feel it absolutely necessary to interfere, I strongly advise you to take up this matter with Clive Johnson."

Hattie shook her head. "I have reason to doubt he'd be candid with his answers."

"That's absurd. Johnson is a man of stellar reputation. If he has dealt with the crimps on occasion, then he has done so with good reason."

She smiled politely, her headache having returned full force.

He opened the door and then turned back. "I will give you one last word of advice, Mrs. Longren. You will be better served in this community if you adopt a more pleasing attitude toward those who have your best interests at heart." He placed his hat on his head and, bowing, bid her good day.

"Pompous ass," she muttered when the door had closed.

She heard a snicker, and turned to find Sara behind her, a hand clapped over her mouth, her eyes bright with mirth. "Land sakes, Mrs. Longren. I never enjoyed myself so much as in these last few moments. That man needed to be brought down a peg or two."

"Yes, well, I doubt I succeeded," Hattie muttered. "Nothing could penetrate that thick skull of his."

Charlotte rushed down the hallway from the kitchen. "Oh, Hattie, how could you! You practically ran him off, and you were unforgivably rude to him! He'll *never* come back to see me," she ended on a wail.

Hattie stared at her in surprise. "Would that be such a terrible thing?"

"Yes! He's handsome and kind and—"

"He's much too old for you."

"You're just jealous!" Charlotte accused. "You don't have anyone calling on you, and you can't stand that he wants me."

"I'm in mourning for Charles," Hattie corrected, exasperated. "No respectable man would call on me so soon after his death." She spread her hands. "Charlotte, Greeley's not the right man for you. You should have someone lighter in spirit, who won't be so stern, whom you can fall in love with—"

"I *am* in love!" Charlotte cried, then let loose a sob.

"You'll just ruin *everything*! I *hate you*!" She ran up the stairs.

Her bedroom door slammed, and Hattie could hear muffled, heartrending sobs. She sighed, rubbing her temples. She'd taken her irritation with Greeley out on Charlotte, which was inexcusable. Charlotte needed her understanding right now, not her disapproval.

"Let her go, ma'am," Sara said. "She's just overwrought."

"It's just that he's—"

"A lot like Mr. Longren," Sara observed shrewdly.

Hattie realized Sara was right. *Oh, God.* She didn't want Charlotte to suffer as she had, to feel guilty because the man she loved couldn't bring himself to return the sentiment.

"I'll have Tabitha take Charlotte some chamomile tea in a bit, along with the latest dress patterns from *Butterick's*," Sara was saying. "After she settles down, you can try to reason with her."

Hattie smiled gratefully, but her thoughts remained troubled. Was she being fair? Or was she allowing her personal dislike of Greeley to cloud her judgment? She couldn't expect Charlotte to want or need the same things from a relationship that she had wanted.

And yet, Greeley's views regarding marriage and women's position in society were decidedly old-fashioned. It had been on the tip of her tongue to inform him that she had no intention of giving Clive Johnson free rein in the business any longer, that she had decided to take a much more active role in its day-to-day affairs. Greeley might well have become apoplectic at *that* news—something she would've secretly loved to witness.

Even more troubling, though, was the fact that Greeley had failed to answer her questions regarding Longren Shipping, choosing to criticize her instead. Surely a kinder man would've been more straightforward, or at least more diplomatic in his criticism. By turning her questions around on her, Greeley had left her no more knowledgeable than before, yet wondering what he knew but refused to reveal.

Perhaps Mona had been correct in her assertion that the police knew what went on under their noses but chose to ignore it. Or even worse, were paid handsomely to look the other way. If Hattie found that to be true, she would forbid Charlotte to have anything to do with Greeley, no matter how crushed Charlotte was by her decision.

She sighed. Realistically, she could ill afford to turn down suitors for Charlotte, but she simply didn't like or trust the police chief. And it was clear she'd have to look elsewhere for the answers she sought.

She could summon Clive Johnson to the house to question him, but she had a different strategy in mind— surprising him with a personal visit to the offices of Longren Shipping. The less prepared he was, the more likely he'd answer candidly—or at least reveal information without thinking.

Tugging on the silver chain of the pocket watch Charles had given her for their six-month anniversary, she checked the time. If she made haste, she could catch

Johnson before he left for the afternoon to board their schooners currently anchored in port. And a brisk walk to the office would clear her head and help her throw off, for a few moments, her unrelenting restlessness.

However, a return to the waterfront would do little to mend the tatters of her shredded reputation.

The Mantle of Ill Intent

AFTER changing into her walking skirt and ankle boots, Hattie descended the stairs to the front entry. "Sara, you'll have to postpone your daily outing to the mercantile to remain here and act as chaperone. I will be making a quick trip down to the office."

Sara frowned. "Are you certain that's wise, ma'am? You're still in mourning, and Mr. Longren always said—"

"Sara," Hattie repeated firmly. "I don't very much care, at this moment, what Mr. Longren said."

The housekeeper huffed and retrieved Hattie's cape, her expression disapproving. She helped Hattie put it on, then opened the door.

"Please inform Charlotte that she is not to leave the house until I return," Hattie said as she walked out.

"Yes, ma'am."

Stepping off the front porch, Hattie paused to breathe deeply, drawing the crisp, clean air into her lungs. The midmorning sun shone brightly, and the sky was a clear blue. With the warming of spring, bulbs had burst into bloom in her neighbors' gardens in the last few days. In the distance, the waters of Admiralty Inlet sparkled. The walk through her neighborhood promised to be pleasant. Her spirits lifting, she set out, her pace brisk, and in no time at all, she had covered the six blocks, traversing the zigzagging footbridge down to the waterfront without mishap.

The offices of Longren Shipping stood next to the Customs House, only a half block up from the huge wooden wharf where ships unloaded their goods and sailors disembarked. Though Charles had proudly explained that few shipping companies had been able to lay claim to such sought-after waterfront real estate, Hattie had always thought this part of town held little aesthetic appeal. Dirt streets separated rows of haphazardly constructed, whitewashed buildings, and the only visual relief to the relentless white and brown mosaic came from the blue waters of the bay beyond. No one had made an effort to plant even the smallest whiskey barrel of flowers.

Yesterday's storm had moved through quickly, tossing the ships about in the harbor but doing no permanent damage. In this morning's bright light, the extensive destruction from the fire was apparent. Only two blocks from Longren Shipping, burned-out, blackened shells and piles of lumber still smoldered. The block to the east of the wharf lay in ashes save a Chinese laundry on the corner, and on the next block, nothing had escaped the fire's wrath.

As Hattie walked along the waterfront, she was careful to stay next to the buildings. Despite the early hour, the boardwalks were crowded, and saloons and brothels had reopened for business. The temperance society was out in full force, its ladies picketing the entrances to the saloons.

The streets, though sloppy from yesterday's rain and the water poured on the fire, teemed with a mix of horse-drawn carriages and flat wagons. Buckboards drawn by draft horses stood ready to be loaded with the cargo crates stacked along the wharf.

Sailors stood at the wharf's edge, holding hand-lettered signs and using megaphones to loudly protest the conditions under which they were forced to toil. Hattie spied Frank Lewis standing to one side, arms folded across his broad chest, observing. He turned his head and their gazes locked, causing Hattie's stride to falter, but he merely raised a sardonic brow.

She turned away, only to find herself looking straight into the disapproving gaze of Chief Greeley. He stood opposite Frank Lewis, feet planted wide and hands fisted on his hips, flanked by several police officers who were keeping an eye on the sailors' demonstration. Hattie stared back at Greeley, her back ramrod straight. No doubt he would choose to believe she had openly defied his edict not to return to the waterfront. *So be it.* She had no control over the man's silly opinions.

Ignoring the curious glances of passersby, Hattie continued down the boardwalk until she stood in front of the entry to Longren Shipping. Dread over the coming confrontation settled deep in her stomach, but the consequences of failure were even more frightening. Drawing a deep breath, she opened the door.

The room she stepped into was long and narrow, each wall lined with wooden file cabinets and glass-fronted bookcases crammed with books and ledgers. Framed pictures of current and past presidents of the United States hung on one wall, along with a calendar. The only windows were those fronting the street, leaving the hallway at the back, which led to storerooms and a rear entrance, shrouded in shadows.

Clive Johnson wielded his authority from behind a massive oak desk placed in the center of the room, halfway back. Only two months ago, that desk had belonged to Charles. A young clerk Hattie had never seen before toiled away, his back to her as he sat on a stool in front of a high, sloping desk situated against the back wall, a thick ledger of accounts at his elbow. A black and gold enamel typewriter rested on a smaller, shorter table to his left.

At the sound of the door closing, her business manager glanced up from the pile of papers he'd been reading. He leapt to his feet.

"Mrs. Longren! If you'd sent word, I would've come up to the house."

"That's not necessary, Mr. Johnson. And the walk was good for me." Determined to appear calm and in control, Hattie took her time unbuttoning her cape, then perched on the edge of the green leather chair he rushed to clear for her. He shouted at the clerk to prepare tea.

As she observed Johnson from under her lashes, she was struck once again by how truly off-putting the man was. His black bow tie, striped black and white silk shirt held in place over his protruding belly with red suspenders, and black wool frock coat reflected his belief that he was now a powerful waterfront shipping master. But the broken, dirty fingernails and Vandyke beard that hadn't seen a trim in days told the story of a man who had failed to leave the rougher side of his life behind.

"I trust your wife and children are well?" she asked politely.

"The missus is fine—"

"And the business?" she interrupted. "It can't be easy, absorbing the loss of the barque Charles commanded."

"We're makin' a profit," Johnson replied, returning to his chair, his expression cautious. "I can write a check for your household expenses—"

"I don't need one at the moment, thank you." The tea the clerk set before her looked as if it had been brewed to within an inch of its life. Prudence dictated she add a small amount of sugar. "I've decided to educate myself about the business Charles left me," she explained as she stirred. "Surely the loss based on the South Seas mutiny, in terms of both the ship and its cargo, was a severe blow."

"We're handlin' it." Johnson's tone had turned abrupt; he didn't appreciate her questions. "We're takin' on extra contracts, pushin' wage cuts on the crews."

She took a cautious sip of tea, then hastily set down the cup. "Won't lowering the wages cause the crews to move to our competitors, leaving us shorthanded?"

He smiled. "You could say I've . . . *encouraged* them not to leave."

"You mean you've threatened them." She nodded. "Or have you actually taken to flogging them?"

He steepled his hands, regarding her in silence. "You've got no reason to worry about whether I use cowhides on the crews. You've got no business experience—"

"I think I know what constitutes inhumane treatment, Mr. Johnson. That knowledge doesn't rely on business expertise."

"It's standard punishment." A carnal light gleamed in his eyes, causing Hattie's stomach to clench. "I wouldn't want to offend a woman of your delicate sensibilities by explainin' the details."

My God, the man actually *enjoyed* the floggings. She shuddered. Quickly changing the subject, she came to the point of her visit. "If you'd be kind enough to fetch the accounting ledgers for me, I'll take them home for review."

Surprise flitted across his face, followed by a scowl. "That's not possible—we make entries in those ledgers every day."

"I'm sure your clerk can simply make notes of the day's business while I conduct my review."

He shook his head. "You don't need to see them. I can provide you with a summary of each week's business in our Friday meetings at the house."

"I'm no longer interested in merely receiving a summary," she argued calmly, holding on to her temper. "I'd like to better understand how we plan to assimilate our recent losses and present some suggestions that don't involve strong-arming the crews into taking starvation-level wages."

"No one is starvin'," Johnson retorted.

"I can't imagine—given that sailors are already poorly paid and endure many hardships—that reducing their pay has improved their lives." She put up a hand, cutting short any further argument. "Regardless, I intend to acquaint myself with the company finances. And I would also like to review the company's policy of procuring crews from shanghaiers."

He seemed to relax a bit, his posture becoming less defensive. "I only use crimps when needs arise. I would've thought Charles told you."

"Yes, he did," Hattie admitted. "However, rumors beg otherwise. And whether or not shanghaiers are openly condoned, their practices are brutal. Therefore, I insist on reviewing your personnel files."

He flushed, small red veins becoming more prominent on his ruddy skin. "If you're suggestin' I would mislead you—"

"Perhaps not *mislead* as much as feel you don't need to bore me with the details." When he opened his mouth to protest, she held up her hand a second time. "I'm sure you know I highly value your services. However, Charles left me in charge of this company—"

"Only by default," Johnson snapped. "He didn't expect to die, leavin' you to deal with the business. He never would've approved of any woman's involvement, much less his wife's. I'm only doin' what he would've wanted."

"Nevertheless, it is my right and my decision to take a more active role."

His knuckles turned white where they gripped the arm of his chair, then his expression turned sly. "Exactly who've you been talkin' to, Mrs. Longren? What're these so-called rumors you made mention of?"

"You needn't be concerned with them."

"If your information came from a union representative," he warned, "then you can't trust 'em. They'll say whatever they need to discredit the shippin' companies. They think we should pay ridiculous wages for no work."

Hattie remained silent. Given that Mona had been the one to first raise questions about Longren Shipping's policies, Hattie didn't have any intention of repeating what Frank Lewis had told her. She didn't want to provide either side with reason for retaliation.

"Please gather the ledgers and any files dealing with the procurement of sailing crews." She made a show of opening her watch. "I have lingered longer than I intended—I must leave immediately."

"But—"

"*Mr. Johnson.*" She stood and leaned over the desk, placing her gloved hands on its dusty surface, though she knew Sara would squawk when she saw the smudges. "The ledgers, *now*. Or I shall be forced to find someone to replace you who is more willing to accept my authority."

He remained in his chair for a long moment. Then he rose slowly, his dark eyes filled with an emotion akin to hatred. "It seems I don't got a choice."

"No, you don't."

He stalked over to the clerk's desk, picking up the large leather-bound book she'd noticed earlier, plus a stack of files, then returned to dump them into her arms. "You have these back by tomorrow mornin'."

She shifted the pile for better balance and met his gaze head-on. "I'll return them when I'm through with them, at which time I will expect a meeting to discuss any policy changes I would like to make."

His face mottled with fury, but he said nothing. She walked to the door and waited, but he made no move to open it for her. It was the clerk who rushed forward to help her.

Outside, she paused for a moment to breathe in fresh air unsullied by the oppressive atmosphere inside the office. Her shoulders sagged as a growing sense of defeat threatened to overwhelm her. She'd gotten what she'd come for, but not without repercussions.

Clive Johnson wouldn't be in a forgiving mood anytime soon.

* * *

ONCE home, Hattie stood in the front hallway, staring at the closed doors to the library. The room had always been Charles's domain. On countless evenings, he'd closeted himself there after dinner on the excuse he had business to conduct. At the time, she'd suspected it was a way to remove himself from the tension that had sprung up between them. But given Clive Johnson's attempts to thwart her, she was now certain Charles had also kept secrets from her. And though she was loath to invade his privacy, his desk might contain answers. Squaring her shoulders, she shifted her burden of ledgers and files to the crook of one arm and slid the doors open.

The stale air coming from the dim room contained a lingering hint of Charles's cologne, and a flood of memories rushed over her. She closed her eyes for a moment, steadying herself, then walked to the huge oak desk in the center of the room. Setting down the files, she circled the room, turning on the lamps that sat on small end tables or stood next to formal groupings of leather wingback chairs. As if compelled, she adjusted a piece of furniture here and there, changing hard right angles to oblique, more pleasing ones.

A small conservatory filled with plants drew her through an arched doorway on the far wall. Double French doors, which looked onto the patio and garden, opened to a fresh, cool breeze. A riot of flowers surrounded the patio, and beyond, she could see her neatly tended beds of vegetables and herbs.

During her short marriage, she had spent most of her time in the garden, because it had been the one place where she'd felt at peace. She now realized that Charles must have frequently watched her from where he sat at his desk. Ignoring the oddly disturbing thought, she walked back into the room.

The corners of her mouth turned down as she studied the furnishings. If she intended to make this room a part of her and Charlotte's lives, the cream-colored Aubusson rug could stay, but the green-and-gold patterned wallpaper would have to go. It made the room far too dark and dismal, as did the deep red brocade cloths, fringed with gold, that draped over the tables. And the portraits of Charles's dour ancestors, which hung in heavy, gilt-edged frames high on the walls, added to the overall gloomy feeling.

Her hands itched to take them down and stack them in an out-of-the-way corner until Sara had time to put them in the attic. To strip the tablecloths off, revealing the golden oak beneath, and to yank the heavy velvet curtains away from the windows, replacing the dark fabric with lace panels that would allow sunlight to pour in.

For the moment, however, that would have to wait— she had more important tasks facing her. But when the time came, she thought on sudden inspiration, she would include Charlotte in the redecorating project. Perhaps it would distract her from thoughts of Greeley.

Returning to the desk, Hattie sat in Charles's high-backed chair and opened the red and black leather-bound ledger Clive Johnson had given her. Page after page of columns of tidy numbers greeted her, with one-line explanations written in minute, spidery script. She removed her kid gloves and tossed them aside, then rang for Sara.

"I'll take a tray here in lieu of lunch," she told the housekeeper. "If Charlotte needs me, let her know where I am."

However, after only a half hour of reading, Hattie closed the ledger, admitting defeat. She had no idea how to decipher the numbers, no inkling of what they meant. Not, she thought wryly, that her parents had ever considered educating her in the art of bookkeeping. They'd fully intended for her to follow in her mother's footsteps, working in clinics for the poor. And until Charles had swept into her life that night at the charity ball on the

Boston Commons, she'd never given her preordained future a second thought.

Truth be told, she had only the vaguest notion of how a shipping office actually conducted its business. Charles had once explained to her that he functioned as a shipping master—a procuring agency, if you will, for both his ships and those owned by other ships' captains. His employees, which included office personnel and the longshoremen who manned the Whitehall boats, acquired crews from ships setting anchor, then provided those crews—for a modest fee—to other ships' captains who were ready to set sail. But beyond that general explanation, she knew little of the details.

The accounting for such activities, which included finding lodging for the sailors while in port, was probably quite complex. It simply wouldn't do to remain in the dark—she had to gain a better understanding of Longren Shipping and its finances. And, she realized, she knew just who could help her, no matter how distasteful the thought was.

Frank Lewis.

She shifted uneasily, uncomfortable with the notion of inviting her husband's nemesis to the house. After all, Lewis's union operated the shipping office that was Longren Shipping's largest competitor. Allowing him access to the books could possibly give him substantial insight and leverage over Longren Shipping.

But did she really have a choice? If she approached Eleanor Canby for help, Eleanor would react as others had, judging her sudden interest in the business as unseemly. And even if Eleanor knew of someone who could help her, she wouldn't provide any names. No, Hattie thought, she was on her own, and Frank Lewis was the one person she knew with the education and intellect needed to help her understand the truth behind the numbers. She could count on him to be plainspoken in his explanations. He would, in fact, relish educating her regarding her deceased husband's amoral business practices.

Her decision made, she quickly penned a thank-you note to Mona Starr, asking her for information about how to contact Lewis, then gave it to Sara to have it delivered.

Once the housekeeper left the room, Hattie began pulling open desk drawers, not certain what she sought. Inside the center drawer, she found a check ledger and their household accounts, which she set aside to look at in a day or two, after she had a better handle on the business. Side drawers revealed rows of files, some seemingly personal in nature, others business related.

She flipped through them, stunned to discover that Charles had kept detailed dossiers compiled by a private investigator on a number of prominent businessmen as well as politicians. Her mouth fell open when she found a file on her family containing confidential information regarding their personal finances, as well as character witness statements. Given the dates of the paperwork, Charles had had them investigated *before* he had proposed to her. Pulling the file out, she read the scrawled notes in Charles's handwriting, her stomach churning.

The family seems honorable enough, though the free clinic connection is of questionable propriety, he'd written. *And the dowry is adequate. Once Hattie is removed from her parents' influence, she will make an obedient enough wife.*

Her hands fisted, crumpling the paper. Methodically shredding the documents, she placed them in a cigar ashtray on the desk, striking a match to them.

The rest of the files contained papers relating to various business ventures. The only one that caught her eye was Charles's substantial investment in the proposed railway from Portland, Oregon, along Hood Canal to Port Chatham—a railway she knew many of the town's businessmen hoped would provide the basis for an ever-expanding local economy. And many of these businessmen, it turned out, were the very same ones on whom Charles had compiled dossiers.

Her late husband, Hattie concluded, had been either a careful businessman or a paranoid one, depending on one's point of view. She was uneasy with this revelation into his business practices, and she had no doubt the men whose dossiers she held would be unhappy to know she had access to such information about them.

At the very back of the same desk drawer that contained the dossiers, she found a slim file with only one small slip of paper, upon which Charles had written what appeared to be a safe combination. Standing, she walked to the wall behind her and swung aside the portrait of Charles's grandfather, revealing a small safe. Using the combination, she opened it.

Her mouth fell open. The small, rectangular space was filled with stacks of cash, along with a nondescript black leather journal. Never before had she seen so much money—it had to be thousands of dollars. Surely Charles didn't conduct that much shipping business on the basis of cash.

Increasingly uneasy, she retrieved the journal and flipped through it, finding mostly empty pages. However, at the far back, Charles had written a short list of dollar amounts with no notations to explain them. Large dollar amounts, she realized with a chill, totaling well over fifty thousand dollars.

Sara entered, holding a calling card. Hattie quickly snapped the book shut, shoving it back inside the wall safe and returning the picture to its place on the wall.

"A Mr. Michael Seavey, ma'am." Sara handed her a card made of white vellum, embossed with ornate engraved script.

Placing the card on the desk, Hattie sat, smoothing her skirt. "I'll receive him in here, Sara."

The housekeeper frowned. "Won't you be wanting to freshen up first, ma'am, and greet him properly in the parlor?"

"I'm in the middle of my work—he'll have to accept me as I am, dust and all. If you would be so kind as to prepare tea for us."

"Very well, ma'am," Sara sighed, obviously despairing of Hattie's negligent attitude toward etiquette.

Moments later, Seavey appeared in the doorway, resplendently attired in a close-fitting gray frock coat with silk lapels, matching waistcoat, gray-on-gray striped silk tie, and black trousers. His pale gaze settled on her, and he bowed, his manner as subtly mocking as it had been that night on the beach. "Mrs. Longren."

She inclined her head, indicating he should take the seat across from her and then clasping her trembling hands in her lap. It did not please her to realize that a man rumored to be involved in shanghaiing and the white slave trade had the ability to undermine her composure. He was beneath contempt, yet she would strive to remain polite. "Your visit comes as a surprise, Mr. Seavey."

He settled into the wingback chair. "Not an unpleasant one, I hope," he murmured. Tugging off his gloves one finger at a time, he placed them on the desk, a slight smile curving his lips. "I've come to inquire after your health."

She raised both eyebrows. "You are the second person to do so today."

"Ah." He feigned chagrin. "I fear I've been disingenuous. Dare I ask what man has bettered me at my own game?"

"Chief Greeley paid us a quick visit this morning. I will tell you what I told him, that the girls and I are fine."

Sara brought in the tea tray, and Hattie busied herself with serving. Though her pulse still beat quickly, she was pleased to see that her hands were steady.

"Greeley was here to see the fair young Charlotte, I presume," Seavey said.

"Yes."

"He'd keep her safe. However, he would also crush her spirit."

Hattie stared at him, teapot in midair. "Yes, that's it precisely, isn't it?"

Seavey gave a nod. "Unfortunately, that is all a woman can hope for."

Hattie held back an automatic retort. This man was dangerous; it would not be wise to openly challenge him.

Seavey sipped his tea in silence, glancing around the room, apparently feeling no need to keep the conversation going. Hattie had to restrain herself from fidgeting.

"This room has always pleased me," he finally commented, surprising her yet again. "I told Charles on numerous occasions that he couldn't have created a more comfortable space from which to conduct business."

"I had no idea you'd been to the house," Hattie said, unwillingly intrigued. "Was it before Charles and I married?"

Seavey's expression turned wry. "On the contrary, I visited frequently after your arrival. I even had the pleasure of a glimpse of you in the garden from time to time, though Charles was usually very careful to keep you tucked away from sight."

She swallowed, feeling unaccountably betrayed. The garden had been her escape, yet now she was discovering she'd never had a moment alone or gone unobserved—even, it appeared, by strangers.

Seavey seemed unaware of her reaction, raising his cup to salute her. "It is easy to see why Charles was so possessive. You are a woman of great beauty as well as strength of character. I confess I find myself equally fascinated by both."

She frowned. "I'm in mourning, Mr. Seavey. Your remarks are inappropriate."

He leaned back, lazily propping a low-cut, black leather boot on one knee. "I rarely worry about propriety, Mrs. Longren. And I was led to believe, given your recent adventure, that we were kindred souls of a sort."

"We are nothing of the kind," she said, alarmed that he would have drawn such a conclusion. "As owner of Longren Shipping, I simply felt an obligation to ensure that my sailing crews were safe."

He looked amused. "You did more than that. I seem to remember you standing shoulder to shoulder with Port Chatham's most famous madam. That takes grit, as well as a certain, shall we say, *flexible* frame of mind."

She shrugged, piqued by his accurate portrayal. "Once I saw the state of things, I could hardly turn my back, could I? You, on the other hand, seem to have been endowed with little or no social conscience. You stood by all through the night and did nothing to help."

He threw his head back and laughed out loud. "My sleek little cat has claws."

She set her teeth. "Where are your bodyguards, Mr. Seavey? Should I ask Sara to take them some tea and cake?"

Her attempt to change the subject only served to amuse him further. "They don't feel the need to protect me from my women."

"I'm not one of your women," she snapped, goaded.

"Not yet, perhaps."

She slashed a hand through the air. "Why are you here, Mr. Seavey?"

He sighed, returning his cup to its saucer. "Very well, if you insist on directness."

"I prefer it."

"Somehow, I'm not surprised, though I thoroughly enjoy sparring with you." He held up a hand to forestall her next retort. "Eleanor Canby's editorial this morning, I'm told, was influenced by remarks you made in public the night of the fire."

Hattie frowned. "I voiced an opinion that the fire might have been started intentionally, if that is what you are referring to. Can you deny it?"

"Why would you think I would have any knowledge of the matter?" he queried, his tone mild.

"You live on the waterfront, do you not?"

"On the top floor of my hotel, yes. I find the energy in that part of town . . . exhilarating."

"Then you must be privy to what goes on."

He studied her for a long moment. "I thought it best to pay you a visit," he said, his tone gentle, "to encourage you not to voice opinions on issues about which you have little or no direct knowledge. Such opinions, when made known to the wrong people, could put you at risk."

She arched her brows. "Are you threatening me, Mr. Seavey?"

He sighed. "You have an overly suspicious nature, my dear. I'm merely concerned for your safety. A widow in this town has little enough security as it is."

She stared at him, trying to discern the truthfulness of

his statement. "Tell me, Mr. Seavey, why were you and Charles so well acquainted that you profess to have a fondness for this library? Were your visits for social or business purposes?"

He drank more tea before answering. "A little of both."

"Given the line of business I'm told you engage in, I can't imagine what Charles could've possibly gained by a liaison with you."

"No, I don't suppose you can. Charles kept you well away from both his business and social affairs."

"Did Charles collude with you to procure crews by any means necessary?" she asked bluntly.

Something shifted in his pale eyes, but he answered calmly enough. "The shipping masters need crews to fulfill sailing contracts, and the sailors need berths. I merely ensure that the two come together, taking a small profit for the effort I expend."

She shook her head. "Your reasoning is self-serving, is it not? Shanghaiing is a reprehensible practice, though few in this town seem to be concerned with that fact. But I intend to put a stop to it, at least with regard to Longren Shipping. As you can see," she said, gesturing at the stacks of papers before her, "my level of involvement in the business is now changing."

He didn't seem alarmed by her announcement. Indeed, his expression was one of polite boredom. "I doubt you'll find the work Charles engaged in either interesting or fulfilling. I shouldn't imagine a woman of your refinement would be pleased to have to deal with such mundane tasks."

"I have little choice in the matter," she said briskly, "if Charlotte and I are to survive. And you didn't answer my question."

"I don't believe I intended to." His tone remained diffident as he toyed with one snowy white cuff. "Your man Johnson seems competent enough. Why not leave the business to him?"

"Clive Johnson was well regarded by my husband. However, by becoming more involved in Longren Shipping, I will have a glimpse into my late husband's life, and therefore perhaps a better understanding of who he was." She opened the desk drawer and withdrew one of Charles's dossiers, handing it to him. "Files such as these exemplify how little I knew about Charles, and they throw into question his judgment."

Seavey opened it and quickly glanced at the contents. His head jerked up, his expression hard, and she wondered how she could've been drawn into believing for even a few moments that his veneer of sophistication was anything but that—a thin camouflage of what lay beneath. She wouldn't, however, allow herself to be afraid.

"I haven't read the file," she assured him. "The letterhead was enough to convince me of the nature of its contents. However, I suspect you'd prefer to keep the information contained within private."

Seavey regarded her for a moment without comment. "It seems I am in your debt," he said finally.

"Not at all. I ran across the file while looking through Charles's desk drawers and thought to return it to you."

"This is the only copy, I presume?"

"Yes."

He abruptly stood, tucking the file inside his coat, then drawing on his gloves. His expression was pensive. "I don't recommend living in the past, Mrs. Longren," he said at length. "It will prove a lonely place."

She shook her head. "I wasn't married to Charles long. I'd like to know more about him before I put his memory to rest."

"A laudable sentiment, perhaps, though I've never been one to appreciate sentimentality."

He walked to the library door, then turned back. "I can sympathize with your need to find answers, Hattie," he said quietly. "However, I shouldn't think you'll be pleased with what you discover."

Chapter 7

"WAIT a minute," Jordan said, now surrounded by piles of newspapers and Hattie's diaries. "I think Charlotte was right in a way—Seavey seemed fond of you."

Hattie, who hovered in the stacks, shook her head. "He wanted to control me, to ensure that I didn't harm his business. He was the kind of man who thrived on acquiring power and holding it over people."

"Maybe, but history is littered with powerful, ruthless men who also loved obsessively. He might have been capable of employing one set of ethics in business, yet another with a woman he cared about. So he may have been a shanghaier and white slave trader, and he may also have had a hidden agenda during that visit. But the way I see it, he definitely was interested in you."

"Hidden agenda?" Hattie looked confused.

"An unspoken reason for his visit," Jordan rephrased.

"Oh, well, yes—he did seem to cut his visit short on that occasion. Then again, I never completely understood what motivated Seavey." Hattie frowned, her expression turned inward. "I'm hoping his personal papers will reveal more than I wrote in my diary."

Jordan perked up and began thumbing through the stacks of documents. Seavey's papers would make fascinating reading. "You put them here?"

Hattie shook her head. "I don't know where they are—you'll have to locate them. He must have relatives in town; surely they'll know what became of them."

She floated over to the next aisle and a book landed in front of Jordan. "That's his memoir, but of course you can't believe a word he wrote in it. It's merely a justification for his business dealings. He wanted to believe he provided a much-needed service."

"The author of the history book I have back at the house *did* claim that many sailors actively participated in the practice of shanghaiing," Jordan pointed out as she flipped through the pages of the thin memoir.

Hattie snorted. "All that means is that they went along so they wouldn't be beaten. Seavey always claimed that he never mistreated the sailors unless they *resisted* his offer."

Footsteps suddenly reverberated through the ceiling, and they both looked up. It took Jordan a moment to realize that ghosts don't clomp, that someone must've entered the building.

Charlotte flew down the stairwell. "The fuzz! The fuzz!"

Hattie sighed. "She read a Kurt Vonnegut book last week that the prior owners left in the library."

The footsteps were now on the risers, and Darcy came into view. Jordan's shoulders sagged in relief. If another of

Port Chatham's finest had appeared, Jordan would've ended up justifying her unauthorized presence in court. *Ghosts made me do it, Judge.* Right. Like that would be admissible anywhere outside of a sanity hearing.

"How's the research going?" Darcy asked.

"*Run!*" Charlotte screeched, flying around the basement.

"Fine. Why are you back so early?" Jordan asked, trying not to duck when Charlotte swooped overhead.

"It's been a couple of hours, actually, and I vary my route. I find it's always good to keep the perps guessing," Darcy said, her tone wry. She folded her arms and propped a shoulder against one of the stacks, completely unaware of the ghosts. "Find anything interesting?"

"Not exactly. I've been reading about the time frame right before Hattie was murdered."

Darcy's eyes lit up. "You're researching the murder?"

"I can get her gun for you!" Charlotte hissed, hovering behind Jordan's left shoulder.

Jordan slipped a hand behind her back and made a shooing motion. "How about I tell you all about it over a beer in about an hour?"

Darcy pursed her lips. "So get out of here and let you get back to it, huh? That's the thanks I get."

"I promise—"

Darcy held up a hand. "I was kidding, though I'll expect a full report. You'll leave the place as you found it, including putting away all those fashion magazines scattered about upstairs? *And* replace the plywood barricade across the entry?"

"You have my word."

She tossed Jordan the key to the front door, then paused. "You know, I wouldn't have thought you'd be the type to spend time reading up on fashions of the rich and famous of yesteryear." When Jordan remained silent, she muttered something under her breath and turned toward the stairs, almost walking straight through Hattie, who flitted out of the way. "One hour, or I'm coming back."

"Deal."

Once Darcy was gone, Jordan turned back to Hattie. "So where were we? Oh, right. So—there's Frank, who had a history of violence and the physical conditioning to easily murder you, and with whom you'd already had a public confrontation, witnessed by the police chief. *That's* the guy you chose to fall in love with. And Clive Johnson hated you and didn't hesitate to use violence against the crews on your ships. But Seavey, who couldn't keep his eyes off you and who acted chivalrously toward you, is the one you believe murdered you."

Hattie shook her head. "You don't understand— Seavey was evil. Longren Shipping was all that interested him, and I was simply in his way."

"You're wrong!" Charlotte cried, and they both looked at her, surprised. "You never saw that he loved you, just like you never saw how much John Greeley loved me!"

"Yeah, Greeley was a real prize," Jordan observed. "If he were alive today, I'd be warning every single woman within three counties to stay clear of him."

Charlotte burst into tears and abruptly disappeared in a puff of particles. Jordan raised a brow at Hattie.

"Faulty materialization—her emotions interfere."

"So I gather she never saw through Greeley, even after you were gone?"

"No. She never believed me when I told her that Greeley was a lot like Charles—cold and controlling. Oh, Greeley was a good enough police chief, I suppose, though he certainly arrested the wrong man for my murder. But he was hard, and cruel." Hattie looked pensive, then shook her head. "I'll take her home and settle her down while you finish reading."

Jordan turned back to Seavey's memoir, then remembered what she'd wanted to ask. "Wait." She called Hattie back as she began to fade. "Why are you so convinced that Seavey was evil?"

"Because he kidnapped Charlotte."

Jordan's jaw dropped.

"He thought he could force me to cooperate." Hattie trembled. "His men held Charlotte in the tunnels. She lay in the dark, bound and gagged so no one could hear her terrified screams, soaked in cold, foul-smelling water with rats only a few feet away, waiting for her to fall asleep."

Hattie drew a breath, her expression distant and filled with loathing. "I have no doubt that Michael Seavey deserved *everything* he eventually got."

Soiled Goods

TWO days hence, Hattie received a reply from Mona that included Frank Lewis's address. She penned a quick note to him, requesting he call upon her that afternoon at Longren House to discuss a business matter.

The night before, she'd found a stack of *Seacoast Journal* issues and located the "Red Letters" column that had incited Charles's crew to mutiny. After reading it through, she admitted to herself it was possible the charges Lewis made against Charles and Clive Johnson might have been accurate. They certainly fit with what Mona had hinted, as well as with her own impression of Johnson.

Lewis had published what appeared to be factual accounts of sailors who had been drugged and shanghaied, and then, after having been turned over to Charles, beaten when they tried to escape to shore. Their stories sickened her. Their treatment was as inhumane as Lewis had indicated to her the morning after the fire, and as owner of Longren Shipping, she refused to condone such tactics.

Still, she felt Lewis should have to prove that the company's practices were as bad as he alleged. And with any luck, his proof would also include the information she needed to understand why the library safe held all that cash.

Hattie knew that by inviting Lewis to review the company books, she was making a pact with the devil. His actions were reprehensible—he had to have known he'd sealed Charles's fate when he wrote that column. After all, it wouldn't be the first time the content of "Red Letters" had been used to justify violence against ships' captains.

Lewis wouldn't arrive until that afternoon, leaving Hattie idle for the rest of the morning. To make up for her inattentiveness the day before, she suggested to Charlotte and Tabitha that they visit the local dressmaker's shop to purchase matching thread and ribbons for the fabric Mona had given them. The girls were thrilled at the prospect, racing to put on their cloaks and gloves.

Though fog enshrouded the ships in the harbor and clung to the headlands, chilling the air, the wind was calm. She and the girls walked the three blocks to the shop in no time. Charlotte seemed to have regained her good humor after Chief Greeley's visit, chattering away with Tabitha about dress styles and ideas for how best to use the new fabric.

"The sun will come out within a few hours, right, Hattie?" Charlotte asked, putting a skip in her stride.

Hattie agreed. "It should be a very pleasant spring afternoon. You girls should plan to spend it in the garden.

There's much to be done to prepare the beds for the next planting of vegetables and herbs."

"I was thinking it might be warm enough to warrant a trip to the ice-cream parlor," Charlotte said, her expression hopeful.

"Unfortunately, I have a meeting this afternoon. It wouldn't do to have you girls visit Mr. Fuller's establishment without a chaperone."

"But it's just a few blocks from the house," Charlotte protested, "and I could take Tabitha with me. Nothing could possibly happen to us!"

"Nevertheless, it wouldn't be appropriate." Hattie didn't want to alarm Charlotte by mentioning what Mona had said about girls from the hill area kidnapped and sold into prostitution.

"Then Sara could take us."

"Sara won't have the time. Now that we've let go the rest of the household staff, she has more duties to fulfill."

"Please?" Charlotte wheedled. "She'd make the time if you asked her."

"And then she'd feel she had to work extra hard tomorrow to make up for the time she took off to indulge you." Hattie gave Charlotte a chastising look. "That would hardly be fair."

As they had arrived at Miss Willoughby's shop, she shushed Charlotte's continued objections. Opening the door, she ushered the girls inside. To her dismay, Eleanor Canby stood at the counter, discussing dress designs with the shop's proprietress.

A satisfied look settled over Eleanor's face when she

saw them. "Hattie," she acknowledged with a slight nod. "You've chosen a nice day to venture out with the girls. I trust you've wisely decided to focus on domestic chores in accordance with the dictates of your period of mourning."

Hattie forced a smile. "The girls and I have the urge to make several new dresses, yes."

"It does get tedious, wearing the same mourning outfits," Eleanor agreed, glancing over Hattie's conservatively cut black muslin day dress and walking boots with approval. "I assume you're hoping to make a few new dresses that will be suitable, once summer is behind us? I'm sure Celeste can advise you as to the latest fashions."

"Yes, that would be lovely." Hattie smiled at the seamstress, who was Eleanor's niece, the daughter of her brother, a well-respected local physician. The diminutive woman was quiet and shy, and easily intimidated by Eleanor. But once away from Eleanor's influence, Celeste tended to relax and chat knowledgeably about the latest styles.

Eleanor seemed to want to continue the conversation, no doubt waiting for an opportunity to bring up her latest editorial. Refusing to be drawn, Hattie gave her a polite nod. "The girls and I will be examining your ribbons, Celeste, while you finish with Eleanor."

A look of frustration passed over Eleanor's face. "I gather you read this week's issue of the *Gazette*?" she demanded.

Hattie turned back, sighing inwardly. "Yes, though you know I don't agree with your views."

"My reporters are never wrong."

"Perhaps, but a second fire could have been started in that location to deliberately mislead the fire department. Have the authorities considered that possibility?"

Eleanor pursed her lips. "I fail to understand why you continue to defend the actions of such depraved individuals."

"I don't like to see innocents accused of wrongdoing. And I sincerely doubt the fire was the result of the actions of a prostitute."

"It will do you no good to voice that opinion in this neighborhood."

Hattie abruptly lost patience. "So it's come to that, has it, Eleanor? I'm not allowed to say what I think in public? I thought members of the press were staunch supporters of the First Amendment."

"This has more to do with your poor judgment than the First Amendment," Eleanor retorted. "It's bad enough that you took the girls down to fight the fire. But to continue to openly accuse this town's businessmen of illegal acts will only further ostracize you, as well as jeopardize any possibility Charlotte will have of making a good match."

Charlotte touched Hattie's arm, her expression beseeching, but Hattie shook her head. "Just what do you fear, Eleanor? The truth? Or your investors? Is Michael Seavey one of them?"

"Surely you aren't accusing me of slanting the news!"

"You don't need to, as long as you control the editorial page."

Eleanor's face flushed dull red, and she stepped closer,

lowering her voice. "Watch your tongue, Hattie. If I should make it known I've cut you from the list of guests for my social events, no one in this town will have anything to do with you. I hold all the power here."

From the corner of her eye, Hattie caught Charlotte's flinch. "To take such a petty action would be beneath you," she said evenly.

Eleanor stepped back and nodded. "Perhaps. But if you become a social liability, I'll have no choice."

Hattie gazed steadily at Eleanor. "If you'll excuse us, we have ribbons to select. Girls?"

As they walked over to the ribbon display, Hattie realized Eleanor hadn't answered her question about whether Michael Seavey was an investor in the *Gazette*.

* * *

UNWILLING to allow her argument with Eleanor to cast a pall on their outing, Hattie indulged Charlotte's whims for ribbons and lace more than she probably should have. But by the time they arrived back at the house, Charlotte was chatting excitedly with her young maid about the dress patterns they would start cutting that afternoon, so Hattie felt the expenditures were justified. And though Charlotte tried once more to convince Hattie of the dire necessity of a visit to Fuller's Ice Cream Parlor, she seemed content enough to remain at home with Tabitha.

Relieved, Hattie retired to the library to continue to read through the business files. She'd barely gotten started, though, when Frank Lewis responded to her summons by presenting himself at the kitchen door. At Hattie's request, Sara brought him to the library, her eyes wide with curiosity.

"There was no reason to assume you have to use the workers' entry, Mr. Lewis," Hattie chided.

"On the contrary." He leaned against the library doors, arms crossed, his gaze cool. "To have come to the front door would've given the wrong impression. I don't aspire to be on equal footing with your neighbors."

"Reverse snobbery?" she asked lightly.

"Nothing so lofty—I simply don't respect many of them." He added, "And you are in mourning, are you not? Your neighbors can't be left wondering whether you're receiving gentlemen callers."

She conceded the point. "You are correct, though I chafe against the societal restraints of the mourning period. A woman is expected to do nothing—sitting in her house with the curtains drawn day after day—going slowly mad from the inactivity." She glanced at the housekeeper, who continued to hover in the doorway behind him. "Tea and sandwiches, please, Sara."

Sara sniffed. "Shall I feed him in the kitchen, ma'am?"

"No, he'll have a light lunch in here with me. We have work to do."

Frank raised his eyebrows but said nothing while Sara huffed her disapproval all the way down the hall. He didn't move from the door. "What is it that you want from me, Mrs. Longren? Last time we talked, you accused me of all but murdering your husband."

"Can you deny that you gave no thought to the potential consequences of what you printed?"

"I printed the truth," he said, shrugging. "I feel no need to justify myself to you, nor do I feel any remorse that your husband is dead. He was not a man who deserved loyalty, from his crew or from a woman such as yourself."

The callousness of his statement shocked her. Still, she managed not to show it. "Please, won't you be seated?"

He studied her for a long moment, his gaze making her nerves skitter. Then he pushed away from the door, wandering over to a wall of bookcases.

Watching him circle the room, she was struck by how tall he was, yet lanky, almost thin, even. He radiated an intense energy she could feel even from where she sat—she suspected he rarely relaxed. He ran his fingers lightly over the bindings of the library's extensive collection of leather-bound books—lightly and reverently, she thought.

She found him to be an intriguingly complex man. Under different circumstances, she would have been drawn to know him better, perhaps to even form a lasting friendship with him. It had been a long time since she'd indulged in the simple pleasure of intelligent conversation. But unfortunately, they'd ended up on opposite sides—she had no choice but to remain guarded around him.

He abruptly turned, facing her. "Longren Shipping is blacklisted by the union. It has been instrumental in forcing lower sailors' wages, and it has condoned violence against union members. I doubt you and I will find any common ground."

"That remains to be seen." She gestured at the stack of files in front of her. "These are the ledgers and files for Charles's business. I brought you here to make a proposal, that you use them to prove you are right about his business practices." She ignored his look of surprise. "By giving you access to my husband's files, you can prove to me whether or not he regularly used shanghaiers, and also whether the company can afford to hire unionized sailors."

His expression was skeptical. "And what do you hope to gain from this arrangement? Do you aspire to salvage your husband's good name?" he mocked. "Or perhaps you wish to let it be known you gave the sailors' union a chance, so that you can continue to support a corrupt system?"

"I could simply wish to derive satisfaction from having improved the rights of workers, could I not?" she asked lightly.

He snorted. "I rarely find that business owners are motivated by humanitarian principles. If not for the reasons I've just stated, why have you brought me here?"

She sighed. "Very well. To be frank, you and Mona Starr both made accusations about my husband that trouble me. I wish to prove them either true or false."

"And you don't have the training to decipher the books," Frank concluded shrewdly.

"No," she replied, loath to admit any weakness in his presence. His brashness annoyed her, but at the same time, she had to admit that after her dealings with Greeley and Johnson, she found Frank's straightforward manner refreshing, even when he was deliberately attempting to rile her.

He remained silent for a moment longer, then shrugged. "Very well. I can hardly resist an opportunity to review the books, can I? But if I prove what I believe to be true about Longren Shipping's policies, you agree in return to change them. All new hires must be union sailors at union-specified wages, and you will give me the chance to talk to your existing crews, to see whether I can convince them to join up. Agreed?"

She shook her head. "You must think me naïve, Mr. Lewis. I can't commit to pay wages of an unspecified amount that could potentially cripple my company. However, I will agree to give your suggestions serious consideration, as well as make every attempt to negotiate a contract with the union that makes provisions for hiring union sailors at fair wages. In addition, if you can prove the sailors are mistreated during voyages, I will immediately alter the practices by the ships' captains and first mates while at sea."

"And what of Clive Johnson? God knows I'd love to see his power on the waterfront diminished, but he'll never agree to what you're proposing. I've seen, and heard first-hand accounts of, his brutal tactics."

"If he doesn't mend his ways," Hattie replied with deceptive mildness, "I'll replace him."

Frank raised his brows but didn't pursue the subject. "You're currently paying your crews twenty dollars per month. The wages that are necessary, at a minimum, are thirty dollars in Puget Sound, thirty-five dollars for out-side ports. Are you willing to consider those figures?"

"Prove to me that I can afford it," she shot back as Sara entered with a tray.

"Fair enough. Where would you like me to start?"

"Well, to begin with," she said, unaccountably frus-trated by his insistence on keeping her at a distance, "I'd like you to be seated."

He smiled slightly, but moved forward to sit across from her. While Sara served, his gaze returned to the walls of books. Hattie made a mental note to offer him the use of her library for the duration of the time they worked together.

Sara plunked down the last of the plates on the desk, rattling the china.

"Sara . . ." Hattie admonished.

"Hmmph." She gave Frank one last hard look, then stalked out.

"You'll have to forgive my housekeeper," Hattie said as she held out a plate of sandwiches, then poured tea. "I seem to shock her daily, and she is dedicated to me."

"On the contrary, I find her loyalty admirable." Frank's tone was wry. "She is right to worry about you." He took the tea she offered and set it down. "Show me the ledger. Perhaps the notations will reveal payments made for pro-curement."

She handed over the heavy book, and he shoved food and drink aside to make room. Selecting a beef and hard cheese sandwich with one hand, he flipped the ledger open and started reading.

She nibbled on a cucumber triangle and waited. He finished his first sandwich, and she handed him a second without thinking, responding to an unconscious urge to feed him. He took it, glancing up at her, and she sat back, embarrassed by her action. His mouth quirked, but he returned to the task at hand.

After a long interlude, he stopped reading to drink some tea. "I may see a pattern," he said. "Deposits are occurring with regularity, probably in the form of advance wages from ships' captains to Longren Shipping. Expenses of corresponding but smaller amounts are then logged to a number of vendor accounts—these would be, in all likelihood, accounts for boardinghouse operators or shanghaiers. One of these vendor accounts is always credited at the time of the deposits, so I'm guessing that amount is the cut Clive Johnson takes. The amounts going to the other vendors are only slightly more than what is required to pay the sailors' 'boarding' expenses. In some cases, if we trace back to where these sailors are renting rooms, we will probably find that the owner of the boardinghouse *is* the shanghaier."

Hattie shook her head, totally confused. "I don't understand."

Frank settled back in his chair. "When a ship drops anchor in the harbor," he explained, "the shanghaiers like Mike Seavey pay longshoremen to take their Whitehall boats out and lure the crews away with promises of jobs and free rent while in port. Though the ships' captains try to protest this practice, the sailors are motivated to desert ship because of the treatment they've suffered while at sea—the lure of better conditions is simply too hard to resist. This frees the ships' captains, by the way, from paying back wages, since the sailors have technically deserted ship. The sailors are then transported to shore and forced into the tunnels. Those more willing to oblige the shanghaiers are allowed to 'rent' rooms in the boardinghouses; the rest are kept in chains in the tunnels."

Hattie set down her sandwich, her appetite gone. "That's appalling," she admitted. "But I don't see where Longren Shipping comes in."

"I'm getting to that. As the time to set sail nears, the ships' captains contract with Longren Shipping for a crew. The captain pays an advance against the sailors' wages, along with a procurement fee to Longren Shipping. Clive Johnson pockets a portion of the wages, deposits the procurement fee to the business, then pays out to the boardinghouse operator—or the shanghaier—the rest. The shanghaier releases the sailors without pay, claiming their room and board are barely covered by the payment received. Once back in Johnson's custody, longshoremen transport the sailors back out to a ship. Anyone attempting to resist is drugged or worse, to guarantee they will be 'accommodating.'"

Hattie thought it through. "So you're saying that the deposits and payments back out to the vendors are proof that Longren Shipping is colluding with shanghaiers. How can you be certain?"

"It's a well-known method of indebting the sailors to their handlers," Frank insisted. "And the pattern of payments backs up what I'm saying."

"Show me the entries," she demanded.

He stood, bringing the ledger around to her side of the desk, placing it open before her and leaning down. She raised her head. Their gazes locked, and her breath backed up in her throat. She suddenly wished she weren't wearing black, that her dress was made of one of the colorful fabrics she'd seen that morning at the dressmaker's. That he would see *her*, not his enemy's widow. Shaken, Hattie forced herself to focus on the ledger page.

After a lengthy pause, he cleared his throat and pointed. "See the third column of figures? The notations refer to account numbers which"—he reached out, his arm brushing her shoulder, and flipped to the back of the ledger—"correspond to names of boardinghouses and saloons that are known to let rooms." He turned to yet a different section of the ledger. "And look here—this is your petty cash account. The dates of these credits match those of the payments associated with the first vendor entry for the crew. They're probably kickbacks to Johnson, but there are no explanations regarding to whom the money goes. Cash is notoriously difficult to track."

He turned his head to regard her, a lock of dark brown hair falling across his high forehead. She had the strongest urge to brush the hair back from his eyes, and she clasped her hands in her lap, mortified. How could she have these irrational feelings, so soon after Charles's death, and with *this* man, of all men?

Returning to his chair, he said, as if nothing had transpired between them, "Longren Shipping is making a tidy profit, but it's coming at the expense of the crews you hire. I'd stake my reputation on it."

"But we have no concrete proof that you are correct."

"No, not without further documentation. You'll need the chart of accounts, which provides a detailed explanation of the purpose of each account represented by a number in the ledger, and you'll have to request from Johnson or his clerk a documented list of the petty cash payments."

She nodded. "Very well. I will return to the office tomorrow and demand that information."

"I'll ask around on the docks, see whether anyone has heard any rumors. I can also verify the dates ships came into port and set sail, which should tie to the dates of the deposits." He hesitated, frowning. "Mrs. Longren..."

"You called me Hattie down at the beach," she reminded him. "We've gone beyond formal names, I believe."

Frank's expression turned self-deprecating. "I doubt that's a good idea, but very well...Hattie." He paused a second time. "Are you certain you want to pursue this line of inquiry? It's not without an element of risk."

"Yes, I'm certain."

He frowned. "As a union organizer, I'm pleased you are acting honorably. And I can't deny that the opportunity to convert Longren Shipping to a union house would be a major coup, in terms of both workers' rights and a boost to the credibility of the union. But...I'm concerned about your welfare." He seemed uncomfortable with the admission, and she was unaccountably touched. "It would be hard enough for a man to take on this task, let alone a woman." He hesitated, then added, "And Johnson won't back you up."

"Clive Johnson has fought me since the day we received word of Charles's death," she pointed. "His lack of support will be nothing new."

"It's in his best interests to keep you away from the business. He's benefiting from the current arrangement, far beyond the salary you pay him."

"Do you know that for a fact?"

"It's rumored on the docks."

Hattie thought about it. A system of lucrative kickbacks would certainly explain Johnson's fury over her "meddling" in the business. She paused, wondering whether she should trust Frank, then went with her instincts. Rising, she opened the safe, careful to keep the door angled so he couldn't see the cash. Removing the small journal, she opened it to the list of dollar amounts in the back and handed it to him. "Do these mean anything to you?"

He glanced down the list, then whistled softly. "This is a substantial amount of money—I've known men to kill for far less." He took back the ledger and searched through the entries once more. "I can find no corresponding payments of these amounts, nor any obvious smaller payments to a similar account or description that would add up to these sums. Have you checked your personal household accounts?"

"No." She felt foolish that she hadn't thought to do so.

"I'll look at those this evening, but surely the amounts are far too exorbitant?"

Frank shrugged. "The explanation could be as simple as payments to workmen and landscapers, perhaps combined with some personal investments, though you're right—I can't fathom the house costing even close to that amount."

She hadn't considered the possibility of other business ventures. Her thoughts returned to the stacks of cash in the safe. It was possible that Charles had invested in side business ventures such as the railroad, and that the cash represented his return on those investments. But why keep so much cash around? Why not deposit it in the bank, unless he hadn't wanted any record of receiving it?

Frank's expression remained troubled. "My advice would be that you don't show these to anyone else. At least, for now."

"Because they could have something to do with Longren Shipping?"

"Possibly. The fact that they don't show up as legitimate accounting entries indicates they might be associated with illegal contraband that wouldn't be listed as inventory. Have you ever heard your husband discuss opium or other smuggled items?"

"Absolutely not." She halted her unconscious defense of him. "Though from what I've been told, Charles evidently did his best to shield me from what he did, even socially."

"You're referring to his visits to the Green Light," Frank said softly.

She flushed. "Then the rumors are true?"

He contemplated her, probably trying to decide what to reveal. "It's not my place to discuss his . . . proclivities. If you want answers, ask Mona."

"I have a right to know."

He hesitated. "You're right, you do. But I'll not be the one to tell you, and if I had my way, I'd make certain you never found out the details."

She wanted to push him, but she could tell by his expression it would do no good. She sighed. "Then I will be in touch. I'll request the documentation you mentioned first thing in the morning."

"Very well." Frank stood, his gaze warm, yet worried. "Most women wouldn't even consider taking this on."

She shrugged. "You may have been right all along—I may not have any clue about the man I married," she admitted. "But I'm determined to find out."

"If Clive Johnson is complicit in what we have discovered today, he won't change his ways without a fight. And the fact that you're a woman won't even give him pause."

"I refuse to be afraid of him," she said, her chin lifting. "I own the company, and I *will* have control."

Frank walked to the door, then turned to quietly study her one last time. She had the oddest feeling he wanted to say something of a personal nature, but he said instead, "I'll expect to hear from you."

With a nod, he walked out as he had come, through the kitchen.

* * *

HATTIE scarcely had time to tidy Charles's desk and return files to drawers before she heard a knock on the front door. Her immediate thought was one of concern that whoever was calling might see Frank Lewis leaving and wonder at the reason for his visit. Then she chastised herself—*she* had been the one to insist that he not worry about such issues. Her business with him was legitimate, and she wouldn't ask him to skulk around. Even in light of Frank's concern over the risk she was taking, she'd be damned if she'd worry that someone would spy on the two of them and inform Clive Johnson.

Rising, she walked around the desk just as Sara received Chief Greeley in the front hallway, Charlotte on his arm. Tabitha trailed a few steps behind, looking anxious. Hattie's brow knit—what had they been doing outside?

Charlotte's cheeks were flushed as she laughed up at the police chief, her young love written across her face for all to see. He leaned down and murmured something to her, his manner slightly cocky, and she blushed.

"Miss Charlotte!" Sara rushed to take the girls' capes and gloves. "Where have you been?"

"Out, Sara," Charlotte answered gaily, waving a hand. "It's a beautiful day!"

Hattie moved forward, stopping at the library doors. "Chief Greeley," she said, nodding coolly. "Charlotte, please explain yourself. You and Tabitha were supposed to be in the parlor, working on dress designs."

Charlotte hesitated, showing the first signs that she

might have done something wrong, then she tossed her head, her gaze defiant. "As I believe I indicated this morning, Hattie," she said, her tone artificially mature, "today was perfect weather for an outing to Fuller's. Tabitha and I were enjoying a delicious raspberry ice when Chief Greeley stopped by." She leaned into the police chief's side, her hand still on his arm. "We had a wonderfully pleasant time, wouldn't you agree, John?"

Greeley smiled down at her indulgently, though his gaze, when he looked at Hattie, was censorious.

Hattie sighed inwardly. "Sara, please take Charlotte into the parlor to wait for me there while I talk to Chief Greeley." She turned her gaze back to Tabitha. "Go with Sara, Tabitha."

"Yes, ma'am," Tabitha said, shooting a sulky look at Charlotte.

Hattie had no doubt Charlotte had pushed Tabitha into agreeing to the outing. She leveled a hard look at Charlotte. "And you and I will discuss *your* rebellious behavior in a moment."

"But—"

"*Now*, young lady."

Charlotte blanched at being chastised in front of the police chief. Her eyes filling with tears, she whirled and stormed across the hall.

Hattie motioned Greeley to follow her into the library. "I'm not in the habit of allowing the girls to go out without a chaperone, if that is what you were about to comment on, Chief Greeley," she said once they stood before the fireplace. "Charlotte left the house without my knowledge and permission, after I expressly forbade her this morning to do so."

"Be that as it may, Mrs. Longren," Greeley said, slapping his gloves against his pant leg, "you clearly weren't attentive enough. You should consider yourself extremely lucky that I happened by Fuller's establishment and noticed Charlotte at one of the tables by the front window. Though I didn't go so far as to reprimand Charlotte publicly, I can't condone such licentious behavior in the girl I intend to marry."

Hattie would've considered herself far luckier if he *hadn't* happened by, but she refrained from saying so. "Rest assured I will be punishing Charlotte for disobeying my orders, as well as questioning the household staff as to how this could have happened."

Greeley rocked back on his heels, his eyebrows arched. "Charlotte merely needs a firm hand, Mrs. Longren. I would point out that this type of behavior—as well as the obviously lax supervision in your household—argues in favor of a brief courtship. I trust you've thought over my request and have agreed to my suit?"

"On the contrary, Chief Greeley," Hattie said, grinding her teeth. "I said I would give you an answer by the end of the week, and I plan to stick to that schedule. I have far too many concerns about a possible liaison between you and my sister to make such a decision in haste. Today's lapse in judgment, though deserving of disciplinary action, does not rise to a level that would justify a precipitous decision. Our parents had the faith to leave Charlotte in my hands. I owe it to them to consider carefully any possible change in that guardianship that might be against their express wishes."

Greeley's expression had hardened as she spoke. "Charlotte's presence at Fuller's, whether or not accompanied by her friend, was reckless and inappropriate. I must warn you that I won't be interested in 'soiled goods.'" Greeley pulled on his gloves. "I'll be back at the end of the week, Mrs. Longren. In the meantime, see that you keep Charlotte's girlish impulses properly in check."

Hattie didn't reply, gripping the edge of the desk so hard she felt a fingernail break.

Once Greeley was out the door, she took a moment to rein in her temper, as well as to congratulate herself for not having given in to the urge to hurl Charles's paperweight at Greeley's retreating back.

Chapter 8

TRUE to her promise, Jordan forced herself to stop reading an hour later and locked up, driving straight from the Historical Society to All That Jazz. On the way out the door, she'd added to her growing list of transgressions by filching several memoirs for her bedtime reading. To her way of thinking, it was better to steal what she needed now, rather than repeatedly sneak back into the building.

Of course, career burglars probably made similar rationalizations.

She *did* have another reason for taking the books, but she wasn't yet willing to admit it, even to herself. After all, no sane, normal person would acknowledge that she now felt compelled to solve a century-old murder for a resident ghost. Right?

The light at the first intersection on the outskirts of downtown turned red, forcing her to stop. Traffic was sparse, though, and moments later, she was on her way again, leaving behind the relatively flat land next to the waterfront and climbing the hills into the residential neighborhoods along the bluff. As she passed block after block of quaint old homes, she realized how peaceful the town seemed today in comparison to its violent past. What must it have been like to live here in the late nineteenth century? Undoubtedly for women like Hattie and Charlotte, life tended to be short, even tragic. But Jordan suspected it had also been more exciting.

Hattie had left the safety of the only home she knew and traveled across the country with a man who was in many ways a virtual stranger. What an adventure! Would Jordan have had that kind of courage? Would she have been lured by the excitement and danger? Would she have initially romanticized the marriage, as Hattie had appeared to?

She wasn't altogether certain, but she doubted it. She *had* leapt into marriage with Ryland while still in school. (And look how *that* had turned out.) But she couldn't deny that every chance she got, she planned her life down to the nth degree before taking the next step. Which, come to think of it, wasn't working out so hot, either.

Okay, admittedly she'd made a few impulsive decisions lately. But once committed, she'd backed up those decisions with solid plans. So she probably wasn't as impetuous as Hattie, nor did she have the same thirst for adventure.

Then again, comparing herself to a woman who'd ended up murdered probably didn't make for the healthiest form of self-analysis.

Parking the Prius around the corner from the pub, Jordan climbed out. The dog knew where to go and bounded in that direction, leaving her to follow at her own pace, shaking her head. After just two days in his company, she was fairly certain he was smarter than she was.

As she turned onto the main arterial, she halted, her gaze drawn down the sloping hill to the inlet beyond. The sunset promised to be stunning—the water already glistened in bands of midnight blue, orange, and neon pink. Lights on the ferry returning from Whidbey Island twinkled against the darkening sky, its wake rippling through the prism of colors. Downtown, the ornate outlines of historical buildings were backlit against the crimson sky. She felt like a tourist, gaping at the picture-perfect, postcardlike scene spread below her.

A young man rode past her on an old-fashioned high-wheel bicycle, completing the charm of the scene.

"Nice evening for a ride," she called to him, and he grinned, giving her a quick salute. Then he spread his arms wide and tilted his head back, coasting down the hill.

A chill wind gusted down the street behind him, dragging pine needles and bits of debris in its wake. She shivered, hugging herself. According to the locals, she could expect wind year-round. Because Port Chatham sat surrounded by inlets and bays, no matter which direction the wind blew, the town sustained a direct hit off water that averaged temperatures in the forty-degree range. She would definitely have to modify her wardrobe before she froze to death.

The tavern was already crowded, heat and bright light spilling onto the sidewalk. Jase stood behind the bar, helping Bill mix drinks. Mellow jazz played from the sound system's speakers but was mostly drowned out by shouts of laughter and loud conversation.

The minute Jordan entered, Darcy pointed to the empty chair at her table, her expression determined. "I might consent to you relaxing with a drink first, but you owe me a detailed report."

"Alcohol loosens my tongue, so that's definitely your best strategy." Jordan dropped into the chair.

"Then allow me to pour it down your throat. Just out of curiosity, how many drinks does it take to get you drunk?"

"Two."

"Huh. Probably best not to admit that in mixed company." Darcy drank some beer. "I suppose the ghosts were there this afternoon?"

"I plead the Fifth."

"Shit." Darcy flopped back in her chair. "I'm pissed that you can see them and I can't."

"Want to trade places?"

Jase brought over a glass of Australian Shiraz. "Figured out who dunnit yet?" he asked.

Jordan narrowed her gaze. "It's early days. Don't you have customers to tend to?"

He shot her a grin. "Yes, ma'am."

She followed his progress back to the bar, then watched him mix drinks. He handled the task the way he handled everything—confidently and capably. "There ought to be a patch," she muttered.

Darcy gave her a sideways glance. "Come again?"

"You know, like those nicotine patches? Only these would provide nice little vanilla orgasms, to take the edge off so you're not inclined to do something foolish."

"Vanilla orgasms," Darcy repeated, shaking her head. "How's that Four-Point Plan working for you?"

"Just peachy."

A dark-haired woman of average height, rail thin and radiating a grim intensity, approached their table. "Are you going to buy that fancy crap at the deli or eat dinner here tonight?"

"Jordan, meet Kathleen, the chef of All That Jazz," Darcy offered.

"Eat here?" Jordan replied faintly.

"Good choice." Kathleen cocked her head at the dog, who had stretched out on his designated patch of floor. "A couple of burgers for him? It's grass-fed, organic beef."

"Sure, okay."

"You name him yet?"

"He doesn't like the names I've come up with so far, but I think I'm making progress."

Kathleen snorted and left.

Jordan looked at Darcy. "She didn't ask what I wanted."

"You'll get whatever she thinks you should have."

"She also didn't seem too concerned about Health Department regulations." Jordan cocked her head at the dog.

"The inspector is someone's stepmother's cousin—I can't remember exactly who—but we don't worry overly much." Darcy made a hurry-up motion with her hand. "Now quit stalling and spill it."

Jordan brought her up-to-date on what she'd read that

afternoon about the men in Hattie's life. "The thing is, any of them could've had a motive to kill Hattie, and any of them could've been either an abusive or pathological personality type."

Darcy drummed her fingers on the table. "I think your problem is that you're viewing this from current-day perspective. Historically speaking, men were possessive, controlling chauvinists."

"You mean, rethink my definition of 'normal.' *Right*— been doing that a lot lately. So there were no laws on the books regarding domestic abuse or sexual harassment?"

"The *terms* weren't even known back then. I whine about men like Holt Stilwell, but the reality is, if he steps over the line, he's broken the law. Back then, not so much. And within a marriage, women had even fewer rights."

Jordan took a healthy sip of wine, enjoying the crisp bite of the Shiraz while she thought about it. "You know, Michael Seavey could be as strong a suspect as Frank Lewis." Jordan summarized his involvement in waterfront crime for Darcy.

"Maybe." Darcy looked unconvinced. "What about potential female suspects? Given a sturdy murder weapon, a woman has the strength to bash in a skull."

"Eleanor Canby, the owner of the *Port Chatham Weekly Gazette*, comes to mind. She disapproved of Hattie's actions, even openly accused her of poor judgment in an editorial. That's a little over the top."

"Who was in the house that night?"

"Besides Frank Lewis? The housekeeper and Charlotte. I doubt either had a motive to kill Hattie."

Kathleen served their dinners—salads of fresh organic greens topped with ahi tuna seared in ginger and garlic, accompanied by warm, crusty chunks of bread to be dipped in olive oil. Jordan abruptly realized how famished she was. She cut the two hamburgers into bite-sized chunks, placing the plate on the floor for the dog, then dug in to her salad.

The first bite registered with her taste buds. "This is good."

Darcy nodded, her mouth already full.

Once Jordan had sated the worst of her hunger and was willing to talk between bites, she continued. "I read that in the 1890s, Port Chatham was the second-largest port on the West Coast behind San Francisco. And that it had all the prostitutes, smuggling, et cetera, et cetera, you typically find in a port town."

Darcy sprinkled sea salt on her olive oil and dipped the bread into it. "Yeah, the waterfront was literally lawless."

"And yet, if the editorial I read today was any indication, Port Chatham did have an upper-crust society."

"As far as I know, that's accurate. I've heard mention of a group of women, referred to as Mercer Girls, who would've been the matrons of Port Chatham society by the time Hattie arrived."

"Was Eleanor Canby one of them?"

Darcy looked toward the bar. "Tom! Eleanor Canby, *Port Chatham Weekly Gazette*—Mercer Girl?"

"Yep." He picked up a box that had been sitting on the bar and brought it over to the table. "Back in the 1860s,

William Mercer, the president of the University of Washington, realized how scarce marriageable women were in the region, so he traveled back East and returned with young, single, educated women from good families." Tom placed the box on the floor beside Jordan's chair, then pulled up his own. "Several Mercer Girls married ships' captains in the area and went on to become socially powerful in their communities."

"That explains the moralistic tone of Eleanor's editorials," Jordan said.

Tom pointed to the box. "My great-granddaddy's diaries. Jase said you wanted to take a look at them."

"Yeah, thanks." Jordan put down her fork and carefully wiped her hands on her napkin before removing the box lid. The cardboard was the acid-free type used for storing rare documents. Inside, each small volume had been sealed in plastic to keep out dust and mildew. Jordan picked up the top one and carefully slid it out of its wrapping. Using the tips of her fingers, she flipped through page after page of neat cursive script. Excitement curled along her spine.

"These should be fascinating. I've got Greeley's memoir, but his personal diaries might provide more insight into his true feelings about the events."

Tom raised a brow.

"Thanks a lot," Darcy said. "You'd think a psychologist would know how to keep her mouth shut."

Jordan realized she'd as much as admitted she'd been at the Historical Society, and that Darcy was complicit. It was too late to do anything but dig herself in deeper, so she gave Tom her most charming smile. "Feel free to forget I said that."

He grinned. "Nah, I think I'll tuck that little tidbit away so I can use it as leverage against Ms. Law and Order over here."

Quickly redirecting the conversation, Jordan said, "No offense, but from what I've read about your ancestor so far, he was a bit on the controlling side."

Tom nodded. "That comes across in his writing. Of course, a police chief in his day would have to be made of pretty stern stuff." He swiped a chunk of bread from the basket and reached over to dip it into Darcy's olive oil. "So your plan is to come up with an alternative theory for Hattie's murder?"

Jordan glanced at him to see whether he looked offended, but he only seemed curious. "From what I've read so far, it's possible the murder could be linked to the practice of shanghaiing," she admitted. "Hattie wanted to eradicate the use of shanghaiers by Longren Shipping, and she was meeting with strong resistance."

Tom frowned. "My great-granddaddy felt Hattie's murder was a crime of passion, pure and simple."

"I'm not ruling that out," Jordan hastily assured him. "God knows, Frank Lewis was capable of it. And to be honest, I still have my doubts about his innocence. If someone is bludgeoned to death, that indicates spur-of-the-moment passion, just as your ancestor assumed." She noticed the speculative looks from Tom and Darcy and stopped herself. "Not that I have any firsthand knowledge of crimes of passion, of course."

"Right," Darcy said.

Moving right along, Jordan said, "These diaries should give me more facts about the events after Hattie's death, which will be very useful. Everything I read today had to do with the time leading up to the murder, and with Hattie's attempts to take control of Longren Shipping." She remembered Hattie's comment about Seavey's family papers. "Do either of you know whether the shanghaier Michael Seavey has any living relatives still in town? I have his memoir—" She winced, then shrugged. "It's possible his personal papers might be worth reading, if any exist."

Darcy exchanged a look with Tom. "That would be Holt Stilwell."

"Oh." Muscle shirt macho guy. Great.

"Seavey had an estranged sister who married into the Stilwell clan and produced several offspring," Tom said. "Holt's the only child of the son of the daughter of one of those offspring, if you followed that. Holt's parents are dead, along with most of his cousins. And the family wasn't exactly into preserving their heritage, for reasons you can probably surmise. But you never know, he might have a box of stuff somewhere at his place. That is, if the rats haven't chewed the contents."

"Yuck," Jordan said, earning a grin from Tom.

"I can ask him, if you want. Holt is less likely to be difficult if the request comes from me."

"And I don't like the idea of you driving out to his place by yourself," Darcy added. "You're Stilwell's type—he's partial to women who are still breathing."

Jordan sputtered out a laugh. "Thanks, but I can handle him. To be safe, though, I'll approach him here at the pub."

"By the way," Darcy said, "I looked through the incident reports this afternoon down at the station. Nothing popped. So if someone is making a habit of watching, they haven't been reported by anyone else."

"Which rules out your garden-variety sex offender."

Darcy shrugged. "Only if they've been at it long enough to get caught. You still getting an itch between your shoulder blades?"

"Sometimes, but it's probably just my overactive imagination."

"Yeah, well, I have the utmost respect for those little itches, so keep your eyes open."

"How's it going with Hattie and Charlotte?" Tom asked with a grin.

Jordan narrowed her eyes. "How come no one in this town seems concerned that I can supposedly talk to ghosts? Even the neighbors are showing up in droves to lend their support."

"Hey, you're big news," Darcy pointed out. "That has a lot of weight around here."

"And if you think about it," Tom said, "you're providing a much-needed community service. Historical preservation and righting old wrongs are important community issues in this town."

"Uh-huh." Jordan's tone was skeptical.

Jase came by with a full tray of empties, stopping to pick up Jordan's.

"Right, Jase?" Tom asked.

"Right." He smiled at Jordan. "Another?"

"Yes, thanks," she said, throwing sobriety to the wind.

"May take a few minutes to get it to you," he muttered, looking harried.

"Are you short a waitress tonight?" Always aware of where he was in the room, she'd noticed him delivering multiple trays of drinks while they'd been talking and eating.

"Yeah. Honeymoon."

"Want some help? I put myself through college by waiting tables—I can probably still balance a tray."

"Would you mind?" he asked, relieved. "Just for a few minutes until I catch up the backlog? I didn't anticipate tonight's crowd."

"So the Ted Rawlins Trio is really bringing them out?" Tom asked him.

The mention of Ted's name reminded Jordan that he would be playing that evening. Glancing toward the stage, she noted that he and his band were already setting up. Jordan had already met the other two musicians who made up the trio, in L.A. But the stunning woman who walked over to where Ted stood on the stage, placing a proprietary hand on his arm and leaning in close to whisper in his ear, looked only vaguely familiar. It took Jordan a moment to place her.

"You know her?" Jase asked, noting the direction of Jordan's gaze.

"Not personally, no, but I'm fairly certain her name is Didi Wyeth."

"Your husband's ex-girlfriend, the Hollywood actress?" Darcy's gaze sharpened, and she turned in her chair to look. "What's she doing with Ted Rawlins?"

Jordan wondered the same. "Oh, wait—Ted and Didi have the same talent agent, I think. Ted dropped his other one last year, according to what he told me. He and Didi must've met through the agent."

"That still doesn't explain what she's doing up here, unless she hopped out of your hubby's bed and right into Ted's."

"Maybe Ryland's death hit her hard—maybe she's on the rebound," Jordan speculated. "He broke up with her a week or so before he died in the accident. It was all over the papers."

Darcy frowned at that bit of information. "Interesting. That gives her motive, possibly. Did you mention her to Drake?"

"Of course."

Jase was waiting, so after telling the dog to stay, Jordan walked over to the bar, hefting a tray of drinks that Bill had mixed. "Where do these go?"

Jase pointed out the tables, then asked her to check others nearby for orders. A few customers noted the efficiency with which she handled the drinks and asked whether she planned to hire on. She laughed, replying that the way her checking account was being depleted, she might have to, which drew a few pained chuckles from people who were also renovating their historic homes.

She walked to the section of the room next to the front

door to take orders. Some looked surprised, then smiled and told her they'd only come for the music, though a few others ordered drinks. She eventually made her way to where a man stood inside the front door, reading a newspaper. He hadn't been there long—she'd noticed him when he walked in.

"What would you like?" she asked, pencil poised over the small order pad Jase had given her.

The man glanced up from the newspaper, his light-colored eyes sweeping over her without expression. She had only a brief moment to realize he made her uneasy before he replied. "Jack Daniel's."

"Neat?" she clarified, writing it down.

"Sure."

"Be right back with that." She turned to go, mentally shrugging. She could feel his eyes on her back, and it occurred to her as she crossed to the bar that the LAPD might have sent him to keep an eye on her.

Controlling a spurt of irritation at the thought, she gave her orders to Jase, made several more trips through the packed room, then returned to lean both elbows against the bar. If she was under surveillance, so be it—she was determined to enjoy herself. She purposefully ignored the stranger, listening to the musicians warm up while she waited for the next round to be mixed.

Ted raised his horn, working his way through a complicated riff, his fingers caressing the valves, and she was reminded once again of his tremendous talent—he truly *was* one of the greats. Or he would've been, if his career hadn't been interrupted by a stint of drugs and alcohol.

He'd always claimed that he could be the next Miles Davis, and his band members had privately admitted to her that he wasn't being arrogant. Perhaps now that his career was back on track, he'd get the recognition he deserved.

She jolted as an arm snaked around her waist. "Well, well, well. If it isn't the pretty lady who offed her old man for sleeping around," a deep, gritty voice murmured in her ear.

She smelled the alcohol on his breath before she looked up into Holt Stilwell's leer. Calmly, she stepped to one side, but his grip tightened, keeping her where she was. Rather than struggle with him, she looked him in the eye. "How convenient, Mr. Stilwell. I've been meaning to ask you about borrowing your family papers."

It wasn't the reaction he'd obviously hoped for. "What're you talking about?"

"I'm looking for any diaries you might have from the late 1800s."

He dropped his hand to her hip. "Well, now, if I do have any, I wouldn't let you see them." He grinned, purposely crowding her. "That is, unless you want to drop by my place later tonight."

"Holt." Jase had approached without her knowledge. His eyes lacked their customary warmth, and his voice was deceptively quiet.

Stilwell stared at him for a long moment. "She yours?"

Jordan gaped at Stilwell, wondering whether she'd time-traveled back a century.

Jase shook his head. "Don't."

Darcy was out of her chair and looking determined, but Jordan shook her head at her. "Excuse me." She took the tray of drinks Jase had set on the bar and moved away, effectively breaking the tension. From a safe distance, she turned back, her expression polite. "If you wouldn't mind looking for those papers, Mr. Stilwell, I'd appreciate it."

He shrugged. "Whatever."

After delivering the drinks, she gave Stilwell time to focus his attention elsewhere by walking over to the stage. "You guys want any water to drink during your set?" she asked the band members.

Ted frowned, wiping down his horn with a soft cloth. "You're working here?"

She shook her head. "Just helping out for the evening."

"That's not okay," he protested. "You shouldn't be hauling our drinks."

He'd always voiced strong opinions about what she should be doing with her life, opinions she felt were inappropriate. She kept her tone light. "I'm just getting a little exercise and helping out a friend."

"Let her bust her butt, hon." Didi Wyeth's clothes and makeup were stunning, her voice artificially sultry, her body slender to the point of emaciation. Her glance flicked over Jordan dismissively as she snuggled up to Ted's side.

Jordan noted that the gesture seemed to annoy him, and given the brittleness of Didi's expression, she suspected the actress had picked up on his reaction as well.

"I'm sure Jordan needs the money, since insurance

companies don't pay out to murderesses," Didi continued, smiling with false sympathy at Jordan.

"Didi," Ted warned.

She shrugged. "Grey Goose martini, double, dirty," she ordered.

"No problem." Jordan smiled politely and wrote down the order, then returned to the bar.

"Is she bothering you?" Jase asked, evidently having observed the interchange.

"You mean, do I mind that she's here?" Jordan shrugged. "Thanks for the thought, but, no, I'm fine. Ryland pretty much killed whatever feelings I had for him long before she arrived on the scene."

"Good to know," Jase said quietly.

Their gazes met and held. She moved to place two pitchers of ice water for the band onto her tray, silently willing her hands to remain steady.

"That should do it for the moment," he said in a more businesslike tone. "Sit with Darcy and enjoy the music— I'll let you know whether I need you again."

"Deal." She hesitated. "And thanks."

He smiled, catching her reference to Stilwell. "Standard knight-in-shining-armor stuff, though my armor may be a bit tarnished here and there."

Tarnished just enough, she suspected, to enhance his appeal.

* * *

DARCY had somehow managed to save her chair from the boisterous crowd. The pub was now standing room only, the roar of laughter and clink of glasses loud enough that Jordan had to strain to hear Darcy. As many people were simply listening to the music as were purchasing drinks, though Jase didn't seem to mind. Tom had decamped to stand with friends at the opposite end of the bar.

"So Ted Rawlins lives most of the year in L.A.?" Darcy asked.

Jordan gave her a questioning look. "As far as I know. Why?"

"Just curious how well you know him."

The light dawned. "Ah, you think maybe I had a relationship with him, and that's what I'm keeping quiet about? That Ryland and I were *both* into kink with our patients? No way."

"Then why is the actress sending you death rays?"

"She probably still feels threatened by my presence, given that she dated Ryland before the divorce was finalized," Jordan replied. She cocked her head. "You have an overly suspicious mind."

"Comes with the territory. I spent five years in the Minneapolis PD as a homicide detective, so I'm more jaded than most."

That certainly explained Darcy's fair coloring—the upper Midwest was heavily populated with Scandinavians. Still, Jordan was surprised. "I thought you were a local."

"Nope. I've been here eight years, which in the locals' eyes still makes me a newcomer. You'd be amazed by the number of folks in this town who have a past life." Darcy cocked her head toward the bar. "Bill, for instance, used to be a Wall Street trader. And Tom was a tenured professor at the University of Washington; he taught chemistry."

Jordan raised her eyebrows. "And he now paints for a living?"

Darcy shrugged. "People around here tend to value quality of life over money."

Jordan wanted to ask whether Jase was one of them, but she didn't want to reveal her curiosity.

"Lawyer." Darcy read her mind with uncanny accuracy. "I'll let him give you the lowdown, though."

Jordan picked up a piece of bread and nibbled while she chewed on that new little tidbit of information. She never would've pegged Jase for a lawyer—he was far too laid back.

"Have you at least mentioned other possible suspects to Detective Drake?" Darcy asked, bringing the conversation back around.

"I gave him a few names." Jordan had mentioned Didi's, and she'd also supplied the names of ex-patients who had sued Ryland for sexual harassment.

"That so? I requested a copy of the case file, which arrived this afternoon, and from what I've read, Drake may not be investigating anyone else."

Jordan refrained from comment, and Darcy shook her head, leaning over so that her voice wouldn't carry. "Look, I know I'm just another cop in your eyes, but unless you really did kill the jerk, I'm not the enemy. Cutting the brake lines on a car takes knowledge and advance planning—in other words, it's a premeditated act. I've spent enough time on the force to know a murderer when I see one, and you aren't the type. Hell, even if you *had* lost your temper and felt like killing the son of a bitch, I figure you would've simply yelled at him to get counseling." Darcy paused. "No offense."

"None taken," Jordan said faintly.

"So if you want my help with this, ask, dammit."

"Thanks," she said, surprised and touched, and also feeling more than a little guilty for continuing to withhold information from her.

Darcy nodded as if that settled it. "Now, are you gonna let me help solve Hattie's murder or not?"

Jordan smiled. "How about nightly updates?"

*   *   *

FOR the next few hours, Jordan listened to music and helped Jase when needed. Twice, she asked the man up front whether he wanted a fresh drink, since he hadn't touched his whiskey. Both times, he turned her down with only slightly more than a grunt. She'd been tempted to ask him to produce his badge, but in the end, she decided to leave him alone and ignore the itch he gave her between her shoulders.

By midnight, she was feeling the effects of the lack of sleep from the night before. She woke up the dog, collected the box of diaries, and headed out the door, yawning.

Half a block from the tavern, though, Stilwell suddenly materialized out of the shadows, blocking her path.

The dog leapt between them, growling. Setting the box on the pavement, Jordan placed a hand on his collar, surreptitiously glancing around to see whether she could count on help from any passersby.

Stilwell caught her action and grinned, obviously enjoying her discomfort. He tossed her a book with a cracked binding held together with string. She fumbled, almost dropping it, scrambling to protect the fragile pages.

"That's all I got from the family," he said with a shrug. "I figure you owe me one now. I'll decide how and when to collect."

"Thanks," she said, ignoring his innuendo. "This will be a great help." She stepped back, pulling the dog with her.

He shifted to block her escape. "What do you want it for, anyway?"

"Just some research I'm doing about the town back when my house was built," she replied, leaving out any specifics. "I'll make sure this gets back to you in a few days or so. All right?"

He shrugged and turned to go. "Makes no difference to me whether I ever get it back." With that, he disappeared into the night as quickly as he'd appeared.

Jordan stood on the sidewalk, frowning after him, willing her pulse to return to normal. He'd just tossed a rare document at her that might well be worth a significant sum of money. In her experience, only the strongest of emotions overrode greed in a man like Stilwell. So why had he been so cavalier about parting with the book? And she had the oddest feeling that he was overplaying a part, trying too hard to make everyone think he was the baddest of bad boys.

She shook her head. On the other hand, she was functioning on only a few hours of sleep, so she probably shouldn't be willing to attribute altruistic motives to the man's actions.

The small spurt of adrenaline caused by his appearance seeped away, leaving her even more exhausted. She took several deep breaths, then leaned down to place Stilwell's packet on top of the box and pick both up. "Time to go home, boy."

By the time she got the dog settled in the back of the car, her responses were so sluggish that she wondered whether she should drive the three blocks to her house. But even though every muscle in her body ached, the lingering uneasiness from the encounter with Stilwell had her eyes wide open.

Enough so that on the way home, she made a detour to an all-night grocery on the edge of downtown, to buy some groceries and the latest issue of *Vanity Fair*.

Chapter 9

BY seven the next morning, Jordan was wide awake and twitching inside her sleeping bag, her overactive brain no longer willing to let her linger in that pleasantly relaxed state between deep sleep and fully alert. She pushed her arms out of the sleeping bag—a feat, since the dog, who seemed to have gotten over his unwillingness to enter the bedroom, was plastered along her right side, pinning her. Luxuriating in a jaw-cracking yawn, she stretched to relieve the stiffness caused by two nights on a hard floor.

She paused, arms over her head, frowning. Actually, her sleep hadn't been deep *or* relaxed. She'd dreamt of the incidents leading up to Hattie's murder, one of those godawful frustration dreams in which the more she'd learned, the further she'd been from discovering the killer's identity. She'd watched herself pace through the deep gloom of the library, pausing to read excerpts from diaries and memoirs, then wearing new tracks in the Aubusson carpet as she puzzled over the clues to the writers' psyches she found hidden in every line of text.

Sighing, she pushed back the edges of the sleeping bag. She had a busy day planned—the movers were due to arrive by midmorning, she'd made an appointment with the local vet to take the dog in for a wellness check and grooming, and Tom and Jase were dropping by to help her assess the work needed on the house.

And she couldn't forget she'd promised Ted a tour. Though he was a distraction she didn't need, she couldn't beg off without upsetting him. He was still fragile and, when thwarted, prone to act inappropriately. As his ex-therapist, she had a responsibility to support his efforts to put his life back on track. She sincerely hoped, though, that he left Didi at home.

She tugged harder on the sleeping bag in an attempt to free herself. The dog took her struggles as a sign that it was time to get up. Rolling over, he slapped a paw across her midsection, almost knocking the breath from her lungs, and reached his head up to lick her face. She laughed and pulled the edge of the sleeping bag over her face, which he took as a sign that it was time to play.

The next thing she knew, she was being dragged—inside the sleeping bag—toward the bedroom door. She wrestled, and he growled and refused to let go, all the while wagging his tail. She managed to crawl out just before he pulled her down the stairs.

Heading for the bathroom, she splashed cold water on her face, then glanced out the window to gauge the weather. No rain, no clouds—a perfect day to escape for an hour before the rush began. Pulling on jeans, a sweatshirt, and high-tops, she ran a comb through her hair, securing the most unruly strands with clips, creating an overall effect that was vaguely—but not quite—stylish. Story of her life.

Hoping to avoid the ghosts, she tiptoed down the stairs, then halted at the library door. She took a tentative step inside, half expecting to see the people from her dream still lurking in the shadows not yet dispelled by the early morning sun. But the room stood silent, refusing to reveal its secrets.

All the men in Hattie's life—the ones who'd had reason to murder her—had at one time stood in this very room. As she peered into the gloom, it took only a quick blink of her eyes to imagine their presence.

Frank Lewis stood to one side, a shoulder insolently propped against a tall bookcase, while Michael Seavey reclined in stylish elegance in the wingback chair. John Greeley, impatient and grim, stood next to the desk, clenching his huge fists. Clive Johnson lurked by the French doors, a feral light in his eyes, waiting for an opportunity to exact his own personal form of brutal retribution.

To a man, their expressions were at once enigmatic and threatening. Yet whenever Jordan came close to understanding their true motivations, she'd discover some new tidbit in a memoir or diary that had her altering her opinion.

Without a doubt, Clive Johnson made her skin crawl. Though it was callous of her, she sincerely hoped to discover that the man had died a horrible, painful death.

And though Tom had a point about his ancestor being a hard man out of necessity, Jordan still couldn't warm to Chief Greeley any more than Hattie had. He reminded her of the sheriff in the movie *Unforgiven*, she realized, whose ethics had been situational at best.

Frank Lewis, on the other hand, was classic alpha male in a literary-bad-boy sort of way, with hints of anger alternating with glimpses of genuine warmth and concern for Hattie. Clearly, he'd been driven to improve the rights of sailors. But had he eventually allowed the reins to slip on his temper? Jordan didn't yet know—but she was keeping her eye on him, not nearly as besotted with him as Hattie seemed to be.

Then again, Jordan found herself unwillingly charmed by Michael Seavey, even though she knew he had to have been a dangerous man. If Hattie was correct, he'd cold-bloodedly kidnapped Charlotte and allowed his thugs to terrorize her. And yet he seemed perfectly comfortable with himself. He exuded confidence and self-knowledge, both of which were attractive traits. Jordan had always had a soft spot for strong, confident men, and she could've sworn he truly cared for Hattie, no matter how much Hattie denied it . . .

Jordan blinked. *Holy God.* Seavey reminded her of Ryland—handsome, elegant, and polished, with just a hint of amused self-deprecation, yet capable of ruthless calculation in his dealings with others. She shuddered. *Just great.* She was allowing her personal blind spot for charming psychopaths to affect her ability to solve Hattie's murder.

Disgusted and more than a little spooked by what had morphed from fleeting glimpses into a full-blown, vivid daydream populated by people from another century, she headed down the hall, slipping out the back door ... and immediately slid to a halt as the dog lunged, barking. Someone had pitched a bright orange single-person expedition tent in her backyard.

Shushing the dog, she walked over and tentatively rapped on one of the tent's aluminum supports. "Hello?"

"Be with you in a minute," a sleepy feminine voice called out.

Jordan heard fabric rustling, then a young woman with pale brown hair caught in a ponytail stuck her head out. Dressed in gray sweats and thick wool socks, she crawled through the low opening, then straightened and stretched on a yawn.

Blinking sleepy brown eyes at Jordan, she said, "Hey."

"Hey yourself," Jordan replied, keeping her tone friendly, then waited.

The girl yawned. "I'm Amanda?"

The neighbor's daughter, Jordan remembered. Landscaper.

"I restore the gardens of haunted houses," Amanda added helpfully.

Jordan couldn't help herself—she had to ask. "Doesn't that limit your potential client base?"

"Not in this town."

Okay. She cleared her throat. "Did you pitch your tent in the wrong yard?"

Amanda looked confused. "*Oh.* No, I like to get a

spiritual sense of the garden I'll be working on. It's all part of my process."

"I see." Jordan didn't, but she was beginning to suspect that the inhabitants of Port Chatham had their own unique approach to life. "I'm headed out for breakfast. Perhaps we should talk when I get back?"

"No problem." Amanda yawned again. "You've got an espresso maker in the kitchen, right? I'll just grab my beans, if that's all right with you."

"Knock yourself out."

The girl retrieved a plastic bag containing coffee beans and some sort of cereal mix from inside the tent, then headed into the house. Shaking her head, Jordan turned in the direction of the alley.

The dog stayed where he was, his head cocked toward the house, his expression dismayed.

"Don't start with me," she warned. "I'm currently without caffeine."

He heaved a sigh, then stood and trotted in front of her through the backyard, leading the way.

They walked a few blocks to a French café she'd noticed the other night just down from the grocery. When she'd spied the small sign for the restaurant, she'd noticed that they served European-style coffee with breakfast and had been intrigued enough to make a mental note to try out the place the first chance she got.

The owner, a plump, cheerful woman in her fifties, showed Jordan to a table in the restaurant's small courtyard where the dog could sit with her. Despite the early hour, the other tables were filled with patrons, some of whom were eating or drinking coffee, others who were reading the newspaper. She smiled at a few of them and received nods, then set the books she'd brought with her on the table, settling back in her chair to peruse the menu.

Clearly, her next order of business needed to be to join a health club. Espresso infused with cream and served in a bowl, lemon pancakes topped with raspberry puree, French toast soaked in vanilla, cinnamon, and orange custard, then grilled—she could *feel* the pounds leaping off the page and onto her hips. Then again, she had a long day ahead of her, unpacking and moving furniture, right?

Rationalization in place, she ordered espresso and French toast. The dog propped his chin on her shoulder, his tail sweeping the flagstones.

"How about Marley? You know, after Bob Marley?" she asked, rubbing his ears while she waited for her coffee to arrive. "You seem like you'd be more into reggae than jazz, am I right?"

"*Raaooomph!*" He closed his eyes, obviously expecting her to continue her ministrations.

The owner returned with the steaming bowl of coffee adorned with a decorative pattern in the cream and mocha-colored foam floating on top, and set it before her. "You're trying too hard," she advised. "He'll eventually tell you what name he wants."

"*Rooooo.*" He yawned in agreement, then closed his eyes again.

The woman chuckled, giving his head a pat before she headed back inside.

Jordan took her first gulp, letting the caffeine reach her

brain, then picked up the book she'd brought on renovation. The introduction, which went into mind-numbing detail about the National Register of Historic Homes, had her eyes immediately glazing over. Leafing through a few more chapters, she skimmed enough to determine that the entire book was written in the same manner, so she flipped it shut. This morning wasn't the time for complex subjects.

Succumbing to temptation, she pulled out the smaller book she'd brought with her, John Greeley's memoir. She'd perused enough of it yesterday to note it contained a discussion of Hattie's murder investigation by the Port Chatham Police Department. Evidently, Greeley had headed up the investigation himself, which made sense. Back then, they would've had a small police department—there wouldn't have been homicide detectives.

Flipping to the table of contents, she located the chapter on the murder investigation and hunted for the page. After another fortifying sip of espresso, she started to read.

Though I am a man whose work exemplifies sobriety and industry, I feel it necessary to record the investigation that resulted in the arrest of the individual who was responsible for the terrible murder of Mrs. Charles Longren on that tragic night of June 6, 1890. It is my intent by recording the details of this horrendous crime that others may learn from the straightforward and

*thorough work of the Port Chatham Police
Department, and that this learning will
influence future investigations, providing a
good example for generations to come.*

*The victim, Mrs. Charles Longren, had
been recently widowed from one of Port
Chatham's most respected businessmen, who
was rumored to have perished at sea at the
hands of a mutinous crew. This unfortunate
incident marked the beginning of a period of
extreme mental instability for his widow,
who it can be said then made several ill-
advised decisions, resulting in her reckless
and inappropriate behavior on more than
one occasion, and ultimately leading to her
own murder, as well as the ruination of her
younger, innocent sister, Miss Charlotte
Walker. Be that as it may, the Port Chatham
Police Department did not shirk in its
duties, as you, dear reader, will soon
surmise.*

Jordan rolled her eyes. The man's gargantuan sense of
self-importance was enough to almost, but not quite, trig-
ger her gag reflex. She refrained from speculating about
the borderline personality required to write such pompous
drivel and continued to read.

*At twelve minutes before midnight on
that fatal night, this author was called upon*

to examine the body of Hattie Longren,
whom it appeared had been bludgeoned with
an auger. Within hours of the commission of
the crime, I had vigorously pursued and
arrested Mrs. Longren's murderer, one
Frank Lewis, a union representative with a
history of violence who also may have been
her illicit lover...

The restaurant owner set Jordan's breakfast before her, the aromas of warm citrus and maple syrup jerking her back to the present. She marked her place with a torn corner of her napkin and shut the book, thinking about what she'd learned as she dug in.

According to Greeley's version of events, Hattie had been hit from behind with an iron hand auger, described as a vise with long handles on either side, weighing approximately eight pounds. Greeley had found it lying next to her body, one handle smeared with blood. Given Greeley's description of the tool, it was obviously heavy enough to have split open Hattie's skull when wielded with sufficient force. Using recently imported European techniques in the science of fingerprinting, Greeley had identified a bloody print on the master bedroom door as Frank Lewis's.

Frank claimed to have been drugged and unconscious in the library at the time of the murder. When he'd regained consciousness, he'd immediately looked for Hattie, concerned for her safety. He'd discovered her body, tried to revive her, then contacted Greeley. Frank had admitted he was woozy from the effects of whatever drug someone had slipped into his tea and was not thinking clearly—he thought he might've left the bloody print on the door handle as he ran out of the room to contact the police.

Greeley had written that he hadn't believed Frank's version of events. Based on Frank's presence at the crime scene and the bloody print, Greeley had immediately arrested him.

Though Frank had vehemently denied killing Hattie and claimed that Greeley should investigate Clive Johnson, the police chief had dismissed his arguments. In the weeks before the trial, Greeley had gone on to establish Frank's motive by interviewing witnesses from the neighborhood who claimed to have heard frequent arguments between Hattie and Frank, though the substance of those arguments was unknown.

Jordan frowned as she chewed. Even with the fingerprint, the evidence seemed circumstantial at best, though perhaps back then it would've been considered sufficient to gain a conviction. However, given what she'd already learned about Hattie's life and her strained relationships with her neighbors, Jordan thought it entirely possible some hadn't given truthful statements—or, at the very least, had been influenced by circumstances to believe the worst. She made a mental note to ask whether any signed statements or witness testimony from the trial might still exist.

What bothered her the most, though, were the parallels between Hattie's murder investigation and Ryland's.

In both cases, an arrogant cop was in charge, and in both cases, one suspect had been the focus from the very beginning. Why hadn't Greeley looked at other possible suspects? Surely Charlotte and the housekeeper had told him about Michael Seavey and Clive Johnson, even if they wouldn't have thought to mention Eleanor Canby. Then again, according to Hattie's diary, Greeley had held Johnson in high regard, and his relationship with Seavey was unknown. Greeley therefore might have discounted what the women had told him; he certainly made a habit of discounting what *any* woman said.

Perhaps Seavey's papers would shed further light on the investigation—that is, if he'd written about it. And Jordan would have to ask Hattie what Frank had been doing in the house that night—why he'd been in the library, and whether she knew who could have drugged him. But no matter how Jordan looked at it, Greeley seemed to have focused on Frank from the very beginning, having arrested him the very same night, then concentrated on building the case against him.

She pushed her plate away, her appetite gone. From what Darcy and Carol had told her, Drake seemed to have focused exclusively on her since the night of Ryland's murder. Did that mean Drake was building a case against her, compiling what he believed to be strong evidence that she'd tampered with Ryland's Beemer? Had people like Didi Wyeth manipulated the facts out of spite? The thought that someone might be deliberately encouraging Drake's tunnel vision...

No. The LAPD was a highly professional organization

with more than a hundred years of technological advances in forensics at their fingertips. Surely, even if Drake *did* suffer from tunnel vision, the prosecutors wouldn't indict on less than damning evidence against her, given the press's laser focus. And that evidence simply didn't exist, because she hadn't killed Ryland.

She glanced at her watch. More time had passed than she'd realized—the movers were probably waiting for her. And she'd wasted far too much time already that morning obsessing. *That* had to stop. Downing the last of her coffee, she paid her bill, then headed home, still lost in thought, the dog in the lead as usual.

The good news, she concluded, was that she seemed to be adjusting to her spectral roommates—as long as she could find peaceful, contemplative moments like these away from them. Obsessing aside, she had a house she loved, a new town she might love even more, and an ancient murder investigation that had her more hooked than most mystery books. The cops would do their job and find Ryland's murderer.

She needed to stay positive.

* * *

THE moving van pulled to a stop at the curb just as she arrived, sending Charlotte into a spastic frenzy, flying from window to window. Doing her best to ignore Charlotte's ceiling-level hovering, Jordan walked the movers through the house and handed out instructions. Downstairs furniture would go in the parlor on the main floor, overflow furniture would be stored in the parlor on the second floor, and boxes would be delivered to the room designated on their labels. Then she and Hattie lured Charlotte into the library, whereupon Jordan produced the *Vanity Fair* she'd purchased the night before. She slipped out, shutting the doors—just in case others could hear ghost shrieks or see magazine pages flying—and taped up a note, declaring the room off-limits.

Walking into the kitchen, she noted that Amanda was already at work, pounding in stakes and marking off quadrants in the garden with red string. Promising herself she'd get the upper hand in the Amanda situation at some point, she made espressos for the movers, then carried a book on home repair and Seavey's papers—the ones Holt Stilwell had tossed at her the night before—out to the porch, sitting down in the swing where she would be available for questions.

Curious, she flipped through a chapter on tools in the home repair book that included useful pictures and clear explanations, hoping to find a picture of a hand auger. No such luck. Evidently, they weren't considered a necessary purchase these days.

She was about to flip the book shut and move on to Michael Seavey's papers when she spied a row of pictures of hammers. There really *was* a wide range of hammers. Framing hammers looked like they could do serious damage, making them her favorite. She was fairly certain Jase had had her buy one the day before. The hammers with the big, curved claws looked more elegant but equally deadly, which appealed to her aesthetic sensibilities. But the cutest ones were the little ball-peen hammers with their round heads, which Jase had failed to have her purchase. She was puzzling over that when she was interrupted.

"Where do you want this?"

She looked up to find a mover standing on the porch, the mattress to her prized king-size bed bent over his shoulder. He sported a short, spiked black haircut and enough prison tattoos to resemble a mass murderer, but if he could set up her bed and she didn't have to sleep a third night on the floor, she was willing to worship at his feet. "Upstairs, master bedroom around to the front. The one with the window seat."

He didn't move. "You sure? Because I could prop it out in the hallway, you know, until you decide."

She raised a brow.

"That room has a weird feeling, is all," he explained. "The boss mentioned a lot of homes in this town are maybe haunted."

"You don't say."

"Well, I couldn't sleep in there."

Her gaze narrowed. "It has a window seat."

He shook his head, his expression indicating he thought she was nuts, then headed inside without another word.

She set aside the home improvement book, picked up Seavey's papers, removing the string that held them together, and settled in to read.

The Invitation

MICHAEL Seavey was under no illusion that he had ever possessed the virtue of patience. In the more than two decades he'd ruled the waterfront, making a comfortable living off the misfortune of others, he'd never tolerated anyone standing in his way.

Fortunately, he no longer had to handle the disposal himself—he employed loyal enforcers who understood it was their job to use whatever methods were required. If anyone encroached upon his business holdings, they were warned. If they didn't heed the warning, they quietly disappeared. Michael had long ago gotten in the habit of simply taking what he wanted. Which was why, as he stood in the offices of Longren Shipping, watching Clive Johnson pace, he couldn't understand his reticence with regard to Hattie Longren.

He'd had other women in his life, of course. In the past, his tastes had run the gamut from young, frightened virgins to older, wiser women who knew not to cross him.

Even his late wife, who'd shown a talent for wielding a bullwhip against rebellious sailors, hadn't had the courage to stand up to him. He'd found her quite amusing until she'd turned that bullwhip on him after he'd discovered her in bed with one of his bodyguards.

He most decidedly didn't find Hattie Longren amusing, however. Stubborn, enthralling, and exasperating, but definitely not amusing. And at the moment, she held enough power to damage his business holdings, which he had no intention of condoning.

Michael leaned over, striking a match against the pointed toe of his ankle boot. He held the flame to the tip of his cigar, slowly rolling it while drawing to create an even burn. The Cuban crackled and hissed, and he breathed its potent fragrance in deep, taking a moment to appreciate one of the many perks of having access to high-quality smuggled goods: cigars, opium, fine liquor, and willing women. Women far more willing than Hattie.

He felt a rare anger take hold. He simply couldn't understand why he was giving her any leeway. Or, for that matter, why he'd backed off from the threats he'd planned to deliver during last week's visit. He must've been momentarily disarmed by that business with the dossier Charles had compiled. Michael should've found Hattie's refusal to read the contents hopelessly naïve, yet he'd found himself thinking it was . . . admirable.

Damnation! The entire affair had him feeling as if he no longer comfortably fit inside his own skin. If he wanted Hattie in his bed, he should simply put her there—he'd never balked before at taking a woman.

She was a widow and, as such, without protection. It would be child's play to abduct her and keep her at his hotel. He doubted Greeley would care or even bother to look for her. After all, Michael would be doing Greeley a favor, removing Hattie so that he had unimpeded access to young Charlotte.

Clive Johnson continued to pace in front of his desk, trying—and clearly failing—to deal with his impotent fury over Hattie's visit to the office. If the man weren't so useful, Michael thought with genuine regret, he would've figured out a way to make him disappear long ago.

The business manager was crass and stupid, but unfortunately also good at following orders, which was probably why Charles had kept him around for so long. However, since Charles's death, Johnson had been running wild, extorting increasingly larger kickbacks from the boardinghouse owners, and when he didn't get what he wanted, exacting brutal retribution when he didn't get what he wanted. Though Michael had always run his businesses efficiently, he'd never employed—or admired the application of—senseless violence. If Michael's enforcers showed up on a man's doorstep, that man knew why.

"You handled her all wrong, you know," Michael finally said, keeping his tone mild. "A spirited woman such as Hattie requires more . . . finesse."

Johnson halted long enough to glare at him. "If we're not careful, that bitch'll take us all down."

Michael sighed inwardly. He found it tedious to have

to explain the obvious, though he supposed there was a certain comfort in knowing that Johnson didn't have the imagination to double-cross him. "You've got nothing to worry about—the worst she'll do is order you to stop using my services."

"And if she does, what then?"

Michael shrugged. "We'll figure out a way to hide the transactions, of course." He pushed away from the wall and tapped cigar ash into Hattie's teacup, which Johnson hadn't bothered to clear from his desk. "I never understood why Charles was so willing to openly document the payoffs."

"Charles was obsessive about more than his women." Johnson scowled. "You read the paper. She's makin' public statements about the fire, for God's sake. It won't be long until she puts that together with the boardin'houses, and makes the connection to Longren Shipping. Once she does that, the trail'll lead right to us."

Michael detected a whine in Johnson's voice. "I warned you to have a care in your dealings with Taylor's establishment. The loss of one boardinghouse to union sailors wouldn't have given us any trouble—we could have used the tunnels for the overflow of crews until we found more suitable lodgings. Setting that fire was a grave error in judgment."

"If I'd let him get away with it, others woulda done the same," Johnson snapped. "I set an example."

"Others would have followed only if you continued to squeeze them. It does no good to extort to a level where people can no longer survive." Michael took another puff on his cigar. "Greed will be your downfall, Johnson, if you don't get your ... *appetites* under control."

"I don't see where that's none of your business, now, is it?"

"It is if you keep taking the kind of risks you did the other night. I covered for you this time, but don't expect the same courtesy in the future."

Johnson shrugged, too clueless to heed Michael's warning. "Word on the docks is that Frank Lewis is askin' about Longren Shipping. He visited Longren House Friday afternoon."

Michael's gaze sharpened through the haze of fragrant smoke. "An unwelcome development," he observed.

"I'm dealin' with the problem."

Michael hesitated, then decided to leave the matter to Johnson. "See that your men aren't overly zealous in their task. Hattie is intelligent and headstrong—you could cause the opposite reaction of what you intend." He smiled slightly. "I find it ironic that a woman may be the downfall of you, given your, shall we say, indulgences."

Johnson's shoulders jerked. "I'm surprised Longren didn't recognize the problem he had with his wife and deal with it—he never hesitated in the past." Johnson bared his teeth in a cocky grin. "She should be taught a lesson. I'd enjoy bein' the one to do it, and I wouldn't bother with none o' your damn finesse."

The thought of Johnson putting his filthy hands on Hattie had bile rising to the back of Michael's throat. It took all of his control not to react.

He settled for grinding out his cigar in the remains of Johnson's lunch. "That wouldn't be advisable," he said softly. "You'll leave Mrs. Longren to me."

* * *

AFTER spending hours in the garden, Hattie and the girls came inside, pleasantly tired, their frocks covered with dirt and bits of plant debris. Sara clucked when she saw their disheveled state, but Hattie merely smiled. There was something about getting down on one's hands and knees and working among the earthworms that made one feel as if all in the world was right. At least, for a few hours.

"I still don't see why you disapprove of the dress design I've chosen," Charlotte pouted as she allowed Tabitha to help her remove her muddy walking boots. "It's very becoming, and sure to catch Chief Greeley's eye."

"Bustles and all those petticoats have been proven to damage a woman's internal organs," Hattie explained patiently for the fifth time that day. "I won't have you physically harming yourself for the sake of fashion."

"Oh, pooh." Charlotte tossed her head, sending the bits of leaves clinging to her golden curls to the floor and drawing an exasperated sigh from Sara. "You've been listening to Aunt Kate far too much." She referred to their maiden aunt who traveled the country lecturing on the dangers of women's fashions and advocating a more sensible approach. "She's a spinster—what could she *possibly* know about catching and holding a man's interest?"

Hattie raised an eyebrow. "So you're saying you think it's more important to have a man appreciate you for how you look, rather than for your intelligence, your good humor, or your talent."

"Well, of course not! But if you don't catch his eye to begin with, you won't ever have a chance to impress him with the rest. Men are frivolous creatures, are they not?"

"For heaven's sake, child," Sara admonished as she handed Hattie the day's post. "I don't know where you get these crazy notions."

"They're not crazy," Charlotte protested. "I've read magazine articles about how to catch a man, which is more than either of you can say."

"Well, notwithstanding the advice of those experts," Hattie said, her tone wry as she shuffled through the pile of newly delivered notes and cards on the hall table, "Chief Greeley made his preferences regarding your dress perfectly clear—he expects you to be conservatively attired. So if you're hoping to catch his eye, and not have him strongly disapprove, you'll take my advice and choose a pattern that shows off your figure in a more demure and understated manner."

She held up an envelope from Eleanor Canby, frowning. Given their recent argument, she would've thought Eleanor would avoid contact with her. With some trepidation, she tore open the envelope, then allowed herself a small sigh of relief. It was an invitation—a very fancy, engraved summons to a dinner party being held by Eleanor that weekend:

MR. AND MRS. ALEXANDER CANBY
WILL BE PLEASED TO SEE YOU AND CHARLOTTE
AT CANBY MANSION THE EVENING OF
SATURDAY, JUNE 6TH, AT EIGHT O'CLOCK, FOR
A DINNER HONORING THE FAMOUS COMPOSER
AND MUSICIAN,
SCOTT JOPLIN.

JUNE 1, 1890

Eleanor had scrawled a handwritten missive across the bottom:

Hattie, I hope you will take this invitation as an opportunity to redeem yourself in the eyes of the Port Chatham business community.

Charlotte peered over Hattie's shoulder to read the invitation and clapped her hands. "Scott Joplin! I simply *adore* his ragtime! And absolutely everyone will be there! You *must* send a reply at once!"

Hattie frowned. "I'm not at all certain we have the appropriate clothes. Eleanor's party will be quite elaborate, and she will expect us to dress accordingly."

"Yes, ma'am," Sara agreed. "The clothes you wear should reflect an appropriate degree of display, as well as indicate that you appreciate the time and expense Mrs. Canby has gone to for the party."

"All the more reason to pen a quick refusal," Hattie replied. Not to mention, she thought, that they would be under scrutiny the entire evening. Eleanor was throwing down the gauntlet—one misstep and they would be cut from all future social events. She expected Hattie to let it be known to all the guests that she had learned her lesson and would henceforth act according to the dictates of proper etiquette.

How utterly galling.

"You *can't* be thinking of not attending!" Charlotte wailed.

"An occasion such as this requires gowns of the finest quality," Hattie explained. "Satins, lace collars and cuffs, expensive evening slippers—we don't have either the time or the money to upgrade our wardrobes." She refused to think of the cash in the safe; she wouldn't use potentially ill-gotten gains for their benefit.

"But Mona gave us material that is well suited," Charlotte protested. "All we need to do is remove and reuse some of the lace from gowns Charles had made for you that you can't wear because of your mourning period. And regardless, Eleanor will expect you to be dressed in a more subdued fashion." Her expression turned pleading. "Please."

"And what of your restrictions? You're still very much on probation because of that stunt you pulled at Fuller's Ice Cream Parlor."

"Oh, Hattie! You can't make me stay home from the most important social event of the season!"

"Charlotte's right, ma'am," Tabitha said. "We can take apart some of your other gowns and use the lace from them for Charlotte's gowns, and use the mousseline de soie that Mona sent to create a gown for yourself."

"To not attend would be an insult to Mrs. Canby you can ill afford," Sara warned.

Hattie sighed. "Very well—" She was drowned out by Charlotte's shriek, then staggered under the force of her hug.

"Come on, Tabitha!" Charlotte said, dragging the poor girl up the stairs. "We must begin at once!"

"Don't remove any gowns from my closet without my express permission," Hattie called after them as they scurried up the stairs, then shook her head. She'd be lucky to have even a fraction of her wardrobe survive the week. She dropped onto a hall chair to remove her muddy boots.

"Ma'am."

Hattie looked over to find Sara hovering by the kitchen door, wearing a troubled expression and wringing her hands.

"Yes, what is it, Sara?"

"If you could come to the back entrance? There's someone who needs to speak with you." Sara's eyes were wide and afraid.

Perhaps Frank Lewis had already sent someone with word of the information he'd sought. "For heaven's sake, Sara, whoever it is, send them in. And bring me some tea, would you please?"

Sara shook her head with vehemence. "I'll not take that chance with your reputation, ma'am. This person should not enter our house. If she hadn't been so insistent, I wouldn't even have announced her arrival."

She? Hattie frowned, intrigued. "Very well, though sometimes I think you worry far too much about my reputation. I'm fairly certain it's irredeemable at this point."

She rose from the hall chair. After the day's work in the garden, her muscles protested the sudden movement, but she followed Sara down the hall and through the kitchen to the back door.

Mona Starr stood on the back stoop in the encroaching twilight.

"Mrs. Starr!" Hattie said, shocked. "Please, come in! I'm ashamed that my housekeeper left you to stand outside."

Mona shook her head, glancing around, clearly uneasy with her surroundings. Though she was immaculately and expensively dressed, her expression conveyed distress. "I've come to ask your aid in a matter of some urgency. If you would be kind enough to follow me out to my carriage?"

"Of course," Hattie replied, even more curious.

"I wouldn't have come at all if the situation weren't so grave."

Hattie stepped outside, shushing Sara's protests. "Don't worry, Sara, if the woman abducts me, you can call Chief Greeley to my aid within moments. Nothing will happen."

She hurried through the gathering darkness behind Mona's quickly retreating figure. When she rounded the stand of trees at the back of the yard, separating the garden from the alley beyond, she came upon an elaborate carriage drawn by a matched pair of bays. Mona waved her over to the open carriage door.

Hesitating, Hattie wondered what she was getting herself into and whether there really was cause to be concerned for her own safety. She shook her head over her own foolishness. This woman had no cause to harm or abduct her—she'd been listening to Sara and Greeley far too much. With a firm stride, she walked over and peered inside, then gave a small cry of distress.

Frank Lewis lay on the floor of the carriage, unconscious, his face so bloody and bruised she hardly recognized him.

Chapter 10

JORDAN slowly became aware that someone was standing on the porch. Now was *not* the time for interruptions. Hattie had never mentioned that Frank had been attacked!

"Look, if the room bothers you that much, I can take the bed in . . ." Her voice trailed off when she saw Jase on the steps, looking tired. Tom stood behind him on the sidewalk. "Oh, hey. Sorry, I thought you were movers."

"You know, some folks consider hanging the porch swing *before* sitting in it," Tom observed with a grin.

"Where's the fun in that?" she quipped, stacking the diaries and books and rising to her feet. The dog raised his head long enough to scope out the situation, then went back to sleep. A nap in the sun apparently trumped human companionship.

"Got any more of that?" Jase asked, pointing to her mug.

"Sure." She led the way down the hall to the kitchen.

While she reheated the espresso machine, she motioned for them to sit down. "Late night?"

"Closed around three A.M." Jase rubbed his unshaven jaw. "A few extra musicians showed up, and they all jammed until the wee hours. My no-longer-twenty-something body is feeling the effects."

Tom turned a kitchen chair around, straddling it with his arms resting along its high back. "You'll survive once you count up the night's receipts. And the music was damn good, I gotta say. Keep it up and you'll become the premier location for live jazz in Port Chatham."

"A mixed blessing," Jase muttered, then gave Jordan a grateful smile when she handed him his cup. "Which reminds me, whoever you served that bourbon to by the front door never paid his bill. I found the drink after closing—it hadn't been touched."

"Damn." She stared at Jase, dismayed. "I knew that guy was trouble. I should've kept a better eye on him." And she should've asked him whether he worked for Drake, but she didn't say that out loud.

She paused while pulling the next shot of espresso, frowning. Why would a cop skip out on a bill? That didn't make sense.

"The money isn't the problem," Jase assured her. "It just had me curious. Did you get a good look at him?"

She described him, but he didn't ring a bell with either of them. "If he shows up again, I'll find out who he is."

Jase shook his head. "I don't want you confronting him. Just point him out and let me handle it."

She shrugged. If he was who she suspected he was, and

if she saw him lurking around the house today, she'd ask him to produce identification. "What's a ball-peen hammer used for?" she asked, thinking about the pictures she'd seen in the home repair book.

"Metalworking," they answered in unison.

Jase added, "You don't have any metalwork on this house. Why do you ask?"

She explained that she'd seen a picture of one when she looked up hand augers, the supposed weapon of choice for bludgeoning in 1890.

"You had a chance to look at my great-grandfather's diaries?" Tom asked.

"Not yet, though I was able to read a few pages over breakfast from his memoir about the murder investigation. And Holt Stilwell approached me with some papers last night after I left the pub." She caught Jase's frown. "I handled him, don't worry. He gave me what turned out to be portions of Michael Seavey's diary, which I was reading when you arrived. Seavey indicated that Clive Johnson, Hattie's business manager, was the one who started the fire on the waterfront in 1890, and that he'd helped Johnson by covering it up."

Tom raised his brows. "Interesting."

"Yeah."

She handed him an espresso, then turned back to pull another one for Jase. While they'd been talking, the Goth kid had delivered two dish packs of her china and kitchen utensils to the center of the room. She finished Jase's espresso, then slit open the dish packs with a box cutter, so that she could hunt for the plates, mixing bowl, and pans she'd need to fix everyone breakfast. She'd bought supplies at the grocery store the night before, in anticipation of today's crowd.

"According to Eleanor Canby's editorial, which it now appears she may have been pressured to write, the fire originated in a brothel," she said, placing her griddle on the stove to heat while she pulled the ingredients for buttermilk pancakes from the cupboards and fridge. "Hattie may have been right all along—she believed the fire had been deliberately set to send a message."

"What kind of message?" Jase asked.

"Don't know, I haven't read that far yet." She pulled a pint of fresh, local strawberries and a package of organic bacon from the fridge, setting the bacon on to fry. "The rest of today's a lost cause, what with the movers here. I won't get back to my research until tonight at the earliest."

As if she'd conjured them up, two movers appeared in the kitchen doorway, asking for instructions. She dealt with their logistical issues, then returned to mixing the pancake batter, talking while she worked. "I have to admit, after reading about the murder investigation in Greeley's memoir, I'm wondering whether he got the right man. The evidence was mostly circumstantial." She filled them in on Frank Lewis's claim that he'd been drugged and the bloody fingerprint. "I haven't asked Darcy whether that would've been enough to convict in the nineteenth century, but I'll run it by her tonight."

Tom looked troubled. "Have you read about the trial itself?"

"No, just portions of the investigation so far. I had hoped to find trial information, either in Greeley's memoir or at the Historical Society." She flipped bacon and pancakes, then washed strawberries. "It would be nice to read the actual witness statements. Depending on who gave damning evidence against Frank, I would be swayed one way or the other. Eleanor Canby, for example, probably wouldn't have hesitated to make things look bad for Frank and Hattie."

"More evidence could've come out during the trial that swayed the jury," Tom argued, accepting plates of pancakes from her.

He was right, she realized as she poured more batter onto the griddle. But if she couldn't find the trial transcripts, it was a moot point. And though she wasn't yet willing to admit as much to Tom, she had a bad feeling about the veracity of Greeley's account. The police chief had clearly felt the need to prove he'd built an airtight case against Frank Lewis. If he'd had doubts at any time, he wouldn't have admitted to them *or* documented them.

Then again, what would have been his motive to bungle the investigation? Had someone who wanted Lewis out of the way put pressure on him? Had Michael Seavey seen an opportunity too good to pass up?

Evidently, the food smells had reached the backyard—Amanda entered through the back door, giving Tom and Jase high fives.

"So you guys know each other," Jordan said, handing

Amanda plates of food with instructions to deliver them to the movers.

"Tom tips me off about which houses are haunted," said Amanda over her shoulder.

"Of course he does," Jordan agreed faintly, and Jase grinned. She busied herself with mixing more batter.

"How does the fire tie in with the murder?" Jase asked as he ate.

"What fire?" Amanda asked as she stepped back into the kitchen.

Jordan handed Amanda a plate while she described the 1890 waterfront fire, then answered Jase's question. "I'm not certain yet, but my gut is telling me it's related." She flipped more pancakes. The dog nudged her thigh, and she fed him a slice of bacon. "I'll search the library and see how many of Hattie's diaries I can find. Maybe if I put her account side by side with your great-grandfather's, I can track through the events from the two different perspectives."

"Hattie's would have ended before the murder, whereas Tom's great-grandfather's probably wouldn't have mentioned Hattie until he investigated the murder," Jase pointed out.

"Damn. You're right." She'd been counting on reading both to see whether she could pinpoint any discrepancies that would lead her to other avenues of research.

"What about Charlotte? Did she have a diary?" Tom asked.

The possibility hadn't even occurred to her. "I don't know. I'll..." Her voice trailed off as she realized she'd been about to say, "I'll ask her," and Jase grinned, following her train of thought. She finished gamely, "...hunt through Charlotte's old room and see whether I can come up with anything. I found a doll hidden in the back of the closet—it's possible I'll discover more."

"Have you searched the attic yet?" Tom asked. "The former owners may have stored it away, not understanding its historical significance."

"Or tossed it in a fit of pique, after being endlessly harassed by a couple of ghosts?"

"That, too." Tom smiled.

"They're already harassing you?" Amanda popped a strawberry into her mouth. "Cool."

"In any event," Tom continued, "you'd be surprised what people around here find in their attics. We could take a look."

Jordan folded her arms. "Are you here to help with the murder investigation or discuss the plan for the renovation?"

Tom looked sheepish. "Both. You gotta admit, the old murder is exciting stuff."

"I might be getting a little hooked," Jordan allowed, then shrugged. "I haven't even stuck my head inside the attic door—I don't even know where the attic is. Wait, I think I saw a closed door next to Charlotte's room that could hide a set of stairs."

Tom gave her a curious look. "You didn't go up there before you bought the house?"

"No, I left that to the guy who conducted the structural and pest inspections."

He and Jase exchanged a look that clearly said "first-time home buyer."

Tom stood and carried his dishes over to the sink. "That was delicious. You mixed those pancakes from scratch, didn't you?" At her nod, he placed his hand over his heart. "Will you marry me?"

"Now, that's just pitiful," Amanda declared, polishing off her fourth pancake.

* * *

AFTER Amanda left to prune the bushes she thought could be saved, Jordan led the men up to the second floor. When she opened the door she thought would lead to the attic, it revealed a second bathroom with a huge claw-foot tub, a pedestal sink, oak wainscoting, and a cracked black and white tile floor. She had an immediate vision of soaking in the tub, surrounded by the soft glow of candlelight, after a hard day's work on the house.

Jase took her shoulders in both hands and turned her away. "Focus."

"Attic. Right."

She hit pay dirt with the door on the other side of Charlotte's bedroom, over the library. Trotting up the stairs, she flipped on the light switch on the wall at the top of the landing.

And promptly let out a bloodcurdling scream, wind-milling her arms.

Both men raced up the stairs.

Jase grabbed her, pulling her behind him. *"What?"*

Tom stood on his tiptoes, peering over their heads, and started laughing.

The entire room was filled from ceiling to floor with vines that crisscrossed every square inch of space, creating an impenetrable jungle. Smaller, dead vines hung down into the stairwell, creating a lacy tangle of twigs, into which Jordan had run headfirst.

"What the *hell* is it?" Jordan asked him, her voice shaking.

"The wisteria, is my bet."

"It grew through the *wall?*" she wailed.

"It grows through *foundations*," Jase corrected, taking a closer look, then chuckling and releasing her. "You okay?" he asked, still smiling.

No, she was mortified that she'd screamed like a ninny.

Tom was already talking on his cellphone. "Yeah, get over here. I'll check the foundation while we wait." He flipped the phone shut. "Bill's on his way over with a chain saw."

"Chain saw?"

"Just to clear inside the room," Tom assured her. "Before we can cut the rest of the vine, we have to make certain the roots haven't compromised the structure." Seeing her stunned expression, he hastily added, "We'll jack up the foundation, if necessary—don't worry."

Don't worry. Jordan closed her eyes.

"I thought you said you had this place inspected," Tom said.

"Of *course* I had it inspected! I have the report out in the car."

"What was the guy's name?" Jase asked. "Because you should seriously consider going after him for negligence."

"I don't know . . . Martin, that's it. Bob Martin."

He and Tom exchanged a look. "There's no Bob Martin doing inspection work in this neck of the woods," Tom told her. "And I would know—my cousin is in the business."

"But that's not pos—" She stopped. "Oh . . . *oh!*"

Her vision of her dream home disintegrating around her, she took the stairs two at a time down to the first floor, almost colliding with the Goth kid, who was wheeling a hand truck loaded with boxes. She shoved open the library doors, advancing on the ghosts, who were sitting at the desk, arguing about the contemporary clothing styles in *Vanity Fair.* "*You altered my inspection report?*"

Tom had followed close on her heels. "Of course not. Why would I have done that?"

Hattie answered Jordan, looking surprised. "We thought it prudent."

"In what *universe?*" Jordan shouted, then put up a hand. "Don't answer that."

"Okay," Tom said, looking confused.

The ghosts wore earnest expressions.

She took a deep breath, then another. "I paid *good money* for this place, and now I have to rebuild it *from the foundation up?*"

Tom said, "Actually, that's the worst-case scenario—"

She rounded on him. "But I don't know that, do I, *since I never saw the original report?*"

Tom now wore the look of a man who believed he was dealing with an escapee from a mental institution. "I thought you said it's in your car?"

"You wouldn't have bought the house if you knew the truth," Hattie explained. "And then you wouldn't have moved here, and we never could've gotten you to help us."

Charlotte nodded enthusiastically.

Jordan belatedly realized she had a growing audience. Jase stood next to Tom just inside the doorway, with the Goth mover next to him. It had to look as if she'd been shouting at an empty room. She turned back, noting that the ghosts had taken advantage of her momentary distraction to disappear. *Wimps.*

"Uh, lady?" The kid ventured forward a step. "If you have, like, Tourette's syndrome? Well, my aunt has it, you know, and it's okay, I can explain it to the other guys. You don't have to feel like you need to come in here to hide your outbursts."

Jase started coughing.

Her cellphone rang, and she pulled it out of her jeans pocket to check the caller ID. She flipped it open. "*What?*"

"Hello to you, too," Carol said. "How are you?"

"Regressing," Jordan snapped. "You?"

"I'm sitting here with a cup of golden oolong tea, watching the local cable news channel, trying to maintain a Zen-like calm while I wait for my next patient to arrive, who is late, dammit. It's going to throw off my entire damn day. I hate it when people think they can show up late."

Jordan rubbed her forehead.

"Right. As I said, I have the news on, and they've been showing excerpts of a press conference from earlier this morning conducted by Detective Drake."

Jordan immediately got a very bad feeling and started a yoga breathing exercise.

"Sweetie, he's saying that new evidence has come to light in the case. Could he have found out somehow? You didn't confide in anyone else, did you?"

"No." Jordan pressed fingers against both eyes. "Maybe a neighbor saw something. I didn't see anyone around that night, though, and most people were still commuting home at that hour."

"Well, brace yourself. He's saying he will be formally interviewing you tomorrow as a person of interest in your husband's murder."

Jordan's eyes locked with Jase's, her knees threatening to buckle.

"Whoa." He jogged forward and led her over to the nearest chair. "Deep breaths, okay? Deep and even."

"Who's that?" Carol asked.

"A friend," Jordan said, her voice sounding funny even to her own ears. "Drake hasn't contacted me yet." She glanced out the window to see Darcy pull her police cruiser up to the curb behind the moving van. "Never mind—I think I'm about to get the news."

"You need a lawyer now."

"I need drugs, but you had your chance."

Carol continued as if Jordan had never spoken. "Drake

is moving fast, so you won't have time to obtain legal counsel—I'd bet my Gucci sandals on it."

Jordan's ears started roaring, and she dropped her head between her knees while Carol jabbered on.

"And do not even *think* about letting him interview you without a damn good criminal defense lawyer present. Cops are sneaky as shit. He'll have your words twisted around until he's got what he needs to swear out an arrest warrant—"

Jase pried the phone out of Jordan's hands. "Who is this?" Jordan heard him ask. There was a moment of silence, then he introduced himself.

Carol's voice rose in pitch, sounding excited.

"Yeah," he replied, "that Cunningham," making Jordan wonder what he meant, but at the moment, she was more concerned with whether she was passing out. The dog, who had followed her inside the library when the commotion started, licked the side of her face, whining. She put an arm around him.

"No, I don't think that's necessarily a good idea." Jase listened for another moment. "Yeah, I'll make sure she checks her email." Then he asked, "So is this cop a head case or what?"

This time, Jordan heard her best friend's reply, clear as a bell. "Already, I like you."

He flipped the phone shut just as Darcy reached the library doors.

Jordan angled her head long enough to see the expression on Darcy's face. "I think I'm about to get arrested," she said to no one in particular, not really able to take it in. "Will you adopt the dog if I'm convicted?" she asked Jase.

She didn't bother to wait for his response—she was too busy putting her head back between her legs.

Chapter 11

"I repeat, I'm not here to arrest you. I'm just setting up a time for the meeting tomorrow."

Jordan nodded but kept her head between her knees, looking no higher than Darcy's black boots.

The boots turned to point at Jase. "Are you going to represent her?"

At that, Jordan did lift her head. "What?"

Jase sent Darcy a rueful look. "I thought I'd managed to keep my past in the past."

"Give me a break—I'm a cop." She looked at Jordan. "Remember I told you last night that Jase used to be an attorney? Well, he was one of the top criminal defense attorneys on the East Coast."

Jordan stared at him uncomprehendingly, then made the connection. "You're *William J. Cunningham?*"

"That's my father. I went by J. Cunningham. And no, I don't still practice, but I keep my licenses current." He frowned at Darcy. "You know I've been out of the business for years, which means representing Jordan is not a good idea."

"But you're a jazz piano player," Jordan said, her mental picture of him crumbling as she remembered the newspaper articles about the wealthy clients he'd defended in some of the nation's most high-profile cases.

"I've always played jazz as a way to let off steam," Jase explained. "The pub gig is more recent, though." He noted the confusion that had to be showing on her face, insisting, "I'm out of that life. I chose to leave because I wasn't comfortable with the ethics of the cases I handled."

Jordan shook her head. "You're not laid back at all, are you? It's just an act." Why hadn't she seen the dichotomies? His easygoing attitude contrasted with his sharp intellect and the competent way he handled everything he did. She hadn't seen the real man at all.

"I wasn't acting." Jase's voice was calm. "I'm a pub owner now."

"No one changes that much, that fast," she said stubbornly.

"*Dammit*—"

Jordan's cellphone rang, interrupting whatever he had intended to say. Without a word, he handed it to her.

She checked the caller ID—it was her mom. Obviously, her parents had seen the press conference. Jordan decided to let the call go to voice mail. If she answered now, her mom would instantly pick up on her distress.

"Yo?" Darcy waved a hand. "We're on a tight timeline here. The reality—whether or not I'm fond of defense attorneys—is that Jordan needs a damn good one, and fast, and that means you, Jase." When he started to protest, Darcy forestalled him. "You tell me where she can find someone as good as you, on short notice, who would be as motivated to help her."

"I can make calls on her behalf to any number of old acquaintances. One can hop a plane—"

"—and be here by tonight *and* come up to speed on the case?" Darcy shook her head. "I don't think so."

"I'm sitting right here," Jordan said irritably, "and I can make my own decisions."

"Jordan?" The call came from the front porch.

Jordan recognized Ted's voice. *Damn.* She'd forgotten all about his visit. "In here," she called.

He walked through the library doors, dressed stylishly in chinos and an Egyptian cotton button-down shirt, finger-combing the damage the breeze had done to his hair. He halted just inside the doors, his smile of greeting fading when he saw the crowd in the room.

Jordan introduced him to Tom and Darcy, whom he hadn't yet met.

"What's going on?" Ted asked Jordan.

She managed a smile. "I may need a rain check on that tour I promised you."

He frowned. "Are you in trouble? What can I do to help?"

"I'm fine. The police just want to talk to me again about Ryland's murder. The detective in charge of the case is flying up tomorrow to interview me."

"That's ridiculous. Who is this asshole? He can't harass you like this—I won't have it." Ted pulled out his cell-phone. "Give me his number, and I'll talk to him."

"Bad idea," Darcy said. "The guy's just doing his job, and any interference from civilians will only make him more pugnacious."

"Well, we can't just sit here and let him run roughshod over her!" Ted snapped.

"We're dealing with it," Darcy told him.

Jordan intervened. "Jase used to be a criminal defense attorney, and Darcy is the chief of police. They'll both be present to ensure Detective Drake doesn't step out of line." She rose to place a hand on Ted's arm. "I'll be all right. But I'm pretty slammed, so . . ."

"You're betting your future on the legal expertise of a *tavern owner?*" Ted's expression was incredulous.

Irritation crossed Jase's face, but Jordan shook her head at him.

"There's no way I'm trusting anyone else to handle this for you!" Ted stated categorically.

She tamped down her impatience. "Ted. We've discussed this—I can take care of myself."

"But you shouldn't have to, dammit!"

"It's what I prefer." She noted his increasing agitation and quickly added, "I really do want to have that coffee with you. How about I give you a call in a couple of days?"

"All right," he said grudgingly, "but promise me you'll call if you need my help. I'm not without influence, you know. I could bring some pressure to bear on that detective. He'll think twice before treating you disrespectfully."

"I appreciate the offer." She guided him toward the door. "So how did you meet Didi Wyeth?" she asked, keeping her tone conversational. "Through your new agent?"

"Yeah, she was leaving Arnie's office one day as I arrived. We got to talking, and one thing led to another. She mentioned she was taking a break this summer, so I offered to let her stay at my house up here."

She drew him onto the front porch. "You know Didi dated Ryland for a while?"

"Sure, she cried on my shoulder about it. The bastard broke her heart. I think that's why she's taking some career downtime, though she hasn't admitted as much." Ted gave Jordan a stubborn look. "I'm sorry Ryland's dead, Jordan, but you deserved better. You understand that now, don't you?"

"Of course," she said lightly. One of the movers came up the steps, obviously needing to talk to her. "I'd better go. See you in a few days, okay?"

After answering the mover's question, she turned back to find Darcy leaning against the doorjamb, arms folded. "What's his problem?" she asked, cocking her head at Ted as he climbed into his car.

Fragile ego, abandonment issues, lack of empathy for others, and maybe a tad too much transference during the therapy process. Not that Jordan could say *that* aloud.

"That screwed up, huh?" Darcy concluded from the look on her face. "Why don't I just pull out a gun and shoot the son of a bitch. Put him out of his misery."

"Difficult call to make, given that I'm in worse shape than he is."

Darcy looked amused. "There is that." She pushed away from the door frame. "The interview is set up for eleven o'clock tomorrow morning. You know where the station is?"

Jordan nodded, tensing again.

"There's nothing you can do for now, so go back to your unpacking. I'll be there, and so will Jase. I threatened to find financial backers for Kathleen's restaurant if he doesn't represent you."

"If he's uncomfortable with the idea, I don't want him pushed into it." Despite what Jordan had told Ted, she didn't yet know how she felt about Jase representing her.

Darcy rolled her eyes. "Get a grip. He won't let any other attorney within miles of you—he's not taking any chances with your defense. And he's damn good, so do what he says tomorrow. No heroics, no rebellious moves. Got it?"

Jordan nodded again.

"Just let Drake go through his routine, answering with only the barest minimum of information. He's holding his cards close to his chest at the moment—I couldn't get much out of him. We'll have a better idea of what he's got after the meeting, and then we can devise a strategy."

Jordan swallowed and nodded a third time.

"You okay?" Darcy peered suspiciously at her.

"Sure."

"You're not going to hyperventilate or faint or anything silly like that, are you?"

"Of course not."

* * *

JASE was waiting for her when she walked back inside. She could hear a chain saw whining upstairs—Bill must have come in through the kitchen door while she was talking to Ted on the porch. Amanda and Tom were arguing in the upper hallway. Jordan heard Amanda say that someone had to stand up for the plant's rights, and she decided to steer clear of that debate. She headed for the kitchen.

Jase followed, standing in the doorway and watching her pull open a moving box to start unwrapping china.

"Are you okay?" he asked.

She shrugged. She knew he'd picked up on her ambivalence, but she didn't trust her instincts where he was concerned. She'd seen no reason not to trust him, but—

"I was young, and it's the family business. I was expected to enter the firm," he explained again. "As soon as I realized what I'd gotten myself into, I bailed."

"But you were good at it."

"Yeah, I was." His voice turned cool. "Why do I feel like that's a criticism?"

Why indeed? She had no answer for either of them—she didn't yet understand why the knowledge of his past upset her so much.

She turned away to stack dinner plates in the cupboard to the right of the sink. "I guess it doesn't matter, does it? I need a lawyer, and you're willing to help. Darcy is right, beggars can't be choosers. I should be grateful."

"But you don't have to like it," he concluded astutely.

She didn't reply, pulling another newspaper-wrapped stack of china out of the box.

He sighed and held out his hand. "Give me five dollars, dammit."

She fished the bill out of her pocket and handed it to him. "In the movies, it's always a dollar," she said lightly.

"I've never been cheap."

She smiled, but it was halfhearted.

He shook his head. "Anything you need to tell me before the meeting tomorrow? Something you might know that never made it into the accounts in the newspapers?"

She hesitated. "No."

"All right." He turned to go, then paused. "Just one more thing." She looked up from her unpacking. "Just in case you're inclined to make comparisons, I'm not at all like your late husband. Got it?"

She nodded. Again.

He certainly wasn't acting laid back any longer.

*   *   *

FOR the rest of the day, Jordan unpacked, focusing on the kitchen, trying to ignore the sounds of the chain saw and large pieces of wood thumping down the stairs. She worked even harder at ignoring the meeting tomorrow and her stark terror of being arrested. Somehow, if she could get the kitchen under control, she told herself, she would be able to handle the chaos in the rest of her life.

The ghosts remained conspicuously absent, for which she was grateful—she couldn't cope with them at the moment. She could only hope they weren't up to anything nefarious.

Tom poked his head in around midafternoon to tell her that the foundation was solid, but that the library wall would have to be rebuilt. Calling Amanda in from the garden, they discussed strategies for saving the wisteria and creating an iron trellis structure that could be attached to the outside wall and support the vine, preventing it from damaging the new wall.

Not too long after, Felicia Warren dropped by to deliver the forms Jordan would need to fill out to have Longren House added to Port Chatham's historic homes register. They spent a pleasant hour discussing the pros and cons of owning and refurbishing a historic home. Jase was right—the woman was a fount of knowledge. Jordan's head was spinning by the time she left.

Just before dinner, Jordan slipped out to deliver the dog to the vet's for grooming and a wellness check, repeatedly promising him that she would be back to pick him up in the morning. She could tell by his expression that he didn't believe her. Clearly, he had as many trust issues as she did—he'd probably been betrayed in his life just as many times.

The movers were finished by the time she returned, and she wrote a check, adding a large cash tip. She even accepted with aplomb the Goth kid's note referencing a Tourette's syndrome hotline and support group.

When the ghosts still hadn't reappeared by dark, she decided to simply enjoy the time on her own. Pouring herself a hefty glass of Merlot, she knocked down empty boxes for recycling, then smoothed and folded a small stack of packing paper, to be saved in case she decided she had to slip over the Canadian border in the middle of the night with the dog and a few belongings. With a second glass of wine in hand, she headed up to the attic to search for Charlotte's diaries. After an hour of digging through boxes covered with debris from the earlier chain saw activity, she'd uncovered nothing of interest and admitted defeat. A search of Charlotte's room yielded similar results.

It wasn't until late that night, after she came back from taking a long walk through her new neighborhood, missing the company of the dog the entire time, that she realized she was still so keyed up over the upcoming interview with Drake that her chances of sleeping through the night were slim to none.

She changed into an oversized football jersey, crawled under her down comforter, and, with a cool night breeze flowing in the window, picked up the stack of Hattie's diaries she'd pulled off the library shelves that afternoon.

Might as well distract herself with a murder investigation she *could* control.

Unintended Consequences

HATTIE reached into the carriage and lifted Frank's hand to feel for a pulse. Fast and erratic, but there. *Dear God.* She'd been the cause of this.

"We have no doctors on the waterfront," Mona said in a low voice behind her. "I didn't know who else to turn to. He's been unconscious for hours—my men found him in the alley behind the Green Light this afternoon. I had hoped he'd come to, but . . ."

Arms wrapped around herself to keep from trembling, Hattie straightened. "Sara!" she yelled.

The housekeeper must have been standing close by, for she appeared within seconds.

"Go quickly and fetch the girls," Hattie ordered. "Have Charlotte rush a note over to Dr. Willoughby's infirmary—we need him on a matter of utmost urgency." Willoughby was Celeste's father and ran the neighborhood medical clinic. "Instruct Charlotte to take Tabitha with her, and to remain vigilant, returning home at once.

Upon their departure, put clean bedding on the cot in the attic bedroom."

"Ma'am!" Sara protested, spying the contents of the carriage. "You can't possibly mean to bring him into our home!"

"That is precisely what I intend. Mr. Lewis may have suffered this beating because of what I asked of him. It's our responsibility to see that he gets the care he needs. Now, *go!*"

The housekeeper fled, and Hattie turned back to Mona. "Can your coachman help us carry him inside?"

"Of course." Mona walked to the front of the carriage and gave a quiet order. "Frank was doing your bidding when this happened?" she asked as they waited for the man to climb down.

"Yes, he was looking into a business matter for me."

"So you might know who did this—or ordered it done."

"I have a very good idea, yes," Hattie replied, her fury building. "Rest assured that I intend to have a word with Chief Greeley."

The coachman had opened the opposite door of the carriage and positioned himself at Frank's head. With Hattie and Mona holding Frank's legs, they eased him out of the carriage and onto the ground.

The coachman leaned down and gently lifted him in his arms. "Where to, ma'am?"

Hattie directed him through the back door, then up two flights of stairs to a room under the eaves. He lowered Frank to the cot Sara had just finished hastily making up, shifting his body to a more comfortable position.

Hattie surveyed the room, mentally rearranging the secondhand furniture to create a small but functional infirmary. If she left the door open to the floor below, heat would make its way up the stairs and keep the room comfortably warm. Frank would be safe, yet well concealed. If anyone made a social call, he or she would be none the wiser.

Sara handed her a blanket, which she shook out and draped carefully over Frank. He hadn't stirred since he'd been removed from the carriage. She turned to Sara, who hovered, sneaking curious glances at Mona. "Prepare a basin of warm water, along with some clean rags, and bring them to me."

"Yes, ma'am. The girls are on their way to Dr. Willoughby's, ma'am."

"Good." Hattie glanced at Mona. "There's nothing more we can do for the moment. If you'd be kind enough to follow me down to the second-floor parlor while we await the physician's arrival, I'd like to ask you a few questions."

Mona inclined her head. "Of course." Turning to the coachman, she ordered him to wait for her in the carriage.

They descended the stairs, Hattie motioning for Mona to precede her into the small, comfortably furnished room in which Sara kept a fire lit most evenings. Moving to a side table that held a tray of crystal glasses and a decanter, she poured Mona a glass of sherry. Hattie indicated they should sit in the two Murphy rocking chairs in front of the fireplace.

"Now, tell me everything you know," Hattie said. "Where did you find Frank? Did anyone witness the attack?"

"My butler found him in back of our house around midafternoon." Mona adjusted the skirts of her brocade gown, then leaned back in the rocker, her beringed fingers gently tapping on the rocker's arm. "Booth asked the merchants in the immediate vicinity, but no one admitted to hearing or seeing anything unusual."

"Could Frank have been beaten in a different location, then dumped at your establishment?"

Mona frowned as she lifted her glass from the small table between them and took a sip of sherry. "Possibly, yes. It does make sense that Frank would've been attacked on the wharf—he rarely comes to our block during the day."

"And an alley sees less traffic, thus ensuring that it would've taken longer for someone to discover him."

"Yes."

So whoever had beaten him had possibly meant for him to die of his injuries, Hattie surmised. "Do you employ anyone who could ask around the wharf without raising too much suspicion? I would like to know anything he can discover about the attack—the number of people involved, whether any of them were recognized. I might be able to track them based on their employment to the person who ordered the attack."

"Booth can make inquiries, yes, but to what end?"

Mona turned concerned eyes on her. "I would strongly advise that you not pursue this—to do so could be very dangerous."

"But I must know whether this attack is related to my business," Hattie insisted, then voiced her deepest fear. "And what of the possibility that Frank doesn't recover?"

"If the worst happens, then you'll send word and I'll make plans to remove his body to a location where it will be discovered by the authorities," Mona replied. "One more body, discovered on the waterfront, will be of no consequence. When you report this to Greeley, do not tell him of Frank's whereabouts until we can be certain he will recover. You must protect yourself from falling under suspicion in the event that Frank dies."

Hattie shuddered, though she knew Mona was only being pragmatic.

"Your physician will be discreet?" Mona pressed.

During Hattie's past interactions with Willoughby, she'd found him to be rather proper, with a grandfatherly manner. He and Charles had been acquaintances though not close friends. "Dr. Willoughby is likely to believe Frank's presence in my house is inappropriate."

"Can his silence be bought?" Mona asked bluntly.

Hattie thought about the stacks of cash in the library. If need be, she would use that cash to ensure Frank's safety. "I'll double his usual fee in return for a promise of discretion."

"Then we'll hope for the best. As soon as Frank can be safely moved to the Green Light, contact me and I will return for him."

Hattie nodded, then hesitated. "I'd like to ask you about comments you made the night of the fire, if I may?" When Mona showed no signs of objection—other than a slight return of wariness in her expression—Hattie continued. "You indicated that my husband, Charles, wasn't a nice man. Precisely what did you mean by that?"

Mona studied her in silence, then seemed to come to a decision. "He beat one of my girls so bad she couldn't work for weeks."

Hattie swallowed, chilled despite the blazing fire. "You're certain? I can't believe— Charles would *never* have treated a woman that way!"

"You mean he wouldn't have treated *you* that way, and you'd be right. He saved his more savage appetites for my girls." Mona leaned forward, lowering her voice. "Remember the young girl who brought you the blankets the night of the fire? The one who was so timid in your presence? You must have noticed the freshly healed cuts and burns on her face and arms."

At Hattie's reluctant nod, Mona continued. "Charles and his man, Clive Johnson, asked to share Isobel one evening. At that time, Isobel was relatively new to the trade, and she still retained an air of fragile innocence that appealed to many of my customers. Of course, I agreed to Charles's request."

Hattie's eyes widened. "You mean, two men with one woman, at the same time?"

Mona looked momentarily amused. "We don't place limits on the sexual practices of our customers. My girls are trained to accept and enjoy all our customers' predilections, no matter how unusual."

"Of course," Hattie said faintly.

She'd heard the girls in the Boston clinic giggle about odd requests from their customers, but she had no first-hand knowledge of such things. The fact that her husband had participated in them stunned her. Though now that she thought about it, many of the young men in town visited the brothels, and perhaps this was part of the allure.

"This wasn't the first time Charles had brought along his business manager for a ménage, of course." Each of Mona's words fell like a blow. "And though I'd had to warn him once in the past when he'd gotten overly rough, he'd been more circumspect since then, so I wasn't concerned. But this time he and Johnson went too far." Mona stopped for a moment, then shook her head. "If another girl hadn't heard Isobel's screams and come to find me, I've no doubt Isobel would've been killed."

Hattie's breathing had become shallow, and there was a faint roaring in her ears. Unable to remain seated, she rose and walked to the window that looked down on the front garden.

The picture Mona drew was one she could hardly fathom. It bespoke of a casual cruelty in her husband of which she'd seen no evidence during their short marriage. Though he'd been cold and distant, she couldn't relate Mona's words to the man she'd known. She now understood why Frank had refused to give her details.

"I can't..." She stumbled to a halt, unsure of what she meant to say, then pressed a hand to her stomach.

"If a man beats on me or my girls, he's not invited back," Mona continued, seemingly unaware of the depth of her distress. "I had Booth throw them both out. Clive Johnson is no longer welcome at my establishment."

Mona drank the last of her sherry and placed the empty glass on the table. "Why do you ask about the incident? Is what happened to Isobel related to what Frank was making inquiries about?"

Hattie thought once again about the cash in the library safe, and about the rumors of the white slave trade. But until she established a connection to Longren Shipping, she had to assume the two matters were unrelated. "No, it was another matter entirely. I simply wanted to know the truth about Charles's visits to the Green Light. You are not the only person to insinuate that Charles had unhealthy appetites." Hattie shook her head, her mind still reeling. "It seems I didn't know my husband at all."

Mona didn't offer sympathy, for which Hattie was grateful.

"Do you think Clive Johnson was behind this attack on Frank?" Mona asked instead.

"Possibly," Hattie conceded. "Though I think it equally likely that Michael Seavey ordered the beating—he visited me two days ago to warn me off."

Mona frowned.

"Hattie?"

Hattie jerked around to find Charlotte hovering at the door to the parlor, her eyes wide and questioning. Dear

God, how much of the conversation with Mona had Charlotte heard?

"Dr. Willoughby is on his way?" Hattie managed to ask calmly. At Charlotte's nod, she turned to Tabitha, who stood behind Charlotte. "Tabitha, please accompany Miss Charlotte to her room and stay with her until I come for you both, is that understood?"

"Yes, ma'am."

Charlotte glanced nervously at Mona. "But . . . we saw someone carry a man up to the attic. That man who visited you that day in the library."

"Not now, Charlotte. I will explain as soon as I am able."

Charlotte nodded, for once not arguing, then turned to Mona. "Thank you for the beautiful fabric, Mrs. Starr."

Mona smiled. "You're welcome, my dear." Charlotte curtsied and left, and Mona said to Hattie, "A charming girl. It would be a shame to see her put at risk because of this business."

"Yes."

Mona stood. "It's best that I leave before the physician arrives—it wouldn't do to have him notice my carriage. And the longer I linger, the more likely it is that a neighbor could note my presence."

Hattie sighed. "You're right, though I don't like the thought that either of us would be judged for our actions this evening."

Hattie showed Mona down the stairs and out through the kitchen.

Mona turned, her hand on the back doorknob. "Frank

wouldn't want it known that this has happened, and I know him well enough to know he wouldn't have wanted me to involve you. If I'd had any other alternative—"

"You made the right decision," Hattie assured her firmly. "I'll send word as soon as I know what his condition is."

Mona continued to hesitate. "And I will send communication of any information I am able to uncover regarding his attack. But please, don't try to deal with whoever did this on your own."

"I will take every precaution," Hattie agreed.

Mona's expression indicated that she'd caught Hattie's prevarication, but she didn't pursue the subject. "As soon as I return to the waterfront, I'll send one of my men to stand guard."

"Do you believe that's necessary?"

"Yes, I do. And don't worry, he'll be invisible—your neighbors won't know he's around."

"Very well." Secretly, Hattie was relieved to know someone would be watching out for them, and for Frank. "I am in your debt."

"Just take care of Frank—he's one of our own. We wouldn't want to lose him."

Shutting the door behind Mona, Hattie took the water and clean cloths Sara was holding. "I've left Mr. Lewis longer than is wise. Please bring Dr. Willoughby up when he arrives."

"Yes, ma'am."

Hattie climbed the stairs to the attic, pausing just inside the door.

Frank lay where the coachman had left him, still unconscious. He must have shifted while she'd been talking to Mona, because one foot had fallen to the side, dangling off the edge of the cot.

Laying a hand on his brow, she was startled by the heat she felt there. Surely a fever was a sign that his body was trying to heal? She gently brushed the hair off his forehead, as she'd wanted to do yesterday in the library, though this time her reason was to pull the hair away from the bloody cuts and bruises covering his face.

One eye had already blackened, and two long gashes—perhaps made by the steel toe of a boot, she realized, shuddering—ran across his forehead and down his left jaw. His nose was bent and badly swollen along the right side, indicating it had been broken. Yet even as battered as he was, the strength of his character was apparent in the uncompromising line of his jaw and squared-off chin. Her gaze traveled down his body, noting that the knuckles of both hands were split and smeared with dried blood, indicating how hard he'd fought back.

"Who did this to you?" she murmured.

She sank into the chair Sara had set beside the cot. How could she have let this happen?

Tears burned behind her eyes. She'd seen far worse in the Boston clinic, she reminded herself, and she'd be no good to him unless she could keep her emotions in check.

Unlacing his work boots, she gently pulled them off, setting them on the floor at the foot of the bed. Fetching a pair of sewing scissors, she carefully cut away his shirt, revealing a broad, muscular chest marred with reddish-black and purple splotches along his ribs.

She was contemplating whether to leave the removal of his pants to Dr. Willoughby when Sara entered with a second basin of cool water. "I thought if you kept cold compresses on his bruises, it would ease the pain a bit."

Hattie smiled at her. "Thank you, Sara. As soon as Willoughby arrives, please do me the favor of keeping a close eye on the girls. Don't allow Charlotte or Tabitha to come up here. Explain as little to them as you can—I will deal with their questions once we know more of Mr. Lewis's condition."

"Yes, ma'am." She hesitated. "Do you think he'll recover?"

"I pray to God that he does."

Hattie closed the door behind Sara as much as she dared, to discourage the girls' curiosity. Then she drew a chair and table over next to the bed. Wetting a cloth in warm water, she began the process of gently cleaning the blood off Frank's face, hands, and torso, biting her lip each time he moaned. As she worked, the anger that had begun to build within her earlier grew into a burning rage.

* * *

WHEN Dr. Willoughby arrived, Hattie retreated once more to the second-floor parlor, to await word of his diagnosis. After an agonizingly long hour, the portly, middle-aged physician knocked on the door. She bade him enter, rising to fix him a glass of his favorite brandy.

He lowered his bulk into the Murphy rocker next to her with a sigh, his face lined with exhaustion.

"How is he?" Hattie perched on the edge of her chair, handing the doctor his drink.

He accepted with a nod of thanks. "That young man sustained a hell of a beating—pardon my language. I'd like to personally thrash the men who did it."

"So there was more than one attacker?"

"I found evidence of at least three." Hattie swallowed her outrage, allowing him to continue. "One man couldn't have overpowered a man of his size. He was surprised from behind, I would guess, by the initial blow to the back of his head, which would have stunned him. After that, he wouldn't have been able to protect himself, though it seems he tried." The physician paused to take a gulp of brandy. "I can see no evidence of compression of the brain, so in that respect, he is lucky. His features remain even and do not slacken to one side, and his pupils are dilated evenly. I suspect, since he continues to sleep so deeply, that he has sustained a concussion. Do you know how long he has been unconscious?"

"At least four or five hours, from what I was told."

"Hmm." He frowned at that, staring into the fire for a long moment. "Well, all you can do is keep him quiet and keep constant vigil, to see whether he awakens. I've elevated his head—keep it that way—and stitched up the various cuts. Under no circumstances should he have any stimulants."

"What of his ribs?"

"Yes, I was getting to that—two are broken. I've taped them to keep them in place so that they do not puncture his lung. You mustn't let him shift about too much. The ribs will be quite painful for a while yet, and he won't like the effect when he breathes. I've left a dram of laudanum in the room, in case he experiences too much pain, but you are only to administer it after he has regained full consciousness and appears to be completely lucid. He's best off with only willow bark tea, if he can tolerate the pain."

"My housekeeper knows how to prepare it."

"Good. He also has numerous bruises in his kidney region. Should those become more tender or swell, notify me immediately." Willoughby turned from the fire with a frown. "If Mr. Lewis had a lesser constitution, I suspect he would've died from the beating he took."

"You know Frank?" Hattie asked, surprised.

Willoughby nodded. "He and I had some dealings recently. He came to me for medical supplies. Some story about a young girl—yes, name of Isobel, if I remember correctly—who had fallen from a carriage, though I doubt he told me the truth. Hard to sustain burns in a fall from a carriage," Willoughby added wryly.

Hattie managed not to react. So Frank had been the one to treat Isobel. That was why he knew the details of what Charles had done to her.

She glanced at Willoughby and found him watching her with a shrewd expression. When she remained silent, he sighed. "I won't push you to tell me what you know, but it's my duty to report this attack to Chief Greeley."

"I've already taken care of it—you needn't trouble yourself," she lied. "I'm sure you've already had a long day."

"Who do you have to nurse Mr. Lewis?"

"I will take care of that as well."

Willoughby's expression turned to one of shock. "Mrs. Longren, that is highly improper. I can't allow it. I will send someone over—"

"*No.* The more people who know, the greater the likelihood Frank's attackers will learn of his location. No one will suspect he is here."

"But—"

"I have extensive experience treating the injured and infirm at my parents' clinic in Boston," she interrupted firmly. "His injuries, though severe, are ones I've handled in the past. And you said yourself that we must simply wait and see whether he returns to consciousness. My housekeeper and I can keep vigil."

The physician continued to eye her with disapproval. "Charles would never have allowed this."

"Charles is no longer here to make the decisions, Dr. Willoughby. If you care about your patient's survival, you will speak to no one about this."

The physician studied her, then sighed. "Very well."

"Thank you." Hattie stood. "If you'll prepare your bill, I can pay you immediately."

He pursed his lips, reaching down to pull a slip of paper from his satchel. "Charles always said you were headstrong—he was concerned that trait would land you in trouble one day. I'm well aware of the good Frank Lewis has done on the waterfront, so I can hardly object to your willingness to take him in. But if you'll take every precaution, I'll sleep better with that knowledge."

Hattie nodded. "If you'll follow me to the library once you've finished your drink, I'll pay you there."

Once he'd left, promising to drop by the next afternoon to see how Frank was doing, Hattie returned to the attic. She sat in the chair next to the cot, one hand rubbing her temple. Frank lay, silent and unmoving, and still unnaturally pale. She lifted one of his hands and held it in her own, willing some of her strength into him.

He didn't respond, his breathing slow and deep.

His hand still in hers, she leaned back and closed her eyes. She would keep watch over him throughout the night, then pay a visit to the police in the morning. And regardless of what she'd told Mona, she would soon deal with the men who had beaten Frank. She had no doubt that Michael Seavey or Clive Johnson had ordered the attack. She would discover which one, then find a way to deal with him.

She had no intention of allowing the perpetrators to go unpunished.

The Warning

THE next morning, Hattie opened the door of the Port Chatham Police Station, a one-story brick building located around the corner from the Green Light and identified by a rough wooden hanging sign that announced, simply, Police. She approached the front desk and asked the uniformed officer to be allowed to speak with Chief Greeley.

While she waited, she watched the passersby on the boardwalk outside the building's plate glass windows. The streets were teeming with tradesmen and sailors going about their business, but she was too distracted to take much notice.

After a restless night, Frank's fever was lower this morning, his sleep deeper and less disturbed. But he still hadn't regained consciousness, which was worrisome. She'd left Sara in charge, changed into a clean dress, and hurried down to the waterfront, unwilling to be absent from his side for any length of time.

"The chief will see you now, ma'am."

The desk sergeant escorted her through a large, open

room furnished with battered oak desks. Uniformed officers sat at several of the desks, filling out paperwork. To her right, cells constructed of iron bars running from ceiling to floor marched down the wall. A few of the cells were empty, but others housed unkempt prisoners who smelled as if they hadn't washed in days. They tracked her passing, a feral light in their eyes. She averted her gaze, wrinkling her nose, and ignored their catcalls.

"Sorry about that, ma'am," the officer muttered.

"It's all right, Sergeant," Hattie assured him. "I've heard, and smelled, worse."

Greeley's office stood against the rear wall, built of whitewashed, half-height wooden walls and closed in by large windows. The design was intentional, she supposed, so that he could see at a glance what was happening in the common area. He sat behind an oak desk substantially larger than those in the other room, reading a sheaf of papers.

As they entered, he looked up, his gaze coolly assessing. "That'll be all, Dobbs."

"Yessir."

"This is a surprise, Mrs. Longren." Greeley indicated that she should take a seat in one of the rickety wooden chairs across from where he sat. "If you wished to discuss Charlotte with me, you could've sent a note requesting that I call on you later this afternoon."

"You mistake the reason for my visit, Chief Greeley." Hattie pulled off her gloves and placed them in her lap. "I come on a matter of some urgency. I wish to file a report of an assault."

Greeley jumped to his feet. "Charlotte is all right? Someone attacked her?"

"No, no," Hattie hastily assured him. "I didn't mean to alarm you. The attack happened yesterday afternoon, here on the waterfront. Frank Lewis was badly beaten and left for dead."

Greeley lowered his large frame back into the chair, his expression now wary. "And how would you know about this alleged attack, Mrs. Longren?"

She hesitated, trying to decide the best way to proceed. "I learned about it from Mona Starr. Mr. Lewis is in serious condition and remains unconscious. His physician has indicated that Frank was attacked by at least three assailants."

"You should have had the physician file a report with us."

She waved that aside. "I wish you to look into this matter immediately, to ascertain who might have perpetrated the crime."

Greeley picked up a fountain pen and fiddled with it. "And what is your interest, may I ask?"

She arched a brow. "To bring his attackers to justice, of course. I agreed to report the attack to you because, as I'm sure you know, people like Mrs. Starr don't believe the police will take them seriously."

Greeley studied her for a moment, his expression giving away little. "Where is Frank Lewis right now?"

"Hidden where the men who tried to kill him will not find him. Mona felt it prudent to keep the location of his convalescence secret for now."

"You can tell me his whereabouts—I am, after all, the police."

If members of the police force knew his location, she couldn't trust that word of it wouldn't leak out. "I don't see the point—Frank can't talk to you until he awakens, and given that he has a concussion, he may not remember the attack at all."

Greeley leaned back and steepled his fingers. "Then I see no way I can help you, Mrs. Longren. I would need access to the victim, to hear his side of the story, before I can investigate."

"But you could ask around on the waterfront, see if you can discover any witnesses to the attack," she insisted.

Greeley shook his head. "A waste of time and resources. I need evidence that the attack actually occurred before I can assign a man to investigate. Lewis is known to have angered a number of businessmen and shipping masters in this town. Someone could've simply been teaching him a well-deserved lesson."

"This was no 'lesson,'" Hattie snapped. "It was attempted murder. I have no doubt once you've seen the extent of his injuries that you'll agree. And regardless, it's your duty to investigate an attack against any citizen, no matter what the provocation."

Greeley looked amused. "If I investigated every waterfront brawl, I'd need a force ten times the current size."

"Then perhaps you should ask Mayor Payton to increase your budget! I fail to see—"

"What concerns me far more, Mrs. Longren," Greeley

interrupted, "is your role in this affair. Precisely what is your involvement with the alleged victim? I would've thought that after your run-in with him the other morning you'd have done whatever necessary to avoid contact with the man."

Hattie stared at Greeley, clenching her jaw. "Frank may have been gathering information for me at the time of the attack," she conceded.

"Ah. What kind of information?"

"Nothing that concerns you—a business matter regarding Longren Shipping."

Greeley sighed, pinching his nose. "Mrs. Longren. I believe I've already talked to you at length regarding your misguided notion that you need to be involved in the day-to-day affairs of Longren Shipping. If you are now consorting with a union representative, you may do grave harm to your business."

"I don't see where that's any of your concern, Chief Greeley."

"On the contrary. If this attack occurred as you say, then it is precisely the kind of situation I've been concerned about. You can't possibly know what you are doing or the type of people you are exposing yourself and the girls to. There's every likelihood your actions directly caused this alleged attack."

Hattie flinched, and he nodded, obviously pleased that his supposition was correct.

"Furthermore, I find this to be yet one more reason why I believe Charlotte should be removed from your household as soon as possible. Your willingness to associate with known criminals is placing her in personal danger, and proving to me that you are not an acceptable role model."

She stared at him. "That's absurd. Whatever involvement I choose to have in Longren Shipping has absolutely nothing to do with Charlotte. In fact, by coming down to the waterfront, I keep her exposure to anyone I employ at an absolute minimum."

"Frank Lewis was seen leaving your home the other afternoon, was he not? That's evidence enough of your casual disregard for Charlotte's safety."

Hattie shuddered, knowing what his reaction would be if he discovered Frank's whereabouts. "How do you know about Frank's business appointment with me?"

Greeley didn't answer, instead leaning across his desk and pinning her with his cold, dark eyes. "I want an answer, Mrs. Longren," he said softly. "Do you consent to my courtship of Charlotte?"

"Will you be investigating the attack on Frank Lewis?" she countered.

"Not at this time. As I've explained, I have no evidence that an attack has taken place."

"Mona Starr can corroborate my story, as can her butler and coachman."

"I don't find Mona Starr's word to be reliable. Nor should you."

"Then it seems I shall have to investigate myself."

"That is both foolhardy and dangerous."

Hattie clenched her hands in her lap. "Furthermore,

given your continued refusal to act in a manner which convinces me of your good moral standing, particularly with regard to criminal activities taking place on the waterfront, I will have to say no, I won't condone your courtship of my sister. My parents would have wanted a better suitor for her."

Greeley stared at her, a muscle in his jaw working. "Very well." He leaned back and stood. "My request was merely a formality—I had hoped to have your approval, but I can act without it."

Hattie stood as well. "I will remind you that I am Charlotte's legal guardian, Chief Greeley. You will not approach her or talk to her without my permission."

"And I would remind you that I'm the law in this town, Mrs. Longren. Any judge will be happy to alter Charlotte's guardianship, given the circumstances and your deteriorating reputation. I can easily argue that, given your recent activities, the death of your husband has unhinged you."

Hattie's spine was rigid as she marched to the door. "Do *not* call at our home, Chief Greeley. You won't be admitted."

"Mrs. Longren."

She paused, her hand on the knob.

Greeley's eyes were cold and hard. "Do not stand in my way, or I'll break you."

* * *

HATTIE was shaking when she left the police station, though not from fear. The sheer outrage of Greeley's position—not to mention his utter lack of concern for Frank's well-being—had her trembling with rage.

Clearly, Greeley possessed no sense of justice, which she found to be the ultimate in hypocrisy, given that he had made his reputation by quickly solving a number of cases. Rather, his specialty appeared to be the wielding of power for his own gain, without regard to the consequences. And for the moment, she feared, his focus was on wielding that power to acquire Charlotte as his wife.

Hattie drew her cape around her, shivering, even though the temperature was quite pleasant. Michael Seavey had been correct—Greeley would crush Charlotte's spirit within days, perhaps even on her wedding night. Hattie jerked on her gloves. To her dying breath, she would protect Charlotte from him.

People passed her, casting curious glances her way as she stood lost in her thoughts. Though the possibility struck terror in her heart, she doubted Greeley could reverse the terms of her legal guardianship within any immediate time frame. Therefore her focus for the moment needed to be to discover who had attacked Frank. As of early this morning, she hadn't heard back from Mona regarding her man's inquiries along the waterfront, which left the task to Hattie.

She withdrew her pocket watch and noted the time. She'd been gone scarcely an hour—she'd have to hope Frank was still resting peacefully. At the next cross street, she turned toward the harbor. If Frank had been attacked because of the questions he'd been asking on her behalf, then it stood to reason Clive Johnson was involved or would know whether Michael Seavey had ordered it. And she had yet to receive the additional financial information she'd requested. Therefore, a stop at the offices of Longren Shipping was in order.

* * *

WHEN she entered the office, her business manager was conducting a conversation with the clerk. Johnson wasn't pleased to see her, though his expression carried a slight smugness that hadn't been there two days before.

She greeted him, closing the door firmly behind her. "I was in town and thought to stop by for those account details I requested."

Johnson shook his head. "I ain't got time to compile files for you, Mrs. Johnson. You don't need to see 'em."

"Indeed." Coming on the heels of her argument with Chief Greeley, Hattie was in no mood to tolerate Johnson's insolence. "I expect my orders to be taken seriously, Mr. Johnson, and to be given the highest priority."

He rocked back on the heels of his boots, looking secretly amused. "I been otherwise engaged."

She realized what he was insinuating, and it made her nauseous. "You ordered the attack on Frank Lewis."

His expression turned sly. "Now, what would you be knowin' about that, Mrs. Longren?"

"It's rumored around town."

He laughed. "I don't think so."

It was all Hattie could do not to react with violence. Her shoulders rigid, she turned to the clerk. "What's your name, young man?"

"Timothy, ma'am."

"Well, Timothy, as of today, you're in charge."

Johnson's amusement turned to shock. "What the hell are you talkin' about?"

"You're fired, Mr. Johnson. Gather your personal belongings and clear out. Stop by my house tomorrow, and I will give you your final pay."

"You can't do that—I control this business."

"Not anymore, you don't." Hattie placed both hands on the edge of his desk, leaning across it. "You've thwarted my every move, blocked every attempt I've made to understand and run this business the way Charles would have wanted it run."

Johnson snorted. "That's rich, by God. You don't have no clue how your husband woulda wanted this business run. I was Longren's friend—I knew more about 'im than you ever woulda, even if he'd lived."

"Yes, I've heard about your trips with my husband to the Green Light, Mr. Johnson, and about the activities you engaged in. They would have been reason enough to fire you, even if you hadn't given me additional cause." She straightened and held out her hand. "The office keys, Mr. Johnson. You have ten minutes to clear out."

"I wouldn't do that if I were you, Mrs. Longren."

The mocking voice had her whirling in the direction of the back hallway. Michael Seavey emerged from the shadows to lean an elegantly clad shoulder against the wall by the clerk's desk.

"Eavesdropping, Mr. Seavey?" she asked with as much poise as she could muster.

"I admit to it being a favorite pastime of mine." He took a moment to light a cheroot. "Haven't you ever heard the Chinese proverb 'Keep your friends close and your enemies closer,' Hattie?"

"Now see here, Seavey—"

"Shut up." Seavey didn't bother to glance Johnson's way, his tone pure steel. "I suggest you reconsider your position, Mrs. Longren. It would be best to leave Johnson in charge for now. Poor young Timothy here hasn't the expertise to run the business, I'm afraid, and if you have to close your doors, even temporarily, your competitors will take advantage."

"I'm not interested in continuing to employ thugs, Mr. Seavey. And it is none of your business how I conduct mine." She stared him straight in the eye. "In attempting to advise me on this issue, you're merely seeking to protect your own business interests, are you not?"

He looked amused. "I've always said you possessed a keen intelligence. However, my argument is not without merit. Longren Shipping can't sustain a loss of clients without permanently closing its doors, I suspect, given the financial loss from the South Seas disaster."

She hated to capitulate in front of Johnson, but she knew Seavey was at least partially correct in his assessment. She was being precipitous in her decision, and for all the wrong reasons. She was furious with Johnson—he'd as much as admitted his involvement in Frank's attack—and she'd acted on impulse.

"Very well. I'll withdraw my demand for now." She turned to Timothy. "Those files, Timothy. And I expect you to visit me each morning at Longren House—you will report directly to me. Your job depends on your utter frankness with me, do you understand?"

"Yes, ma'am." Timothy handed her two file folders while casting a wary glance at Johnson. "I'll do my best."

Johnson folded his arms. "I won't have no employee spyin' on me."

"Yes," she replied quietly, "you will. You have no choice in the matter."

* * *

SEAVEY followed Hattie out to the boardwalk. "You really must control that temper of yours, my dear."

"You will address me properly, Mr. Seavey," she snapped.

He executed one of his maddeningly mocking little bows. "As you wish, Mrs. Longren."

Reining in her temper, she said, "Though you raised good points, I will *not* tolerate your interference in the future. Johnson must go. And I suggest you find some way to replace the business revenue you've enjoyed from your arrangement with Longren Shipping, because it won't be continuing. I intend to unionize."

He drew on his cheroot, then flicked it into the alley,

where it sizzled in a puddle of water. "Unionization will take time—you can't convert your crews overnight. And the other ships' captains using Longren Shipping for their procurement won't go along with your plans—at least, not initially."

She crossed her arms. "I beg to differ."

"You can't expect people to accept a cut in profits without good reason." His expression turned wry. "When it comes to money, I believe you'll find few as altruistic as yourself."

She shrugged. "Perhaps not, but I will be converting my own ships immediately, and I will also be shutting down any other questionable activities associated with them." She cocked her head. "Rumor has it you are heavily involved in the white slave trade, Mr. Seavey. Was that the nature of your business with Charles? You control the tunnels, do you not?"

Something flickered in Seavey's eyes, and he glanced around them. "These are not subjects to be discussed in public—they are far too dangerous."

Taking her arm, he led her around the side of the building and into the alley. His bodyguards followed at a discreet distance, though they did little to ease her sudden nervousness. It was hardly safe to enter an alley with him, but then again, her thirst for answers overrode her sense of caution.

"Now tell me, Mrs. Longren, why you are asking about this?" Seavey asked once they were well away from passersby.

She debated how much to reveal. Seavey couldn't be

trusted, but she suspected he had knowledge of Charles's affairs that no others were privy to. "Do you know whether Charles was involved in smuggling contraband on his ships?"

Seavey stared at her, his expression unreadable. "I suppose it's possible. Precisely what do you know of smuggling activities concerned with Longren Shipping?"

"I'll only say that I have in my possession evidence that leads me to believe Charles was involved in something illegal. You're denying any personal involvement?"

He regarded her in silence, then shrugged. "I might bring in the odd box of cigars now and then, but I have no stomach for trafficking in humans."

She frowned, unsure whether to believe him. "But human trafficking *is* occurring, is it not? Was Charles involved? Did he use your tunnels for that purpose?"

Seavey's expression remained bland. "The tunnels run all along the waterfront, Mrs. Longren. I control only a small portion of them. Whoever is telling you this is either lying or has a personal reason to spread such rumors."

"You're prevaricating, Mr. Seavey. I strongly suspect you know more than you're admitting."

He merely shrugged. "I suggest you cease this avenue of inquiry. It's an extremely dangerous one."

"I can take care of myself," she retorted, though she had no such confidence.

"I doubt that very much." Seavey moved closer. "I have a proposition for you, Hattie. Protection in return for certain, shall we say, pleasurable 'favors.' "

She took a step back, in the direction of the board-walk, casting a glance behind her. "You must be mad—I would never agree to such an arrangement."

He advanced a step for every one she retreated. "And why not?" he asked lightly. "You might find me to be very … entertaining."

She raised her chin. "Hardly. I find you distasteful."

"That's most unfortunate." Her back met the side of the building, and he closed the remaining gap between them, reaching out to run a gloved finger lightly down her jawline, causing her to shiver. "I would treat you very, very well—I can guarantee you pleasure beyond anything you experienced with Charles. And Charlotte would no longer need to worry about Greeley's advances."

He knew how to tempt her, knew that Charlotte was her Achilles' heel. Nonetheless, the idea sickened her. "Please step back, Mr. Seavey. Your behavior is outrageous."

He smiled. "I hope so." But he acquiesced, stepping back with an exaggerated sigh. "Very well. But know this, Hattie—your time as a widow in mourning will soon come to an end. And you need my protection, whether or not you'll admit as much."

"I find your suggestion disgusting."

He nodded. "I understand you'd view it as such. Nonetheless, you'd do well to consider my offer."

"Never." With the small amount of poise she had remaining, she stepped around him and exited the alley, her head held high.

* * *

As soon as she was out of sight, Michael's two body-guards silently appeared at his side.

"Find out who is spreading rumors about me," he ordered. All charm had vanished. "I want a name by nightfall."

Chapter 12

A few minutes before eleven the next morning, Jordan parked her car on the main street running through the heart of downtown Port Chatham. After shutting down the power to the Prius, she sat for a moment, gazing out the window.

Since her arrival, she hadn't had the time to walk around the picturesque downtown district. Many of the buildings were more than a century old—three-story, imposing Victorian structures built of granite or brick with ornately decorated moldings around their windows and doors. At the street level, galleries and boutiques catering to tourists displayed an array of handmade gifts and custom clothing, while the floors above housed offices and residential apartments.

Given the frigid wind coming off the water, Jordan was surprised by the number of people crowding the sidewalks. Tourists shivered in shorts and sandals, warming their hands around cups of coffee while they window-shopped. Locals, dressed more practically in denim and flannel, cut through the crowds, walking purposefully with some destination in mind. Between the beautiful old buildings, she caught a glimpse of the ferry departing, and of fishing trawlers coming and going in the bay. The overall effect should have been quaint and charming, but the fact that she was about to face interrogation for murder lent a surreal atmosphere to the scene. Then again, pretty much everything seemed surreal to her at the moment.

She'd parked across the street from the police station, which was housed in a small, one-story, distressed-brick building that blended well with the historical feel of the business district. Three antique divided-light windows at the front of the building were filled with posters advertising community watch groups and outreach programs. A hand-painted white sign saying Police hung above the glass door. Flowers overflowed planters and hanging baskets, trees shaded the sidewalk, and wooden benches had been provided for those who wanted to rest their feet.

Was this the same building in which Hattie had visited Chief Greeley the morning after Frank's attack? Jordan thought it very possible. She noted the windowless annex on the right side of the building. Had the prisoners Hattie had been forced to walk past been housed there? Did Darcy use that same space now to detain people who obstructed justice by withholding key information during the course of a murder investigation? Or would she simply allow Drake to slap cuffs on her and haul her back to L.A.?

Rolling her shoulders to ease tense muscles, Jordan

once again pondered the enigma that was LAPD Homicide Detective Arnold Drake. People generally liked her, and they instantly felt comfortable confiding in her, a talent she'd put to good use as a therapist. However, Detective Drake appeared to be the exception. Beginning with his questioning the night of the accident, his enmity toward her couldn't have been more obvious.

When she'd mentioned his reaction to Carol, her friend had written it off as a cop's knee-jerk suspicion of the spouse in a murder investigation. But Jordan suspected Drake's feelings ran deeper. She sensed she'd somehow touched off a long-buried resentment, and that his feelings related to a personal incident in his past.

Knuckles rapped on her window, jerking her out of her reverie. Jase stood on the sidewalk, dressed in pressed jeans and a button-down shirt—evidently Port Chatham's version of professional attire. She opened the window.

"Getting up your courage?"

"Something like that."

He opened her door and hunkered down. "I suppose it will only make things worse to tell you that you need to appear relaxed and confident. Cops are trained to note changes in breathing. He'll know whether you're nervous, and if you are, he'll assume the worst."

"Yeah, that helps—I'm thinking about throwing up now. How do ordinary citizens *do* this?"

He smiled, his gaze sympathetic. "Ordinary citizens don't, typically. Most of the populace is law-abiding and has very little interaction with cops. Those who do come into contact with the police in this context are usually guilty."

She nodded glumly.

"Of course, most innocent people also don't lie during a police investigation," he said mildly. "I'd say that isn't helping your stress level."

Busted. She closed her eyes. "I didn't kill Ryland," she insisted.

"I never said I thought you did. But you have a pretty good idea why Drake thinks you did, don't you?"

"Yes." She met his gaze. "Why are you agreeing to represent me, when you know I'm holding back on you?"

"All clients lie to their lawyers, for all kinds of reasons."

"That's certainly a cynical outlook."

He shrugged. "You'll confide in me when you're ready."

She took a deep breath, then another. Straightening her shoulders, she nodded to Jase. "Let's do this."

"Attagirl."

Climbing out, she hit the button to lock the car, then pulled her jean jacket close, chilled. He placed a hand on her arm, stopping her before she could step off the curb. "Just remember, I'm here to protect you from any strategies Drake may use to trap you into saying something you shouldn't. Check with me before you answer his questions, got it?"

"Yeah. And Jase—don't push this guy, okay? He's passive-aggressive, and for some reason I don't understand, he's holding a grudge."

Jase cocked his head for a moment, studying her, then nodded. "I'll trust your judgment."

They waited for a break in the traffic, then jogged across the street. Darcy stood waiting for them on the other side of the front door. The inside of the police station was utilitarian, furnished with standard-issue metal desks. Black file cabinets had been shoved against the walls at haphazard intervals. Rectangular fluorescent lights hung from the ceiling. No jail cells in sight, thank God.

"Drake's already here and waiting." Darcy directed them down a hallway to a room toward the back of the building. "I'll be observing from the other side of that glass mirror." Holding Jordan back for a moment, she said, "Simple answers, don't volunteer information. And—"

"—check with Jase before I say anything," Jordan finished for her. "I know."

Darcy searched her face for a moment, then nodded. "Good luck."

The conference room was empty except for a gunmetal gray table and four folding metal chairs with padded seats. The walls were painted white but had their share of nicks and smudges. Arnold Drake rose from his chair as they entered.

"Mrs. Marsh." He shook her hand, his grip slightly damp. "Please, have a seat."

A man of slight stature, Drake had the rumpled look—though lacked the charm—of the fictional Lieutenant Columbo. She wondered whether he had a physical condition that caused his hands to sweat, or whether he was nervous. Observing his confident, relaxed demeanor, she suspected the former.

"J. Cunningham," Jase supplied as he indicated where

he wanted Jordan to sit—across but kitty-corner from Drake. He chose the chair directly across. "Mrs. Marsh's attorney."

Drake's brow had risen at the mention of Jase's name. "In my book, Counselor, people who retain high-priced legal talent such as yourself are guilty as hell."

"Come now, Detective—I just happen to live here in town." Jase gave him a relaxed smile. "Mrs. Marsh has agreed to this interview for the purpose of helping you with your investigation. However, only a fool would talk to the police without legal representation."

Jordan gave him a sideways glance. He'd morphed into a glib, polished attorney, right before her eyes.

He asked that they skip any small talk and get right to the business at hand, managing to leave the impression that Jordan's time was valuable and not to be wasted. Even so, they were forced to wait while Drake reviewed his notes. Jordan's tension grew as the silence stretched out, though she recognized the interrogation tactic for what it was—an attempt to rattle her even before the interview began.

When she shifted in her chair, Jase shot her a quick warning glance.

"I'd like to review once more the events leading up to the time of the accident, Mrs. Marsh," Drake said finally. "What time did your husband arrive at your condominium in Malibu Canyon?"

"Around seven P.M., I believe. Ryland had called around six to tell me he was leaving his office in Beverly Hills."

Jase pressed his foot down lightly on hers, reminding her to restrict herself to answering the question.

"And he came to your residence—excuse me, the residence you both still owned until the divorce finalized, correct?"

"Yes."

Drake made a note, then continued. "He remained at the condo for how long?"

"Until just after nine P.M."

"Two hours. That's quite a long time, Mrs. Marsh. What did the two of you talk about for two whole hours? You weren't on good terms, according to the newspapers."

"Don't answer that," Jase interrupted. "Respond only to the content of your conversations with your husband."

"We discussed the upcoming court date and the terms of the settlement." That much was true, though "discussed" was probably too mild of a term. Ryland had been furious with her.

"Did you offer your husband any alcoholic beverages?"

Jordan hesitated, wondering what he was getting at. "He asked for, and I gave him, Scotch on the rocks."

"Why would you give him hard liquor if you knew he would be driving back after dark on dangerous, winding canyon roads? Was it your intent to get him drunk? Did you hope that he would lose control of his car?"

"Don't answer that." Jase pinned the cop with a hard look. "You know better, Detective."

Drake shrugged. "How many drinks did your husband have?" he asked, acting as if he found it absurd to have to rephrase the question.

Jordan's breathing sped up slightly. "Just the one drink, Detective. Ryland knew better than to drive while intoxicated."

"Surely the autopsy included a blood alcohol test," Jase said. "What were the results of that test?"

"That his blood alcohol level was within legal limits," Drake admitted.

"Then move on."

Drake gave Jase a quiet look, then returned to his notes. "Did you and your husband argue about the terms of the divorce settlement?"

Jordan waited for Jase's nod, then answered truthfully. "No." They hadn't argued about the settlement, per se, but she knew she was splitting hairs. Dangerously.

"Then what did the two of you take two whole hours to chat about?"

"You're fishing," Jase said. "Do you have any more questions for my client of a substantive nature?"

"Who suggested you meet that evening, Mrs. Marsh? Was your little get-together your idea, or your husband's?"

Jordan tensed, knowing they were now on quicksand. "Ryland had called me earlier in the week, expressing a desire to talk. I suggested that he meet me at the condo after we'd both dealt with the workweek."

"So the rendezvous was your idea."

Jordan frowned at his use of the term "rendezvous," and Jase held up a hand. "Asked and answered, Detective. Ryland Marsh initially suggested the meeting, and my client suggested the location and time."

"Which is odd, don't you think?" Drake asked in a bland tone. "After all, wouldn't it have been more convenient to meet in town, closer to both of your offices? Did you have a reason for luring your husband out to the condo?"

"I didn't lure Ryland anywhere," Jordan answered, increasingly irritated with his innuendos. "If you'll recall from our original conversation, I wasn't at work that day. The paparazzi were being annoyingly persistent because of the civil suit, so having Ryland come out to the condo, where we could talk in privacy, made sense."

"But you suggested the location, didn't you? Had Mr. Marsh wanted the meeting to take place closer to his office?"

"Well, yes, but—"

"And you demanded that he meet you at the condo, which conveniently happens to be located at the end of a very dangerous canyon road—"

"Don't answer that," Jase interrupted, placing his hand on Jordan's shoulder. "Move on, Detective."

Drake glared at Jase, then seemed to pull himself back. "Did you and Mr. Marsh argue that night?" he asked abruptly.

"We weren't on good terms," Jordan replied vaguely. She felt Jase tense beside her.

"So you argued."

Jordan hesitated. "Yes," she said finally.

Drake pounced. "What about?"

She tried to think of a way to answer without revealing the whole truth. "The divorce."

"But that's not exactly true, is it?"

"What are you getting at?" Jase asked.

"What I'm *getting at*, Counselor, is that we have a reliable witness who claims that prior to that evening, Mrs. Marsh knew her husband was hoping for a reconciliation, and that she suggested the meeting to discuss it. That Mr. Marsh drove out to the condo, hoping to reconcile with his wife, who, it now appears, had no intention of doing so. That they argued violently. And further, that she had to have understood that her chances of a substantial divorce settlement were evaporating."

Jordan managed—just barely—not to show her dismay. He knew everything. Who had told him? "There wouldn't have been a huge cash settlement, regardless," she managed calmly as her mind raced. "Ryland had used most of our joint assets to fight the civil suits against him."

"Which means your only hope of benefiting from any kind of financial settlement was to ensure that your husband died, so that you could receive an insurance settlement."

"Don't answer that," Jase said, but Jordan slashed her hand through the air.

"Any assets that still existed were in my trust fund, set up by my maternal grandmother at her death," she said. "I didn't need an insurance payout."

Drake flipped through his notes. "It says here that you purchased a home in Port Chatham recently, is that true? And that you needed a down payment for that home that exceeded the amount you could legally withdraw from the trust fund, correct? So you had planned to use any money you received from the divorce settlement to make that down payment."

"I didn't expect to receive—"

"If so, an insurance death benefit would've come in mighty handy, now, wouldn't it?"

"Don't—" Jase began.

"We also have witnesses who claim to have overheard an extremely heated argument between the two of you that night, just prior to Mr. Marsh storming out of the condo and driving away." Drake leaned across the table, his gaze triumphant. "You had motive and means and opportunity, Mrs. Marsh. I should just arrest your ass right now."

Darcy opened the door to the conference room and came inside, leaning against the wall. Jordan found her presence enormously reassuring, given that she was moments away from hyperventilating.

"This interview is terminated." Jase's tone was arctic.

"Not by a long shot," Drake snapped. "I still have questions for Mrs. Marsh."

"Even if your witnesses are as reliable as you claim," Jase pointed out, "cutting the brake lines on a car is a premeditated act. And my client was inside with the victim at the time the lines would have been cut."

"She could've had an accomplice."

"And the moon could be made of cheese," Jase retorted. "People like Mrs. Marsh don't normally come into contact with killers for hire, as you well know. You can't have it both ways, Detective. Either they argued and Ryland

Marsh left in anger, with my client remaining inside the condo, indicating that she in fact had *no* opportunity to cut the brake lines, or the murder was planned in advance, which would mean that your questions regarding any argument that took place at the condo would have no basis for the crime committed."

"Bullshit, Counselor. She could've planned the whole thing in advance, then used the meeting to goad Marsh into an argument, in an attempt to ensure that he would drive more recklessly. Between the anger and the cut brake lines, the crash would've been a slam dunk."

"Ryland's anger was always cold and controlled," Jordan pointed out. "He *never* drove recklessly, and if he'd been angry, he would've driven even more methodically."

"Perhaps, but his judgment would've been impaired by the booze you insisted he drink, now, wouldn't it?"

"You've got nothing but circumstantial evidence and speculation, Drake." Jase stood, his fingers tightening on Jordan's elbow as he pulled her from her chair. "You have no forensic evidence to tie my client to the crime, and you're basing all your suppositions on eyewitness accounts, which we both know can be flawed. Either arrest my client or let her go."

Jordan felt the blood drain from her head. *Really, really bad way to phrase it.*

Drake shrugged. "Fine with me." He stood and reached behind his back to produce a set of handcuffs. "Given Mrs. Marsh's propensity to flit about the country, I have no guarantee she will stay put in Port Chatham during the investigation. I believe an arrest is warranted at this time."

Jordan's breathing deteriorated to shallow gasps. "Easy," Jase said under his breath.

Darcy stepped forward. "I'll place her under surveillance and guarantee that she remains in my jurisdiction for the duration."

Drake glared at her. "Just whose side are you on, Chief Moran?"

"I'm simply protecting the rights of my citizens, Detective Drake." He started to explode, and Darcy held up a hand. "Your case is circumstantial, Detective. You know as well as I do that Mr. Cunningham will have Mrs. Marsh out on bail ten minutes after your plane touches down in California, and your D.A. will be gunning for you."

"At least she'd be back in *my* jurisdiction."

"Bring me evidence of her fingerprints on the brake lines, or a fingerprint that can be tied to a person who has been in contact with Mrs. Marsh and received some form of payment from her. Better yet, corroborate your witness's account of the events that night. Until then, I will guarantee that Mrs. Marsh won't flee my jurisdiction."

Drake tossed his handcuffs onto the table, then gathered his notes together, his movements jerky. "If she has a passport, I want her to surrender it to you immediately."

"Though your demand typically requires a court order, my client would be more than happy to voluntarily hand over her passport to the Port Chatham police, since she has no reason to flee," Jase inserted smoothly.

Jordan was glad *he* had confidence in her willingness to

stay put—frankly, fleeing was looking damn good to her at the moment.

Drake shoved files into his briefcase, locking it. Straightening, he shot Jordan a look full of loathing. "This isn't over, Mrs. Marsh. I'll be back."

Jordan started breathing again.

*　*　*

DARCY suggested they go to lunch at a Chinese restaurant a block from the police station. The hostess seated them quickly, and a waitress immediately came over to take their order. Jordan wasn't even certain she could eat, and the tension among them was only increasing the acid production in her stomach.

"Of all the monumentally stupid things to do," Darcy began, breaking the silence after the waitress departed, "keeping us in the dark tops the list."

Jordan shook her head. "I come to town, and I find out you already know I'm part of an ongoing investigation. So I say, casually, 'Oh, by the way, Ryland decided he didn't want a divorce after all, and we had a hell of a fight the night he died—'"

"Yeah, you figured we'd think you'd done it—I get that." Darcy rubbed her face. "But dammit, we can't help you if we don't know the facts. Drake blindsided both of us back there."

"I'm sorry."

"Why don't you tell us what really went down that night." Jase's tone was mild.

"All right." She took a deep breath. "Ryland called me Monday night—three nights before the accident. He claimed he wanted to reconcile, that he'd made a huge mistake letting me go." She shook her head. "I was stunned. He'd spent almost a year directing his lawyer to pull every stunt in the book to keep all of our assets in the divorce, and now he wanted me to take him back? I said no way and hung up on him."

"What reason did he give for the reconciliation?" Darcy asked.

"That's just it—he didn't have one, at least not one that made sense. He called right back, begging me to listen and making a big deal out of how much he missed me, how the other women hadn't meant anything, how much he loved me." Jordan rolled her eyes. "Right. I didn't buy that for one minute. But after I calmed down, I thought the kindest thing I could do was to meet with him, hear him out, and try to find a way to let him down gently."

Darcy gave her a look of disbelief.

"I know, I know. But I was married to him for seven years—I figured I owed him the chance to explain himself. Besides, I'd already committed to the house up here, and I didn't want the divorce to drag out. Yes, I could've handled the down payment out of the small inheritance from my grandmother and some outstanding receivables from my therapy practice, but it would've required me to cash out long-term investments on short notice. The settlement from the divorce—a small amount from the sale of the condo—was sufficient and simply more convenient. So I called Ryland and asked him to meet me at the condo Thursday evening after work. My plan was to *minimize* the conflict between us, not goad him into a heated argument."

"Why meet him at the condo?" Jase asked.

"You mean, did I lure him out there with the intent of murdering him?"

He gave her a chiding look. "Drake was right to ask—the condo was much farther away for both of you than some bar or restaurant closer to town, right?"

"But much less public," Jordan pointed out. "And believe me, the paparazzi had taken every opportunity to follow us around. The last thing I wanted was to be the subject of another front-page article claiming that the divorce settlement was in contention again. We'd just managed in recent weeks to make it *off* the front page."

"What happened after Ryland got there?" Darcy asked.

"We fought, and he got very angry." She frowned. "In fact, I'd never seen him that way before—almost desperate to convince me we should be together. I put it down to his possibly running out of money, because of the civil suits that had been adjudicated against him. The damages from those suits would've set him back years, and it was questionable whether he could ever get his license to practice reinstated."

"So if anything, Ryland was the one who needed *your* assets," Darcy concluded. "Did he know about the inheritance from your granny?"

Jordan nodded. "Probate was finalized while we were

married. But the account was always in my name only—the probate lawyer said Grandmother's will stipulated that the money was mine and mine alone."

"Sounds like Granny knew what kind of man you'd married," Darcy observed.

"Long before I did, it seems." Jordan sighed. "That's it—we argued, Ryland pleaded with me, I refused, he got angrier, I asked him to leave, and he stormed out." She looked at both of them. "I have no idea *how* to cut the brake lines on a car—I don't even know where to look for them. And I didn't have anyone else do it for me."

"I can certainly vouch for your lack of DIY experience," Jase said, relenting enough to smile a little. "It's difficult to envision how you could tamper with the brakes when you don't know one tool from another. The D.A. will argue, though, that such things are easily researched. And Drake is convinced you did it."

"That much is obvious."

The waitress returned with their food, and they let the subject drop while they filled their plates. Jordan discovered that she was ravenous, but when she tried to use her chopsticks, she found her hands were shaking too badly to make them work.

Jase was watching her carefully. "Are you all right?"

"No, I'm not—I'm mad." She realized it was true. She was angry at a system that allowed such flawed investigations, and angry with Drake for focusing exclusively on her. She looked at Darcy. "Drake's not interested in finding out who really did this, is he?"

Darcy speared a pot sticker. "Nope. He's got you in his sights, and he's got witness statements that evidently corroborate his assumptions." She chewed for a moment. "God knows I'm a suspicious soul, but if I didn't know better, I'd think someone was setting you up."

Jordan's chopsticks wobbled, the food falling back to her plate. Darcy was right—it was possible someone was feeding the police information in an effort to keep Drake focused on her.

"The question is, who?" Darcy mused.

Jordan shook her head. "The only person who comes to mind as a remote possibility is Didi Wyeth. Maybe she thinks I did it, and she wants revenge."

"She could've followed Ryland to your condo, witnessed the argument, and decided to take advantage of the situation," Jase said. "How angry was she when Ryland broke up with her?"

Jordan shrugged. "Carol mentioned that the gossip columnists had plastered pictures of their breakup all over the tabloids, speculating that Didi was washed up as an actress. If her career was harmed by the press coverage, I suppose that's a motive."

"Or, in the spirit of keeping her motive simple," Darcy countered, "she could've just been really pissed off at the son of a bitch for dumping her and wanted him dead. Your argument presented the perfect opportunity, and she took it. Then you come along, telling Drake to talk to her and find out whether she had an alibi, and she uses that opportunity to redirect Drake's attention right back to you."

And if not Didi, Jordan had to wonder how many other women were floating around out there with similar levels of anger.

As always, Darcy seemed to be on the same wavelength. "Who in your opinion are the most likely suspects in Ryland's murder?"

"Besides Didi? Anyone Ryland diddled who failed to win a judgment against him."

"Names?"

"Marcy Brentworth—she comes from old Hollywood producer money. Alice Langston, another actress." Jordan thought about it, then shook her head. "Those are the only two I can come up with off the top of my head, but if we look at the civil suits, we'll come up with at least a dozen names."

"Any of them stand out as being particularly strident or furious during the trial?"

"I don't know. I wasn't in court, and I avoided reading the press coverage. My goal was to stay as far away from that circus as possible." She turned to Jase. "Do you know any good private investigators in L.A.?"

He raised an eyebrow, then nodded. "Yeah, someone I used in the old days. He's thorough, and he's also one of the good guys."

"Give him a call." She pulled out a piece of paper and started writing down names. "While Drake is indulging his personal prejudices against me, a killer is walking around loose. And I want him found." She handed Jase the paper. "I'll hire your guy to look into the whereabouts and alibis of these people. That should be a start."

Jase read the names on the slip of paper, then added Drake's. "When a homicide detective in a case holds a personal grudge, I want to know why," he said by way of explanation when he saw her questioning look. "It could come in handy if we ever have to go to trial."

Jordan reflected on it, then nodded. "Go for it."

"No more Ms. Nice Guy, huh?" Darcy asked.

"No more Ms. Nice Guy, no more Ms. Gullible. Someone killed Ryland, and though he had many faults, he didn't deserve it. The least I can do is find his murderer. Then maybe I can put this behind me."

"As long as you're being proactive, I don't much care why," Darcy said, "though I'd rather you were doing this for yourself, not Ryland."

"I am, believe me."

* * *

DARCY left them outside the restaurant with the explanation that she had paperwork to catch up on. Jordan walked with Jase a half block to the wharf on the waterfront. She stood leaning against the railing, watching wisps of fog float on the waters of the bay. A refurbished nineteenth-century clipper ship was tied to the end of the wharf, and Jordan took a moment to study its intricate rigging and graceful lines.

"They use it to take tourists out at sunset during the warmer months," Jase explained, following her gaze. "Port Chatham has its own Wooden Boat Society, dedicated to keeping alive the art of building wood-hulled boats and refurbishing the historic ships."

She knew he was giving her time to say whatever was on her mind. "I'm sorry," she said again.

Jase nodded, then said in an even tone, "I'll cut you slack on this one. But for the record, if you continue to keep me in the dark, I'll *encourage* the prosecutor to toss you in jail. If I'm to defend you to the best of my ability, I need to know everything."

"I didn't want you to think badly of me," she admitted.

He gave her a chiding look, but his tone remained businesslike. "I'll call JT and get him started on the investigation."

"Do you think he'll have time in his schedule?"

"He'll have to make time. I doubt Drake is going to wait long before he returns to town, this time armed with an arrest warrant."

Chapter 13

JORDAN swung by the vet's office on her way back to the house, arriving hours later than she'd promised the dog and feeling more guilt than she'd ever felt over the failure of her marriage. At the sound of her voice, the dog started howling from the back area.

The receptionist grinned. "He's been despondent since you dropped him off yesterday. I think you just reaffirmed his faith in human beings." She told the technician who was sitting beside her to bring him out. "You didn't give us his name though. We need it for our records."

Jordan felt her face heat. "We haven't agreed on one yet."

The receptionist didn't seem to find her comment the least bit odd. "Then we'll use your name for now. But call us when you decide so we can properly file his records."

Jordan handed her a credit card to pay the bill, then quickly braced as the dog exploded through the door from the kennel area, dragging two people in his wake. He ran straight at her, planting his paws on her shoulders.

Jordan staggered under the impact, laughing and letting him lick her face and neck.

"Aren't you gorgeous!" She hugged him, stunned by the change in his appearance.

The vet, a trim woman in her midforties and attractive in a natural, farm-girl sort of way, helped pull him off Jordan. "I'm so sorry—he's a little hard to control once he gets an idea in his head. You didn't leave a leash—"

"He doesn't like them," Jordan explained. "Any health problems?"

"None that we found." The vet rubbed his head. "He's around four years old and in good health, other than being underweight. We brought him current on his shots, so he may sleep a little more than usual today. I've prepared a list of foods and supplements you'll want to consider, to bring his weight back to normal and boost his immune system."

Jordan signed the credit card receipt, then leaned down to give him another hug. "I can't believe how handsome he is, now that he's clean."

"He's a mix of Great Pyrenees, Saint Bernard, and German shepherd, all smart breeds. He's very gentle and intelligent, and—we seem to have established—loyal."

"I'd already figured out the intelligent part," Jordan said wryly. "So you have no idea who owned him before me?"

"Nope." The vet smiled. "And it doesn't really matter, does it? He's chosen the person he wants to be with."

* * *

AFTER loading the dog plus all the food and supplements she'd purchased into the Prius, she drove to the house. The men were gone, along with the detritus from the wisteria. Though Amanda's tent was still in the backyard, she was nowhere to be found. Tom had left notes taped to a kitchen cupboard indicating he'd get back to her within a couple of days with the remodeling plan.

When Jordan stuck her head into the library, she found Hattie and Charlotte still mysteriously absent, which had her wondering whether they were occasionally called back to wherever ghosts came from, for some kind of confab with their superiors. Surely there was some sort of society, complete with its own laws that ruled the spectral realm. It made sense, didn't it?

Feeling antsy and unable to settle, she headed for the kitchen to retrieve her portable CD player. She'd take advantage of the ghosts' absence while keeping her mind off the meeting with Drake by putting some work into those stacks of books in the library. Restoring a sense of order to the room would make her feel as if she'd accomplished something productive for the day.

She put one of Ted's CDs in and set the player atop the stacks of newspapers on the corner of the old oak desk. With the trio playing in the background, she started sorting through piles of books. The dog collapsed on the floor, stretching out to sleep with a grateful sigh.

Ancient, leather-bound volumes of classics had been heaped together with modern fiction—everything from *The Complete Works of Henry James* to Vonnegut and Grisham. Alphabetizing the collection, which had to number in the thousands, was out of the question, though she actually considered it for a brief, insane moment. The thought of establishing that level of control over even a small corner of her life held great appeal. In the end, she settled for sorting out the worst of the moldy volumes to be taken to a used-book dealer for assessment, then dusting and stacking the others in the bookcases.

At dinnertime, having organized one entire wall, she knocked off for the day. She was about to wake up the dog when she spied a stack of small, thin volumes that she'd set aside while filling the last bookcase. They didn't look like published books. Curious, she picked one up and flipped through it. They were diaries—more of Hattie's, by the look of the writing. She picked them up and headed upstairs to add them to the growing pile of reading materials next to her bed.

Fifteen minutes later, she and the dog were on their way to the pub. Though clouds were building to the southwest, she decided they could both use the walk to stretch their legs. If they were caught in the rain on the way home, it was only a few blocks—they wouldn't melt.

As they walked, Jordan realized she was feeling more confident, and less panicked, now that she'd decided to hire a private investigator. Despite the nerve-wracking interview with Drake, and despite knowing he had every intention of arresting her for Ryland's murder, she felt, well, *good*. Charged up. Ready to take on the world.

She shoved both hands into her jeans pockets, frowning. Over the last year, she'd become far more insular than she'd been at any other point in her life. She'd always been a planner, but she'd never been one to avoid problems. Her MO was to analyze, consider alternative strategies, then take action. Since when had she become so passive, so willing to rely on others to come up with solutions?

Because of the public nature of Ryland's legal problems and their divorce, she realized, she'd gotten in the habit of lying low to avoid the press, and of waiting for others to take action. But in the case of Ryland's murder, she now saw she'd been far too trusting, assuming the cops would find the real murderer.

Well, no more of that, she decided as they reached All That Jazz. Deciding to launch her own investigation, albeit from afar, was a step in the right direction. Hopefully, she thought as she and the dog entered the pub, Jase would tell her this evening that the private investigator was already on the case, working to develop viable suspects.

"Well, aren't you just the handsome guy." Darcy reached out to run a hand down the dog's back as Jordan followed him over to her table. "He cleans up good."

Jordan took a seat. "According to the vet, he sailed through his homeless phase with no health problems. Good genes, evidently. He'll probably become even more insufferable, now that he knows."

"What makes you think he hasn't known all along?"

"Valid point." She pulled her passport out of her jacket pocket and held it out. After a brief tug of war that had Darcy raising one eyebrow, she forced herself to let go.

She glanced around—the pub was already filling up,

some people standing around and chatting, others ordering drinks or food. Jordan was once again impressed that Jase felt laid back enough about the business to allow folks to drop in simply to enjoy the music. Most tavern owners would have required people to pay a cover charge and purchase at least one drink.

"Is Ted scheduled to play again this evening?"

"Yeah, I think so," Darcy replied. "He came in earlier with his band members and Didi Wyeth."

"Good." Jordan had questions for Didi. She wanted to know whether the actress was the "witness" who had told Drake about Ryland's attempts to reconcile. Didi would've known, because according to what Ryland had told Jordan the night he died, he'd used his desire to patch up his marriage as the reason to break off the affair with Didi.

Kathleen stopped on her way past the table, raising her eyebrows at Jordan in an unspoken question.

"Yes," she said hastily.

Jase brought her a glass of red wine. "It's an old-vine Zinfandel I'd like to start carrying. Let me know what you think."

His manner was once again friendly, and Jordan was able to relax a bit. In truth, she was grateful for his help, but she still didn't know how she felt about his past. What she knew for certain, though, was that a slight distance had been created between them, and she regretted it.

She held the wineglass up to breathe in its bouquet, then sipped. Her eyes drifted closed.

"I take it that's a solid yes vote," Jase said.

She nodded. She took another sip, savoring, then asked, "Did you get ahold of the private investigator?"

He gave the room an assessing glance, evidently deciding he had a few minutes to relax, and pulled up a chair. "JT's already digging up information. He should have something by tomorrow."

"That's fast." Jordan was surprised.

"He owed me."

"Ah. Thanks for calling in favors. As soon as he has any information to report back, I'd like to set up a conference call with him."

Jase nodded. "I'll arrange it."

Kathleen arrived with plates of food—tonight's selection was grilled salmon, steamed local asparagus, and rice pilaf. She'd included a plate of home-baked treats for the dog.

"They probably don't serve food like this in the California State Penitentiary System, huh?" Jordan asked as she put the dog's plate on the floor.

"You're not going to jail," Jase and Darcy said simultaneously, glowering at her.

"No, I'm not," Jordan said calmly. "Geez. Lighten up— it was a joke."

Jase's expression remained tense, and Darcy gave her a halfhearted smile.

Bad sign. Jordan swallowed nervously. "But maybe I should take my passport back, just in case."

"Maybe," Jase acknowledged, earning a glare from Darcy.

Jordan sighed and dug into her food. "Look, the PI will find something Drake overlooked, or I'll dig up information on my own." When they didn't look reassured, she decided a change of subject was in order. "So how about I bring you up-to-date on what I've learned about Hattie's murder?"

"Right, good," Darcy said, looking relieved.

Jase took that as his cue to excuse himself to help out behind the bar.

While they ate, Jordan told Darcy about the attack on Frank, and Hattie's coming to the conclusion that Clive Johnson was behind it, then about how Michael Seavey had thwarted Hattie's attempt to fire Johnson. "The two were definitely in cahoots, but I still think Seavey was torn between his growing feelings for her and her jeopardizing his business with Longren Shipping. And I think part of his motivation for offering her his protection was that he was truly worried for her safety."

"That's plausible." Darcy forked up a bite of salmon. "So now we know how Frank ended up in Hattie's home around the time of the murder?"

"Yeah. And Greeley's reaction was over the top, don't you think? Why wouldn't he have investigated the attack on Frank, as Hattie asked?"

"Actually, I can see his point. It doesn't make sense to file an incident report based on third-party information." Darcy hesitated. "Not that they probably had incident reports back then, but still. He would've needed to see and/or talk to Frank, and Hattie was denying him access."

"But given her suspicion that the police might be corrupt, it made sense to withhold Frank's location. Especially since Greeley had made it clear he thought Frank had the beating coming to him."

"Yeah, you've got a point." Darcy chewed, her expression pensive. "You gotta wonder what else was driving Greeley."

"And why he never considered Clive Johnson a suspect in Hattie's murder," Jordan added. "From everything I'm learning, Johnson had the strongest motive by far to get rid of Hattie. And yet, Greeley never even mentions him in his memoir." Jordan shook her head. "No offense, and present company excluded, of course, but I'm dealing with a few too many cops right now who don't seem interested in approaching their jobs in a fair and impartial manner."

Darcy shrugged. "Cops are human, and they lead very stressful lives. They don't always do a good job of separating the personal from the public." Her expression was worried. "But yeah, I'm concerned about Drake. More than once, I watched detectives on the Minneapolis force be influenced by their personal baggage—the divorce they were going through, the child who'd just entered drug rehab—and watched how those problems drove them to inaccurate conclusions on their open cases."

Jordan reached down to rub the dog's stomach. "Well, I have to believe Jase's buddy will come up with something we can use. Otherwise, I'll go mad." She glanced in the direction of the stage, spying Ted and Didi. "Then again," she muttered, shoving back her chair, "maybe *I* can come up with something. Be right back."

She intercepted Jase halfway across the room, commandeering a tray of drinks he had intended to deliver to the band.

"Jordan," Ted greeted her, his expression lighting up. "How did the meeting go this morning? Everything okay?"

"Just fine," she lied, handing out the drinks to the band members. "In fact, that's one of the reasons I came over to chat." She turned to the actress, holding out her martini. "I'd like to ask you a few questions, if you don't mind, Didi."

Didi was sitting in a chair just off the edge of the stage. Tonight's outfit consisted of tight leather pants, a bustier, and knee-high black boots. She looked like she planned to visit a BDSM club later on, though Jordan doubted Port Chatham had one.

Eying Jordan with distaste, Didi said, "Why would I talk to you? You murdered the man I loved."

"Because I *didn't* murder him," Jordan replied evenly, "and because you want his real murderer found just as badly as I do."

Didi shrugged. "Ryland told me about the insurance policy you took out, you know. I figure you just never expected the cops to find those cut brake lines."

Jordan tamped down her irritation. "Did Detective Drake interview you about your relationship with Ryland?"

"Sure. I told him Ryland and I were in love, that he was only trying to reconcile with you long enough to get his hands on your granny's inheritance." Didi paused to light an imported cigarette, blowing the smoke in Jordan's face. "He wouldn't have stayed with you."

"I wasn't interested in him staying with me," Jordan said automatically, then realized Didi's version of Ryland's reasons for the reconciliation made as much sense as any she'd been able to come up with. "So you're the one who told Drake about Ryland wanting to patch up the marriage."

"Yeah. I figured anything I could say that got him looking in your direction was good. I knew you'd done it, and I wanted to make damn sure you didn't get away with it." Jordan started to protest, but Didi added, oblivious, "Drake also wanted to know where I was that night, and unlike you, I have an airtight alibi."

"And it is?"

"Not that it's any of your business, but I was at a party in Beverly Hills, hosted by the producer of the next film I'm starring in."

Jordan shot a curious glance at Ted, but he had his back turned to them, talking to his band members. He'd indicated to Jordan just yesterday that Didi was on vacation. "I thought you were taking some time off from your career?"

"You can't believe everything you read in the newspapers, darling."

Jordan thought she detected a hint of anger behind Didi's reply. So Ted had been at least partially correct—the press had had a field day with the news of Didi and Ryland's breakup.

The actress flicked ash on the floor, her expression

bored. "Look, why don't you just confess and be done with it? We all know you resented the fact that Ryland cheated on you. That the only reason you'd been so accommodating during the divorce was because you thought you were going to take him to the cleaners. I'll bet you got the shock of your life when you realized the lawsuits would eat up that nice settlement you'd been fantasizing about."

"If I didn't know better, I'd think you were attributing the kind of motives *you* would have to my actions." Jordan kept her tone mild.

"I *loved* Ryland," Didi shot back. "I would *never* have done anything to hurt him."

"Oh, for..." Jordan gave up, letting her irritation rule. "Get a clue. The man you fell in love with screwed his way through half his patient list! You've got serious self-esteem issues if you think he could've *ever* been any good for you."

"How could you possibly understand anything about me? You killed your husband because he cheated on you!"

Ted turned to look at them, his expression alarmed.

"I'm a therapist—I see women like you all the time," Jordan retorted. "You can't sustain a loving relationship because you've never worked through your childhood abandonment issues. Trust me, I get that. But *self-regulation* does *not* translate to dating every father figure you happen to cross paths with."

"Well, you would know, now, wouldn't you?" Didi taunted. "You were married to the man for seven years! If anyone had daddy issues, it's you!"

"*Excuse* me?"

"Jordan, calm down," Ted said, looking shocked. "You're embarrassing yourself."

"I've had a particularly trying day," Jordan snapped. "And I'm losing patience with needy, dysfunctional people who think they can mess with my life by feeding false information to the police!"

"Whoa," Ted's bass player murmured, looking up from applying rosin to his bow. "Catfight!"

Didi screeched and lunged for her.

Jase wrapped an arm around Jordan's waist and pulled her behind him, removing her from the reach of Didi's manicured claws. "Get your girlfriend under control," he told Ted, fending her off, "or I'm throwing her out."

"She's not my girlfriend," Ted said, and Didi howled. He grabbed both her arms. "Be quiet!"

"*Get counseling!*" Jordan shouted over Jase's shoulder, blocked from moving any closer.

"You'd be the *last* therapist I'd call, you murderous bitch!"

Jase planted his hands on Jordan's shoulders, turning her toward Darcy's table and pushing her across the room. "I've got JT verifying her alibi," he said in a tone only Jordan could hear. "If she's lying, he'll figure it out."

"Oh, she's lying all right," Jordan growled, dragging her feet. "I'm *trained* to know when someone is lying."

"I'm sure you are. You might want to dial back on the 'proactive' just a bit, though," he advised, a thread of laughter running through his voice.

Angling a glance up at him, she saw that he was grinning. *Great.*

She dropped into her chair, her cheeks heating as she realized the scene she'd caused. "I can't believe I did that." What was the *matter* with her? She'd *never* used her training in such an inappropriate and damaging way. Yes, she cared that Ryland's murderer was found, but still...

"You did have ample provocation," Darcy pointed out, then grinned as well. "And though you are so terminally *nice* it makes my teeth hurt, the entertainment factor is way up there. Listening to the trio this evening will be anticlimactic."

"Cute." Jordan ventured a glance around the room, noting the number of covert stares aimed her way. "And I'm *not* nice, I'm tough as nails."

"Right."

"Oh, shut up." She concentrated on her breathing.

Jase set another full glass of wine before her, then gave her a quick shoulder rub. "Drink up. In a little bit, you won't feel a thing."

"That would be good." She took a large gulp. "I'm so sorry—I didn't expect it to get that out of hand."

Jase looked amused. "No problem. The pub is getting quite the reputation. Business is bound to pick up."

"Ha-ha, funny." But she noted that during her talk with Didi, the room had become twice as crowded. "Though I like the way you let folks simply hang out, that you don't force them to buy drinks to be here," she added.

He exchanged a confused look with Darcy. "Come again?"

"All the people who've been coming to the jazz performances and just hanging out."

322 · P. J. ALDERMAN

They glanced at each other again, then Jase shook his head, clearly not understanding her.

"All the people standing around by the entrance? At the bar?" She wondered whether the two of them were particularly oblivious this evening.

"There aren't any people standing by the entrance," Darcy said, her expression becoming intrigued. "Exactly what do you see?"

Jordan felt a chill. "Oh, no." She shook her head. "No, no, no. Do *not* pull that crap on me—I've had a bad day."

"What do you think you see?" Jase repeated.

She turned toward the entrance, counting the patrons that stood there. "A couple dozen people, mostly men in work clothes, crowded just inside the door." She'd had a fleeting impression that their clothes were a little odd, but her mind slid away from that fact. "Right?" she asked a little desperately.

Darcy grinned. "Hey, Tom!" she shouted, waving him over, and Jordan watched him walk right through several "people" standing next to the bar.

She closed her eyes and laid her head down on the table.

Jase rubbed her back with one hand. "It'll be all right," he said, chuckling. "To tell you the truth, I've always wondered whether there were any ghosts hanging around in here. It's an old building."

"There are ghosts in here?" Tom turned in a circle, scanning the room.

Jordan thudded her head against the hard surface of the table.

It all began to sink in—the little girl with the antique doll, the elderly couple in the porch swing, the young man on the old-fashioned bicycle. The woman in the *cape* leaving the grocery that first night. Half the *people* she'd seen in the damn town!

Darcy was having a look around herself. "So what are they doing?"

Jordan quickly glanced up, then laid her head back down. The table's cool surface was such a comfort. "Hanging out, talking to each other? Listening to the music? I don't know."

"I wonder if they like my selection of bands," Jase said.

"What do you suppose they want?" Tom asked her.

"How the hell should I know? You want me to go take a poll? First, I'd have to poke each one with a finger, just to make sure I'm talking to a ghost, which could be a bit embarrassing to explain to the humans I accidently poke . . ." Her voice trailed off as she realized the import of what she was saying. "Oh, God—I can't tell the difference," she wailed, mortified. "They're *everywhere*, and they all look just like real people to me."

"Is that really a problem?" Jase asked, and she gave him a dirty look.

"An entire community of ghosts, huh?" Darcy said. "*Seriously* cool. Maybe you can help me figure out what I need to do, to be receptive enough to see them."

"I think either you can see them, or you can't," Tom said. "It's not like you can develop powers you don't have."

"Why the hell not?" Darcy asked.

Jordan's head shot up as a new thought occurred to her. "Oh, *oh.*"

She jumped up, scanning the crowd until she found the man from two nights ago who'd never paid for his drink. He held her gaze for a fraction of a second, then turned and slipped through the crowd.

Dammit! He was getting away. She hurriedly nudged the dog awake with her foot.

"Whoa, hold on." Jase took hold of her arm. "Where're you going?"

"There's someone I need to check out." She folded the rope for the dog.

"*Wait* a minute—with all that's been happening, you're not chasing after someone on your own."

"No, really, I'm okay," she assured him. "I don't think I'm in any danger."

"Dammit—"

"I'll explain later." She was already out the door, jogging toward home.

* * *

She followed the stranger, keeping a half block between them. Though she was fairly certain he knew she was there, he didn't stop or look back, instead disappearing around the corner. As she and the dog turned onto her street, she spied him standing next to a streetlight across from her house.

The dog planted all four paws, the hair on his back raised, and growled low in his throat. She halted, barely avoiding somersaulting over him. Putting a hand on his neck, she murmured, "Go up on the porch, boy. I'll be okay."

He cast a distrustful glance toward the man, then reluctantly did as she asked. Sitting on the top step, he kept watch as she jogged across the street.

The man straightened as she approached, his expression becoming resigned. She had a fleeting moment to wonder whether she was out of her mind, walking up to a stranger on a deserted street, and that thought had her stopping a safe distance from him. She shoved her hands into her pockets and met his hard gaze.

"You're Frank Lewis, aren't you?" she accused.

Chapter 14

THE ghost gave her a blatant once-over that had her wondering whether even after crossing over...well, to wherever ghosts cross over to, men continued to be plagued by a preoccupation with women and sex. She carefully returned his perusal.

Actually, now that she could see him rather than relying on Hattie's written description of him, she could understand the attraction. Attitude radiated from him in waves, and in a rough-hewn, antiquated sort of way, she figured he pretty much personified "bad-boy hunk" for the nineteenth century.

The fact that his clothing was a century out of style and hung loosely on his hard, angular frame did little to lessen his impact. And though Jase held far more appeal for her, she wasn't completely immune.

She brought herself up short. Okay, she hadn't just compared the sex appeal of a ghost to that of a real man, right?

"Does Hattie know you're here?" she asked.

He shook his head, settling himself more comfortably and shoving his hands into the pockets of his baggy work pants. "You're not to tell her, either."

Jordan crossed her arms. "You know, that would've gone over a whole lot better as a request. Just in case you need tutoring in twenty-first-century customs vis-à-vis the gender wars."

His expression turned wary. "Pardon?"

"Never mind."

Glancing around the darkened neighborhood, she wondered whether any neighbors were watching. If so, they would think she was standing on the street conversing with a light pole. It was a safe bet she wasn't enhancing her reputation. Then again, given the most recent rumors that were bound to be flying around, talking to a light pole might be considered a minor infraction.

"So why are you here?" she asked.

"To keep an eye on your investigation." One corner of his mouth lifted in a slight smile. "You could say I have an uncommon interest in your findings."

She eyed him suspiciously. Either she'd had too much to drink, or he'd just made a spectral pun. "Have you been following me since I arrived in town?"

He snorted. "If I had been, you wouldn't have known I was there. We can be present without revealing ourselves."

"So why reveal yourself at all?"

"Because I thought it was time to impress upon you the importance of finding Hattie's murderer. From what I've seen so far, you're rather inept."

She gaped at him. Not only was she delusional, her imaginary friends were now criticizing her performance. This had to represent a new low in methods of self-recrimination. "Did *you* kill Hattie?"

"Of course not." His tone was chiding, as if he thought she was dull-witted.

"You were in the house that night, which makes you the most likely suspect," she pointed out stubbornly. "You had opportunity."

"How ironic. Aren't you currently criticizing the police detective on *your* case for thinking you're the most likely suspect in your husband's murder, simply because you were there when he was murdered?"

She could've argued that *she* wasn't the one with the reputation for violence, but he had a point. Still, his people skills definitely could use some improvement. "You claimed you were drugged. How?"

His brow furrowed. "I don't know," he said finally. "At first I thought it was possible Hattie had slipped laudanum into my tea. We'd argued about my refusal to take the drug—I was concerned with remaining alert, but she didn't like to see me suffering. But I brewed my tea after she retired upstairs for the evening, so I had to rule out that possibility. I did add brandy to my tea, though. I doubt I would've tasted the laudanum, had it been added to the decanter."

"And the physician left the laudanum in the house when he'd examined you after your attack."

"Yes."

"Clive Johnson ordered the attack on you, didn't he?"

"I never knew for certain. Two of the men who attacked me were employed by Johnson, but the other two worked for Seavey. Hattie believed Johnson had ordered it, though."

Jordan frowned. "So who do *you* think killed Hattie?"

"That's what you're supposed to find out, isn't it? With all that expertise you have digging around inside people's heads?"

"You must've had your suspicions."

"Seavey was the perfect suspect—he was in love with Hattie, and he had a reputation for destroying what he couldn't have. He also wanted the union neutralized, so framing me for her murder would have been an efficient solution." Frank's mouth twisted. "He looked quite pleased at my hanging."

Jordan couldn't quite wrap her mind around experiencing one's own hanging and then "living" to tell about it. But in the face of Frank's suspicions of Seavey, she had to wonder once again whether she was letting her weakness for charming psychopaths color her impressions. After all, there was no question Seavey hadn't been a good man. So why didn't she believe he'd killed Hattie? "I've been bothered by the fact that John Greeley didn't pursue any other suspects."

Frank lifted one shoulder in a shrug. "Don't forget, Greeley hated Hattie. He blamed her for Charlotte's ruination. Had it not been considered a society murder, he might not have investigated at all."

"Clive Johnson had good reason to kill Hattie, not

to mention frame you for the murder. That's pretty damning."

Frank shook his head. "Not from Greeley's perspective. I mentioned Johnson, of course, but Greeley held him in high esteem—I doubt he would've investigated him." Frank rubbed his jaw. "Seavey came to see me one night after the trial. I told him I was innocent and that I believed Johnson had committed the murder."

"What did he say to that?" Jordan asked, curious.

"Nothing. He just nodded and left."

The dog approached, growling. She put out a hand to bring him to her side, shushing him.

"What's his name?" Frank asked.

"You know, I'm getting tired of people asking me that." He smiled slightly. "Try Malachi."

"Why?"

"I had a friend, an Irishman and a ship's carpenter, who was shanghaied out of New York City on the same boat I was on. He completed a lot of the work on your house for Charles Longren. He had this dog, Malachi, who looked a lot like your fellow."

"I'll think about it," she said.

Frank nodded, straightening. "Are you going to solve Hattie's murder or not?"

Jordan's exasperation returned. "Do you have any suggestions as to how I might do that?"

"Hattie wrote about everything up to her murder. Also, read Greeley's personal papers. If he wrote in a daily journal, he might've let something slip. Or he might've regretted his actions after the fact." Frank stared at Jordan, his expression brooding. "It's important that Hattie find some peace. I couldn't give it to her when she was alive."

Jordan softened a bit. "Look, why don't you come inside with me? I suspect seeing you would go a long way toward making her happy."

He shook his head, and for the first time, Jordan saw the pain and sorrow in his eyes. "I didn't stop her murderer—I don't deserve to see her."

* * *

JORDAN'S cellphone buzzed as she and the dog walked up the front porch steps. She pulled it out of her pocket to check the caller ID. Carol.

"You left me *hanging*," Carol complained the minute she answered. "How did the interview go with Drake?"

"About like you'd expect," she answered as she walked down the hall to the kitchen in search of a drink of water.

She skidded to a halt. Hattie and Charlotte sat at the kitchen table, smiling. "Where have you been?" she asked them.

"At work, where else?" Carol said. "Why?"

"Not you, the ghosts."

"At the telekinesis seminar," Hattie replied. "We thought we'd give you some time to calm down after discovering the inspection report."

"And it gave us an opportunity to practice our skills," Charlotte added, beaming.

Frightening thought.

"You mean, you don't just see the ghosts, you talk to them like regular human beings?" Carol asked.

"It's a little difficult to tell them apart," Jordan muttered.

"Ah." Hattie nodded, looking pleased. "So you're now noticing the rest of our community. Excellent."

"We've been staying away from the tavern," Charlotte explained. "We didn't want you to think we were harassing you."

"Perish the thought." Jordan headed for the sink, opening the cupboard door directly above.

"Interesting one-sided conversation," Carol observed.

"Self-destructive and delusional," Jordan corrected. She reached for a glass, only to find that they weren't where she'd put them—the cupboard was full of cleaning supplies.

She frowned. She could've sworn she'd put them there yesterday afternoon...She opened the cupboard to the right, where she'd put the dinner plates, and found cereal.

"What are you trying to find?" Charlotte asked, looking helpful.

"Glasses. I know I put them in here."

"We moved the crystal, china, and cutlery into the butler's pantry, where they belong."

"*You rearranged my kitchen?*"

"They did?" Carol asked, laughing. "Fantastic."

"A well-organized home is the foundation—" Charlotte began.

Jordan turned on her heel and stalked out of the kitchen, heading upstairs. "You've *got* to take pity on me and at least prescribe some nice tranquilizers," she said to Carol.

"I'm far more worried about what Drake's up to."

"He wanted to arrest me, but Darcy and Jase talked him out of it." Jordan used the glass she'd brought up to the hall bath the evening before to gulp down some water, then summarized the meeting for Carol.

"I'm definitely taking the next flight up there." Carol sounded worried. "You need me."

"What can you do, other than sit around and wring your hands? I asked Jase to hire a PI, and as we speak, he's busy investigating, trying to crack people's alibis and find out who fed the police information. Really, all we can do is wait and see what he digs up."

"So Jase took your case? *Good.* I Googled him—he used to be hell on wheels."

He still is.

Jordan blocked that thought and headed for the bedroom, but she was halted at the doorway by the dog, who was sniffing the air and growling. She glanced inside. Nothing seemed out of place.

Shrugging, she walked around the dog while she described her interactions with Didi Wyeth to Carol. "What's your off-the-cuff profile? Is she capable of murder?"

There was a moment of silence while Carol thought. "Well, of course, I'd need to interview her to be certain, but yeah, I think she'd probably be willing to skewer anyone who messed with her career. And you said her breakup with Ryland was picked up by the gossip columnists, right?"

"Yes, but what's the saying—'Any publicity is good publicity'? So why would having the sordid details of their breakup splashed across the front page of *The Hollywood Reporter* harm her career?"

"Sweetie, she jumped into bed with L.A.'s most notorious psychiatrist, who was in the middle of being sued for sexual harassment by his client. That doesn't exactly make her look stable. And whereas the general consensus was that you deserved sympathy, given Ryland's slimy morals, I'm sure most folks thought Didi had a screw loose. If I were a film producer with two hundred million of my investors' cash at stake and a bonding company to keep happy, I'd think twice about casting her."

Jordan sighed. "You may be right, but she has an alibi."

"Wait and see what the PI turns up—I'll bet she's lying. My money is on her infamous temper."

"Well, I can vouch for the temper," Jordan said wryly.

"You sure I can't visit for a few days and at least provide moral support?"

Jordan thought about the wisteria and the gritty film that had settled over everything. Definitely *not* Carol's preferred milieu.

"I've got two words for you," she replied. "*Plaster dust.*"

"I just became the least supportive best friend you've ever had."

"I thought you'd see it that way." She flipped the phone shut, setting it on the nightstand next to her bed.

Given the revelations of the day, she felt eerily calm. Of

course, there was probably only so much stress her nervous system could take before it completely shut down its fight-or-flight response. Maybe she was a walking zombie at this point. So the possibility loomed that she might hang just like Frank Lewis, for a crime she didn't commit. So what? So there were a few extra ghosts populating her reality. Not a problem.

She changed into sweats. Glancing out the bay window, she noted that Frank hadn't stirred from his post across the street. Their gazes locked for one long moment, and he inclined his head. She closed the fragile lace sheers, ridiculously reassured that he was standing watch for the night.

Climbing into bed, she turned on a lamp and started thumbing through the stack of memoirs and diaries on her nightstand. She'd already read Greeley's diary and hadn't found anything of note, but she still had those volumes of Hattie's diary she'd found earlier to finish. Pulling them from the stack, she settled back against the pillows.

Maybe before she landed on death row, she could clear another suspect's name.

The Abduction

MORE than two days had passed, and Frank hadn't regained consciousness. The increasing fear that he wouldn't awaken at all had Hattie's nerves stretched as thin as the thread the girls were using to sew Charlotte's new gown. Sleepless nights were taking an additional toll.

Hattie sat in the chair beside the bed in the waning afternoon light, reading Henry James aloud and hoping Frank could hear her voice. Exhaustion had her stumbling over the lyrical prose; she could only hope the famous author would forgive her.

Her life felt as if it were temporarily suspended. Surely Frank would awaken, and he would remember the names of his attackers. But until then, she felt as if she were useless, doing nothing more than waiting.

Timothy had shown up faithfully each morning to report on the prior day's business at Longren Shipping, and she'd taken bits of time away from the attic to have him help her decipher the files she'd brought home after her last visit to the office. She now knew that Longren Shipping made regular payments to a vendor whose name was unknown to the Port Chatham business community. In all likelihood, that vendor was no more than a dummy account to accumulate the cash skimmed by Clive Johnson. But she needed more proof to make any formal accusation of wrongdoing. Her only hope was that Frank had managed to discover more before he'd been attacked, and that he would eventually be able to tell her what he knew.

The girls had proceeded with their plans to make Charlotte's gown for Eleanor's soirée, which was scheduled to occur the next evening. They'd even sewn a beautiful mourning gown for Hattie, made from the mousseline de soie and trimmed in dark green velvet. She would wear her dark green velvet cape as a wrap, though she knew it would likely cause Eleanor's eyebrows to inch ever higher. But the excitement over the upcoming social event had yet to take hold of Hattie—she couldn't think past the moment when Frank might awaken.

She'd struggled through a portion of the next chapter in James's *Portrait of a Lady* when she felt rather than heard a slight shift of the blankets. She looked up, her voice trailing off midsentence, to find Frank's eyes open and fixed on her, his expression confused and grimacing with pain.

She dropped the novel on the blanket and reached out to grip his hand in both of hers. "Don't try to move— your ribs are broken, and you have a concussion. Do you understand?"

"Yes . . . water?"

She poured a small amount into a glass from the

pitcher on the table next to his cot, then held it to his lips so that he could swallow.

He leaned back against the pillows, exhausted by the effort. "Where?" His voice was hoarse from disuse.

"You're in my attic, and safe for now," she said softly. "No one knows where you are."

He nodded slightly, closing his eyes.

"Frank, who did this to you?"

"Don't...know. There were...four." Each word seemed to tax him further, bring him ever more pain. "Seavey's...I think."

"Mona is asking around. We'll get names, then I'll take them to Greeley."

"No." He opened his eyes, his expression fierce. "Too dangerous...Greeley...paid by Seavey."

His agitation increased, and she strove to reassure him. "Very well, I won't go to the police."

One corner of his mouth rose. "You...must've been very worried...aren't arguing with me."

She laughed softly. "I'm fine, now that you're awake. Do you know why you were attacked?"

"Know...too much. Seavey...Johnson bribing boardinghouses...Johnson started fire..." His voice trailed away, then he seemed to rouse himself. His grip tightened on her fingers. "Henry James...kept hearing your voice...brought me back."

She smiled. "Rest."

"Don't leave..."

"I won't," she promised.

* * *

SHE left his side only after his breathing had deepened, and only long enough to return to the second-floor parlor to pen a note. She rang for Sara. "Have Charlotte and Tabitha deliver this to Dr. Willoughby at once. Also, prepare some chamomile tea—strong enough to mask the flavor of laudanum, if possible."

"Yes, ma'am." Sara slipped the note into her skirt pocket, then fidgeted.

"Yes, what is it?" Hattie asked impatiently.

"Mrs. Starr is at the kitchen entrance again, asking to see you."

"Ah. Bring her to me, please."

"Is that wise, ma'am?"

"For heaven's sake, Sara! Do as I say!"

Sara fled, leaving Hattie feeling guilty for having snapped at her. The housekeeper only had her best interests at heart. An apology was in order, she feared. She rubbed her face, exhausted.

At the telltale swish of satin skirts, she dropped her hands back to her lap. "Please come in, Mrs. Starr."

"You really should call me Mona." She walked over to the chair next to the fire. "And how is our patient this evening?"

"He awakened a short while ago and was able to talk a bit, but he's in great pain. I've sent for the physician."

"Yet he was aware of his surroundings and recognized you?" When Hattie nodded, Mona looked relieved.

"Then the worst is over—he'll likely recover. Tell me, does he remember the attack?"

"Yes. He said there were four, not three as Dr. Willoughby had surmised. He indicated they were in Seavey's employ."

Mona frowned. "Hmm. My man Booth was able to persuade two witnesses to take him into their confidence, though they have no intention of speaking as candidly to the police. Their stories and descriptions of the attackers were remarkably similar."

"Was Booth able to uncover the attackers' identities from the information he was given?"

"Yes." Mona pulled a slip of paper from her watch pocket, unfolded it, and handed it to Hattie.

As Hattie read, her hands began to shake with fury. "Two of the names appear on the payroll for Longren Shipping."

Mona nodded. "Our sources tell Booth they are long-shoremen. Clive Johnson has used them for similar work, though the targets in the past have been sailors and boardinghouse operators." She leaned back, staring into the fire. "The other two have had occasion to visit my establishment. They are under Seavey's employ, as Frank thought."

"Then the attack was planned by both men."

"So it would seem."

Hattie recalled Seavey's offer of protection, now recognizing it for the smoke screen it was. Oh, she had little doubt he'd planned to take full advantage of her, should she have actually agreed to his protection. But he'd never intended to do more than keep her distracted from the activities of Longren Shipping so that he and Johnson could continue to run the company as they saw fit.

Sara interrupted with a tray of tea and cakes. Hattie poured for herself and Mona.

"Will you take the information to Greeley?" Mona asked, stirring fragrant wildflower honey into her tea.

Hattie shook her head. "He was of no help when last I talked to him, and Frank claims he is in Seavey's pocket. I didn't tell Frank I'd already visited Greeley. I can see now that my actions were naïve."

"You did what you felt was right, what any ordinary citizen would assume was the correct course of action under the circumstances," Mona pointed out.

"Yes, but I thank God I had enough caution not to reveal the location of Frank's convalescence."

"So what now?"

Hattie's expression turned wry. "I believe I can count on Greeley's rigidly held views to render him blind to the possibility that Frank might be staying here. In Greeley's mind, I wouldn't risk the condemnation of my neighbors by harboring a single man in my own home, particularly while I am in mourning. Though Greeley believes I lack good judgment, I doubt it would occur to him that I would so risk my reputation."

Mona pursed her lips. "Perhaps you're correct, though we must remain vigilant. This will be my last visit. However, I will leave my guard in place."

"Thank you. And rest assured that I will apprise Frank of your invaluable role in this affair."

Mona set her cup on the tray and stood to take her leave. "There is one more bit of information Booth was able to learn."

Hattie gave her an inquiring look.

"The rumor along the waterfront is that Clive Johnson started the fire of three weeks past."

"Yes, that corroborates what Frank told me."

"According to what my man learned, a boardinghouse operator named Taylor refused to pay a bribe to Clive Johnson. Taylor subsequently made it known around town that he would run a boardinghouse only for union sailors. Clive Johnson burned down the boardinghouse to set an example to anyone else who might contemplate such a move. He paid a brothel patron to set the second fire for the purpose of misleading the investigators."

She'd been correct in her supposition after all, Hattie realized.

"No doubt your business manager never dreamed the fire would spread as it did, though that certainly in no way excuses his actions," Mona concluded.

"And I suppose there's no proof, which means he'll get away with having murdered the people who died as a result of the fire," Hattie said bitterly.

"Yes, I suspect that will be true. Unless," Mona said thoughtfully, "you could persuade a reporter for the newspaper to run a story mentioning an unnamed source?"

Hattie shook her head. "I have no credibility with Eleanor Canby on this subject. I still don't understand, though, who would've felt it necessary to pressure Eleanor to run the editorial condemning me. Seavey would have had the most to lose if Johnson were arrested, but it doesn't seem like Seavey's style."

"Michael Seavey can employ subtlety when it is called for," Mona said. "Though Greeley is another possibility. He and Eleanor are good friends, and he knows what goes on between the ships' masters and the boarding-house operators. He wouldn't want it known that he turns a blind eye, particularly when people have died."

Hattie brooded for a long moment. "Thank you for telling me."

"It was the least I could do, given the great risk you are undertaking for a close friend of mine. I might point out that you seem to make a habit of doing so."

Hattie smiled sadly. Then she leaned over and tossed the slip of paper Mona had given her into the fire. She watched in silence as it burned to ash.

"This will be the last time we speak of what we've learned this evening," she said quietly. "But all actions have consequences. I will personally see that they do."

* * *

HATTIE had no sooner seen Mona to her carriage than a loud scream had her hiking her skirts and dashing for the front hall. Tabitha stood, sobbing in Sara's arms. The young maid's braid had fallen into disarray, lying against her back in a snarled mess, and her eyes were wild with fear.

"Oh, Mrs. Longren!" Tabitha sobbed. "I tried my best, I did! But I couldn't stop them!"

The Betrayal

HATTIE'S heart stopped beating. She grasped the maid's thin shoulders and gave her a quick shake. "Calm down, Tabitha! Tell us where Charlotte is."

"They took her!"

"Describe to me exactly what transpired," she ordered from what felt like a great distance.

"We didn't think there was any harm in it, you see," Tabitha explained, her voice quavering. "We did just as you told us to—we took the note to Dr. Willoughby's clinic. Then Charlotte..." Tabitha's voice trailed off as she burst anew into tears.

"*Tabitha!*" Hattie gave her another hard shake. "If you can't tell us what happened, we can't get Charlotte back."

"Yes'm," Tabitha sniffled. "You see, Charlotte wanted an extra-nice ribbon for her dress for tomorrow evening, and so she thought we could make just the one stop on the way home."

"At Celeste's?"

"Yes'm. I tried to tell her you wouldn't approve, that we should ask your permission first, but—"

"Never mind that. What happened next?"

"We went to Miss Celeste's, like I said." Tabitha wiped her eyes, then continued. "It was after we left the shop and were walking along the street ... these two men ran out of the bushes and grabbed Miss Charlotte right off the sidewalk and dragged her into a carriage! I screamed, but there weren't no one around, so I ran back here." She started crying again. "It's my fault, Mrs. Longren ..."

Hattie realized her fingers were digging into the poor girl's shoulders. She forced herself to loosen her grip. "We'll sort all that out later," she said, "but you acted decisively by running back to tell us. Now, this is very important, Tabitha. Can you describe the two men for me?"

"Well, they were big and they wore clothes like the men we saw on the waterfront the night of the fire."

"So the men were sailors?"

The maid looked confused. "Their arms and legs were as big as trees, they were. And they were tall."

"Longshoremen, possibly," Hattie murmured. "Or lumberjacks."

Tabitha screwed up her face. "Maybe."

Dear God. Two men of that size easily could've grabbed Charlotte and put her into a carriage without risking detection, especially if they'd planned the location of the attack so that it was shielded from view by the landscaping at the entrance to an alley. The carriage could've been waiting just out of sight. They must've watched the house, then followed the girls, waiting for the right moment.

"What about the carriage?"

Tabitha's face was blank. "I think it was black."

"Was it a brougham carriage or a gentleman's phaeton?"

The girl didn't know the difference.

Hattie paced the hall, forcing air in and out of her constricted lungs. It would've been easier to conceal Charlotte in a carriage, but the phaeton would've been faster. And if they'd used chloroform, they could've gotten away with the phaeton—she would no longer have been struggling or screaming. God knew, chloroform could be had at any saloon along the waterfront. Either way, the vehicle could've been any of several available for hire from the waterfront liveries. She'd have no luck tracking it down—no one would be willing to talk to her.

She continued to pace. It was entirely possible Seavey had kidnapped Charlotte. Did he intend to use her to force Hattie to agree to his proposition, or would he smuggle Charlotte out of the country, sending her to the Far East to be used as a child prostitute? Either prospect was horrifying. She had to act, and quickly.

"My cape, Sara. I must speak to Chief Greeley at once—in this matter, he will be of assistance." Sara quickly helped her into her wrap as she spit out orders. "Stay with Tabitha and fix her some tea to calm her nerves. Dr. Willoughby is due at any moment. When he arrives, take him upstairs. I should be back within the hour."

With that, she flew out the door.

* * *

SHE arrived at the police station, breathless from the six-block run. Not bothering with the desk sergeant, she dashed past desks and prisoners' cells to Greeley's office. At her entry, he stood, his face set in rigid lines.

"Mrs. Longren, it's inappropriate to burst in without warning—"

She halted next to his desk, her hand at her throat, gasping for air. "The situation is dire, Chief Greeley. Charlotte has been kidnapped."

He was around the desk in an instant, his large hands gripping her arms. *"What are you saying?"*

"She was taken by two men outside our house, not moments ago. You must help me."

His hands were punishing—she would no doubt have bruises by morning. "Were you with her? Did you recognize her assailants?"

"Please—you're hurting me."

He seemed to realize where he was; he loosened his hold on her. "Tell me what you saw."

"I didn't see the attack—I was inside the house. Her lady's maid, Tabitha Dumont—"

"Charlotte was without a chaperone?" Wrath blazed in Greeley's eyes. *"You fool woman, what have you done?"*

Hattie tried to edge away. "Condemning my actions serves no useful purpose at the moment, Chief Greeley. If you'll allow me to relate what I know—"

Greeley let go of her with a shove, and she had to grab the edge of the desk to remain on her feet. He paced the small confines of the office. "Tell me."

She summarized the trip to Celeste's and the abduction, leaving out the real purpose of their outing, which was to deliver the note to Willoughby's clinic. "Tabitha immediately ran home to inform us, and I left within moments to come down here. The attack couldn't have happened any more than a half hour ago, at the most. If you act with haste—"

"And do what?" Greeley rounded on her. "In a carriage of any reasonable speed, they could be halfway to a neighboring town by now, or have Charlotte well concealed in the depths of the tunnels. *It's too late.*"

Hattie gaped at him. "You're the law—surely you have resources at your disposal to ascertain who has abducted her."

"To what end?" Greeley roared. "Whether or not we find Charlotte, she is lost to us now. Her captors no doubt have compromised her—her reputation is ruined."

"You can't possibly know that for certain!" Hattie said hotly. "If we act at once, they may not have had time to do more than simply conceal her."

"Charlotte is beyond all possible redemption," Greeley muttered, staring through her as if he were talking only to himself.

"Surely you don't equate the potential loss of Charlotte's good reputation with her very life!" Hattie cried, desperate to make him see reason.

Without warning, he backhanded her, sending her careening off the desk and to the floor. She lay there, her hand raised to her face, staring at him.

The desk sergeant rushed into the office, helping her to her feet. Two other patrolmen came to stand in the doorway, their wary gazes on Greeley.

"Are you all right, ma'am?" the sergeant asked, keeping an eye on Greeley, who stood like stone in the middle of the office.

"Yes . . . I think so," she answered shakily. "Thank you."

"Get out," Greeley said to her in a low voice.

"What?" Hattie asked, confused.

"I said, *get out of my office.*"

"Chief—" the sergeant began.

"*Shut up.*"

Hattie drew in a breath and straightened her shoulders. "So you will do nothing to help save Charlotte's life."

Greeley's face was devoid of all emotion. "The moment you allowed Charlotte to leave the house unattended, Mrs. Longren, you may as well have put a bullet in her brain. She is dead to us all."

He turned to the sergeant. "Get this woman out of my sight."

* * *

HATTIE stood on the boardwalk outside the police station, her breath hitching. She had no one to turn to, no one who could help. And she had no notion of how to proceed. Should she wait for a ransom note? But what if none were delivered? She would only be giving Charlotte's kidnappers the time they needed to transfer her aboard a ship bound for the Orient.

She didn't know how long she'd been standing there before she became aware of Michael Seavey's approach.

"Mrs. Longren," he said smoothly, removing his top hat to execute a bow. "And what brings you out on such a fine—"

She slapped him, putting her weight behind her swing. "You *son of a bitch*! I want her back *right now*!"

Seavey held her so her fists could no longer reach him. "Contain yourself, Mrs. Longren!"

"What is it that you hope to gain?" She spit the words at him. "Money?"

"I have no notion of what you're saying," he replied evenly, still holding her. "Please explain yourself."

She ceased her struggles, going limp under his hands. "Just give me back my sister."

His eyes shifted, and she *knew*. He was the worst kind of animal, preying on innocents. "Name your price, and I will meet it," she said, trying to mask her terror and failing. A sob escaped. "Please don't hurt her. I've heard what your men are capable of."

He shook his head, frowning, then his gaze suddenly sharpened. "You've been hit." He ran fingers with surprising gentleness across the reddened skin, then along the swelling at her jawline. "Who did this?" he asked quietly, a note of steel having entered his voice.

She stepped back, shuddering, and he dropped his hands. "Please, if you have an ounce of decency left in you, I beg of you ..." She stopped, shaking her head.

He studied her broodingly. "And what will you give me, Hattie, for the safe return of Charlotte? Money? Or more? Will you give me everything I want?"

Hattie closed her eyes. As she suspected, he meant to bargain Charlotte—for control of Longren Shipping, for the demise of the sailors' union, and for her own freedom. He wanted everything. She cared nothing for herself, but what of Frank? What would happen to him if she gave in to Seavey's demands? Would Seavey insist that she turn Frank over to him? She couldn't bring herself to trade one life for another. And yet, she couldn't think about what was happening to Charlotte at this very moment.

Perhaps she had one more option, one more strategy at her disposal. And if that didn't work, then she would force herself to make the more wrenching decision.

"What happens to me, or to Longren Shipping, is no longer of any consequence," she said. "But I won't bargain with the lives of others."

Seavey studied her, a muscle ticking in his jaw. "Then it's truly a pity," he said finally, "that you won't allow me to help you." He replaced his top hat, nodding. "Good day, Mrs. Longren."

He stepped around her and walked away. With shaking fingers she pulled her cape close to ward off the chill that seemed to permeate even her bones, never noticing the warmth of the late afternoon sun.

Pray to God my idea works.

Turning, she stepped into the alley. Walking to the door at the back of the building across from the courthouse, she raised a hand and knocked on its weather-beaten whitewashed exterior. Within moments, the door opened, revealing the young prostitute Hattie recognized from the night of the fire.

"Isobel. Please tell Mrs. Starr that I must speak with her immediately."

* * *

FROM one block away, Michael Seavey watched Hattie enter the Green Light. So Hattie thought to secure assistance from Mona Starr. He found Hattie's resolve, her courage in the face of truly frightening circumstances, curiously admirable. His late wife would've acted only to save her own skin, not out of principle or concern for others. Not that asking Mona would do Hattie any good—the wealthy madam was not without resources, but she didn't have the power to affect the outcome of this little drama. Whereas he did. However, the question was, what outcome did he desire?

He turned to his bodyguard. "Remy."

"Yessir."

"Fetch Clive Johnson and bring him to my hotel room."

"Yessir."

"And, Remy?" The bodyguard turned back. "Don't be gentle about it."

Remy's eyes gleamed with anticipation. "How much time do I got, Mr. Seavey?"

"One hour should be sufficient, I believe."

The Rescue Plan

TWENTY-FOUR hours later, Hattie sat in the second-floor parlor, sewing a hidden pocket into the skirts of her evening gown. She'd already pricked her fingers with the needle more times than she could count.

No ransom note had been delivered, as she'd prayed would happen. At least a ransom note would've cast a different light on Charlotte's abduction, raising doubts as to her presumption about Seavey's plans to use Charlotte as leverage. With no such note forthcoming, she'd been forced to accept the worst.

Sleep had been impossible, eating even more so. All she could hope was that the plan she and Mona had devised would be successful.

"Give me time to gather information regarding Charlotte's location," Mona had told her the day before at the Green Light.

"But the longer we wait—"

"Acting in haste, and in the absence of a solid plan, will be even riskier," Mona had pointed out. "Think with your head, not your emotions, Hattie. Charlotte's life is more important than whatever temporary discomfort, or even abuse, she experiences at the hands of her captors."

Hattie had forced herself to nod her agreement. "How long?"

"Twenty-four hours, at least. You must also attend the soirée tomorrow evening—it will be your cover."

"To expect me to act normal, as if nothing has happened, as if Seavey and Greeley, who are bound to be in attendance, haven't had a hand in this . . . *no*. You ask too much."

"If anyone asks later, dozens of people will say that you were at the party, that you couldn't have been involved," Mona had insisted.

Though Hattie had been forced to admit the wisdom of Mona's plan, she'd been incapable of more than a shudder by way of response.

Mona had taken her silence as acquiescence. "Slip out no earlier than midnight, and make certain no one sees you. Come to the alley door—we will proceed from here."

So she had come home to wait, firming her resolve for what she must do. Struggling to assure Sara and Tabitha that all would eventually be well, that Charlotte would return home safe.

Hattie closed her eyes for a moment, then bent over her sewing once again. She would never forgive herself for her own naïve actions that had brought about this chain of events.

She heard a slight movement and turned. Frank stood,

one shoulder propped heavily against the doorway, his face white with pain. Setting aside her sewing, she leapt to her feet. "You shouldn't be out of bed—whatever were you thinking?"

Frank shook his head, working to get his breath back and, she realized, to keep his balance. "Willoughby said I could walk around as soon as I felt well enough."

"Yes, I'm certain you're feeling fine at the moment," Hattie said, her tone acerbic. Though his improvement had been rapid since his awakening, he was by no means miraculously cured of either the concussion or the broken ribs. She grasped his arm. "Let me help you back up the stairs."

He didn't move, instead gazing down at her grimly. "The walls have ears, Hattie. I heard Tabitha's screams, and her sobs late into the night. And Sara informed me of your plans for this evening."

Hattie stiffened. "I gave Sara no such permission."

"I was persuasive in my arguments." Hattie watched him deal with a new wave of dizziness before continuing. "She's concerned, as am I. I'm asking you to reconsider."

"There's no other way."

She began to turn away, but Frank placed his hand on her arm, halting her. "I can't . . . be there to protect you."

She covered his hand with her own. "I must do this— I'm Charlotte's only hope."

"Take Seavey's offer," he urged. "I could accept that before I could bear seeing any harm come to you."

"And you don't believe *he'd* harm me?"

"At least you'd be safe. He's a hard man, but I don't think he'd mistreat you."

"And what of you?" she argued, unaccountably angry. "Do you truly believe I'm capable of trading Charlotte's life for yours? If so, you must think very little of me."

After a long moment, Frank sighed, dropping his hand. "At least give me assurances that Mona is taking adequate precautions for your safety."

"Yes, Booth will be accompanying us, along with two hired bodyguards."

"Very well." His tone was grudging.

"Please, allow me to help you back to bed—"

"*No.*" He ran a hand through his hair, his expression rife with frustration. "I'll await your return in the library."

* * *

AT precisely eight o'clock that evening, Hattie presented her engraved invitation to the butler at the door of the Canby Mansion. While he studied it, she slipped a hand into her pocket to assure herself the roll of cash she'd taken from the library safe was still there.

"If you'll follow me, Mrs. Longren." The butler ushered her inside.

Eleanor stood with her husband in the mansion's spacious front entry hall, receiving guests. She wore an eggplant moiré gown trimmed in creamy white Venetian lace that Hattie couldn't help but admire. The gown's rich fabric bespoke of the wealth Eleanor and her husband enjoyed, while its subdued color had been carefully chosen so as not to eclipse the outfits of her guests. Hattie knew she'd never possess a fraction of the social skill Eleanor so effortlessly exhibited.

She moved forward, injecting as much warmth into her voice as she could. "Eleanor, thank you for allowing me to attend this evening."

Eleanor noted the dark green velvet trim on Hattie's mourning gown, pursing her lips. "Hattie." She inclined her head. "I believe my invitation included Charlotte. Is she not attending this evening?"

"I'm afraid my sister came down with a severe headache this afternoon and is quite indisposed," Hattie lied.

"A pity. I'll send my maid over presently with a powder that may ease her discomfort."

"No . . . that is, no, thank you, Eleanor. Sara has already prepared a tincture for Charlotte, and she's gone to bed for the night. I'm certain she'll be fully recovered by morning."

If Eleanor noticed her agitation, she didn't remark upon it. "Very well, I'm sure you know what's best."

"Yes."

"May I present my husband, Alexander? Alex, this is Charles Longren's widow, the lady I've mentioned to you frequently of late."

"Mr. Canby," Hattie managed politely.

After a quick glance in the direction of his wife, Canby bowed over her hand. "Mrs. Longren. I hope you enjoy the evening we have planned." She caught the barest hint of a twinkle in his eye. "The music promises to be entertaining."

"Yes, I look forward to it," she replied. Casting about desperately for an appropriate topic of conversation, she seized upon the design of the grand, three-tiered staircase behind them that was the talk of the town. "You must be quite proud of your home, Mr. Canby. The architecture is astonishing."

"Why, yes, my dear!" Canby smiled, looking relieved. "Do note the eight panels of the domed ceiling—the frescoes of graces and nymphs depict the Four Seasons and Four Virtues. You'll have to return for a visit during the first few days of a season—sunlight shines through the ruby glass of dormer windows, causing a red beam to point at the appropriate season—"

"Alice," Eleanor interrupted firmly, glowering at her husband. "Please show Mrs. Longren into the parlor, where she can await the arrival of our other guests."

Canby shot Hattie a rueful glance but remained silent. Hattie gave him a small smile of apology before turning away. Evidently her own contretemps with Eleanor were indicative of the manner in which she also treated her family members.

Hattie was shown into a lushly furnished parlor graced with a high ceiling decorated by stencils and elaborate murals. Because she was the first to arrive, she had a moment alone to collect her thoughts. She'd probably committed some small slight of etiquette, showing up *exactly* on time, but her nerves hadn't given her a choice. She wanted the hours until she could slip away *gone*, the evening *over*. Concentrating on breathing deeply and evenly, she took in her surroundings.

Tall windows adorned with allegorical corner carvings of lions, doves, and ferns looked onto formal gardens. Groupings of velvet-upholstered, baroque-style furniture crowded the room, and on the farthest wall stood the largest music organ she'd ever seen in a private home. No doubt Eleanor had her own personal organist who played hymns each Sunday for the family.

Unable to remain still, Hattie paced around the ornate room, noting it contained no fireplace. Eleanor's pronouncement to the world, Hattie suspected, that she could afford central heating and therefore no longer saw the need for wood fires. Stopping at a window, Hattie gazed out, trying to calm the pounding of her heart, which sounded unnaturally loud to her own ears. It wouldn't do to faint, she silently chastised herself.

"Alexander commissioned the house's interior finish work by his ships' carpenters, as you know." The deep voice came from behind her, chilling her.

She swallowed and turned from her view of Eleanor's immaculate gardens. Michael Seavey stood inside the door of the parlor, elegant in his charcoal gray dress jacket and kid gloves, his pale eyes watching her the way a powerful cat watches its prey.

Think of Charlotte, she reminded herself, *only of Charlotte*. All that mattered was that he not learn of her plan for later that evening.

"It's said that the design of the supporting structure for the hall staircase remains a secret even to this day," he added, smiling slightly. "And Eleanor does love her secrets."

"Stay away from me." Hattie kept her voice low.

He strode across the room to stand before her, his demeanor too familiar by half. She held her ground. The gesture did not appear to be lost on him. He smiled. "I do greatly admire your spirit, my dear."

She took a deliberate step backward, allowing him to see the revulsion she felt. An indefinable emotion flickered in his eyes, gone in an instant, then his expression turned neutral. He made a production of removing his gloves and lighting a cigar.

"I'm told we are to be entertained by the great Scott Joplin this evening," he said lightly, obviously enjoying the acrid fragrance of the smoke.

"I doubt I'll find Joplin's music relaxing."

"On that we agree." He looked amused, clearly choosing to misinterpret her remark. "The jarring melodies that enthrall Antonín Dvořák elude me. Rumor is that the composer might use their essence in his New World symphony, as I'm sure you've heard."

"Yes, though I'm surprised you took note. I don't see you as a man of refinement."

If her affront bothered him, he didn't show it. He puffed on the cigar, then sighed. "I feel the need to impress upon you once again that I can help you, Hattie, if only you'll allow me."

"In return for the surrender of everything I hold dear, no doubt," she replied bitterly.

He leaned toward her, keeping his voice low. "Say the word, and Charlotte is returned to you, unharmed."

She remained silent. In the hallway, more guests had arrived, and she could hear Greeley's booming voice, causing her stomach to knot even harder.

"Men have base instincts, Hattie," Seavey murmured. "Ones that Charles may have chosen to shield you from during your brief marriage. And my men...well." He spread his hands. "I can't predict, nor can I control how long they will wait before acting upon those...instincts."

"You bastard."

He stepped closer, so close she feared she'd gag. "I've proposed a lucrative business alliance, one that will make you a rich woman overnight. And I can guarantee you'd enjoy my touch."

"I don't want your money. Or your hands on me."

"Yes, I've come to that lamentable conclusion." He straightened away from her. "You have the rest of the evening to decide. After that, it's out of my control."

She kept her tone cold, though fine tremors ran the length of her spine. "Do not approach me again, Mr. Seavey, or conventions be damned—I will scream this house down. And I will tell *everyone* what you've done to Charlotte. Do you understand?"

He sighed, inclining his head. "More than you do, my dear."

* * *

SHE thought dinner would never end.

As poor luck would have it, she'd been seated across from Seavey, which gave him an excellent vantage point from which to observe her barely disguised terror. Mayor Payton, jovial to the point that she wanted to scream, had been seated next to her. When she'd seen the name cards placed among the glittering lead crystal and china on the dinner table, determining the seating arrangement as Eleanor decreed, it had been all Hattie could do not to snatch them up and rearrange them.

She could be thankful for one small bit of serendipity, though—Chief Greeley had been seated to Eleanor's right at the far end of the table, well away from her. To that end, he was forced to limit his treatment of her to icy, rage-filled stares. Hattie had no doubt that had she been forced to remain in close quarters with him for the duration of the six-course meal, they'd have come to blows.

As it was, she was forced to endure Payton's inane chatter and Seavey's cat-and-mouse barbs, all the while willing herself not to throw up the rich food. The butler oversaw the serving of each course—Quilcene oysters on the half shell, mock turtle soup, filet of beef in morel mushroom sauce, escarole salad, salmon in dill sauce.

At last, waiters removed the tablecloth, providing finger bowls before the serving of dessert. Hattie dipped trembling hands in the lemon-scented water, wiping her fingers on a paper doily. She'd made it this far; surely she could survive floating island with fresh raspberry ice.

At Eleanor's signal, they rose en masse to retire to the music room for the evening's entertainment. Hattie made certain she positioned herself close to the doors leading onto the patio, opened to allow a small amount of fresh air into the room, which was a crush of warm bodies sated on heavy food and strong spirits.

As discreetly as possible, she checked the time on her pocket watch. A few moments before midnight.

Scott Joplin appeared beside the grand piano, formally dressed in a black suit and vest, snowy white shirt, and silk tie, bowing to the adoring crowd. Seating himself, he paused for a moment, eyes closed and hands suspended over the ivory keys, then launched into his ragtime songs.

After one last glance around the room to ensure Seavey and Greeley stood some distance away, Hattie quietly slipped out the French doors, escaping into the night.

Chapter 15

JORDAN swore, slamming Hattie's diary shut and tossing it onto the bed. It simply *stopped*, and at the worst possible moment. Of course, it probably ended in that place because Hattie had been murdered shortly thereafter, but to Jordan's way of thinking, that was no excuse. She refused to be left hanging. It wasn't as if she could just snuggle down and drop off to sleep without knowing whether Hattie and Mona had succeeded in freeing Charlotte.

She glanced at the alarm clock on her nightstand. Three o'clock. This was ridiculous—she hadn't pulled an all-nighter since graduate school and had no intention of doing so now. Reaching out, she switched off the light, then lay back, pulling the covers over her as best she could, given that the dog had most of them pinned beneath him. Two minutes later, she turned the light back on and glared at the watermarks on the ceiling.

Throwing back the covers, she climbed out of bed and trotted downstairs to the kitchen. How did one go about conjuring up ghosts, exactly?

"Come out, come out, wherever you are!" she called.

After enough time had elapsed that Jordan was contemplating some sort of ritual dance to awaken sleeping spirits, the air shimmered, and the ghosts appeared in their assigned spots at the kitchen table. Both were wearing high-necked, ankle-length flannel nightgowns sporting lace and ruffles. Their hair hung in single braids down the center of their backs.

"Really," Hattie admonished her, yawning. "It's the middle of the night."

"Why do you care? Do ghosts actually sleep?" There had to be at least four yards of material in their nightdresses. Thank God football jerseys had been invented.

"Well, of course! We need our beauty rest, after all. And it's not as if we're part of some children's parlor game. 'Come out, come out, wherever you are'? *Please.* Simply call our names and we'll appear."

"My apologies." Jordan's tone was sarcastic as she dealt with the espresso maker. "I just finished your diary. You have to tell me what happened the night of Eleanor's soirée."

"And you needed this information so badly you had to awaken us at three A.M.?" Hattie's tone was querulous.

While the machine heated, Jordan ground beans. "I still don't know who killed you," she admitted. "I know about Frank's attack, the abduction, and Seavey's proposition. But that's far from the proof I need to convince anyone Seavey murdered you." *And as added inducement, I now have another ghost breathing down my neck, criticizing my performance.*

"What do you need to know?" Hattie asked.

Jordan poured her espresso and sat down at the table. "Tell me *exactly* what happened the night of the party."

"Well, Charlotte was kidnapped the day before Eleanor's soirée, as you probably know by now." She smiled sadly at Charlotte. "Remember? You had wanted so badly to attend."

Charlotte nodded, then gave her a look of encouragement.

Hattie's eyes lost their focus, her mind in some distant place. "Mona and I had come up with a plan to free you, you see. She would have Booth find out who was holding you, and the location within the tunnels where you were being held. Then we would bribe the guards to turn you over to us. Once you were back at the house, we'd decide whether to try to force Greeley to press charges against your kidnappers."

"You must have been so scared," Charlotte murmured.

"Yes. The party was torture. Seavey was watching my every move. I thought it would never end. But around midnight, I slipped through the library doors while Scott Joplin was playing. He traveled the country back then, you may remember, playing at opera houses and brothels to support himself while composing his songs." Hattie's expression turned momentarily wry. "I always thought it ironic that Eleanor, of all people, would allow him into her home. But his music was so popular she probably overlooked his questionable connections."

"Never mind that." Jordan noted Hattie's careful

omission of Greeley's refusal to help find Charlotte, assuming it was to spare Charlotte's feelings. "Go on," she urged.

Hattie drew a breath. "The guests were so enthralled with the music that no one ever saw me leave. Or if anyone did notice, they must've thought I was slipping out to the garden for some fresh air.

"The moon was bright, and there was already dew on the grass. My evening slippers were soaked through before I'd even made it halfway across the garden. Isn't it funny the impressions you're left with? I can still feel the cold damp soaking through my stockings." She sighed. "Anyway, all I could think was that damp feet and ruined shoes were of no consequence, that I had to get to Charlotte. Seavey's men had had almost thirty-six hours to do whatever they wanted, and though Mona wasn't saying as much, I knew she feared the worst."

Charlotte placed her hand on Hattie's arm. "They never touched me. Seavey must've given them an order not to harm me. Oh, they talked about what they'd do to me when they got the chance, and they kept me petrified with the descriptions, probably so I wouldn't fight to get away. But mostly, they just forced me to drink a foul-tasting tea of some kind."

"Probably drugged," Jordan surmised. She nodded at Hattie to continue.

"After a block or so," Hattie said, "I thought I'd gotten away without Seavey realizing it. So I moved as fast as I could, trying to stay in the shadows of the buildings along the waterfront, hoping no one would see me." She clasped trembling hands on the table. "I was afraid I'd be waylaid, you see. Danger abounded on the waterfront that late at night. If I'd had the bad luck of some group of drunken sailors spying me, keeping me from my destination..." Her face twisted. "As it turned out, I needn't have worried."

"Why?"

"Because Seavey caught me and dragged me into a dark alley before I could get inside the Green Light. Mona never even knew I'd arrived."

Jordan almost dropped her espresso. "So Seavey *did* follow you."

"Oh, yes."

The Price Paid

MICHAEL Seavey wrapped an arm around Hattie's waist, lifting her away from the Green Light's door and clapping his gloved hand across her mouth to muffle her screams. He dragged her into the darkness at the end of the alley, silently swearing when her teeth sunk through leather into the fleshy part of his palm.

Holding her pressed between his body and the rough brick wall of the courthouse, he whispered into her ear, "Cease your struggles, my dear, if you ever want to see Charlotte again."

She went limp.

"Excellent." He turned his head as the back door to the Green Light opened. "*Ssshhh.*" Mona's butler leaned out and scanned the alley, listening. After a moment, the man shrugged and went back inside, closing the door.

Michael loosened his grip slightly. He turned her so that her back was to the wall, his hand still firmly pressed against her mouth. From the look in her eyes, she would have spit at him if he'd given her the chance.

He said quietly, "If you promise not to scream for help, I'll remove my hand."

She nodded her head fractionally, and he lessened the pressure of his glove, waiting to see whether she'd keep her end of the bargain. When no sound other than her harsh breathing was forthcoming, he took a step back but kept hold of her upper arms.

"Unhand me!" she spat in a harsh whisper.

"I'm afraid that's not possible. Though I suspect you've already ruined an expensive pair of kid gloves," he added wryly, "and I'll probably have a sore hand for days."

"How dare you follow me, *attack* me!" One cheek was already reddening where it had scraped against the brick wall, and her eyes shone with unshed tears.

He shook his head. "Your plan to rescue Charlotte was foolhardy and doomed to fail—my bodyguards can't be bribed. However, I will take you to her now."

Hattie's breath hitched, her expression turning wary. "There is a condition—I must know it."

"Yes, very astute of you. I need your promise that you will tell no one of the events leading to Charlotte's rescue." He noted her confusion, but he added to forestall any further questions, "On this I am unyielding, Hattie. I will not explain myself, nor will I tolerate any prevarication on your part. I won't risk arrest on kidnapping charges."

"But—"

He felt her jolt when he once again placed gloved fingers against her lips. "Do I have your promise? Yes or no."

She hesitated, then nodded. However, once he removed his hand, she added, her voice cold, "But never my forgiveness."

He sighed. "I don't expect it, though trust me when I say you don't know the entire story of what has transpired." He dragged her farther down the alley to the corner of the courthouse, peering into the adjoining street. "Come," he said, motioning with his head for his bodyguards to follow.

They walked the two blocks to his hotel in minutes, no one save his bodyguards bearing witness. The building comprised two parts—the original structure, still frequented by a well-heeled clientele, and a newer annex used to house sailors and provide access to the tunnels. The customers intermingled only in the saloon, located on the ground floor of the older hotel. Seavey bypassed the lobby, forcing Hattie to climb an outside set of stairs at the back of the annex.

Once inside, he pushed her ahead of him, up another half flight and down a dim hallway to the room to where he'd had his men transfer Charlotte. At their approach, a third bodyguard at the door nodded deferentially, moving aside.

Seavey opened the door and Hattie flew over to the bed where her sister lay. Though the girl's clothes were soiled and her hair disheveled, he knew Hattie could see for herself that Charlotte was unharmed by her ordeal.

"Satisfied?" he asked.

Hattie laid a hand on Charlotte's forehead. "She sleeps deeply."

"I had my men give her a drug earlier—she will awaken by morning. It has no lasting effects." He crossed his arms. "And now I think it's time you and I discussed business."

Hattie's fists clenched. "I have money—I can pay you." She reached into her skirt pocket and removed the roll of money, holding it out.

He took it, quickly assessing the amount, his mouth twisting as he realized its probable source. There was a certain sense of poetic justice, he mused, in receiving cash Charles and Clive Johnson had no doubt acquired through the transport of prostitutes to the Far East, given that they'd spread rumors intimating his own involvement in the scheme.

"This is a start," he agreed smoothly, pocketing the cash. "I'll reluctantly drop my earlier proposition, but I'll also need your assurance that you won't alter the arrangement I have with Longren Shipping."

She said nothing, her eyes filling with anger.

"May I remind you," he said, hardening his tone, "that you and Charlotte aren't safe. I can give an order, and the two of you will disappear this night, your bodies never to be found. And I can get to you and your sister anytime, anywhere."

Her shoulders sagged, her tone bitter. "I won't interfere with the running of Longren Shipping in the future."

He nodded, straightening. "Then we are agreed. I will arrange for the two of you to be taken home."

"I only have one question, Mr. Seavey." He paused and

turned to meet her cold gaze. "How does a man like you sleep through the night?"

"More easily than you would imagine, my dear. Much more easily."

* * *

HATTIE didn't break down until Seavey's men had safely delivered Charlotte to her bed and departed from the house. After assuring herself that Charlotte was indeed sleeping comfortably and well cared for, she let herself into the second-floor parlor, collapsing into a chair by the fire.

She shook uncontrollably from head to toe. At least they were safe—for now. And as long as she did as Seavey bid her regarding the business, they could remain safe. She had to cling to that thought.

Frank entered the room, concern etched into his features. "Those were Seavey's thugs."

"Yes." She quickly wiped the tears from her eyes and stood. "They brought the two of us home. Sara and Tabitha are tending to Charlotte."

Frank said nothing, his sharp eyes searching hers, then held open his arms. She knew she shouldn't, that etiquette dictated an extended period of mourning for good reason. She shouldn't crave the touch of another man so soon after Charles's death. She walked into Frank's arms, taking care to avoid his ribs. And for the first time all night, as she laid her head on his shoulder, she felt a moment's peace.

"You're safe...you'll be fine," he murmured, one hand coming up to cup the back of her neck, his fingers massaging.

She shivered at his touch.

After a long moment, she forced herself to pull away, incapable of meeting his eyes. She clasped her hands in front of her skirt. "I had to agree to conditions that will make it impossible for Longren Shipping to unionize. And I suspect I've put you in further jeopardy."

"We'll deal with that eventuality. For now, you're both safe."

She turned to the fire, feeling oddly melancholy. "Yes."

He walked over to a side table and poured her a small glass of brandy, bringing it to her. "Drink this—you need it."

She did as he requested, grimacing. "I much prefer the taste of sherry."

"Brandy has more medicinal benefit in situations such as these." He studied her, frowning. "You should go to bed, get what rest you can before Charlotte awakens. I suspect you'll have your hands full tomorrow morning, dealing with the aftereffects of her imprisonment."

"Who's the patient in this house?" she asked lightly, smiling for the first time in two days.

"At the moment, you are," he said firmly. "I must admit, it feels good to order you around for a change." He smiled. "I've no doubt you'll revert to your position of authority once you're rested."

"I trust you are on your way to bed as well?" she asked, blushing when she realized the boldness of her question.

He smiled. "Though I would like nothing better than to come to bed," he said in a soft tone that had her coloring further, "I have some reading I want to finish in the library. I've had all the sleep I can stand for the moment. I plan to help myself to a cup of your tea and retire a bit later."

"Very well," she said, more disappointed than she would admit. "Good night."

For a moment, he looked as if he would block her exit, but in the end, he inclined his head, standing aside.

* * *

AN hour later, Hattie sat at her dressing table in her bedroom, brushing her hair. She was still too anxious to sleep, yet too exhausted to even raise her arms to braid her hair. The night was silent and still, the Canbys' party having finally wound down and the guests departed.

She dropped the brush and buried her face in both hands. She'd been so utterly foolish, thinking she could go up against men the likes of Seavey and Johnson. She'd failed, and she'd almost lost Charlotte altogether. It was doubtful Charlotte's reputation would ever recover from the incident—she might never make a good match.

Hattie stood and walked over to the window seat that looked out over the street below. Earlier, she'd sent Sara down to the Green Light with a short note of explanation so that Mona wouldn't continue to worry about her. But what to do about Frank's situation? About Clive Johnson?

A slight sound came from behind her. She smiled and started to turn. "So you've changed your mind—"

The pain was crushing. In less than a heartbeat, her world went black.

She never felt her fall, never felt the blood flowing from her, soaking the floorboards beneath her.

Chapter 16

THE kitchen was filled with the sounds of sobbing. Hattie held Charlotte, comforting her, and even Jordan found herself blinking rapidly.

A handful of Kleenex flew at her, which she used to swipe at tears. She blew her nose, then gave a mental eye roll.

Great. She was crying over the death of the person who was sitting across the table from her. Her life couldn't get any more *Twilight Zone*–like unless she invited the ghost of Rod Serling to dinner.

"I still don't think Seavey murdered you," she said for what felt like the twentieth time.

"How can you say that?" Hattie glared through eyes swimming in tears. "He kidnapped Charlotte, he threatened me—"

"He *loved* you," Charlotte countered, sniffling. "If you'd simply *looked*, you would've seen it. I don't care what kind of man he was, he fell for you the moment he set eyes on you, the night of the fire."

Jordan agreed. "He tried to tell you he was innocent—you just didn't want to believe him."

"Right after he took me to the hotel room where *his* men were holding Charlotte," Hattie pointed out.

"Okay, true. But what about Clive Johnson? If you unionized, Johnson had as much to lose as Seavey. Johnson easily could have murdered you and framed Frank. Did you have any contact with Johnson again after you tried to fire him?"

"No," Hattie replied. "But remember, Timothy was coming to the house with daily reports, so I had no reason to visit the office. And once Charlotte had been kidnapped, Johnson could've burned Longren Shipping to the ground—all I cared about was bringing her home safe. But I'm certain Timothy would've informed me if Johnson were up to something."

"Only if he witnessed it, and I doubt Johnson would've allowed that to happen." Jordan propped her elbows on the table, resting her chin in her hands while she thought. "No, it's all wrong—Seavey's profile doesn't match that of a murderer."

Hattie gave her a look of sheer incredulity.

"Okay, what I meant was, he didn't have the psychological profile of a man who would've murdered *you*. I'm betting anyone who got a visit from Seavey's thugs knew exactly what they'd done to deserve it. Seavey didn't kill in anger—he killed for cold-blooded *convenience*, for business reasons." Hattie opened her mouth to argue and Jordan raised her hand. "And let's not forget that you agreed to his conditions that night. So really, he had no reason to kill you—at least, not unless you failed to live up to your end of the bargain."

"He could've worried I'd go behind his back and tell Greeley who had kidnapped Charlotte."

Jordan shook her head. "Seavey had warned you of the consequences. He knew you were too smart to risk Charlotte a second time. No, if he had anyone to fear, it was Frank. And it would've been far easier to kill Frank— Seavey would've had to get past him to get to you. Why not simply kill him?"

"Because Seavey needed someone convenient to take the blame," Hattie said. "I doubt Chief Greeley could've overlooked murder, even if Seavey *did* have him on his payroll."

She had a point. Jordan rubbed her face with both hands. Outside, the sky was lightening to the east. She'd actually stayed up all night, trying to solve a century-old murder. She ought to have her head examined. "I know I'm missing something, but I'm too tired to figure out what it is."

"Who do *you* think killed Hattie?" Charlotte asked, speaking up for the first time.

"Good question," Jordan admitted. "And at this point, I don't even know where to look for the answer."

"What about Seavey's personal papers? If he loved Hattie as much as I believe he did, then he would've written about her death. He would've been devastated by it."

"Well, of course he would've." Jordan stared at her, amazed that she hadn't thought of it herself. "Not only that, he had the resources to hunt down the killer himself. Brilliant!"

Charlotte preened, then her smile slid a little. "Maybe not. You're assuming Seavey didn't believe that Frank murdered Hattie."

Jordan started to tell them she knew Seavey had visited Frank after the trial, then realized she'd have to explain how she knew that. It was getting damned confusing, trying to keep straight what information she could tell which ghost. She stood to leave. "It's worth a shot, anyway."

They gave her blank looks.

"It's worth the time it will take me to at least check out the theory."

"Oh. Where're you going?" Hattie asked as Jordan jogged toward the front hall, the dog on her heels.

"Upstairs to find Seavey's papers. Charlotte's right—the clues have to be in his personal journal entries between the time of the murder and Frank's trial, because he wouldn't have been able to sleep until he knew who'd killed you." She grabbed the kitchen door frame, halting her progress long enough to ask, "What was the date of the soirée?"

"June 6, 1890," Charlotte said.

"Do you want us to make you an espresso?" Hattie called after her. "We've been watching how you—"

"*Do not touch my espresso machine!*"

* * *

JORDAN located Michael Seavey's papers, then sorted through them until she found a packet of loose, yellowed pages in handwritten script, bounded by a rubber band. The minute she tried to pull the rubber band off, it disintegrated. Pages fanned out, dropping onto the bed and the floor. Gathering them up and stacking them in their original order, Jordan sat down on the edge of the bed and began to read the entries around the date of the soirée.

> *June 3rd*—I've come to the unfortunate conclusion I must take action to halt the rapidly escalating situation with regard to Clive Johnson. Sadly, the man has become more of a liability than an asset. I've always felt his unhealthy predilections regarding young girls would cause him trouble one day. To kidnap girls to appease his appetites, then once tired of them, to smuggle them overseas, is certainly distasteful. However, since being barred from the local brothels following the incident with the prostitute Isobel, his activities have begun to affect his business judgment. Still, I remained uninvolved, though increasingly concerned—that is, until I discovered he had decided to spread the rumor that I am behind the kidnappings. This, of course, is unacceptable and has to be dealt with.

Jordan resisted the urge to scream, because of course Seavey hadn't felt the need to explain *how* he had dealt with the situation. If Seavey had pressured or beaten Johnson, he'd actually increased the man's motivation to murder Hattie, whom he would've considered the source of his problems. Jordan started flipping through pages, looking for another reference to Clive Johnson.

> *June 5th*—Today saw a disturbing development. Hattie Longren, whom I've come to admire, accused me of kidnapping young Charlotte. Though it will no doubt take me a period of time to recover from learning Hattie could think me capable of such an act, I am determined to get to the bottom of what has happened. To this end, I have ordered my men to bring Clive Johnson to the hotel. Clearly, my procrastination in dealing with him has jeopardized the sister of someone I care for. I can only hope I'm not too late to save the lovely Charlotte from Johnson's disgusting proclivities.
>
> With regard to Hattie, I find myself tormented by a personal dilemma most unusual . . . I'm deeply angry that she could suspect me of such a heinous crime, and yet, when I would typically strike back in kind, I find myself unable to. My instinct is to help her and to keep her safe, not to destroy her. I must overcome this new weakness in my character.

Jordan laid the papers on her nightstand. So she'd been correct about Michael Seavey all along—he'd loved Hattie, whether or not he understood the emotion well enough to recognize it. Her faith in charming psychopaths was entirely restored.

After thinking about what she'd read for a few minutes, she picked up the rest of Holt Stilwell's package, sifting through its contents and looking at the dates. There were none beyond June 5—the day before Eleanor's soireé. And that meant there were possibly pages still missing.

Jordan took the stairs two at a time, leaping down the last three to land in the front entry. "Hattie!"

No answer.

"Hattie! Charlotte!"

The ghosts materialized in the hallway, their hair now tied with strips of fabric that stuck out all over their heads.

"What?" Hattie's arms were crossed over the bodice of her nightdress, and she was glaring.

Jordan took in their appearance without a blink. "When did Seavey die?"

"He was murdered a few years later, in August of 1893," Charlotte replied.

"Someone finally gave him what he deserved, in my opinion," Hattie added.

Jordan waved that aside. "So we should find personal diary entries from him up to that date, right?"

"I suppose."

"Yeah, well, the ones I have stop the night before the soirée, so I'm *missing* a chunk of pages."

Jordan glanced at her watch—8 A.M. Late enough that Jase should be up and about, and she needed a favor. She headed back upstairs to grab a clean pair of jeans, only to find all her clothing rearranged. "*Dammit!* Did you have to reorganize my closet, too?" she yelled.

"What are you talking about?" Hattie materialized beside her with a frown. "We would *never* assume it appropriate to handle your toiletries and clothes."

"Never mind." Jordan headed for the door. "By the way," she told Hattie on her way out, "according to Seavey, he didn't kidnap Charlotte—Clive Johnson did. Seavey *saved* her."

* * *

JASE answered the door of his Mission-style bungalow, still in the act of pulling on a shirt and with his jeans half buttoned, his jaw cracking from a yawn. Two days' growth of beard shadowed his jaw, and his blue eyes had a sleepy look.

He pushed the door open farther. "Come on in."

She followed him into his living room, a large space filled with comfortable-looking overstuffed furniture. Though the room was obviously well cared for, she liked that it wasn't perfectly neat—a pile of newspapers lay on the floor, and a couple of abandoned coffee mugs were shoved together by a stack of books on the coffee table. "Nice," she said.

He perched on the arm of the sofa. "I was coming to find you in a few minutes, anyway. I set up a conference call with JT for nine o'clock at the pub. He's got something for us—he emailed me last night."

They had an hour, then. "I need directions to Holt Stilwell's place."

"I don't want you approaching him on your own, and I sure as hell don't think it's safe for you to go to his house."

"I'm missing pages from the papers he gave me that night outside the pub," she explained. "And I'm so close, I can taste it."

"So you know who murdered Hattie?"

"No," she admitted. "But I think Holt's ancestor knew, and I think he would've avenged Hattie's death. He was in love with her."

Jase sighed. "Okay, I'll drive you out there." He rubbed a hand over his unshaven jaw. "This means I have to wait on a shower, a shave, *and* coffee. You're going to owe me."

"I'll make it up to you, I promise."

His eyes crinkled. "I'll hold you to that. Give me five minutes."

* * *

THE drive out to Stilwell's place was shorter than she would've expected. The dog stretched out on the king cab seat behind the front seat, doing what he seemed to do best, napping.

"Who'd you go haring off after last night, anyway?" Jase asked, keeping his eyes on the two-lane blacktop road that headed south of town along the bluffs overlooking Discovery Bay.

"Remember the man who didn't drink the Jack Daniel's and didn't pay his tab? He's the ghost of Frank

Lewis, the guy who hanged for Hattie's murder. I saw him slipping out the door and followed him to my house."

Jase merely shot her a curious look. "What does he want?"

"He had the nerve to criticize my lack of progress on solving Hattie's murder." When Jase grinned, she narrowed her gaze. "Anyway, I thought maybe Frank was the person who has been following me, but he claims not."

He glanced at her as he negotiated a curve high on a bluff overlooking the bay. "So you still think you're being followed?"

"Sometimes."

"Have you told Darcy?"

"Not since she reported that she'd been through the incident reports and hadn't found anything suspicious."

"I don't like it—let's mention it to JT and see whether he can send someone up for security detail."

Jordan rolled her eyes. "Please. I've got at least three ghosts hovering, and Darcy's already tracking my every move for Drake. And let's not forget the dog. I think I'm covered." She reached a hand back to rub his head. "Speaking of whom, how about Malachi?"

The dog barked, then attempted to climb over the seat and lick her face, grinning and showing his huge canines. His tail thumped against the back window.

"That would be a yes vote," Jase said wryly. He turned into Stilwell's driveway. "How'd you come up with that name?"

"Trust me, you don't want to know."

As they drove up and parked, Holt was coming out his

front door. He paused on the front porch of his run-down rambler, looking surprised to see them.

Jordan was out of the truck before Jase had the engine shut off. "I need you to help me search for some missing papers," she told Stilwell without preamble. "It's important."

He rocked back on his heels. "Looks like those favors you're gonna owe me just keep piling up."

"Can we cut the crap?" she asked as Jase reached her side. "Your act isn't all that convincing."

Holt's expression turned wary.

"For your information, your ancestor wasn't nearly the bad guy you and the rest of the town seem to think he was. So you can quit trying to live down to your family's reputation. You do *not* descend from the long line of thieves and murderers you think you do."

She felt Jase's sidelong glance. "If you'd let us search for more family papers," he said to Holt, "we'd appreciate it."

Holt shrugged. "Whatever. I gotta get to work, but go for it. The place is unlocked."

"Of course it is," Jordan muttered, noting the rotting porch, peeling paint, and moss on the roof. "Anyone knows better than to burglarize it."

"Hey, if you're gonna criticize my house—"

She shook her head. "Where would the papers be stored? I don't have much time."

"The attic—boxes along the far wall."

"Thanks." They left Holt standing in the driveway as they headed into the house.

"Enjoy my housemates," Holt called after her.

While Jordan checked out filthy rooms on the main floor, Jase located the stairs to the attic, which were in the kitchen next to the back door. She walked past kitchen counters filled with dirty dishes and boxes of half-eaten pizza that had been there awhile, wrinkling her nose. Darcy hadn't been exaggerating when she'd described the state of the place.

The attic proved to be equally scary. She climbed the sagging stairs with trepidation. Jase shoved aside piles of boxes and other debris scattered on the floor to get to the piece of string that hung down from the single lightbulb at the peak of the ceiling. The bulb put out low wattage, so turning it on didn't help dispel the gloom.

Jordan stayed where she was, searching along the far wall until she identified several boxes that might be the right ones. She had to climb over broken chairs and piles of old clothes to get to them.

Kneeling, she opened the cardboard flaps of the first box, then fell back with a yelp. A mouse nest made from chewed bits of paper and filled with tiny, squirming babies sat right on top. The answers she needed might have been torn into insulation. She ground her teeth while Jase used an old rag to carefully move the nest aside, trying not to worry about contracting hantavirus.

That box yielded nothing of interest. Halfway down into the second box, however, she found what she was looking for underneath a stack of old photos of stern-looking family members. Tucking those under her arm for future perusal, she lifted out sheets of paper covered with cursive handwriting that looked like it matched Seavey's.

She carefully shuffled through them, looking for dates. She found them: June 6, 1890, June and July of the same year, all the way through August 1893. *Bingo.*

She held up the papers. "Let's go."

* * *

As they drove back to All That Jazz, Jordan forced herself to set aside Seavey's papers and focus on the upcoming conference call.

"So JT is a good friend? Tell me about him."

"Used to have a gold shield with the NYPD." Jase turned onto the main drag that ran through their neighborhood. "JT left to go into security work about five years ago. My dad's firm has used him on some large cases. Then last year, he moved to the West Coast to escape the bad weather."

Jase parked the truck in its designated slot behind the pub and climbed out. "JT and I go way back—we grew up in the same neighborhood. I went to Harvard, and he went into the police academy."

Jordan whistled at the dog to follow them. "I can trust him?"

"Yeah, and you can assume the information he digs up is solid."

Jase unlocked the back door and was opening it when Ted drove into the small lot, parking next to Jase's truck.

"Hey, Jordan," Ted said, getting out of his car. He

walked over to them, his attire as immaculate as usual. She felt decidedly grungy standing next to him.

"I'm glad I caught you, man," he said to Jase, perfunctorily patting the dog's head, which earned him The Look. "I have to supervise the guys while they knock down our equipment. It needs to go back to the sound studio at the house today."

Jase held the door open wide. "Not a problem. If you need anything, Jordan and I will be in my office on a conference call."

Jase led the way through the back of the building, past the kitchen where Kathleen was already hard at work chopping vegetables. The smells emanating from the sauté pan on the stove were enough to make Jordan's mouth water and remind her that she hadn't eaten since the evening before.

Jordan entered Jase's office, curious about his work environment. The room was utilitarian, with bare walls and simple fixtures. A small table holding an espresso machine sat in the corner. Natural light came from a bank of windows up high on the wall. The desk was large and modern, and held a state-of-the-art computer, fax machine, and printer. A phone system similar to ones in most small businesses, with a larger base unit and multiple phone lines, sat next to the desk blotter.

Jase logged on to his computer and pulled up JT's email, then called the number he'd been sent, placing the phone in speaker mode. He leaned back in his chair, propping his running shoes on the desk. Jordan chose a captain's chair across the desk from him.

"Speak." The gruff voice came on the line after only two rings.

"JT," Jase said. "I've got Jordan Marsh with me."

"Hi, JT."

"Ahh, nice voice. Once this case is closed, you let me give you a call, sweetheart. I'm a lot cuter than that glorified barkeep you've hooked up with."

Jase merely shook his head. "What've you got for us?" he asked.

"Right." JT rustled some papers. "Okay, first off, Jordan's assumption was correct—her husband was dead broke after the civil suits were adjudicated. Sorry, sweetheart— your granny's inheritance was the most likely motive for his suggested reconciliation."

"Didi Wyeth intimated as much," Jordan replied.

"Yeah? Speaking of her, her alibi doesn't check out. She told the cops she was at a party at some big-shot producer's place out in Beverly Hills, but no one remembers seeing her there. Her name also never got checked off the list at the gate."

Jordan felt the first stirrings of excitement. "Any idea where she really was?"

"Not yet, but I'm working on it."

She turned to Jase. "You should've let me keep pushing her last night—I might've gotten the truth out of her."

"More likely, you would've gotten your eyes scratched out," Jase countered.

"I missed a fight?" JT's voice approximated a whine. "Buddy, you *gotta* keep me better informed."

Jase looked amused. "What about the other names we gave you?"

"Let's see...Marcy Brentworth and Alice Langston check out. I pulled the court records for more names, but all the other plaintiffs who sued the dead hubby have rock-solid alibis—I couldn't shake them. Drake's a piece of work, though. Got divorced a couple of years back, and the ex took him to the cleaners."

"So the case is dredging up some emotional baggage," Jase concluded.

"Yeah, but that's not all. I ran across a picture of Drake's ex and just for kicks put it side by side with a current photo of Jordan from the *L.A. Times.* The resemblance is striking—build, hair, even eye color. And his ex won the settlement against him by claiming he cheated on her. The guy's doing some major transference onto Jordan right about now."

Jordan groaned. "So Drake was hoping to find the evidence he needs to believe I offed Ryland, and now someone has obligingly supplied it."

"Yeah. Or maybe he just needs to get back at a woman for what happened to him and wants to make you miserable, who knows? But I can guarantee he isn't working from an objective viewpoint."

"We can use that at trial, if necessary," Jase said. "Good work."

"What about the supposed witnesses?" Jordan asked. "Drake claimed he has reliable witnesses to our argument the night of Ryland's death."

"Still working on names," JT replied. "The LAPD is so paranoid about the high-profile nature of this case, they've got the documents locked down tight."

"Can you get to them?" Jase asked.

"Do you even need to ask?" JT replied, his tone smug.

Jase looked amused. "Killing two birds with one stone, are you?"

"Hey, a man's gotta do what a man's gotta do. Give me another hour, and I'll shoot you an email."

Jase's eyebrow went up. "We interrupt something?"

"Please. Do you think I would've answered the phone? And I don't do quickies—I savor."

"Sure you do."

"I appreciate the personal sacrifice, JT," Jordan said, smiling.

They heard papers being shifted again. "The only other issue is your friend Carol. Per Jase's instructions, I took a quick look at any possible connection she might have with your hubby, and something interesting turned up."

Jordan glared at Jase. "You had him investigate my *best friend?*"

Jase held up a hand. "I was simply covering all bases. Let's hear what JT has to say."

JT cleared his throat. "About a year ago, your hubby and your best friend attended the same business conference."

"I remember it—in San Francisco, right?" Jordan asked. "That's hardly suspicious. We all run therapy practices, and Carol's discipline is similar to Ryland's."

"I would agree, except for one thing," JT said. "There was no hotel room registered in your friend's name. I checked around with a few of her colleagues, and their recollection is that she stayed with a man—your husband, to be precise."

Jordan felt a chill along her spine. "I don't believe you."

"I've got two witnesses who will swear to it." JT's voice had turned gentle.

"Then there has to be an innocent explanation. Carol would *never* have had a relationship with Ryland. I know her—she wouldn't have betrayed me that way."

"It gives her motive," Jase said quietly. "And she knew he wanted to reconcile. You told me yourself that you confided in her."

And Carol had talked to Drake, though she'd sworn she hadn't told him anything. Jordan swallowed around a huge lump in her throat.

"You don't know Carol," she insisted. "She's even less capable of recognizing brake lines than I am. This is crazy."

"Think back to that night," Jase urged. "After you called her, how long did it take her to arrive? Did she show up at the condo more quickly than you expected? Could she have been somewhere in the area?"

"Hell, I don't know," Jordan said, exasperated. "I wasn't paying attention to those sorts of details. Ryland had just been killed." She hunched her shoulders and leaned forward. "I want you to drop this, JT. I will talk to Carol myself and ask her about the conference. There's an innocent explanation," she insisted stubbornly. "I'm certain of it."

"You're the boss, darlin'."

She drew a deep breath. "Thanks."

"You'll get my bill."

Jase punched the disconnect button. The silence stretched out between them.

"So Didi is the most viable suspect," Jordan concluded out loud.

"JT may still come up with interesting names for those witnesses."

They were both leaving unspoken the information about Carol, and Jordan preferred it that way. Even asking about the shared hotel room would put a strain on their friendship, and Jordan couldn't do that. Carol had always been there for her. If—and *only* if—Didi came up with a verifiable alibi would Jordan then call Carol.

Jordan stood to stretch out the kinks. If she didn't get some coffee in her, her sleepless night would soon have her flat on her face. "I need to track down Didi and have a little talk with her."

Jase shook his head. "Not alone, you aren't. If she's killed once, she won't hesitate to do so again." He glanced at his watch. "Why don't we get cleaned up, then I'll pick you up and we'll grab brunch on the way out to Ted's house."

"Sounds like a plan, as long as you add caffeine to the brunch portion of the agenda."

Jase glanced at his watch. "I've got some emails and a

supplier I have to deal with. How does two hours from now sound?"

* * *

ONCE back at the house, Jordan took a long shower, slowly graduating the water temperature from hot to cold in the hope that it would wake her up. With a towel wrapped around her wet hair, she looked through the last of Seavey's papers. She was convinced she'd find the clue she needed to nail Hattie's murderer.

Locating an entry from the night of the soirée, she began to read while she towel-dried her hair.

> *June 6th*—I find I'm barely able to put pen to paper this night, for I suffer from intense emotion unlike anything I've experienced in my lifetime. Though I was able to return Charlotte unharmed, my relationship with Hattie has been irreparably damaged. For I looked into her eyes this evening and saw the truth of her feelings. No matter what I have done—and she will never know the truth of it—she hates me with a deep and abiding passion. I find the pain of this knowledge almost unbearable.
>
> Remy just now brought me word of Hattie's murder. I will not rest until I find her killer. How ironic that I was incapable of understanding what I

felt for her was love until it was too late. She
would've told me it was no less than I deserve.

Jordan flipped through the pages, hunting for additional references to Hattie, but what she found instead was even more intriguing.

July 23rd—For the first time in my life, I
have killed out of the need for personal vengeance.
Once Remy had persuaded him to talk, he
admitted to murdering Hattie in retribution. He'd
laughed, thinking I wouldn't care what he'd done.
He sealed his fate in that moment. I had the
pleasure of watching the man who took from me
everything I hold dear die a slow, agonizing death.
Perhaps now I can rest.

Jordan set the papers down, her hands trembling with excitement. Frank *had* been innocent, and Seavey had avenged Hattie's murder. The question was, who had died on July 23, 1890? Clive Johnson? It certainly made sense. How tragic that Greeley had been too blind to investigate Johnson. To know for certain, though, she needed a name—an official record of who had died on that date.

She reached for her phone.

"Darcy, I need to get back inside the Historical Society building. Are you up for a little B and E this morning?"

"Gee, why the hell not? I live to break the law," Darcy replied. "Pick you up in ten minutes."

* * *

THIS time, Jordan left Malachi at home, explaining that Darcy didn't want dog hairs in the police cruiser. He let it be known he thought that reasoning was suspect at best.

While Darcy drove, Jordan filled her in on what she'd learned.

"So we're looking for some kind of official report of a murder on July 23, 1890?" Darcy asked as they turned into the parking lot of the Historical Society.

"Yeah. Seavey, in a journal entry on that date, indicates he killed Hattie's murderer. My bet, given the prior entries in which he said he needed to deal with Johnson, is that that's who he killed."

"Maybe, if you believe that Seavey was being truthful in his journal."

"Why wouldn't he have been?"

"Anyone in that time frame who wrote journals or diaries had to believe the documents would be read by whoever survived them."

"You have a point," Jordan said grudgingly. "But he admitted to murder, and I don't see Seavey as a man who spent a lot of time agonizing over his reputation."

Darcy moved the plywood from in front of the door. "He might've wanted his relatives to believe he'd done the right thing, simply because he knew he *hadn't* and felt remorse. It's one thing to kill off your competitors, but it's another entirely to be a party to the murder of a defenseless woman."

"Maybe." But Jordan wasn't convinced. She opened the door and they made their way across the dusty room and down the stairs to the basement.

Jordan ran her fingers down the spines of the boxes holding the *Port Chatham Weekly Gazette* from 1890, pulling out the one that was the correct range of dates. Taking it over to the small table, she opened it and handed half its contents to Darcy. "Look for July 23, 1890, or a date close to that, since the newspaper was a weekly."

It took her only a moment to find what she was looking for, her surprise growing as she read. She held out the yellowed newsprint, pointing at the front-page leading article. "Police Chief John Greeley was killed in the line of duty the night of July 23, 1890. He'd been beaten, then shot in the abdomen in the alley behind the police station. He bled to death before he was discovered."

"Whoa," Darcy murmured, skimming the article.

"Yeah." Jordan rubbed her face, trying to process the information in a way that made sense.

"There must've been more than one murder that night." Darcy was flipping through the rest of the newspaper.

"I don't think so, actually."

"Come on. A cop? You think Greeley killed Hattie, then set up Frank to take the fall?"

"Actually, it fits, and for reasons I wasn't even taking into account, dammit. Greeley was furious with Hattie for putting Charlotte at risk and causing her kidnapping.

And I don't care how chauvinistic men were back then, he was obsessed with Charlotte. Men like that are easily capable of killing the person they hold responsible for the destruction of their carefully planned world. And it also makes sense that Greeley would frame Frank—he could buy himself some favors with Seavey for neutralizing a business rival."

Darcy's expression was skeptical.

"Okay, look," Jordan said, warming to her subject. "Seavey said in his journal entry that the man he killed had murdered Hattie 'in retribution.' He indicated he'd 'persuaded' the man to talk. That sounds an awful lot like Seavey had his thugs beat him until he talked. Seavey also said he enjoyed watching the man he'd killed die a 'slow and agonizing' death. A gunshot to the abdomen would qualify as slow and agonizing."

"Okay, I might buy that. But what happened to Clive Johnson?"

"Good question . . . wait. Seavey talked about handling the problem with Johnson around the time of the kidnapping—he felt that by not acting sooner, he'd allowed Charlotte's kidnapping to occur." Jordan picked up the stack of newspapers, shuffling them to find the ones from early June. After some quick skimming, she grinned and handed an issue to Darcy, folded open to the police report. "An unidentified man was fished from the bay on the morning of June 7—the day after the soirée. The corpse was beaten beyond recognition."

"People died almost every night on the waterfront—that proves nothing."

"Yes, but if Seavey had rescued Charlotte by the night before, he'd already gotten hold of Johnson, forced him to reveal Charlotte's location, then 'handled' the problem."

Darcy folded the paper and handed it back to her. "You realize all you have is supposition and circumstantial evidence, right?"

"Yes, but strong supposition, and all the dates match." Jordan replaced the newspapers and set the box back in its place on the shelf. "We know that's what happened, even though it will never be proven in a court of law. And the psychological profile of Greeley fits Hattie's murder—it was a crime of passion."

Closing up, they walked back out to the police cruiser. Darcy's expression was troubled. "This will devastate Tom."

Jordan's steps faltered, and she stared at Darcy in consternation. In her zeal to solve the crime, she hadn't thought of the consequences of revealing the murderer's real identity. Darcy was right—the family's reputation could be irreparably harmed in the community. "So what do I do?"

Darcy started up the car and backed it out of its parking place, looking thoughtful. "Tom deserves to know. Tell him what you've uncovered, then show him the journal entries. Let him decide how he wants it handled. After all, you can tell Hattie and Charlotte without revealing the information publicly, right?"

Jordan thought about it, then nodded. "That makes sense. I also need to find a way to break it to Charlotte—

she still believes Greeley loved her. I doubt she'll take the news well that he was a violent, narcissistic stalker whose love for her was so twisted he murdered her sister."

"Now, that would be an understatement." Darcy turned onto Jordan's street.

Jordan's cellphone rang and she pulled it out as Darcy stopped in front of Longren House. "I'm here," she said by way of answering. "I just had Darcy run me on a quick errand—we're a bit late getting back."

"Actually," Jase replied, "I was calling to tell you I'd gotten tied up with the supplier and was on my way out the door. I'll be there in about twenty minutes."

"I'll wait for you here." Jordan walked up the steps onto the porch with Darcy behind her.

"Oh, and JT called back—he got the name of Drake's reliable witnesses. One, not surprisingly, is Didi Wyeth. But the other—get this—is Ted Rawlins."

"But that doesn't—" Jordan abruptly halted at the front door, causing Darcy to slam into her from behind.

Darcy sidestepped around Jordan. "*Jesus*, Marsh—" she swore, then shut up. Ted stood in the front hall, a handgun in his hand.

Jordan heard an odd coughing noise just as she saw Darcy reach for her gun.

Darcy went down without a sound.

Chapter 17

JORDAN'S phone dropped from nerveless fingers. *Oh God, oh God.* She fell to her knees beside Darcy, frantically searching for a pulse.

"Get up, Jordan," Ted said calmly. "It would be best if I didn't have to shoot you just yet."

From somewhere deep inside the house, she could hear Malachi barking furiously and scratching. She slowly rose, keeping her eyes on the gun pointed at her, which looked really, really big. "What have you done with my dog?"

"Shut him in the butler's pantry, where he won't be a nuisance. I don't like to harm animals." Ted gestured with the gun toward the library. "Let's have a chat, shall we?"

Jordan gave Darcy one last glance, then walked ahead of him, her heart pounding so hard it felt like a fist hitting her chest from the inside.

Charlotte was hovering at ceiling level, fading in and out, and hissing. Hattie stood in the shadows next to the

French doors, her eyes on Jordan, waiting, Jordan realized, for some kind of sign from her. She glanced at Ted, who was frowning distractedly to himself. Surreptitiously, she splayed one hand out at her side, hoping Hattie understood her signal to wait.

"Hold still, Charlotte, and wait for Jordan to tell us what to do," Hattie said.

"But I can get his gun!" Charlotte swooped right over Ted's head, but he didn't seem to notice.

Jordan shook her head slightly, and Charlotte retreated to ceiling level with a loud sniff.

Think, Jordan told herself. Jase would've heard the commotion and realized she'd dropped her phone—he was on his way, and he would have called the police. She just had to stall until the cavalry arrived. "Why don't you let me call the EMTs, Ted? You don't want Darcy to die."

Ted shrugged. "Why would I care? She was in the way." He used the barrel of the gun to scratch the side of his head, mussing his hair.

For the first time, Jordan noted that his clothes were wrinkled. *Changing personal hygiene habits—a sign of deteriorating mental stability.* Not that shooting Darcy without hesitation hadn't already illustrated that salient fact.

"Killing a cop, Ted—that's not good. You can get the death penalty."

"Only if I'm caught, and I won't be."

"Just let me make the phone call," Jordan urged. "Then you can take me to your house."

"Don't give him any ideas, Jordan," Hattie admonished. "He could abduct you!"

"No. Just shut up while I think," Ted snarled.

He paced slowly around the room, keeping the gun pointed in her direction. Through the French doors, Jordan could see Amanda weeding with her back to them, her butt swaying to whatever tune she had on her MP3 player. Chances of getting her attention were slim at best.

"I'm disappointed, Jordan," Ted said, drawing her focus back to him. "I came to you because I lost the record contract. And you helped me, remember? I'm back on the road to greatness, and I deserve that greatness. But you've fucked it all up."

She didn't have to fake her confusion. "How?"

"You moved! Did you really think you could just relocate up here and I wouldn't be upset?"

"But you were the one who invited me up here last year—"

"For the goddamn festival, not to buy some run-down old heap!" he shouted, straightening his arm and shoving the gun at her. "*You* belong at my side, in L.A. You're perfect for me—you are the person I need to help me in my career."

Charlotte hissed and swooped, and Jordan shot her a warning glance. "I have a career of my own, Ted." Falling into therapist mode, she kept her tone even, her reasoning rational. If she persuaded him of his flawed logic, she might be able to get him to give her the gun. "How did you think that would work?"

He snorted, his expression derisive. "Other people don't need you—*I* do. You told me you were taking a sabbatical, and that you needed to *reassess*. I assumed you understood."

Malachi's barking stopped. In the ensuing silence, Jordan forced herself to keep her eyes on Ted. "What about Didi? You're dating her, aren't you?"

"I *told* you, she's just staying up here this summer. Why won't you *listen* to me?" Ted's agitation was clearly escalating.

Hattie floated forward, her expression alarmed, and Jordan put up both hands. "Okay, okay—I'm listening now, aren't I?"

Ted ran a hand over his face. "I just can't make you *understand*," he muttered, resuming his pacing.

Keep him talking. "The private investigator says Didi lied about her alibi," Jordan said. "Do you know anything about that?"

"Yeah, I heard you two on the phone with him at the pub. That's when I knew I had to do something. If you'd just left well enough alone. But *no*. You had to *investigate*." Ted laughed, the sound unnaturally harsh. "Didi was sleeping with our agent that night. He told her if she did, he'd get her a big movie contract. She didn't want anyone to know about it." He gave Jordan an accusing look. "She wouldn't have needed an alibi if you'd just stayed away from that asshole you married—he wouldn't have dumped her. Why'd you have to invite him out to your condo, Jordan?"

Jordan's stomach clenched. "*You* killed Ryland?"

"What choice did you give me? I wasn't about to let him move back in, but I could see you were wavering. He was in our way."

"You followed him that night."

"I'd been following him for *weeks*. I listened to everything, and I could tell you were waffling. So I cut the brake lines."

Jordan felt a sharp pang for Ryland. "And then you told Drake about our argument to point the cops at me."

"Of course. Clever of me, I must admit."

Jordan took a calculated risk. "But your logic just isn't holding up at all, is it, Ted? You murder Ryland, then you implicate me in his murder by telling the cops about our argument? If I'm in jail, I can't be with you, now, can I?"

Ted shook his head. "No, no—you just don't get it, do you, Jordan? I'm beginning to wonder whether you're as smart as I thought you were."

She spread her hands. "Tell me what I'm missing, because from where I stand, your logic sucks."

"*Don't* you dare criticize *me*!"

"Do you think it's wise to provoke him, Jordan?" Hattie asked.

"Let me throw books at him!" Charlotte screeched, flying toward the bookcases.

"*No, wait!*" Jordan said.

"Don't order me around!" Ted snapped, waving the gun. "Do you really want to piss me off right now? I'm still thinking about shooting you."

"No, no," Jordan said hurriedly. She thought she heard a slight movement in the hall. "Listen, Ted, just explain it to me, why don't you? How am I supposed to be with you when I'm rotting in jail for my husband's murder?"

"Well, I can come and visit you, right?" Ted's tone indicated he thought he was reasoning with a five-year-old. "And no one else can have you if you're locked up. Plus, you would've been convicted in California, so you'd be brought back to a California state penitentiary. I can work with that."

Jordan gaped at him, stunned. Rational Therapy hadn't done a damn thing for him. If she decided to go back into counseling, she *seriously* needed to reassess her chosen discipline.

Ted suddenly moved toward her, and she jogged backward. He stopped, shaking his head. "See? Now *that's* the problem—you just don't get that you belong to me. Despite all your mistakes, I still loved you, you know. My world would have been complete with you in it."

He was using past tense. *Not a good sign.*

"I don't have to shoot you, if you'll just come with me." He leaned forward, his tone confidential. "I can call the cops off, you know. I've got contacts. I'm important."

Jordan acted as if she were considering his offer while her mind raced. "Well, *hell.*" She made herself glare at him. "Get a clue, Ted."

Ted's face turned red. At that moment, Jase edged around the library door, his expression grim, just outside of Ted's line of sight.

Jordan signaled with her hand for him to wait. "You know why some people become therapists, Ted? No? It's because they're so messed up, they need to figure out how to fix themselves. And I'm *that* messed up, believe me."

He scowled. "No, you're *not*. You're just a little off track right now. We can fix that."

"*Off track?* I don't think so. I've got a Four-Point Plan for Personal Renewal, did you know that? Around here, we call it the FPP for short. And you know what? It's in shambles."

"What're you talking about?" he asked, confused. "You've always run your life perfectly. And you can do the same for me—"

"Oh, please." She threw her hands up in the air. "I can't even handle my own life, much less someone else's."

"That's not true!"

"I'm the laughingstock of the town."

"Don't be ridiculous," Ted said.

"You are *not* the laughingstock of this town," Charlotte said loyally. "How could you think that?"

"*Shut up and wait.*"

"Don't use that tone with me," he snapped, but he seemed less certain of himself.

Jordan turned back to him. "Here's the thing, Ted— I'm delusional. *I see ghosts.*" His eyes widened. "That's right," she nodded, smiling triumphantly. "*Ghosts.*"

Jase again took a step forward, looking alarmed. She gave a slight shake of her head. She'd counseled Ted for months, and she knew every one of the jerk's hot buttons.

"You're just trying to trick me," Ted said nervously.

"It's no trick—I not only *see* ghosts, I can tell them *what to do.*" She turned her head slightly. "Charlotte, go for it."

"Who are you talking to?" Ted's voice rose.

Charlotte stopped pulsing spastically, her expression confused. "Go for what?"

Jesus. "Take him out," Jordan rephrased.

"Out where?"

"Shut up, or I'll shoot," Ted shouted, his eyes wildly darting around the room.

"Attack, for God's sake!" Jordan yelled.

"Well, why didn't you just say so?"

An entire wall of books flew at Ted, and he screamed, dropping the gun and putting his hands up to protect his face.

Malachi and Jase launched from the doorway, and all three of them went down in a heap of flying fur, growls, and thudding fists. Jordan dove, scrabbling for the gun. More books flew off the shelves, hitting her in the back, almost knocking the wind out of her.

"Charlotte, stop!" she yelled, rising.

No one listened. Jase and Ted rolled, locked in combat. She jogged backward, avoiding being flattened by them while she fumbled with the gun.

Ducking more books, she closed in and stomped her running shoe on the back of Ted's right wrist, pointing the gun. *"Freeze,* or I'll shoot your *hand.* You'll never caress the valves of your horn again." Steadying the shaking gun with her other hand, she added as an afterthought, "You fucking creep."

Ted froze, and Jase landed a solid punch that had his eyes rolling back in his head.

Malachi grabbed Ted's neck and held, growling. More books flew.

"*Charlotte!*"

"Okay, okay!"

"It's easier to start than it is to stop," Hattie explained apologetically.

"Call off the damn dog!" Ted screamed.

"Malachi, *come.*"

Jase shoved books aside and flipped Ted over, planting a knee in the middle of his back. He yanked Ted's arms up and back, holding his wrists with one hand, holding out the other. "Give me the gun, and then go get Darcy's handcuffs."

Darcy. Jordan did as he said, then ran into the hallway and knelt beside Darcy. Blood soaked her chest, and when Jordan pressed fingers to the side of her neck, her pulse was fast and thready. Jordan felt her pockets for the handcuffs, tossing them to Jase.

"Hattie! Dish towels from the kitchen." She grabbed her cellphone and dialed 911, praying the phone was still functional. Towels flew at her. She snagged them out of the air with her free hand and pressed them to Darcy's wound.

"Nine-one-one operator. State your emergency."

Jordan babbled out her address and something about an officer down.

"A neighbor already called it in, ma'am. Units are on their way. Describe the location of the shooter."

Blood immediately soaked through the towels, and she pressed harder. "He's facedown, in the library, cuffed." She craned her neck, then added, "He's crying."

There was a moment of silence. "Crying's good," the

operator finally said, her tone wry. "Stay on the line, ma'am, until the police arrive. Can you do that for me?"

Jordan could hear the sirens in the distance. She let out a sob, giving Jase a wobbly smile. "Yeah. I can do that."

Amanda took that moment to come strolling down the hall from the kitchen. "Hey, there're cop cars all over the place. What's up?"

Chapter 18

JUST after dawn the next morning, Jordan sat in the hospital room next to Darcy's bed, punch-drunk from lack of sleep. She, Jase, and Tom had spent the night at the hospital, helping each other stay positive while they awaited word of Darcy's condition.

After four hours of surgery, she was stable. The bullet had entered her upper right chest, then bounced around a bit, nicking her lung and shattering a rib. After another two hours of recovery, Darcy had been moved to the ICU, and the nurse had consented to Jordan's request that she be allowed to stay in the room, even though she wasn't family.

A number of Darcy's officers and administrative staff had been in and out during the long night, waiting to find out whether their police chief would recover. The mayor had even supposedly stopped by, though Jordan had been in the cafeteria at the time, trying to find coffee while she called Carol to give her the news that they'd caught Ryland's murderer.

According to Tom, a detective by the name of Bert Park had taken over the logistics of contacting Detective Drake. Drake had made arrangements to fly to town later today, to retrieve Ted and transport him to the L.A. County lockup, to be arraigned on murder charges. Tom had told Jordan that Drake had not been pleased to find out he'd been investigating the wrong person all along.

Jordan stretched. Closing her eyes, she rolled her neck to relax the muscles that were giving her a screaming headache. Or maybe it was the fatigue and the gallon of coffee she'd ingested in the last sixteen hours. She'd seen better dawns, that was for sure.

"You've been a pain in the ass from the very beginning." Darcy's voice cracked on the words, but they were lucid.

Jordan's head jerked up. She tried to smile but failed. "Taking out the chief of police within days of hitting town definitely constitutes a personal best for me," she agreed, then added, "This is all my fault."

"I was kidding, for chrissakes," Darcy tried to shift one hand and winced. "You know that stalkers, once they reach that level of violence, can't be rehabilitated. And the smart ones cover their tracks. There was nothing you could've done."

"I could've recognized his pathology."

Darcy managed to snort. "At least tell me that jerk is either dead or in a jail cell where I can get to him and beat the crap out of him."

"It might be a while before you can do that." Jordan held a spoonful of ice slivers to Darcy's lips.

Darcy glared as she sucked on the ice. "Just give me a

couple of days. I'm *motivated*," she grumbled. "Talk to me—what's happening?"

Jordan brought her up-to-date. "Jase demanded that Drake immediately hold a press conference and announce that I was no longer considered a suspect."

"Good man." Darcy closed her eyes, starting to drift.

"As I hear it, Drake was *not* pleased."

"Even better."

Tom appeared in the doorway, holding a large bouquet of flowers and looking embarrassed. "She awake yet?"

"I'm here," Darcy mumbled. She opened her eyes and saw the flowers. "You must've been *really* worried."

"Just shut up." Tom placed them at her bedside. "You scared the crap out of us. Couldn't you have gotten shot in the leg or something?"

"Hard to control the shooter's aim." Darcy looked at Jordan. "You tell him yet?"

"You mean about Hattie's killer?" Tom nodded. "I told Jordan to contact a reporter with the newspaper and see if she can get a human interest story published. The community needs to know the truth about Michael Seavey. It's not right to keep the information from Holt, either. My family can weather the hit."

"Good." Darcy shifted uncomfortably, wincing. "So tell me how you stopped that son of a bitch after he shot me."

"I didn't—Charlotte did."

Darcy's eyes shot wide open. "*I don't friggin' believe it!* Are you telling me I missed a teenage ghost taking out a violent stalker, just because I was out cold?"

Jordan and Tom grinned.

* * *

Jordan parked the car at the curb in front of her house and sat for a moment with the car door open, petting Malachi. She didn't relish the task ahead of her. It had been hard enough to explain to Tom.

"Have you told them yet?" The deep voice brought Jordan out of her thoughts. She turned to find Frank Lewis standing about ten yards away, hands in his pockets, watching her.

"You mean Hattie and Charlotte?" Jordan shook her head. "I'm headed in to talk to them now."

"Hattie will be upset that she misjudged Seavey so badly." Frank grimaced. "I can't say I like that he never tried to stop my hanging, though."

"I wouldn't exactly call him an angel," Jordan agreed. "It's hard to tell from his papers, but I suspect he was responsible for more than a dozen deaths over the years."

"Then again, if he killed Clive Johnson, he just might've redeemed himself for the rest."

"There you go." Jordan paused. "Are you coming inside? Hattie could use the company after I tell her, I'm certain. And she'll have her hands full, caring for Charlotte."

Frank shook his head. "My reasons haven't changed."

Jordan studied him. "As a psychologist, I can recommend you'll be far healthier if you let go of all that guilt."

"And I don't remember asking your opinion," Frank retorted.

" 'Guilt upon the conscience, like rust upon iron, both

defiles and consumes it, gnawing and creeping into it, which eats out the very heart and substance of the metal.'" She shook her head. "That was close, anyway. And being an old-time union man and sailor, you should relate."

He scowled. "Who said that?"

She shrugged. "Some British bishop from the seventeenth century. It's one of my favorite quotes, actually."

"Yeah, well, most ships in my time were made of wood, so I can't relate all that well."

She gave up and climbed out of the car, heading toward the house. "Just think about it," she said over her shoulder.

* * *

SHE found Hattie and Charlotte waiting for her in the kitchen. After fixing the espresso she was convinced she couldn't survive without, she knew she couldn't stall any longer. She sat them both down and explained what she'd discovered in Michael Seavey's papers.

Hattie sat quietly, her expression horrified. "I had it all wrong." She pressed her lips together. "I treated Michael Seavey horribly."

"Let's keep a little perspective," Jordan countered. "He propositioned you, pressured you to drop your plans to unionize Longren Shipping, took your money, and watched Frank hang without a qualm, all to save his own skin. It's not like he was the model of an upstanding citizen."

Charlotte had started crying, and her sobs showed no

signs of abating. "This is all my fault," she wailed. "If I hadn't encouraged John, he wouldn't have murdered you."

Hattie put an arm around her shoulder. "Nonsense. You did nothing wrong."

"But you suspected how bad he was, and I didn't listen!"

"Once you become the obsession of a pathological personality," Jordan said gently, "there's almost nothing you can do to alter his behavior. And it's very hard to see the behavior for what it is, unless you've got specific training." *And not even then,* she thought. She'd never seen the pattern in Ted at all; she'd simply thought he was suffering from transference.

"So he never loved me." Charlotte sniffled.

Jordan shot a glance at Hattie, who frowned. "He loved you," Jordan explained, "but his love wasn't very healthy."

They were interrupted by a knock at the back door and Jordan got up to answer it. Frank stood on the back steps, his hands fisted at his sides, his expression tortured.

Jordan smiled and turned. "Hattie? There's someone at the door for you."

Hattie floated out of her chair, her expression confused. When she saw Frank, she gave an inarticulate cry, her hands covering her mouth.

She flew into his arms.

* * *

GIVING them some privacy, Jordan called to Malachi, and the two of them retired to the front porch to sit in the early morning sunshine. They settled on the top step, and she closed her eyes, propping her shoulder against a column and raising her face to the warmth of the rays.

Jase sat beside her on the step.

He handed her a latte. "So about this Four-Point Plan of yours."

Jordan let out a small laugh. "Fuck the FPP. Of course, I still talk to ghosts, and I don't know what I'm doing with my life, or what I'll want to do after I fix up the house."

He didn't even blink. "We admire 'quirky' around here—you'll do just fine. And personally, I think you should revamp the FPP and stick with it."

She gave him a sidelong glance. "Really?"

"Really." He paused for a moment, as if he were gathering his thoughts. "You've had a lot of turmoil in your life in the last year. You lost your husband, and you were stalked by a psychopath. And those are just the normal-world stresses you've faced."

She rolled her eyes.

"I'm serious—you should take all the time you need to come to terms with the changes in your life." He shot her a grin. "In the meantime, I'll hire you to tend bar and keep me informed about the needs of my spectral customers."

"Since I can't exactly charge my clients my normal fee, I probably will need the money." She took a sip of her latte, a new thought occurring to her. "Oh, hell. I think Ted was the one who got into my underwear drawer."

Jase raised a brow.

"The ghosts were at a telekinesis seminar," she explained, getting another grin out of him, "and Malachi was at the vet's. Ted must've gotten into the house and rifled through my clothing. I found it all rearranged, and Hattie swore they hadn't done it." She shuddered as she pictured Ted pawing through her lingerie. *Major ick.* "I think I need to buy all new underwear."

"Hmm. The purchase of lingerie is a symbolic act and not to be taken lightly." Jordan narrowed her gaze. Jase's expression was solemn, but his eyes held a twinkle. "There's this great shop downtown," he added. "Talk to Mary Ann—tell her I sent you."

"Right." Amused, Jordan leaned back, closing her eyes.

They sat together, not speaking, listening to the neighborhood wake up. And for the first time in a very long time, she felt at peace.